THE CASTLE OF OTRANTO
By HORACE WALPOLE

VATHEK
By WILLIAM BECKFORD

THE VAMPYRE
By JOHN POLIDORI

And a Fragment of a Novel by Lord Byron

THREE GOTHIC NOVELS

Edited by
E. F. BLEILER

DOVER PUBLICATIONS, INC., NEW YORK

Published in Canada by General Publishing Company, Ltd., 30 Lesmill Road, Don Mills, Toronto, Ontario.
Published in the United Kingdom by Constable and Company, Ltd., 10 Orange Street, London, W.C. 2.

This Dover edition, first published in 1966, is an unabridged republication of the following editions of these works: *The Castle of Otranto*, Second Edition; Sir Walter Scott's *Introduction* to *The Castle of Otranto*, as first published by Ballantyne, Edinburgh, 1811; *Vathek*, as edited by Richard Garnett, published by Lawrence and Bullen, London, 1893; *The Vampyre*, as published by Sherwood, Neely, and Jones, London, 1819; *Fragment of a Novel*, from *The Works of Lord Byron, Letters and Journals*, Vol. III, edited by Rowland E. Prothero, published by John Murray, London, 1899.
The introductory material by E. F. Bleiler has been prepared specially for this Dover edition.

Standard Book Number: 486-21232-7

Library of Congress Catalog Card Number: 64-16338

Manufactured in the United States of America
Dover Publications, Inc.
180 Varick Street
New York, N.Y. 10014

Contents

INTRODUCTION

Horace Walpole and
The Castle of Otranto

During much of the first half of the eighteenth century England was ruled by Sir Robert Walpole, later Lord Orford, one of the most successful rough-and-tumble politicians of the time. His son Horace (1717–1797) did not share his fierce energy, but was a gentle, sickly, somewhat effeminate boy. Indeed, one of the speculations several generations later was that Horace Walpole was not the son of Sir Robert, but of a friend of the family, Carr, Lord Hervey. This scandal is not taken too seriously nowadays, but it points up the strong concern in Walpole's two major works of fiction with questions of paternity.

His youth was uneventful. He spent three years at Cambridge University with the poets Thomas Gray and William Mason, who were his close friends, but left without a degree. In 1739, accompanied by Gray, he set out on the Grand Tour of France and Italy, and returned in 1741. He had been intended for the law and politics, but he showed no aptitude for legal matters, and after a brief attempt at a political career, he wisely limited himself to sitting occasionally in Parliament. But even after his father's death he had powerful connections among the Whigs, and he occasionally tried his hand at pamphleteering and small scale behind-the-scenes manipulations.

Sir Robert Walpole, although not a man of great fortune, had left Horace a good income, and when this was combined with the salary from various political sinecures which Horace held most of his life, he hovered in a reasonably satisfactory financial milieu. He was neither poor, like his friend Gray, nor fantastically wealthy like the later William Beckford. He could satisfy most of his wants, as long as they remained within reason, and yet was in no danger of becoming jaded with acquisition.

Walpole became primarily a man of society. He made friends easily, and he was an indefatigable enthusiast, perpetually ferret-ing about contagiously among antiquities of various sorts. Since he had little else to do and his acquaintance numbered many people of much the same intellect, temperament and circumstances as himself, he corresponded voluminously. One of the glories of English literature is the enormous corpus of thousands of letters that he wrote to his many friends in both England and France.

Several pictures survive of Horace Walpole in his early maturity, and they show him a man well suited to the correspondence. He was a handsome man, very reminiscent in physical feature and expression of some of the more ineffectual roles played by the modern actor Sir Alec Guinness: an air of refinement, whimsicality, intelligence, slightly chagrined embarrassment, zest, and a slight touch of malice.

In 1749 Horace Walpole began his unique contribution to European culture by buying Strawberry Hill, a small farm with a broad view of the Thames, on a main road near Twickenham, not far from London. He had rented the property for two years earlier. What he first intended to do with Strawberry Hill, beyond using it as a summer residence, we do not know, although apparently he toyed with the idea of building in various picturesque architectural styles. By late 1749 or early 1750, however, he had come to a decision: he would enlarge the cottage on the property and turn it into a "castellino" in the English Gothic style. He wrote to his friend Sir Horace Mann, who was in the diplomatic service in Florence, and requested whatever "Gothic fragments" (by which he meant medieval artifacts) could be found cheaply. He also took counsel with his friends Bentley, Chute and (later) Gray, as to what should be done.

One difficulty in creating the new Strawberry Hill was that Walpole was neither an architect nor an antiquary (although he later became skilled in antiquities), and a somewhat nebulous "taste" had to function in creating the castle. He seems never to have realized that Gothic was an art of construction, and not simply a decoration, and his interpretation of the form was peculiarly limited to surfaces and visibilities. He could not afford groining or fretwork for the stairways, but he felt they were necessary. According to his practice he might have made them out of plaster and lath; he might have made them out of carved cardboard; but what he actually did was simply paste up wallpaper with groining painted on it. For battlements he nailed cardboard on the framework of the cottage. One of the quips of the day was that Horrie had outlived four sets of battlements.

The work on Strawberry Hill progressed slowly, for Walpole was forced to live and to build upon his income. Perpetually in building, the castle grew from a small cottage into a long sprawling concatenation of rooms, about each of which Walpole became enthusiastic as it took form. The library and refectory were added in 1754; the gallery, round tower, great cloister and cabinet by 1760 and 1761; the north bedchamber in 1770. The guiding principle for the edifice was imitation of whatever building or architectural feature Walpole and his friends happened to like at the moment. The result, even though Walpole and his friends grew in antiquarian knowledge, was an architectural monstrosity, but apparently a monstrosity with charm, since it represented the interests, enthusiasms and achievements of an intelligent, gracious man.

Walpole tried to furnish his castle appropriately—that is, with a mixture of period pieces and quaint oddities which conveyed the mood of Gothicness to him. He imported stained glass windows showing saints in various torments or benedictions. He stuffed "niches full of trophies of old coats of mail, Indian shields made of rhinoceros hide, broadswords, quivers, longbows—all supposed to be taken by Sir Terry Robsart [a humorously invented apocryphal ancestor] in the Holy Wars." He also started a library and art collection, both characterized by the same whimsy, taste, intelligence and resourcefulness. Walpole was never a profound scholar or a true bibliophile, but his collection was nevertheless remarkable.

The significance of Strawberry Hill and its furnishings is that it marks the first important occasion that anyone had waxed enthusiastic over the life and artifacts of the Middle Ages. Before Walpole (apart from Bishop Hurd's less important *Letters on Chivalry*) the word "gothick" was almost always a synonym for rudeness, barbarousness, crudity, coarseness and lack of taste. After Walpole the word assumed two new major meanings: first, vigorous, bold, heroic and ancient, and second, quaint, charming, romantic, perhaps a little decadent in its association with Romanism, but sentimental and interesting.

Strawberry Hill rapidly became one of the showplaces of England, all the more so because of Walpole's political and cultural connections, and visitors from all over England, even from the Continent, were to write Walpole for permission to visit and admire it. Walpole graciously set aside certain days for tours through his creation. It became the symbol of a new aesthetic experience, and to Walpole, after a time, it became more than just a dwelling and a fanciful hobby. It may well have assumed the status of a macrocosm of himself. Just as William Beckford's Fonthill became interlinked with the personality of its builder and owner, Strawberry Hill became Horace Walpole—so much so that it formed a new image of itself in his novel *The Castle of Otranto*.

A project that Walpole had long fancied was the establishment of a printing press, from which he could issue whatever he felt worthy of preservation. In 1757 he founded the famous Strawberry Hill Press (Officina Arbuteana), beginning its existence with the publication of works by Gray. For thirty-two years the Press remained in existence, producing, as Wilmarth S. Lewis has stated, more lasting work, proportionately, than any other press in British history.

It is something of a surprise, therefore, to learn that Walpole's most important work, *The Castle of Otranto*, was not printed at Strawberry Hill, as is sometimes claimed, but was prepared commercially in London in a five-hundred-copy edition. Proclaimed to be a translation from the Italian text of Onufrio Muralto (which name is obviously reminiscent of Horace Walpole), it appeared on Christmas Eve, 1764. Walpole immediately sent out copies to his friends and to reviewers, displaying tactics common to pseudonymous authors: an eager desire to claim the credit if the work is praised, and an equally strong urge to disclaim responsibility if it is damned. As a result, many of Walpole's letters which mention *The Castle of Otranto* are very coy about it, and many of his acquaintances (who have been followed by some modern critics) considered the book to be an enormous, pointless joke.

Walpole's true attitude would seem to have been complex and not easily summarized. He was a whimsical man, and even when he was serious, he found it difficult to avoid flights of fancy. He was also a shy man, despite his gregariousness and social virtuosity, who could pretend an attitude of detached irony toward something about which he had strong feelings. While it is often said that *The Castle of Otranto* was a very elaborate spoof, because Walpole referred to it with diffidence and flippancy, it is much more likely that there is a solid center of sincerity within the story.

The origins of *The Castle of Otranto* are a confused welter of conscious and unconscious material. In Walpole's preface to the second edition of the novel, he declares that he wished to bridge a gap between the romances of old, which were all marvel and wonder, and the realistic novel of his own day, by which he probably meant the work of Richardson and Fielding. There is no reason to doubt this statement; it fits his novel reasonably well. But beyond this conscious literary attempt were other factors. Walpole, in his letter of March 9, 1765, wrote to Rev. William Cole:

> Your partiality to me and Strawberry have, I hope, inclined you to excuse the wildness of the story. You will even have found some traits to put you in mind of this place. When you read of the picture quitting its panel, did you not recollect the portrait of Lord Falkland, all in white, in my Gallery? Shall I even confess to you, what was the origin of this romance! I waked one morning, in the beginning of last June, from a dream, of which, all I could recover, was, that I had thought myself in an ancient castle (a very natural dream for a head like mine filled with Gothic story), and that on the uppermost banister of a great staircase I saw a gigantic hand in armour. In the evening I sat down, and began to write, without knowing in the least what I intended to say or relate. The work grew on my hands, and I grew fond of it. . . . In short, I was so engrossed with my Tale, which I completed in less than two months, that one evening, I wrote from the time I had drunk my tea, about six o'clock, till half an hour after one in the morning, when my hand and fingers were so weary, that I could not hold the pen to finish my sentence, but left Matilda and Isabella talking in the middle of a paragraph.

Strawberry Hill is the setting of Walpole's novel, and even small items of decoration are represented, as much as fictional necessities permit.

Elements of cryptamnesia also entered the novel. When parallels between the historical dukedom of Otranto and Walpole's novel were pointed out, Walpole denied the connection, even though references could be found among his books and there was no reason (if Walpole had remembered it) to deny it. Similarly, reminiscences of his old college at Cambridge were to be found in the castle of Otranto, as Walpole himself later recognized in a letter that is often overlooked:

> Two or three years later [after *The Castle of Otranto*] I went to the University of Cambridge, where I had passed three years of my youth. In entering one of the colleges, which I had entirely forgotten, I found myself exactly in the court of my Castle. The towers, the gates, the chapel, the great hall, everything answered with the greatest exactness. In fine, the idea of this college had remained in my head without my thinking of it and I had used it as the plan of my Castle without being conscious of it myself.

Walpole's life after the appearance of *The Castle of Otranto* was uneventful and continued the same patterns as had already been established. He went to Paris in 1765, was presented at the French court, and became entangled in the quarrel that broke out between Hume and Rousseau. He returned to England the following year, and continued his literary work. In 1768 he was approached by Chatterton, who sent copies of "Rowley" poems to him. Walpole submitted them to Gray and Mason, who declared them hoaxes, and Walpole rejected them. Chatterton committed suicide not long after this, and Walpole was unjustly condemned for not having helped him. Strawberry Hill continued to expand. The gout bothered Walpole more and more, and there are gruesome stories of calculi that emerged from sores on his knuckles and toes. Disabled most of the time and barely able to hobble around, he still remained the great epistolographer of his age, continuing his correspondence almost until his death. He inherited the title Lord Orford in 1791, when he was seventy-four, but was too old and feeble to sit in the House of Lords. He died in 1797.

ii

Horace Walpole was a very prolific writer if his many varied areas of activity are all taken into account. Much of his production was trivial, but his contemporaries considered several of his works important. These were (apart from *The Castle of Otranto*) his *Anecdotes of Painting in England,* a compilation of material about British artists, based on notes taken by George Vertue; *The Mysterious Mother,* a tragedy in blank verse; and *Historic Doubts on the Life and Reign of King Richard III,* which was the first attempt to prove Richard III innocent of murdering the two little princes. Today, however, Walpole is remembered for two achievements: the largest, most vivacious, most revealing body of letters in the English language, and his novel, *The Castle of Otranto.*

This novel has been called one of the half-dozen historically most important novels in English. The founder of a school of fiction, the so-called Gothic novel, it served as the direct model for an enormous quantity of novels written up through the first quarter of the nineteenth century; at one or more steps removed, it has inspired imitations and influenced other forms on up to the present. It was probably the most important source for enthusiasm for the Middle Ages that suddenly swept Europe in the later eighteenth century, and many of the trappings of the early nineteenth century Romantic movement have been traced to it. It embodied the spirit of an age. There are several full studies of the development of this Gothic spirit within the English novel and it is not necessary to provide a detailed recapitulation of it here, but it is always interesting to see how a concept becomes changed by transmission and how individuals wittingly or unwittingly manipulate an accepted form and mirror other conditions around them.

A generation or so often has to pass before awareness of a prototypical work can seep down to readers and writers of popular literature. Such was the case with the detective story form crystallized by Poe around 1841, which did not become a truly popular form until the 1880's and 1890's in the hands of Doyle, Richard Marsh, Fergus Hume, "Dick Donovan" and others. Such was also the case with the early science-fiction works of H. G. Wells (1895–1905); it took approximately thirty years before American science-fiction was able to use them as foundations. And such was the history of Walpole's *Castle of Otranto.* Appreciated at first only by a coterie of friends and fellow spirits of Walpole's, it received tempered praise in *The Monthly Review* and was damned by *The Critical Review.* It went into a second printing of five hundred copies in April 1765, and it was translated into French in 1767. Its first adaptation into a play—an important barometer of public taste during this period—occurred in 1781 at Covent Garden, where Robert Jephson, assisted by Walpole, dramatized the romance under the title of *The Count of Narbonne.* It

was not especially successful, though it was later printed in a standard collection of plays. Actually, it does not resemble *The Castle of
Otranto* very much; all the supernaturalism has dropped out
and only the disinheritance and alienation plot remains.

Imitation began very slowly. In 1777 Clara Reeve wrote in her
preface to *The Champion of Virtue* (which is better known under
its later title, *The Old English Baron*), "This story is the literary
offspring of The Castle of Otranto." But not until the last decade
of the eighteenth century was the influence of Walpole's romance
felt strongly. Within this decade the Gothic novel achieved the
status of a truly popular genre. Even the most superficial relationship to Walpole's romance, the inclusion of the word "castle"
in the title of a book, can be indicated for hundreds of novels
found in this period. Some of these novels were long, and filled
several volumes; others were small chapbooks issued to sell for
sixpence, luridly illustrated with crude woodcuts.

Conventions were rigorously followed in the Gothic chain
that followed Walpole's work. In most such novels the action
takes place in the past, usually the Middle Ages, normally in and
around a castle. Yet there is seldom any attempt to create
verisimilitude or to build up antiquarian detail; in many cases
the authors seem ignorant of the commonplaces of history. The
Latin countries and Germany are most favored for a locale,
although occasionally England is used. The supernatural is
almost always present, although its nature and its quantity vary
greatly from novel to novel. On the whole, the earlier novels used
supernatural effects very sparingly, and as often as not explained
those effects away at the end. The ghost might be a hermit who
wants solitude; it might be a trick of coiners or bandits to keep
away unwanted visitors; or it might simply be chance illusion.
In all the novels of Ann Radcliffe, for example, there is only
one genuine ghost, and that is in her posthumous novel *Gaston
de Blondeville*. As the nineteenth century drew nearer, however,
the amount of supernaturalism in the Gothic novel increased,
so that by the day of Matthew Gregory Lewis's *The Monk,* supernatural devices included magic, witchcraft, true ghosts who took
an active part in the story, a devil, and much else. No apology
is made for this weird company.

Walpole's strongest contribution to the Gothic development
lies in the inner dynamics of his story. Almost all Gothic novels are

motivated in the same way. At some time in the past a crime was committed but was not avenged. The criminal is usually a murderer and usurper. At the time the story takes place the true heir to the usurped estate lies hidden in another identity, unconscious of his destiny. It would seem that he is permanently swindled of his patrimony, and that murder will not out. But the criminal, or villain, persecutes the true heir, and through a chain of circumstances, which usually involve the supernatural, the ancient crime is detected, the villain is punished, and the heir receives his birthright. It might be said that the Gothic novel is a primitive detective story in which God or Fate is the detective.

Gothic novels up through the first decade of the nineteenth century retain this basic plot. But gradually a change occurs in the fleshing of this skeleton. In the earlier novels, as in Walpole's *Castle of Otranto,* the "hero" is a passive character who merely responds to the buffetings of the "villain's" energy until Fate takes a hand. Gradually, in the evolution of the novel, however, the center of interest shifts toward the "villain," who acquires a Mephistotelean, Byronic fascination for the reader. The former "hero" is gradually pushed into the background. By the time of Charles Maturin's *Melmoth the Wanderer* [1820], which is the flower of the Gothic school, the "villain" Melmoth is the center of the story. It might be said that the understanding of evil, within the Gothic novel, has shifted from the Hamlet situation which Walpole recognized he had taken from Shakespeare, to the Lucifer of *Paradise Lost,* on the part of the Protestant clergyman Maturin.

So saturated was the literature of this period with Gothicism that a reaction set in and prose parodies appeared satirizing individual novels or the form in general. Best known of these works (although it contains other elements as well) is Jane Austen's *Northanger Abbey,* where *The Horrid Mysteries, The Necromancer of the Black Forest* and other Gothic novels are mentioned and discussed. William Beckford, the author of *Vathek,* also parodied his half-sister's sentimental Gothic novels with his *Modern Novel Writing* and *Azemia.* Perhaps the best strict parody of the Gothic form, however, is E. S. Barrett's *The Heroine,* which is partly a pastiche of elements from many popular novels. It has been reprinted several times, up to the 1930's, and is still worth reading. Peacock's *Nightmare Abbey,* which is a brilliant burlesque of Romantic ideas of many schools, even brings Coleridge and Byron into a Gothic plot.

A satirical poem by C. J. Pitt, *The Age: A Poem, Moral, Political, and Metaphysical, with Illustrative Annotations* [London, 1810], tells how a Gothic novel may be created; extended footnotes to the poem even give a recipe for transmuting the Gothic apparatus into the sentimental novel:

> (1) The conduct of the poet in considering romances and novels separately, may be thought singular by those who have penetration to see that a novel may be made out of a romance, or a romance out of a novel with the greatest ease, by scratching out a few terms, and inserting others. Take the following, which may, like machinery in factories, accelerate the progress of the divine art.
>
> From any romance to make a novel.
>
> Where you find —
>
> | | |
> |---|---|
> | A castle, ... | put An house |
> | A cavern, ... | A bower |
> | A groan, ... | A sigh |
> | A giant, ... | A father |
> | A bloodstained dagger, ... | A fan |
> | A knight, ... | A gentleman without whiskers |
> | A lady who is the heroine,. . | Need not be changed, being versatile. |
> | Assassins, ... | Telling glances. |
> | A monk, ... | An old steward. |
> | Skeletons, skulls, &c. . . . . . . | Compliments, sentiments, &c. |
> | A gliding ghost, ... | A usurer, or an attorney |
> | A midnight murder, ... | A marriage |
>
> The same table of course answers for transmuting a novel into a romance.

Some time later Sir Walter Scott said, in a similar vein, while reviewing a Gothic novel, "We strolled through a variety of castles, each of which was regularly called Il Castello, met with as many captains of Condottieri, heard various ejaculations of Santa Maria and Diabolo; read by a decaying lamp and in a tapestried chamber dozens of legends as stupid as the main history; examined such suites of deserted apartments as might set up a reasonable barrack, and saw as many glimmering lights as would make a respectable illumination." The references are to a novel of Ann Radcliffe's school, but the general conclusions are valid for the earlier Gothic novels.

Terms are relative and classification is sometimes a personal exercise, but it is safe to say that Charles Maturin wrote the last major novels that can be considered Gothic. Later works may still contain medieval castles, supernatural happenings, crimes, persecutions, mistaken identities, anticlericalism and other Gothic motives; but there is so much new material and the authors' intentions and techniques are so changed that referring to these novels as Gothic is pointless and misleading.

If Walpole's chain of immediate succession died with Maturin, Walpole's influence persisted in other areas of literature. Many of the genres and subgenres that arose in the following century are heavily indebted to the tradition that he established. To name only a few of the less obvious forms: The novel of crime and detection, which received its major crystallization before Poe in the work of William Godwin (*Things as They Are, or The Adventures of Caleb Williams* [1794], *Cloudesley* [1830], *Deloraine* [1833]) adds the Gothic concept of crime and persecution to a novel that is primarily a novel of social ideas. The historical novel, too, gradually emerged out of the somewhat nebulous interest in the past that characterized the Gothic tradition. In this case it was Sir Walter Scott who transcended the older form and created a novel of Romantic realism. Even as late as his *Bride of Lammermoor,* however, strong Gothic elements appeared in his work. Many of the nationalistic schools of fiction, such as the Irish, in the work of the Banims, or the American, in the early work of William Gilmore Simms, attempt to strike the Gothic mood with material of local origin. On the Continent, particularly in Germany, the Gothic novel became metamorphosed, on one level, into a novel of symbolism, psychopathology, and ideas, as in the work of E. T. A. Hoffmann. His *Devil's Elixir,* for example, is a fine transformation of Lewis's *Monk.*

In popular literature one sort of thriller of obvious Gothic provenience continued to flourish in England and on the Continent. This was the early Victorian "blood," as composed by George Prest and G. W. M. Reynolds in England, Victor Hugo (as in *Hans of Iceland* and *The Hunchback of Notre Dame*) in

France, and George Lippard (*The Quaker City, or The Monks of Monk Hall*) in America. Theirs was a novel of extremely intricate plot, great range of characters, sentimentalism and cheap emotion, sadism and half-submerged eroticism, hairraising incident (often with supernatural overtones), and as a rule poor craftsmanship. E. S. Turner in his fascinating *Boys Will Be Boys* has traced the gradual degeneration of this form into the juvenile literature of the early twentieth century.

Walpole himself might have been annoyed at the aftermath of his architectural involvement, or he might have felt flattered that generations of readers found his novel interesting. *The Castle of Otranto* is not, of course, a great novel, and it would be absurd to claim greatness for it. But Walpole was an intelligent man and a lively personality, and his individual charm can be perceived in his novel. The question whether his horrors are truly frightening or simply ludicrous is a matter for the individual reader to decide. Still, most authorities would agree that the same sort of thing was probably done better by Ann Radcliffe and M. G. Lewis, and certainly by Charles Maturin.

William Beckford and *Vathek*

In October 1817, Samuel Rogers the poet happened to be not too far from Salisbury, when he received an invitation to visit Fonthill Abbey, the home of the eccentric millionaire and author William Beckford. Fonthill Abbey was surely the most remarkable building in England at the time, and a contemporary letter by Lady Bessborough describes Rogers's impressions:

> He was received [at the thirty-eight-foot-high doors, which were opened] by a dwarf, who, like a crowd of servants thro' whom he passed, was covered with gold and embroidery. Mr. Beckford received him very courteously, and led him thro' numberless apartments all fitted up most splendidly, one with Minerals, including precious stones; another the finest pictures; another Italian bronzes, china, etc. etc., till they came to a Gallery that surpass'd all the rest from the richness and variety of its ornaments. It seem'd clos'd by a crimson drapery held by a bronze statue, but on Mr. B.'s stamping and saying, 'Open!' the Statue flew back, and the Gallery was seen, extending 350 feet long. At the end an open Arch with a massive balustrade opened to a vast Octagon Hall, from which a window shew'd a fine view of the Park. On approaching this it proved to be the entrance of the famous tower—higher than Salisbury Cathedral [over 285 feet]; this is not finish'd, but great part is done. The doors, of which there are many, are violet velvet covered over with purple and gold embroidery. They pass'd from hence to a Chapel, where on the alter were heaped Golden Candlesticks, Vases, and Chalices studded over with jewels; and from there into a great musick room, where Mr. Beckford begg'd Mr. Rogers to rest till refreshments were ready, and began playing with such *unearthly* power. . . . They went on to what is called the refectory, a large room built on the model of Henry 7 Chapel, only the ornaments gilt, where a Verdantique table was loaded with gilt plate fill'd with every luxury invention could collect. They next went into the Park with a numerous Cortege, and Horses and Servants, etc., which he described as equally wonderful, from the beauty of the trees and shrubs, and manner of arranging them, thro' a ride of five miles . . . and came to a beautiful Romantick lake, transparent *as liquid Chrysolite* (this is Mr. Rogers's, not my

expression), covered with wildfowl. . . . [On the next day Mr.
Rogers] was shewn thro' another suite of apartments fill'd with
fine medals, gems, enamell'd miniatures, drawings, old and modern, curios, prints and Manuscripts, and last a fine and well-
furnish'd library, all the books richly bound and the best editions,
etc. etc. An Old Abbe, the Librarian, and Mr. Smith, the water-
colour painter, who were there, told him there were 60 fires
always kept burning, except in the hottest weather. Near every
chimney in the sitting rooms there were large Gilt fillagree baskets
fill'd with perfum'd coals that produc'd the brightest flame.

The creator and ruler of this almost unbelievable Gothic
empire of some six thousand landscaped acres, a huge cathedral-
like building with the highest tower in England, to say nothing
of a fifteen-mile-long outer wall, twelve feet high and topped with
spikes, was of course William Beckford (1760–1844), the author
of *Vathek.*

Beckford was the only legitimate son of William Beckford the
Elder, an important political and mercantile figure of the day.
Pitt's lieutenant and John Wilkes's friend, the elder Beckford had
been Lord Mayor of London twice. Licentious, colorful, shrewd
yet reckless, he was the firebrand of the Whig opposition. He
was also probably the richest man in England, with a family
cloth business, extensive property holdings in England, and a
fortune in government bonds. A West Indian by birth, he was
also one of the largest land and slave owners in Jamaica. As later
events proved during the lifetime of his son, this wealth was not
all honestly gained. He died in 1770, when his son was ten
years old.

The Lord Mayor obviously planned to mould his son into an
empire builder. Young William was brought up bilingually on
English and French, started Latin at six, and Greek and philosophy at ten. Italian, Spanish, Portuguese, law, physics, and other
sciences were added at seventeen. His tutors were selected from
the best practitioners in various fields. Foremost among them was
young Wolfgang Mozart, who gave him piano lessons while in
England. In his old age Beckford claimed to have given the tune
"Non più andrai" to Mozart in their childhood; he also claimed
that Mozart had written him telling him that he planned to use
it in *The Marriage of Figaro.* Unfortunately, since no trace of this
correspondence has survived, the whole story is very suspect.

The senior Beckford's plans did not work out. It was true that young William was precociously intelligent, very gifted verbally, musically and artistically, and a handsome and appealing child. He certainly had many qualities which might have carried out his father's hopes. But he was also emotionally unbalanced, passionate, haughty, vindictive, and a thoroughgoing hedonist. He did not care about manipulating men in his father's way; he simply bought them, as needed, with his enormous fortune. Politics meant little to him, and in later life he became an M.P. mostly to protect his own interests at Fonthill. Worst of all, from his father's point of view, he was either not interested in business or had no aptitude at all for it; money to him was simply something that flowed in and could be used to buy pleasures.

Another facet of his personality that emerged when he was very young was an escapism focused on the Near East. He devoured *The Arabian Nights* and its imitations, and gathered together everything that he could about the Moslem world. All through his later life, no matter where he travelled, no matter what he was doing, the magic world of medieval Islam encompassed him. While this interest may have been fostered by his Orientalist art tutor, Alexander Cozens, perhaps a deeper reason lay within his own personality; Beckford often referred to himself as a Caliph, and where better than in the whimsical, irresponsible world of the fictional Harun al-Rashid could he find his dreams made real?

Beckford's early life was scandalous, even by eighteenth-century standards. His early maturity followed a pattern: he could remain in England for only short periods of time, for scandal soon would mount so high that his family would be forced to ship "the fool of Fonthill" to the Continent until things could cool off. During this period he took his cousin's wife as a mistress. This caused a family schism, but the situation was made worse when it was discovered that this was mostly a tactic to establish a homosexual relationship with young "Kitty" Courtenay. On the Continent, he travelled with such magnificence (including musicians and artists) that his entourage was at times taken for the Austrian Emperor's. Such ostentation he could well afford, for during the 1780's he had a fortune of about a million pounds and a yearly income of one hundred and fifty thousand pounds, both of which figures should be multiplied by twelve, in most areas, to indicate their present purchasing power. Attracted by the wealth, the worst adventurers from the stews of Venice became his intimates, and the shadiest circles of Paris and Naples knew him well.

Around the end of 1781 Beckford became acquainted with Samuel Henley, who was to be his collaborator on *Vathek.* Henley, who was currently tutoring cousins of Beckford's at Harrow, had been professor of moral philosophy at William and Mary in Virginia, but as a Tory had returned to England at the Revolution. Although his personal life was not the most reputable, he was in orders, was a very competent scholar, and had some pretensions to being an Orientalist. Beckford first employed him to edit *Dreams, Waking Thoughts and Incidents,* which was based on Beckford's travels in Spain and Portugal. The book was prepared for the press, was printed, and ready to be distributed in 1783 when Beckford's family forced the book to be suppressed. It is not known why the family took such violent measures, since the book is harmless enough, but it has been suggested that it was too frivolous for a future ruler of empire. Just what Henley contributed is also not exactly known.

Some time early in 1782 Beckford began to work on his Arabian tale, *Vathek.* In his old age, he claimed to have written it in three days and two nights, but references in his letters indicate that the book took considerably longer, perhaps three or four months. On April 25th he referred to it as "going on prodigiously," and by the end of May it was finished.

Beckford wrote his novel in French, and then decided to translate it. He was dissatisfied with his own translation, however, considering it too Gallic. He then recruited Henley to help him. For the next couple of years, while Beckford flitted back and forth between England and the Continent, the two men worked on it desultorily.

In 1783 the scandal with "Kitty" Courtenay was on the point of breaking disastrously. Beckford's family seems to have feared a criminal prosecution, and persuaded him to marry and beget a couple of children. In this year he married Lady Margaret Gordon, by whom he had two children before her death in May 1786. In 1784 he returned to Paris, where in addition to moving in high social circles he became involved in the shabby occultism that surrounded the court. In the same year, back in England, he became a Member of Parliament, was proposed for a baronage, but was rejected, presumably because of his personal life.

By the spring of 1785 *Vathek* was basically finished, except for notes which Henley was to provide, and four nouvelles (the Episodes) which Beckford planned to insert in the framework of the story. These were still incomplete. In June 1785 Beckford left for Switzerland, leaving both the French and English manuscripts of *Vathek* with Henley, who wanted to continue work on them. In February 1786 Beckford may have begun to suspect that Henley was moving too fast, for he baldly ordered him not to publish: "The Publication of Vathec must be suspended at least another year. I would not have him on any account precede the French edition. . . . the Episodes to Vathec are nearly finished, and the whole thing will be completed in eleven to twelve months."

In the first week of June 1786, however, *The History of the Caliph Vathek, An Arabian Tale from an Unpublished Manuscript, with Notes Critical and Explanatory* appeared on the London bookstalls. Henley had broken faith. Beckford did not learn of publication for several months, but was understandably furious at Henley's breach of confidence. He raged at Henley, who replied disingenuously that he thought Beckford wanted the book published. He also referred adroitly to the scandal that had caused Beckford's marriage, and hinted that his association with Beckford was really an attestation of faith in him.

Henley unquestionably acted badly, but it is difficult to understand why he risked alienating a wealthy and powerful patron. Greed for money may have motivated him, or perhaps (since it is known that he felt proprietary toward the English *Vathek*) he feared that *Vathek* would follow the way of *Dreams, Waking Thoughts and Incidents* and never see publication. Needless to say, his actions led to a breach with Beckford, who never forgave him. Henley spent the rest of his life in poverty, making a poor living at teaching, hack writing, and editing. Beckford even had the satisfaction of rejecting an appeal for financial help. Henley died in 1815.

The further history of *Vathek* is confused, since soon after Henley's English translation appeared, two French language editions were published, one at Lausanne, the other at Paris. It used to be believed that Beckford had rushed the Lausanne edition into print from his original manuscript, and then, recognizing that it needed improvement, had corrected his text and reissued it at Paris. Now, however, the situation is believed to have been more complex. According to the modern reconstruction of events, Beckford had no copy of his French manuscript, which may have been lost in the mails or retained by Henley. Beckford thereupon obtained a copy of the English book and hired Jean-David Levade, a hack translator, to turn it back into French. This version of *Vathek* was published at Lausanne; Beckford apparently did not see it until it was printed. When he saw it, he recognized that it was unworthy of him. He invoked the help of French literary friends, and set about retranslating it himself. This translation was then published at Paris. In 1815 Beckford prepared a third, revised French edition, which also appeared in Paris.

The text of *Vathek,* too, has presented problems. Four stories, told by denizens of Hell whom Vathek met in the halls of Iblis, were to have been inserted in the framework. Beckford spoke of working on them, but after the appearance of Henley's translation, he seems to have put them aside. They remained a legend during Beckford's lifetime, and as the novel rose in critical estimation, many persons asked to see them, including Lord Byron. But Beckford would not show them to anyone, and after a time it came to be believed that they had never existed at all.

At the turn of the present century, however, three French manuscripts were found in a document chest in the possession of one of Beckford's collateral descendants, the Duke of Hamilton. These manuscripts turned out to be the two long stories, "The Story of Prince Alasi and the Princess Firouzkah" and "The Story of Prince Barkiarokh," as well as a fragment entitled "The Story of the Princess Zulkaïs and the Prince Kalilah." These three stories, which are in the same vein as *Vathek,* were published in French and in Sir Frank Marzials's English translation from 1909 to 1912.

ii

Around 1793 Beckford's energies took a different turn, and he decided to build on the family estate at Fonthill, Wiltshire. He engaged the foremost British architect of the time, Sir James Wyatt, and tentatively decided to erect a Gothic ruin, a not uncommon picturesque project for the time. Two years of travel in Portugal, where he was feted at the most splendid palaces and religious edifices, however, crystallized his unformed yearnings, and he returned to Fonthill determined on a full abbey with the highest tower in England.

He had already enclosed his land behind a twelve-foot wall, to keep out fox hunters. From 1795 on crews of hundreds of laborers, both local and from London, worked incessantly behind the wall. On occasion they even worked by torchlight at night to meet the impossible schedules that Beckford set. Many were the disagreements between the dilatory Wyatt and the irascible, impatient Beckford. On the whole Wyatt stood for period architecture in the English perpendicular style, while Beckford insisted on incorporating special features that he had seen on his Iberian travels. As a result, although much of Fonthill Abbey was suggested by Salisbury Cathedral, just as much came from Batalha in Portugal. Beckford, too, wanted to mix styles to obtain a romantic impression, while Wyatt often urged purism. On one occasion Wyatt seems to have finished a balustrade in a style that Beckford had rejected. When Beckford saw it, he raced up to the gallery, braced his feet against the balustrade and sent it crashing down onto the furniture and floor below, both of which it demolished.

Building a medieval cathedral often took centuries, and the late eighteenth century was not so far beyond the fourteenth in technology that an enormous building mass like Fonthill Abbey, with a 285-foot tower, could safely be thrown up in a few years. To meet Beckford's demands Wyatt was forced to compromise, and to sacrifice stability for surface effects. The great tower was built of wood and plaster, and after a succession of minor collapses, the entire structure collapsed during a gale in the spring of 1797. Beckford was not so much annoyed at his architect as at having missed the spectacle of the fall. The tower was begun again, this time with stone walls, and although even this was shoddy work—without a supporting arch in the foundations— the second tower stood until 1825.

Work continued on Fonthill intermittently until 1812 or so, when Beckford considered his work as finished as his means permitted. He had completely neglected his fortune, and a succession of unfavorable court decisions on the estates that his ancestors had gathered by questionable means, enormous embezzlement and alienation by his agents, and abolition of the slave trade had all combined to reduced his splendid tax-free £150,000 per annum to a meagre £30,000 in the first decade of the century, and eventually to less. Still, even if Fonthill was not finished in the imperial style that Beckford had first proposed, it was at least regal. The grounds were laid out in the most picturesque manner, with streams, riding paths, American forests, and ponds. Trees and plants from many parts of the world were all planted naturalistically, to present ever varied prospects. Wild animals roamed almost fearlessly, for Beckford strictly forbade hunting. A state of war existed between him and his neighbors, who both resented him personally and were outraged by the enclosure of his lands. According to one story that circulated about Beckford, his private militia captured a trespasser on his grounds. Beckford received the man amicably and dined with him. He then had the man put out of the buildings, and urged him with great solicitude to beware of the packs of bloodhounds that roamed the estate nights.

Beckford lived in solitude, apart from his servants, and did not encourage visitors. Just how he spent his time is not known for a certainty. Beckford certainly spent considerable time in study, for he was a much more serious scholar than Walpole. He also perpetually rewrote and revised his letters, years after they had been delivered. He made trips to London galleries to buy paintings and books and other collectables; and he took such occasional trips to the Continent as his straitened means allowed. Contemporary opinion regarded the Abbey as the scene of nameless orgies held with the disreputable servants, including the dwarf, that he had gathered in Portugal and Italy. Some modern biographers (and a few earlier students) believe that a psychosexual upheaval had taken place in his middle age, and that his retirement to Fonthill was as an ascetic withdrawn from fleshly pursuits. The evidence is ambiguous, since such matters would be secret, but there was no mellowing of his personality and no maturation.

Beckford's later life passed without incident (or important literary work) until the 1820's, when his finances became so disordered that Fonthill was mortgaged and he was living on borrowed money. It now became clear that Fonthill must go, both buildings and fabulous collections. It was announced for auction, but in 1823 Beckford sold it to a gunpowder maker and war profiteer for £350,000.

After clearing his debts he bought an estate near Bath, and here in a new caliphate recreated Fonthill on a smaller scale and in a different style of architecture. There were hundreds of acres of parks, an ambitious house, and an Italianate tower—although on this occasion it rose to only 125 feet. Beckford called it Lansdown Baghdad. The legend of his eccentricities grew, *Vathek* was successfully reprinted, and by the time of his death at the age of eighty-four, in 1844, he was still one of the most talked-of men in England.

Beckford was a very complex personality, and it is doubtful if he can be completely understood from the records that remain. Most authorities agree in considering him a very disagreeable man. One of his foremost modern biographers, Guy Chapman, has called him "one of the less pleasant characters in English literary history." Even the eighteenth century, which was usually tolerant of abnormalities, regarded him with abhorrence; polite society, for the most part, ostracized him, despite his intelligence, political influence, and enormous wealth. It is significant that the chronicler of eighteenth-century social life, Horace Walpole, in his thousands of letters and in his memoirs, mentions him only once, and that time with disparagement.

Today Beckford is remembered only for *Vathek* (and Fonthill), and his other writings are neglected. Even the *Episodes,* which waited one hundred years for publication, are seldom read except by specialists in eighteenth-century literature. Yet certain of his other works are worth preservation. Three books tap the same vein of sardonic humor that is to be found in *Vathek*: *Biographical Memoirs of Extraordinary Painters* [1780], *Modern Novel Writing* [1796], and *Azemia* [1797]. The first, *Memoirs,* is a juvenile work burlesquing pretentious gallery notes to private art collections, and is said to have been based on the foolish comments his father's housekeeper made when showing visitors the Alderman's remarkable collection. The other two books, which appeared under pseudonyms, parody the sentimental Gothic novel of the day; they are probably pointed at the works of his novelist half-sister Mrs. Hervey, and are amusing and capable.

More important were Beckford's accounts of his travels in Europe, especially the Iberian peninsula. His first travel book, *Dreams, Waking Thoughts and Incidents* [1783], owes much to Sterne. It is a strange combination of dream fragments, reveries, travel impressions and data, all intermingled in eager vividness. It was suppressed after being printed and bound. Many years later Beckford revised it, enlarged it considerably with material from his other travels, and reissued it in 1834 as *Italy, with Sketches of Spain and Portugal.* Together with *Recollections of an Excursion to the Monasteries of Alcobaca and Batalha* [1835] it is one of the best travel accounts of the nineteenth century. If the literature of travel were not greatly neglected in modern studies, Beckford's work would be better known.

iii

Beckford's *Vathek* is almost universally recognized as a minor work of genius and as the best Oriental tale in English, but paradoxically there is strong doubt whether *Vathek* really should be placed in the stream of English literature. It was written in French, and all its major predecessors and sources were French. In English literature it stands isolated; it had no real forerunners and no worthy successors.*

The development of the Oriental tale in the eighteenth century was overwhelmingly a French phenomenon. Its manifestations in other languages, such as in the work of Gozzi and Wieland, are obviously derivative and of secondary importance. The genre began with Galland's French translation of *The Thousand and One Nights* (1704–1712), which was received with delight and enthusiasm. There had been earlier Oriental material in Italian and French, it is true, but none of this had the overwhelming power that *The Thousand and One Nights* demonstrated. These stories appealed strongly to the Rococo mind, what with the wide range of opportunities they offered: delicacies of style, elaboracies of construction, adventure, eroticism, moralism, sensibility, fantasy, philosophy and irony.

Many great authors contributed to the development of the Oriental tale in France. There were Voltaire's *contes philoso-*

---

* M. G. Lewis, who shared with Beckford the characteristics of great wealth, West Indian possessions, moral turpitude, and a taste for the marvelous, and the young George Meredith are the only authors who seem to have produced even entertaining work in this tradition immediately after Beckford. The Oriental ethnographic novel of Thomas Hope, James Morier and Meadows Taylor was a different phenomenon, with roots in both the picaresque novel and Sir Walter Scott.

phiques (*Zadig, La Princesse de Babylone,* etc.), Montesquieu's satire on French institutions (*Lettres persanes*), and the humorous half-parodies of Caylus (*Contes orientales*) and Count Anthony Hamilton (*Les quatre Facardins,* etc.). There were also many collections of less distinguished stories imitating *The Arabian Nights,* but which were simply more or less successful thrillers. T. S. Gueullette, for example, wrote collections of Chinese tales, Moghul tales, Tartarian tales, and even Peruvian tales, all of which provided dreary imitations of Galland's spirited translation. At one time, during the last part of the eighteenth century, a compilation of such "Arabian" material was published; entitled *Cabinet des fées,* it runs to several hundred volumes.

In English literature the Oriental tale is far less important. It remained a half-subliminal form, sometimes used as a vehicle for criticism; sometimes as an embodiment for a moral sentiment or an allegory; sometimes as a frame for an essay, as with Addison; and sometimes even as a story for its own sake. Goldsmith's *Citizen of the World* and Johnson's *Rasselas* are the only members of the form that survive at all (except *Vathek*), and there seems little else that deserves to live, with the possible exception of certain of Dr. Hawkesworth's stories. Most Oriental material is poverty-stricken in both idea and execution.

Beckford's contribution lies in the imagination that he brought to a basically dull genre. He was successful in regaining the sense of wonder that permeated the original Islamic stories. His was a recreation of the Gothicism of Islam, a cultural milieu as medieval as the European Gothicism of Walpole and his contemporaries. Beckford created afresh the Magic culture in its most delightful as well as its most horrific form.

Vathek is a skilfully plotted, amusing story, pervaded with a strong feeling for irony and a sense of the ludicrous that emerges from even the sinister activities of the mad caliph and his frenzied companions. The story is original with Beckford, for no Islamic sources have ever been found, although there does seem to have been a Caliph Watik. What parallels exist between *Vathek* and other works of literature are mostly of French origin. Yet part of his story he found very close at hand. Carathis, as his contemporaries recognized, is the image of his mother; Nouronihar is probably based on his mistress and cousin, Mrs. Peter Beckford, who shared impiety, lust and stupidity with Nouronihar; and Vathek is obviously and admittedly Beckford himself in his headlong quest for new sensation, new beauty, and peace. A forewarning of Vathek is to be found in one of the dreams reported in Beckford's *Dreams, Waking Thoughts and Incidents:* "I hurried to bed, and was soon lulled asleep by the storm. A dream bore me off to Persepolis; and led me thro' vast subterraneous treasures to a hall, where Solomon, methought, was holding forth on their vanity." Equally, the domains of Vathek came to be represented in Fonthill, and just as Walpole's *Castle of Otranto* is the embodiment of a building, *Vathek* is a man, a building, and a mode of thought all remarkably hypostatized as a novel.

John Polidori and *The Vampyre*

By the beginning of 1816 it was inevitable that the great poet Lord George Gordon Byron and his wife Anne were to separate, and Byron announced his decision to leave England. As T. L. Peacock, Shelley's friend and correspondent, phrased it in *Nightmare Abbey*, "Sir, I have quarrelled with my wife; and a man who has quarrelled with his wife is absolved from all duty to his country. I have written an ode to tell the people as much, and they may take it as they list."

Byron caused a gigantic coach to be built containing in compressed form all conveniences for life on the Continent, including a bed, a library, a plate chest, and even a dining area. In this anticipation of a modern trailer, he planned to work his way across Europe to Switzerland, where he would meet the Shelleys, and from there proceed to Italy, and perhaps ultimately to points farther east. He hired a doctor to accompany him as both companion and medical attendant, a procedure that was not too unusual among more wealthy travellers.

The doctor himself, however, was unusual. He was John Polidori (1795–1821), the son of an Italian resident in London who had translated *The Castle of Otranto* into Italian; the uncle of the future Dante Gabriel and Christina Rossetti; and the youngest man ever to receive a medical degree from the University of Edinburgh. Intelligent, lively, enthusiastic, he was probably selected as much for his personality as for his qualifications in medicine and Italian. Byron was to learn not too much later that the intelligence was only a superficial glibness; that the liveliness could be succeeded by cycles of depression and sullenness; and that the enthusiasm very often emerged as irresponsible impetuosity. All in all Polidori stood to gain more than Byron would from their association. He had the honor of travelling as a near-equal with the most famous man in England. He had also been promised five hundred pounds or guineas by John Murray, Byron's publisher, for a full diary of Byron's activities.

Difficulties arose almost as soon as the two men reached the Continent, and the remainder of the trip soon became a succession of tantrums and retreats by Polidori. One incident will suffice to show the personalities of the two men: When the entourage reached Cologne and the Rhine, Polidori, who had been musing over the inequities of fate, said unexpectedly to Byron, "Pray, what is there excepting writing poetry that I cannot do better than you?" Byron calmly faced him and replied, "Three things. First, I can hit with a pistol the keyhole of that door. Secondly, I can swim across that river to yonder point. And thirdly, I can give you a damned good thrashing." Polidori stalked out of the room.

Just why Byron tolerated Polidori as long as he did is something of a mystery. One reason may be that Byron at times took a mildly sadistic delight in laughing at Polidori's mooncalf behavior. On a later occasion, in Switzerland, Byron and his friends discovered that Polidori was in love with a local girl and twitted him about it. Polidori immediately denounced Byron as a cold-hearted monster, and it was Byron's turn to fly into a rage.

The Byron party reached Geneva on May 25, 1816; there they met the Shelleys—the poet, his wife Mary Godwin Shelley, and Claire Clairmont (Mary's half-sister), who had been Byron's mistress in England and was anxious to resume the relationship. There is no record of the meeting of the two great poets, which took place on the shore of Lake Geneva on May 27th, but they seem to have been pleased enough with each other's company to spend considerable time together. The Shelleys settled at the Maison Chappuis in the first week of June, while several days later the Byrons leased the Villa Diodati, which was about fifteen minutes' walk away, through a vineyard.

The two companies saw much of each other, and while details are not known, certain areas of their conversation can be recreated. There was, it is true, a certain range of disagreement between the two poets: Byron, according to the notes of his friend Hobhouse, was contemptuous of Shelley's "vague Wordsworthianism," and Shelley, on the other hand, did not like Byron's feelings of class. As Shelley wrote to Peacock, Byron was "an exceedingly interesting person . . . but slave to the vilest and most vulgar prejudices, and as mad as the winds." But these feelings aside, the two parties got along famously, and days and evenings were spent together on or along the lake, or in their quarters. We know that Byron spoke much of the London literary men that he had met or knew by reputation, and that Shelley told of the Godwin circle. Both men were interested in contemporary science, particularly galvanism, which seemed to give a semblance of life to dead limbs, and there was speculation about the possibility of reviving the dead with electricity. Byron sang a wild Albanian song for the Shelleys, and in solitary moments wrote scraps of "Childe Harold" on odd pieces of paper, which he stuffed into his pockets.

Shelley and Byron, on the whole, talked. Polidori glared at Shelley, to whom he had taken a violent dislike. Mary Shelley listened shily and quietly, while Claire Clairmont was visibly annoyed that the others, particularly the thick-skinned Polidori, would not leave her alone with Byron.

For the purposes of this introduction, the high point of this Geneva period in the lives of Byron and Shelley came during June 15th to 17th, give or take a day. The weather was miserable, rainy and cold, and the two parties spent most of their time in the Villa Diodati conversing. Mary Shelley describes this moment in her introduction to the second edition of *Frankenstein:*

> Some volumes of ghost stories, translated from the German into French fell into our hands.* There was the "History of the Inconstant Lover," who, when he thought to clasp the bride to whom he had pledged his vows, found himself in the arms of the pale ghost of her whom he had deserted. There was the tale of the sinful founder of his race, whose miserable doom it was to bestow the kiss of death on all the younger sons of his fated house, just when they reached the age of promise. His gigantic, shadowy form, clothed like the ghost in *Hamlet* in full armour, but with the beaver up, was seen at midnight. . . . "We will each write a ghost story," said Lord Byron; and his proposition was acceded to. There were four of us. The noble author began a tale, a fragment which he printed at the end of his poem of Mazeppa. Shelley, more apt to embody ideas and sentiments in the radiance of bril-

---

* *Fantasmagoriana; ou Recueil d'Histoires d'Apparitions, de Spectres, Revenans, Fantomes, &c.* Traduit de l'Allemand, par un Amateur. Paris, 1812. The Byron and Shelley parties were probably not aware that this work had been translated into English by Mrs. Utterson as *Tales of the Dead,* London, 1813.

liant imagery, and in the music of the most melodious verse that adorns our language, than to invent the machinery of a story, commenced one founded on the experiences of his early life. Poor Polidori had some terrible idea about a skull-headed lady, who was so punished for peeping through a keyhole—what to see I forget—something very shocking and wrong, of course; but when she was reduced to a worse condition than the renowned Tom of Coventry, he did not know what to do with her, and was obliged to dispatch her to the tomb of the Capulets, the only place for which she was fitted. The illustrious poets, also, annoyed by the platitude of prose, speedily relinquished their uncongenial task.

Despite Mary Shelley's comment about the "platitude of prose," Shelley had previously written two Gothic novels, *Zastrozzi, A Romance* [1810] and *St. Irvyne; or, The Rosicrucian, A Romance* [1811], both of which he had published privately. Nothing ever came of the Lake Geneva novel, however, and it is questionable if Shelley put anything on paper. Claire Clairmont's novel also came to nothing. Polidori started a novel, but abandoned it. His diary, however, contains a good summary of Byron's fragment and its planned continuation.

Strange experiences sustained the supernatural mood of these three or four days. One evening, while Byron was reciting lines from Coleridge's "Christabel," Shelley suddenly shrieked and ran from the room. The other followed him and found him near collapse, leaning against a fireplace. Podidori administered ether, which was considered a restorative in small doses, and Shelley then told of envisioning a woman, perhaps Mary Shelley, with eyes instead of nipples. Mary Shelley, too, shared the mood. As she lay half-asleep at night, the conversation of the previous day about Darwin's experiments in creating life, the possible revivification of the dead by electricity, and the impiety of it all swirled through her head. She dreamed the central situation of her *Frankenstein*. She awoke, and recognizing that what had terrified her might terrify others, began to write the novel *Frankenstein, or, The Modern Prometheus* which was published in 1818.

Byron seems to have worked on his novel for several days, writing it down in full text in a notebook. Polidori summarizes Byron's tale: after swearing his travelling companion to secrecy, a vampire, in modern Greece, undergoes a mock death and is buried. Some time later, the travelling companion returns to London and finds the vampire alive, preying on society. Bound by his oath, the traveller can say nothing. This summary, of course, fits both Byron's *Fragment* and Polidori's *Vampyre*.

After the supernatural soirées, which are probably more significant to us in restrospect than they were to the participants, life at the Villa Diodati proceeded along its usual emotional course. Polidori became more and more impossible as a companion. When Shelley beat him in a boat race, Polidori considered himself insulted and challenged Shelley to a duel. Shelley simply laughed, but Byron told Polidori that he, Lord Byron, had no conscientious objection to duels, and that he would be happy to take Shelley's place. Polidori sullenly retired. In his letter of June 17th, 1816 to Murray in England, Byron wrote about Polidori, "I never was much more disgusted with any human production than with the eternal nonsense, and tracasseries, and emptiness, and ill humour, and vanity of that young person."

By the end of the summer Byron recognized that Polidori's amusement value was less than his nuisance value, and dismissed him. Surprisingly enough, Polidori took his dismissal with good grace. When the Byron party removed to Milan, Polidori appeared and presented his compliments, and the two men met amicably. In the Opera, on October 28th, an incident occurred. Polidori found his vision blocked by a tall fur hat worn by an Austrian officer sitting in front of him, and requested the officer to remove it. Perhaps Polidori was less than polite, or perhaps he unwittingly insulted the military authorities. The officer asked Polidori to step outside. Polidori obliged, expecting a duel, but the officer simply had him arrested for disorderly conduct.

The French novelist Stendhal, who was present, has left a perceptive, detailed account of this incident. Byron and his Italian friends hastened to the guardhouse to effect Polidori's release, and a near riot took place. Polidori became scarlet with rage; Byron turned white. Finally one of Byron's Italian friends suggested that only *titolati* (titled persons) remain. The others left, and the *titolati* wrote their names on a card, guaranteeing Polidori's good behavior. Polidori was permitted to leave, but the next day he was ordered out of Milan, and nothing that Byron and his friends could do served to change the situation.

Exact dates are not available, but by the spring of 1817 Polidori had returned to England. He had originally planned to migrate to Brazil, but for one reason or another he settled at Norwich as a physician. He did not prosper in medicine or literature, despite several publications: *An Essay on the Source of Positive Pleasure* [1818]; *Ximenes, The Wreath, and Other Poems* [1819]; *Ernestus Berchtold, or The Modern Oedipus* [1819]; and *The Fall of the Angels* [1820]. In August 1821, what with gambling debts, his finances became desperate, and he committed suicide by poison. Byron's comment when he learned of Polidori's death was, "Poor Polly is gone."

Two and a half years before his death, however, Polidori had committed the single act that has ensured the preservation of his name. In the April 1819 issue of Colburn's *New Monthly Magazine* there appeared a short novel entitled *The Vampyre.* A long preface, which also discussed the Byron menage in Geneva, and referred to a correspondent there, attributed the story to Byron. As we now know, however, Polidori wrote *The Vampyre,* basing it on the novel that Byron was to have written at the Villa Diodati. Polidori's diary contains a summary of what Byron had planned to write.

Just what happened, or why it happened, is still not entirely clear, but a letter from John Murray to Lord Byron (April 27, 1819) provides some background, even though the interpretation of events may be biased:

> . . . a copy of a thing called The Vampire, which Mr. Colburn has had the temerity to publish with your name as its author. It was first printed in the New Monthly Magazine, from which I have taken the copy which I now enclose. The Editor of that Journal has quarrelled with the publisher, and has called this morning to exculpate himself from the baseness of the transaction. He says that he received it from Dr. Polidori for a small sum, Polidori saying that the whole plan of it was yours, and that it was merely written out by him. The Editor inserted it with a short statement to this effect; but to his astonishment Colburn cancelled the leaf on the day previous to its publication, and contrary to, and in direct hostility to his positive order, fearing that this statement would prevent the sale of this work in a separate form, which was subsequently done. He informs me that Polidori, finding that the sale exceeded his expectation, and that he had sold it too cheap, went to the Editor, and declared that he would deny it. . . .

In the following, May, issue of the *New Monthly,* a letter from Polidori was printed: "I beg leave to state that your correspondent has been mistaken in attributing that tale, in its present form, to

Lord Byron. The fact is, that though the ground-work is certainly Lord Byron's, its development is mine, produced at the request of a lady, who denied the possibility of anything being drawn from the materials which Lord Byron had said he intended to have employed in the formation of his Ghost Story." Nevertheless, when the separate reprint of *The Vampyre* appeared, Colburn took no heed of either Byron's disavowal which appeared in *Gallignani's Messenger* (published in Paris) or Polidori's letter, and managed to insinuate that the story was by Byron.

A short time later, in the preface to his novel *Ernestus Berchtold,* which is a tragic novel about a Byronic egotist, Polidori made the following surprising claim about *The Vampyre:*

> The tale here presented to the public is the one I began at Coligny, when Frankenstein was planned, and when a noble author having determined to descend from his lofty range, gave up a few hours to a tale of terror, and wrote the fragment published at the end of Mazeppa.* *The tale which lately appeared, and to which his lordship's name was wrongfully attached, was founded upon the ground-work upon which this fragment was to have been continued. . . . it appears to have fallen into the hands of some person, who sent it to the Editor in such a way, as to leave it so doubtful from his words, whether it was his lordship's or not, that I found some difficulty in vindicating it to myself. These circumstances were stated in a letter sent to the Morning Chronicle three days after the publication of the tale, but in consequence of the publishers representing to me that they were compromised as well as myself, and that immediately they were certain it was mine, that they themselves would wish to make the *amende honorable* to the public, I allowed them to recall the letter which had lain some days at that paper's office.

At this point it is difficult to judge motivations, and we have no real way of knowing what Polidori's intentions really were. It would seem unlikely that a man as egotistical as Polidori would have been satisfied to see his own work printed under another man's name; it is reasonable to consider Colburn guilty. After stealing Byron's plot, Polidori may well have salved his conscience by his not inaccurate statement about authorship. He may have felt that theft was acceptable if one admitted it frankly—and he probably also needed the money. On the other hand an element of malice must also be assigned to Polidori's actions, for to a contemporary reader it would have been obvious that Ruthven the vampire is in part at least a fictionalization of

Byron. Byron was an internationally notorious personality, known more at this time for his scandalous life than for his works. Many of Ruthven's characteristics fit well into the image of Byron that had been forming. Indeed, even the name Ruthven is significant, for Byron's former mistress Lady Caroline Lamb in her novel *Glenarvon* had attacked Byron under this name. This personal aspect of *The Vampyre,* though it is now nearly forgotten, must have added to Byron's rage, for he took personal attacks very seriously.

Yet despite the many disclaimers and apologies that saw print and probably passed in correspondence and conversation, *The Vampyre* was generally accepted as Byron's work and became enormously popular, particularly on the Continent. It was immediately translated into French, in three different versions, and into German at least twice. E. T. A. Hoffmann comments on Byron's "remarkable knack for the weird and horrible" in his *Serapion Brethren*. In 1824 A. Pichot published a critical essay on Byron, and came to the conclusion that *The Vampyre* had more to do with Byron's popularity in France than all his poetry.

Almost immediately *The Vampyre* appeared as a stage presentation in France, and by the early 1820's the theatrical life of Paris was almost obsessed by the vampire theme. Several versions of Polidori's play were on the boards at the same time, among the playwrights being such prominent literary figures as Eugène Scribe and Charles Nodier. As an amusing anticipation of modern motion picture practice, there were even plays entitled *The Three Vampires* and *Son of the Vampire*. Alexandre Dumas *père's* memoirs use a performance of Nodier's vampire play as background for an extended image of Parisian theatrical life. He summarizes the absurd story in detail, comments on the many errors and misunderstandings that permeated it, and describes with great vivacity the doings of the audience and the claque.

Polidori's story returned to England when J. R. Planché translated Nodier's *Le Vampire* (which was supposed to be the best of the French productions) into English. As *The Vampire, or The Bride of the Isles,* it was performed at the English Opera House in London in 1820. Planché had objected strongly to setting the play in Scotland, but since Scottish situations were popular and the management had Scottish costumes to be used, Scotland it remained; the play was very successful. Later Planché had his own way when he staged an English adaptation of Marschner's opera *Der Wampyr* (which was also based on Polidori's story), and set the play in Hungary. Other vampire plays followed Planché's. To mention a typical specimen: *The Vampire Bride, or The Tenant of the Tomb* by George Blink is set in medieval times. The vampire Brunhilda, who had been brought back from death by magic, says in her monologue: "Children pass from life into eternity, pale, bloodless and emaciated they have died, and no visible sign hath yet denoted what has been the cause of this dire malady. The village I have thinned of its young inmates and but two remain. . . ."

In the history of the English novel Polidori's *Vampyre* has interest beyond its literary merits. It is probably the first extensive vampire story in English, and it served as the model for many later developments. It showed the direction that Romantic supernatural fiction was taking: the abandonment of the disinheritance plot that used to be almost universally present in the longer Gothic forms; the increased employment of local color and folklore, in this case modern Greek instead of Germanic; and a much heavier use of supernaturalism, which is no longer rationalized or explained away as illusion or fraud, but is accepted within its own terms. Polidori's novel also marks a stage in the gradual shift of interest away from the earlier "hero," who was a passive, suffering figure, to the more dynamic, action-initiating "villain." This change of focus is, of course, simply one aspect of Byronism.

For the remainder of the nineteenth century fiction based on vampirism is heavily in debt to Polidori's work. Prest's crude *Varney the Vampire,* which repeats the incidents and situations of Polidori's story over and over until Varney finally repents and commits suicide by leaping into Vesuvius; LeFanu's pleasing and melancholy *Carmilla;* and Bram Stoker's *Dracula*—to name a few of the more important works in this subgenre—all show the influence of Polidori's work. *The Vampyre* also influenced the development of the occult or magical novel. Episodes in Alexandre Dumas's *Balsamo the Magician,* which romanticized the life of Cagliostro, are obviously indebted to Polidori's work, while Bulwer Lytton's *The Haunted and the Haunters* (also known, in a slightly different version, as *The House and the Brain*) and *A Strange Story,* lean heavily on it. Margraves, the evil magician of

A Strange Story, is simply a restatement of Ruthven. Even super-natural fiction from authors not normally associated with the genre, such as W. H. Ainsworth's *Auriol, or The Elixir of Life* shows this influence. To carry the tradition farther, when Poli-dori's own work was nearly forgotten, Bulwer Lytton's novels served as the stimulus for still further generations of works warning against the evil aspects of egoism.

Lord Byron's vampire story, however, is another matter. When Byron heard of Polidori's fraud, he tore his fragment from the notebook in which he had written it, and sent the leaves to Murray for publication. It was characteristic of Byron to remark that this notebook was once the household book of his former wife, and that he kept it as the sole example of her writing he owned, except for her signature on the bill of separation.

Murray published Byron's fragment at the end of *Mazeppa* in 1819 and there it has remained, forgotten and unread except by specialists. Yet it is an interesting work, full of the vitality that permeated Byron's remarkable letters, and we must regret that Byron did not finish it, or at least write more. It is still worth reading.

New York, 1965   E. F. BLEILER

THE CASTLE OF OTRANTO

A Gothic Story

Sir Walter Scott's Introduction

The Castle of Otranto is remarkable not only for the wild interest
of the story, but as the first modern attempt to found a tale of
amusing fiction upon the basis of the ancient romances of chivalry.
The neglect and discredit of these venerable legends had commenced so early as the reign of Queen Elizabeth, when, as we
learn from the criticism of the times, Spenser's fairy web was
rather approved on account of the mystic and allegorical interpretation, than the plain and obvious meaning of his chivalrous pageant. The drama, which shortly afterwards rose into splendour,
and versions from the innumerable novelists of Italy, supplied to
the higher class the amusement which their fathers received from
the legends of Don Belianis and *The Mirror of Knighthood;* and
the huge volumes which were once the pastime of nobles and
princes, shorn of their ornaments, and shrunk into abridgements,
were banished to the kitchen and nursery, or, at best, to the hall-
window of the old-fashioned country manor-house. Under Charles
II the prevailing taste for French literature dictated the introduction of those dullest of dull folios, the romances of Calprenède
and Scudéry, works which hover between the ancient tale of chivalry and the modern novel. The alliance was so ill conceived, that
they retained all the insufferable length and breadth of the prose
volumes of chivalry, the same detailed account of reiterated and
unvaried combats, the same unnatural and extravagant turn of
incident, without the rich and sublime strokes of genius, and vigour of imagination, which often distinguished the early romance;
while they exhibited all the sentimental languor and flat love-in-
trigue of the novel, without being enlivened by its variety of character, just traits of feeling, or acute views of life. Such an ill-imag-
ined species of composition retained its ground longer than might
have been expected, only because these romances were called
works of entertainment, and there was nothing better to supply
their room. Even in the days of the *Spectator,* Clelia, Cleopatra,

and the Grand Cyrus (as that precious folio is christened by its butcherly translator), were the favourite closet companions of the fair sex. But this unnatural taste began to give way early in the eighteenth century; and, about the middle of it, was entirely superseded by the works of Le Sage, Richardson, Fielding, and Smollett; so that even the very name of romance, now so venerable in the ear of antiquaries and book-collectors, was almost forgotten at the time *The Castle of Otranto* made its first appearance.

The peculiar situation of Horace Walpole, the ingenious author of this work, was such as gave him a decided predilection for what may be called the Gothic style, a term which he contributed not a little to rescue from the bad fame into which it had fallen, being currently used before his time to express whatever was in pointed and diametrical opposition to the rules of true taste.

Mr. Walpole, it is needless to remind the reader, was son of that celebrated minister, who held the reins of government under two successive monarchs, with a grasp so firm and uncontrolled, that his power seemed entwined with the rights of the Brunswick family. In such a situation, his sons had necessarily their full share of that court which is usually paid to the near connections of those who have the patronage of the state at their disposal. To the feeling of importance inseparable from the object of such attention, was added the early habit of connecting and associating the interest of Sir Robert Walpole, and even the domestic affairs of his family, with the parties in the Royal Family of England, and with the changes in the public affairs of Europe. It is not therefore wonderful, that the turn of Horace Walpole's mind, which was naturally tinged with love of pedigree, and a value for family honours, should have been strengthened in that bias by circumstances which seemed, as it were, to bind and implicate the fate of his own house with that of princes, and to give the shields of the Walpoles, Shorters, and Robsarts from whom he descended, an added dignity unknown to their original owners. If Mr. Walpole ever founded hopes of raising himself to political eminence, and turning his family importance to advantage in his career, the termination of his father's power, and the personal change with which he felt it attended, disgusted him with active life, and early consigned him to literary retirement. He had, indeed, a seat in parliament for many years; but, unless upon one occasion, when he vindicated the memory of his father with great dignity and eloquence, he took no share in the debates of the house, and not much in the parties which maintained them. The subjects of his study were, in a great measure, dictated by his habits of thinking and feeling operating upon an animated imagination, and a mind acute, active, penetrating, and fraught with a great variety of miscellaneous knowledge. Travelling had formed his taste for the fine arts; but his early predilection in favour of birth and rank connected even these branches of study with that of Gothic history and antiquities. His *Anecdotes of Painting and Engraving* evince many marks of his favourite pursuits; but his *Catalogue of Royal and Noble Authors,* and his *Historical Doubts,* we owe entirely to the antiquary and the genealogist. The former work evinces, in a particular degree, Mr. Walpole's respect for birth and rank; yet may, perhaps, be ill calculated to gain much sympathy for either. It would be difficult, by any process, to select a list of as many plebeian authors, containing so very few whose genius was worthy of commemoration. The *Historical Doubts* are an acute and curious example how minute antiquarian research may shake our faith in the facts most pointedly averred by general history. It is remarkable also to observe how, in defending a system which was probably at first adopted as a mere literary exercise, Mr. Walpole's doubts acquired, in his eyes, the respectability of certainties, in which he could not brook controversy.

Mr. Walpole's domestic occupations, as well as his studies, bore evidence of a taste for English antiquities, which was then uncommon. He loved, as a satirist has expressed it, "to gaze on Gothic toys through Gothic glass"; and the villa at Strawberry-Hill, which he chose for his abode, gradually swelled into a feudal castle, by the addition of turrets, towers, galleries, and corridors, whose fretted roofs, carved panels, and illuminated windows, were garnished with the appropriate furniture of scutcheons, armorial-bearings, shields, tilting lances, and all the panoply of chivalry. The Gothic order of architecture is now so generally, and, indeed, indiscriminately used, that we are rather surprised if the country-house of a tradesman retired from business does not exhibit lance-olated windows, divided by stone shafts, and garnished by painted glass, a cupboard in the form of a cathedral-stall, and a pig-house with a front borrowed from the façade of an ancient chapel. But, in the middle of the eighteenth century, when Mr. Walpole began to exhibit specimens of the Gothic style, and to show how pat-

terns, collected from cathedrals and monuments, might be applied
to chimney-pieces, ceilings, windows, and balustrades, he did not
comply with the dictates of a prevailing fashion, but pleased his
own taste, and realised his own visions, in the romantic cast of
the mansion which he erected.*

Mr. Walpole's lighter studies were conducted upon the same
principle which influenced his historical researches, and his taste
in architecture. His extensive acquaintance with foreign literature, on which he justly prided himself, was subordinate to his
pursuits as an English antiquary and genealogist, in which he
gleaned subjects for poetry and for romantic fiction, as well as for
historical controversy. These are studies, indeed, proverbially
dull; but it is only when they are pursued by those whose fancies
nothing can enliven. A Horace Walpole, or a Thomas Warton, is
not a mere collector of dry and minute facts, which the general
historian passes over with disdain. He brings with him the torch
of genius, to illuminate the ruins through which he loves to wander; nor does the classic scholar derive more inspiration from the
pages of Virgil, than such an antiquary from the glowing, rich, and
powerful feudal painting of Froissart. His mind being thus stored
with information, accumulated by researches into the antiquities
of the middle ages, and inspired, as he himself informs us, by the
romantic cast of his own habitation, Mr. Walpole resolved to give
the public a specimen of the Gothic style adapted to modern literature, as he had already exhibited its application to modern
architecture.

As, in his model of a Gothic modern mansion, our author had
studiously endeavoured to fit to the purposes of modern conven-
ience, or luxury, the rich, varied, and complicated tracery and
carving of the ancient cathedral, so, in *The Castle of Otranto,* it
was his object to unite the marvellous turn of incident, and im-
posing tone of chivalry, exhibited in the ancient romance, with
that accurate exhibition of human character, and contrast of feelings and passions, which is, or ought to be, delineated in the
modern novel. But Mr. Walpole, being uncertain of the reception
which a work upon so new a plan might experience from the
world, and not caring, perhaps, to encounter the ridicule which

* It is well known that Mr. Walpole composed his beautiful and lively fable
of the Entail upon being asked, whether he did not mean to settle Strawberry-
Hill, when he had completed its architecture and ornaments, upon his family?

would have attended its failure, *The Castle of Otranto* was ushered into the world as a translation from the Italian. It does not
seem that the authenticity of the narrative was suspected. Mr.
Gray writes to Mr. Walpole, on 30th December, 1764: "I have
received *The Castle of Otranto,* and return you my thanks for it.
It engages our attention here [*i. e.* at Cambridge], makes some of
us cry a little; and all, in general, afraid to go to bed o' nights.
We take it for a translation; and should believe it to be a true
story, if it were not for St. Nicholas." The friends of the author
were probably soon permitted to peep beneath the veil he had
thought proper to assume; and, in the second edition, it was altogether withdrawn by a preface, in which the tendency and nature
of the work are shortly commented upon and explained. From the
following passage, translated from a letter by the author to Madame Deffand, it would seem that he repented of having laid aside
his incognito; and, sensitive to criticism, like most dilettante authors, was rather more hurt by the raillery of those who liked not
his tale of chivalry, than gratified by the applause of his admirers.
"So they have translated my *Castle of Otranto,* probably in ridicule of the author. So be it—however, I beg you will let their raillery pass in silence. Let the critics have their own way; they give
me no uneasiness. I have not written the book for the present age,
which will endure nothing but *cold common sense.* I confess to
you, my dear friend, (and you will think me madder than ever),
that this is the only one of my works with which I am myself
pleased; I have given reins to my imagination till I became on
fire with the visions and feelings which it excited. I have composed it in defiance of rules, of critics, and of philosophers; and it
seems to me just so much the better for that very reason. I am even
persuaded, that some time hereafter, when taste shall resume the
place which philosophy now occupies, my poor *Castle* will find
admirers: we have actually a few among us already, for I am just
publishing the third edition. I do not say this in order to mendi-
cate your approbation.* I told you from the beginning you would
not like the book—your visions are all in a different style. I am
not sorry that the translator has given the second preface; the first,

---

* Madame Deffand had mentioned having read *The Castle of Otranto* twice
over; but she did not add a word of approbation. She blamed the translator for
giving the second preface, chiefly because she thought it might commit Walpole with Voltaire.

however, accords best with the style of the fiction. I wished it to be believed ancient, and almost everybody was imposed upon." If the public applause, however, was sufficiently qualified by the voice of censure to alarm the feelings of the author, the continued demand for various editions of *The Castle of Otranto* showed how high the work really stood in popular estimation, and probably eventually reconciled Mr. Walpole to the taste of his own age. This Romance has been justly considered not only as the original and model of a peculiar species of composition, but as one of the standard works of our lighter literature. A few remarks both on the book itself, and on the class to which it belongs, have been judged an apposite introduction to an edition of *The Castle of Otranto*, which the publishers have endeavoured to execute in a style of elegance corresponding to the estimation in which they hold the work, and the genius of the author.

It is doing injustice to Mr. Walpole's memory to allege, that all which he aimed at in *The Castle of Otranto* was "the art of exciting surprise and horror"; or, in other words, the appeal to that secret and reserved feeling of love for the marvellous and supernatural, which occupies a hidden corner in almost every one's bosom. Were this all which he had attempted, the means by which he sought to attain his purpose might, with justice, be termed both clumsy and puerile. But Mr. Walpole's purpose was both more difficult of attainment, and more important when attained. It was his object to draw such a picture of domestic life and manners, during the feudal times, as might actually have existed, and to paint it chequered and agitated by the action of supernatural machinery, such as the superstition of the period received as matter of devout credulity. The natural parts of the narrative are so contrived, that they associate themselves with the marvellous occurrences; and, by the force of that association, render those *speciosa miracula* striking and impressive, though our cooler reason admits their impossibility. Indeed to produce, in a well-cultivated mind, any portion of that surprise and fear which is founded on supernatural events, the frame and tenor of the whole story must be adjusted in perfect harmony with this mainspring of the interest. He who, in early youth, has happened to pass a solitary night in one of the few ancient mansions which the fashion of more modern times has left undespoiled of their original furniture, has probably experienced, that the gigantic and preposterous figures dimly visible in the defaced tapestry, the remote clang of the distant doors which divide him from living society, the deep darkness which involves the high and fretted roof of the apartment, the dimly-seen pictures of ancient knights, renowned for their valour, and perhaps for their crimes, the varied and indistinct sounds which disturb the silent desolation of a half-deserted mansion; and, to crown all, the feeling that carries us back to ages of feudal power and papal superstition, join together to excite a corresponding sensation of supernatural awe, if not of terror. It is in such situations, when superstition becomes contagious, that we listen with respect, and even with dread, to the legends which are our sport in the garish light of sun-shine, and amid the dissipating sights and sounds of every-day life. Now it seems to have been Walpole's object to attain, by the minute accuracy of a fable, sketched with singular attention to the costume of the period in which the scene was laid, that same association which might prepare his reader's mind for the reception of prodigies congenial to the creed and feelings of the actors. His feudal tyrant, his distressed damsel, his resigned, yet dignified, churchman—the Castle itself, with its feudal arrangement of dungeons, trap-doors, oratories, and galleries, the incidents of the trial, the chivalrous procession, and the combat—in short, the scene, the performers, and action, so far as it is natural, form the accompaniments of his spectres and his miracles, and have the same effect on the mind of the reader that the appearance and drapery of such a chamber as we have described may produce upon that of a temporary inmate. This was a task which required no little learning, no ordinary degree of fancy, no common portion of genius, to execute. The association of which we have spoken is of a nature peculiarly delicate, and subject to be broken and disarranged. It is, for instance, almost impossible to build such a modern Gothic structure as shall impress us with the feelings we have endeavoured to describe. It may be grand, or it may be gloomy; it may excite magnificent or melancholy ideas; but it must fail in bringing forth the sensation of supernatural awe, connected with halls that have echoed to the sounds of remote generations, and have been pressed by the footsteps of those who have long since passed away. Yet Horace Walpole has attained in composition, what, as an architect, he must have felt beyond the power of his art. The remote and superstitious period in which his scene is laid, the art with which he has furnished forth its Gothic decorations, the sustained, and, in general, the dignified tone of feudal manners, prepare us gradually for the favourable reception of prodigies which, though they could not really have happened at any period, were consistent with the belief of all mankind at that in which the action is placed. It was, therefore, the author's object not merely to excite surprise and terror, by the introduction of supernatural agency, but to wind up the feelings of his reader till they became for a moment identified with those of a ruder age, which

Held each strange tale devoutly true.

The difficulty of attaining this nice accuracy of delineation may be best estimated by comparing *The Castle of Otranto* with the less successful efforts of later writers; where, amid all their attempts to assume the tone of antique chivalry, something occurs in every chapter so decidedly incongruous, as at once reminds us of an ill-sustained masquerade, in which ghosts, knights-errant, magicians, and damsels gent, are all equipped in hired dresses from the same warehouse in Tavistock-street.

There is a remarkable particular in which Mr. Walpole's steps have been departed from by the most distinguished of his followers.

Romantic narrative is of two kinds—that which, being in itself possible, may be matter of belief at any period; and that which, though held impossible by more enlightened ages, was yet consonant with the faith of earlier times. The subject of *The Castle of Otranto* is of the latter class. Mrs. Radcliffe, a name not to be mentioned without the respect due to genius, has endeavoured to effect a compromise between those different styles of narrative, by referring her prodigies to an explanation, founded on natural causes, in the latter chapters of her romances. To this improvement upon the Gothic romance there are so many objections, that we own ourselves inclined to prefer, as more simple and impressive, the narrative of Walpole, which details supernatural incidents as they would have been readily believed and received in the eleventh or twelfth century. In the first place, the reader feels indignant at discovering he has been cheated into a sympathy with terrors which are finally explained as having proceeded from some very simple cause; and the interest of a second reading is entirely destroyed by his having been admitted behind the scenes at the conclusion of the first. Secondly, the precaution of relieving our spirits from the influence of supposed supernatural terror, seems as unnecessary in a work of professed fiction, as that of the prudent Bottom, who proposed that the human face of the representative of his lion should appear from under his masque,* and acquaint the audience plainly that he was a man as other men, and nothing more than Snug the joiner. Lastly, these substitutes for supernatural agency are frequently to the full as improbable as the machinery which they are introduced to explain away and to supplant. The reader, who is required to admit the belief of supernatural interference, understands precisely what is demanded of him; and, if he be a gentle reader, throws his mind into the attitude best adapted to humour the deceit which is presented for his entertainment, and grants, for the time of perusal, the premises on which the fable depends.† But if the author voluntarily binds himself to account for all the wondrous occurrences which he introduces, we are entitled to exact that the explanation shall be natural, easy, ingenious, and complete. Every reader of such works must remember instances in which the explanation of mysterious circumstances in the narrative has proved equally, nay, even more incredible, than if they had been accounted for by the agency of supernatural beings. For the most incredulous must allow, that the interference of such agency is more possible than that an effect resembling it should be produced by an inadequate cause. But it is unnecessary to enlarge further on a part of the subject, which we have only mentioned to exculpate our author from the charge of using machinery more clumsy than his tale

* Honest Bottom's device seems to have been stolen by Mr. John Wiseman, schoolmaster of Linlithgow, who performed a lion in a pageant presented before Charles I, but vindicated his identity in the following verses put into his mouth by Drummond of Hawthornden:

> Thrice royal sir, here do I thee beseech,
> Who art a lion, to hear a lion's speech:
> A miracle! for, since the days of Aesop,
> No lion till those times his voice did raise up
> To such a majesty: Then, King of Men,
> The King of beasts speaks to thee from his den,
> Who, though he now inclosed be in plaster,
> When he was free, was Lithgow's wise schoolmaster.

† There are instances to the contrary however. For example, that stern votary of severe truth, who cast aside *Gulliver's Travels* as containing a parcel of improbable fictions.

from its nature required. The bold assertion of the actual existence of phantoms and apparitions seems to us to harmonise much
more naturally with the manners of feudal times, and to produce
a more powerful effect upon the reader's mind, than any attempt
to reconcile the superstitious credulity of feudal ages with the
philosophic scepticism of our own, by referring those prodigies to
the operation of fulminating powder, combined mirrors, magic
lanthorns, trap-doors, speaking trumpets, and such like apparatus
of German phantasmagoria.

It cannot, however, be denied, that the character of the supernatural machinery in *The Castle of Otranto* is liable to objections. Its action and interference is rather too frequent, and
presses too hard and constantly upon the same feelings in the
reader's mind, to the hazard of diminishing the elasticity of the
spring upon which it should operate. The fund of fearful sympathy which can be afforded by a modern reader to a tale of
wonder, is much diminished by the present habits of life and
mode of education. Our ancestors could wonder and thrill through
all the mazes of an interminable metrical romance of fairy land,
and of enchantment, the work perhaps of some

> Prevailing poet, whose undoubting mind
> Believed the magic wonders which he sung.

But our habits and feelings and belief are different, and a transient, though vivid, impression is all that can be excited by a tale
of wonder even in the most fanciful mind of the present day. By
the too frequent recurrence of his prodigies, Mr. Walpole ran,
perhaps, his greatest risk of awakening *la raison froide,* that cold
common sense, which he justly deemed the greatest enemy of the
effect which he hoped to produce. It may be added also, that the
supernatural occurrences of *The Castle of Otranto* are brought
forward into too strong day-light, and marked by an over degree
of distinctness and accuracy of outline. A mysterious obscurity
seems congenial at least, if not essential, to our ideas of disembod-
ied spirits, and the gigantic limbs of the ghost of Alphonso, as
described by the terrified domestics, are somewhat too distinct and
corporeal to produce the feelings which their appearance is intended to excite. This fault, however, if it be one, is more than
compensated by the high merit of many of the marvellous incidents in the romance. The descent of the picture of Manfred's

ancestor, although it borders on extravagance, is finely introduced, and interrupts an interesting dialogue with striking effect.
We have heard it observed, that the animated figure should rather
have been a statue than a picture. We greatly doubt the justice of
the criticism. The advantage of the colouring induces us decidedly
to prefer Mr. Walpole's fiction to the proposed substitute. There
are few who have not felt, at some period of their childhood, a
sort of terror from the manner in which the eye of an ancient
portrait appears to fix that of the spectator from every point of
view. It is, perhaps, hypercritical to remark (what, however, Walpole of all authors might have been expected to attend to), that
the time assigned to the action, being about the eleventh century,
is rather too early for the introduction of a full-length portrait.
The apparition of the skeleton hermit to the prince of Vicenza
was long accounted a master-piece of the horrible; but of late the
valley of Jehosophat could hardly supply the dry bones necessary
for the exhibition of similar spectres, so that injudicious and repeated imitation has, in some degree, injured the effect of its
original model. What is most striking in *The Castle of Otranto,* is
the manner in which the various prodigious appearances, bearing
each upon the other, and all upon the accomplishment of the ancient prophecy, denouncing the ruin of the house of Manfred,
gradually prepare us for the grand catastrophe. The moon-light
vision of Alphonso dilated to immense magnitude, the astonished
group of spectators in the front, and the shattered ruins of the
castle in the back-ground, is briefly and sublimely described. We
know no passage of similar merit, unless it be the apparition of
Fadzean in an ancient Scottish poem.*

That part of the romance which depends upon human feelings
and agency, is conducted with the dramatic talent which afterwards was so conspicuous in *The Mysterious Mother.* The persons
are indeed rather generic than individual, but this was in a degree
necessary to a plan calculated rather to exhibit a general view of
society and manners during the times which the author's imagination loved to contemplate, than the more minute shades and dis-
criminating points of particular characters. But the actors in the
romance are strikingly drawn, with bold outlines becoming the

* This spectre, the ghost of a follower whom he had slain upon suspicion
of treachery, appeared to no less a person than Wallace, the champion of Scotland, in the ancient castle of Gask-hall.—See Ellis's *Specimens*, vol. I.

age and nature of the story. Feudal tyranny was, perhaps, never better exemplified, than in the character of Manfred. He has the courage, the art, the duplicity, the ambition of a barbarous chieftain of the dark ages, yet with touches of remorse and natural feeling, which preserve some sympathy for him when his pride is quelled, and his race extinguished. The pious monk, and the patient Hippolita, are well contrasted with this selfish and tyrannical prince. Theodore is the juvenile hero of a romantic tale, and Matilda has more interesting sweetness than usually belongs to its heroine. As the character of Isabella is studiously kept down, in order to relieve that of the daughter of Manfred, few readers are pleased with the concluding insinuation, that she became at length the bride of Theodore. This is in some degree a departure from the rules of chivalry; and however natural an occurrence in common life, rather injures the magic illusions of romance. In other respects, making allowance for the extraordinary incidents of a dark and tempestuous age, the story, so far as within the course of natural events, is happily detailed, its progress is uniform, its events interesting and well combined, and the conclusion grand, tragical, and affecting.

The style of *The Castle of Otranto* is pure and correct English of the earlier and more classical standard. Mr. Walpole rejected, upon taste and principle, those heavy though powerful auxiliaries which Dr. Johnson imported from the Latin language, and which have since proved to many a luckless wight, who has essayed to use them, as unmanageable as the gauntlets of Eryx,

> ————————*et pondus et ipsa*
> *Huc illuc vinclorum immensa volumina versat.*

Neither does the purity of Mr. Walpole's language, and the simplicity of his narrative, admit that luxuriant, florid, and high-varnished landscape painting with which Mrs. Radcliffe often adorned, and not unfrequently encumbered, her kindred romances. Description, for its own sake, is scarcely once attempted in *The Castle of Otranto;* and if authors would consider how very much this restriction tends to realise narrative, they might be tempted to abridge at least the showy and wordy exuberance of a style fitter for poetry than prose. It is for the dialogue that Walpole reserves his strength; and it is remarkable how, while conducting his mortal agents with all the art of a modern dramatist, he adheres to the sustained tone of chivalry, which marks the period of the action. This is not attained by patching his narrative or dialogue with glossarial terms, or antique phraseology, but by taking care to exclude all that can awaken modern associations. In the one case, his romance would have resembled a modern dress, preposterously decorated with antique ornaments; in its present shape, he has retained the form of the ancient armour, but not its rust and cobwebs. In illustration of what is above stated, we refer the reader to the first interview of Manfred with the prince of Vicenza, where the manners and language of chivalry are finely painted, as well as the perturbation of conscious guilt confusing itself in attempted exculpation, even before a mute accuser. The characters of the inferior domestics have been considered as not bearing a proportion sufficiently dignified to the rest of the story. But this is a point on which the author has pleaded his own cause fully in the original prefaces.

We have only to add, in conclusion to these desultory remarks, that if Horace Walpole, who led the way in this new species of literary composition, has been surpassed by some of his followers in diffuse brilliancy of description, and perhaps in the art of detaining the mind of the reader in a state of feverish and anxious suspense, through a protracted and complicated narrative, more will yet remain with him than the single merit of originality and invention. The applause due to chastity and precision of style, to a happy combination of supernatural agency with human interest, to a tone of feudal manners and language, sustained by characters strongly drawn and well discriminated, and to unity of action producing scenes alternately of interest and of grandeur—the applause, in fine, which cannot be denied to him who can excite the passions of fear and of pity, must be awarded to the author of *The Castle of Otranto*.

Preface to the First Edition

The following work was found in the library of an ancient Catholic family in the north of England. It was printed at Naples, in the black letter, in the year 1529. How much sooner it was written does not appear. The principal incidents are such as were believed in the darkest ages of christianity; but the language and conduct have nothing that savours of barbarism. The style is the purest Italian. If the story was written near the time when it is supposed to have happened, it must have been between 1095, the era of the first crusade, and 1243, the date of the last, or not long afterwards. There is no other circumstance in the work, that can lead us to guess at the period in which the scene is laid. The names of the actors are evidently fictitious, and probably disguised on purpose: yet the Spanish names of the domestics seem to indicate that this work was not composed until the establishment of the Arragonian kings in Naples had made Spanish appellations familiar in that country. The beauty of the diction, and the zeal of the author (moderated, however, by singular judgment), concur to make me think, that the date of the composition was little antecedent to that of the impression. Letters were then in their most flourishing state in Italy, and contributed to dispel the empire of superstition, at that time so forcibly attacked by the reformers. It is not unlikely, that an artful priest might endeavour to turn their own arms on the innovators; and might avail himself of his abilities as an author to confirm the populace in their ancient errors and superstitions. If this was his view, he has certainly acted with signal address. Such a work as the following would enslave a hundred vulgar minds, beyond half the books of controversy that have been written from the days of LUTHER to the present hour.

This solution of the author's motives is, however, offered as a mere conjecture. Whatever his views were, or whatever effects the execution of them might have, his work can only be laid before the public at present as a matter of entertainment. Even as such, some apology for it is necessary. Miracles, visions, necromancy, dreams, and other preternatural events, are exploded now even from romances. That was not the case when our author wrote; much less when the story itself is supposed to have happened. Belief in every kind of prodigy was so established in those dark ages, that an author would not be faithful to the manners of the times, who should omit all mention of them. He is not bound to believe them himself, but he must represent his actors as believing them.

If this air of the miraculous is excused, the reader will find nothing else unworthy of his perusal. Allow the possibility of the facts, and all the actors comport themselves as persons would do in their situation. There is no bombast, no similes, flowers, digressions, or unnecessary descriptions. Every thing tends directly to the catastrophe. Never is the reader's attention relaxed. The rules of the drama are almost observed throughout the conduct of the piece. The characters are well drawn, and still better maintained. Terror, the author's principal engine, prevents the story from ever languishing; and it is so often contrasted by pity, that the mind is kept up in a constant vicissitude of interesting passions.

Some persons may, perhaps, think the characters of the domestics too little serious for the general cast of the story; but, besides their opposition to the principal personages, the art of the author is very observable in his conduct of the subalterns. They discover many passages essential to the story, which could not be well brought to light but by their naïveté and simplicity: in particular, the womanish terror and foibles of Bianca, in the last chapter, conduce essentially towards advancing the catastrophe.

It is natural for a translator to be prejudiced in favour of his adopted work. More impartial readers may not be so much struck with the beauties of this piece as I was. Yet I am not blind to my author's defects. I could wish he had grounded his plan on a more useful moral than this: that "the sins of fathers are visited on their children to the third and fourth generation." I doubt whether, in his time, any more than at present, ambition curbed its appetite of dominion from the dread of so remote a punishment. And yet this moral is weakened by that less direct insinuation, that even such anathema may be diverted, by devotion to St. Nicholas. Here, the interest of the monk plainly gets the better of the judgment of the author. However, with all its faults, I have no doubt but the English reader will be pleased with a sight of this performance. The piety that reigns throughout, the lessons of virtue that are inculcated, and the rigid purity of the sentiments, exempt this work from the censure to which romances are but too liable. Should it meet with the success I hope for, I may be encouraged to re-print the original Italian, though it will tend to depreciate my own labour. Our language falls far short of the charms of the Italian, both for variety and harmony. The latter is peculiarly excellent for simple narrative. It is difficult, in English, to relate without falling too low, or rising too high; a fault obviously occasioned by the little care taken to speak pure language in common conversation. Every Italian or Frenchman, of any rank, piques himself on speaking his own tongue correctly and with choice. I cannot flatter myself with having done justice to my author in this respect: his style is as elegant, as his conduct of the passions is masterly. It is a pity that he did not apply his talents to what they were evidently proper for, the theatre.

I will detain the reader no longer, but to make one short remark. Though the machinery is invention, and the names of the actors imaginary, I cannot but believe, that the ground work of the story is founded on truth. The scene is undoubtedly laid in some real castle. The author seems frequently, without design, to describe particular parts. "The chamber," says he, "on the right hand; the door on the left hand; the distance from the chapel to Conrad's apartment." These, and other passages, are strong presumptions that the author had some certain building in his eye. Curious persons, who have leisure to employ in such researches, may possibly discover in the Italian writers the foundation on which our author has built. If a catastrophe, at all resembling that which he describes, is believed to have given rise to this work, it will contribute to interest the reader, and will make *The Castle of Otranto* a still more moving story.

Preface to the Second Edition

The favourable manner in which this little piece has been received by the public, calls upon the author to explain the grounds on which he composed it. But, before he opens those motives, it is fit that he should ask pardon of his readers for having offered his work to them under the borrowed personage of a translator. As diffidence of his own abilities, and the novelty of the attempt, were the sole inducements to assume that disguise, he flatters himself he shall appear excusable. He resigned his performance to the impartial judgment of the public; determined to let it perish in obscurity, if disapproved; nor meaning to avow such a trifle, unless better judges should pronounce that he might own it without a blush.

It was an attempt to blend the two kinds of romance, the ancient and the modern. In the former, all was imagination and improbability: in the latter, nature is always intended to be, and sometimes has been, copied with success. Invention has not been wanting; but the great resources of fancy have been dammed up, by a strict adherence to common life. But if, in the latter species, Nature has cramped imagination, she did but take her revenge, having been totally excluded from old romances. The actions, sentiments, and conversations, of the heroes and heroines of ancient days, were as unnatural as the machines employed to put them in motion.

The author of the following pages thought it possible to reconcile the two kinds. Desirous of leaving the powers of fancy at liberty to expatiate through the boundless realms of invention, and thence of creating more interesting situations, he wished to conduct the mortal agents in his drama according to the rules of probability; in short, to make them think, speak, and act, as it might be supposed mere men and women would do in extraordinary positions. He had observed, that, in all inspired writings, the personages under the dispensation of miracles, and witnesses to the most stupendous phenomena, never lose sight of their human character: whereas, in the productions of romantic story, an improbable event never fails to be attended by an absurd dialogue. The actors seem to lose their senses, the moment the laws of nature have lost their tone. As the public have applauded the attempt, the author must not say he was entirely unequal to the task he had undertaken: yet, if the new route he has struck out shall have paved a road for men of brighter talents, he shall own, with pleasure and modesty, that he was sensible the plan was capable of receiving greater embellishments than his imagination, or conduct of the passions, could bestow on it.

With regard to the deportment of the domestics, on which I have touched in the former preface, I will beg leave to add a few words.—The simplicity of their behaviour, almost tending to excite smiles, which, at first, seems not consonant to the serious cast of the work, appeared to me not only not improper, but was marked designedly in that manner. My rule was nature. However grave, important, or even melancholy, the sensations of princes and heroes may be, they do not stamp the same affections on their domestics: at least the latter do not, or should not be made to, express their passions in the same dignified tone. In my humble opinion, the contrast between the sublime of the one and the naïveté of the other, sets the pathetic of the former in a stronger light. The very impatience which a reader feels, while delayed, by the coarse pleasantries of vulgar actors, from arriving at the knowledge of the important catastrophe he expects, perhaps heightens, certainly proves that he has been artfully interested in, the depending event. But I had higher authority than my own opinion for this conduct. The great master of nature, SHAKE-SPEARE, was the model I copied. Let me ask, if his tragedies of *Hamlet* and *Julius Caesar* would not lose a considerable share of their spirit and wonderful beauties, if the humour of the grave-diggers, the fooleries of Polonius, and the clumsy jests of the Roman citizens, were omitted, or vested in heroics? Is not the eloquence of Antony, the nobler and affectedly-unaffected oration of Brutus, artificially exalted by the rude bursts of nature from the mouths of their auditors? These touches remind one of the Grecian sculptor, who, to convey the idea of a Colossus, within the dimensions of a seal, inserted a little boy measuring his thumb.

"No," says Voltaire, in his edition of Corneille, "this mixture

of buffoonery and solemnity is intolerable."—Voltaire is a genius*
—but not of Shakespeare's magnitude. Without recurring to dis-
putable authority, I appeal from Voltaire to himself. I shall not
avail myself of his former encomiums on our mighty poet; though
the French critic has twice translated the same speech in *Hamlet,*
some years ago in admiration, latterly in derision; and I am sorry
to find that his judgment grows weaker when it ought to be farther matured. But I shall make use of his own words, delivered on
the general topic of the theatre, when he was neither thinking to
recommend or decry Shakespeare's practice; consequently, at a
moment when Voltaire was impartial. In the preface to his *Enfant
Prodigue,* that exquisite piece, of which I declare my admiration,
and which, should I live twenty years longer, I trust I shall never
attempt to ridicule, he has these words, speaking of comedy (but
equally applicable to tragedy, if tragedy is, as surely it ought to
be, a picture of human life; nor can I conceive why occasional
pleasantry ought more to be banished from the tragic scene, than
pathetic seriousness from the comic), *"On y voit un mélange de
sérieux et de plaisanterie, de comique et de touchant;* souvent
même une seule aventure *produit tous ces contrastes. Rien n'est
si commun qu'une maison dans laquelle* un père gronde, une fille
occupée de sa passion pleure; *le fils se moque des deux, et quel-
ques parents prennent différemment part à la scène, &c. Nous
n'inférons pas de là que toute comédie doive avoir des scènes de
bouffonnerie et des scènes attendrissantes: il y a beaucoup de
très bonnes pièces où il ne règne que de la gaieté; d'autres toutes*

* The following remark is foreign to the present question, yet excusable
in an Englishman, who is willing to think that the severe criticisms of so masterly a writer as Voltaire on our immortal countryman, may have been the effusions of wit and precipitation, rather than the result of judgment and attention. May not the critic's skill, in the force and powers of our language,
have been as incorrect and incompetent as his knowledge of our history? of
the latter, his own pen has dropped glaring evidence. In his Preface to Thomas
Corneille's *Earl of Essex,* Monsieur de Voltaire allows that the truth of history
has been grossly perverted in that piece. In excuse he pleads, that when Corneille wrote, the noblesse of France were much unread in English story; but
now, says the commentator, that they study it, such misrepresentations would
not be suffered—yet forgetting that the period of ignorance is lapsed, and
that it is not very necessary to instruct the knowing, he undertakes, from the
overflowing of his own reading, to give the nobility of his own country a detail of Queen Elizabeth's favourites—of whom, says he, Robert Dudley was the
first, and the Earl of Leicester the second. Could one have believed that it
could be necessary to inform Monsieur de Voltaire himself, that Robert Dudley and the Earl of Leicester were the same person?

sérieuses; d'autres mélangées: d'autres où l'attendrissement va jusques aux larmes: il ne faut donner l'exclusion à aucun genre; *et si on me demandoit, quel genre est le meilleur, je répondrois, celui qui est le mieux traité."* Surely if a comedy may be *toute sérieuse,* tragedy may now and then, soberly, be indulged in a smile. Who shall proscribe it? Shall the critic, who, in self-defence, declares, that *no kind* ought to be excluded from comedy, give laws to Shakespeare?

I am aware that the preface from whence I have quoted these passages does not stand in Monsieur de Voltaire's name, but in that of his editor; yet who doubts that the editor and author were the same person? or where is the editor, who has so happily possessed himself of his author's style, and brilliant ease of argument? These passages were indubitably the genuine sentiments of that great writer. In his epistle to Maffei, prefixed to his *Mérope,* he delivers almost the same opinion, though, I doubt, with a little irony. I will repeat his words, and then give my reason for quoting them. After translating a passage in Maffei's *Merope,* Monsieur de Voltaire adds, *"Tous ces traits sont naïfs; tout y est convenable à ceux que vous introduisez sur la scène, et aux moeurs que vous leur donnez. Ces familiarités naturelles eussent été, à ce que je crois, bien reçues dans Athènes; mais Paris et notre parterre veulent une autre espèce de simplicité."* I doubt, I say, whether there is not a grain of sneer in this and other passages of that epistle; yet the force of truth is not damaged by being tinged with ridicule. Maffei was to represent a Grecian story: surely the Athenians were as competent judges of Grecian manners, and of the propriety of introducing them, as the parterre of Paris. "On the contrary," says Voltaire (and I cannot but admire his reasoning), "there were but ten thousand citizens at Athens, and Paris has near eight hundred thousand inhabitants, among whom one may reckon thirty thousand judges of dramatic works." —Indeed!—but allowing so numerous a tribunal, I believe this is the only instance in which it was ever pretended that thirty thousand persons, living near two thousand years after the era in question, were, upon the mere face of the poll, declared better judges than the Grecians themselves, of what ought to be the manners of a tragedy written on a Grecian story.

I will not enter into a discussion of the *espèce de simplicité,* which the parterre of Paris demands, nor of the shackles with which *the thirty thousand judges* have cramped their poetry, the chief merit of which, as I gather from repeated passages in the *New Commentary* on Corneille, consists in vaulting in spite of those fetters; a merit which, if true, would reduce poetry from the lofty effort of imagination, to a puerile and most contemptible labour—*difficiles nugae* with a witness! I cannot, however, help mentioning a couplet, which, to my English ears, always sounded as the flattest and most trifling instance of circumstantial propriety, but which Voltaire, who has dealt so severely with nine parts in ten of Corneille's works, has singled out to defend in Racine;

> *De son appartement cette porte est prochaine,*
> *Et cette autre conduit dans celui de la Reine.*

IN ENGLISH.
To Caesar's closet through this door you come,
And t'other leads to the Queen's drawing-room.

Unhappy Shakespeare! hadst thou made Rosencrantz inform his compeer, Guildenstern, of the ichnography of the palace of Copenhagen, instead of presenting us with a moral dialogue between the Prince of Denmark and the grave-digger, the illuminated pit of Paris would have been instructed *a second time* to adore thy talents.

The result of all I have said, is, to shelter my own daring under the canon of the brightest genius this country, at least, has produced. I might have pleaded that, having created a new species of romance, I was at liberty to lay down what rules I thought fit for the conduct of it: but I should be more proud of having imitated, however faintly, weakly, and at a distance, so masterly a pattern, than to enjoy the entire merit of invention, unless I could have marked my work with genius, as well as with originality. Such as it is, the public have honoured it sufficiently, whatever rank their suffrages allot to it.

THE CASTLE OF OTRANTO

A Gothic Story

CHAPTER I

Manfred, Prince of Otranto, had one son and one daughter; the latter, a most beautiful virgin, aged eighteen, was called Matilda. Conrad, the son, was three years younger, a homely youth, sickly, and of no promising disposition; yet he was the darling of his father, who never showed any symptoms of affection to Matilda. Manfred had contracted a marriage for his son with the Marquis of Vicenza's daughter, Isabella; and she had already been delivered by her guardians into the hands of Manfred, that he might celebrate the wedding as soon as Conrad's infirm state of health would permit. Manfred's impatience for this ceremonial was remarked by his family and neighbours. The former, indeed, apprehending the severity of their prince's disposition, did not dare to utter their surmises on this precipitation. Hippolita, his wife, an amiable lady, did sometimes venture to represent the danger of marrying their only son so early, considering his great youth, and greater infirmities; but she never received any other answer than reflections on her own sterility, who had given him but one heir. His tenants and subjects were less cautious in their discourses: they attributed this hasty wedding to the prince's dread of seeing accomplished an ancient prophecy, which was said to have pronounced, that *the Castle and Lordship of Otranto should pass from the present family whenever the real owner should be grown too large to inhabit it.* It was difficult to make any sense of this prophecy; and still less easy to conceive what it had to do with the marriage in question. Yet these mysteries, or contradictions, did not make the populace adhere the less to their opinion.

Young Conrad's birth-day was fixed for his espousals. The company was assembled in the chapel of the castle, and everything ready for beginning the divine office, when Conrad himself was missing. Manfred, impatient of the least delay, and who had not observed his son retire, dispatched one of his attendants to summon the young prince. The servant, who had not stayed long enough to have crossed the court to Conrad's apartment, came running back breathless, in a frantic manner, his eyes staring, and foaming at the mouth. He said nothing, but pointed to the court. The company were struck with terror and amazement. The princess Hippolita, without knowing what was the matter, but anxious for her son, swooned away. Manfred, less apprehensive than enraged at the procrastination of the nuptials, and at the folly of his domestic, asked imperiously, what was the matter? The fellow made no answer, but continued pointing towards the court-yard; and, at last, after repeated questions put to him, cried out, "Oh! the helmet! the helmet!" In the mean time, some of the company had run into the court, from whence was heard a confused noise of shrieks, horror, and surprise. Manfred, who began to be alarmed at not seeing his son, went himself, to get information of what occasioned this strange confusion. Matilda remained, endeavouring to assist her mother; and Isabella stayed for the same purpose, and to avoid showing any impatience for the bridegroom, for whom, in truth, she had conceived little affection.

The first thing, that struck Manfred's eyes, was a group of his servants, endeavouring to raise something, that appeared to him a mountain of sable plumes. He gazed, without believing his sight. "What are ye doing?" cried Manfred, wrathfully; "where is my son?" A volley of voices replied, "Oh! my lord! the prince! the prince! the helmet! the helmet!" Shocked with these lamentable sounds, and dreading he knew not what, he advanced hastily; but, what a sight for a father's eyes! he beheld his child dashed to pieces, and almost buried under an enormous helmet, a hundred times more large than any casque ever made for human being, and shaded with a proportionable quantity of black feathers.

The horror of the spectacle, the ignorance of all around how this misfortune had happened, and, above all, the tremendous phenomenon before him, took away the prince's speech. Yet his silence lasted longer than even grief could occasion. He fixed his eyes on what he wished in vain to believe a vision; and seemed less attentive to his loss, than buried in meditation on the stupendous object that had occasioned it. He touched, he examined, the fatal casque; nor could even the bleeding mangled remains of the young prince, divert the eyes of Manfred from the portent before him. All, who had known his partial fondness for young Conrad, were as much surprised at their prince's insensibility, as thunderstruck themselves at the miracle of the helmet. They conveyed the disfigured corpse into the hall, without receiving the least direction from Manfred. As little was he attentive to the ladies who remained in the chapel: on the contrary, without mentioning the unhappy princesses, his wife and daughter, the first sounds that dropped from Manfred's lips were, "take care of the Lady Isabella."

The domestics, without observing the singularity of this direction, were guided by their affection to their mistress, to consider it as peculiarly addressed to her situation, and flew to her assistance. They conveyed her to her chamber, more dead than alive, and indifferent to all the strange circumstances she heard, except the death of her son. Matilda, who doted on her mother, smothered her own grief and amazement, and thought of nothing but assisting and comforting her afflicted parent. Isabella, who had been treated by Hippolita like a daughter, and who returned that tenderness with equal duty and affection, was scarce less assiduous about the princess; at the same time, endeavouring to partake and lessen the weight of sorrow which she saw Matilda strove to suppress, for whom she had conceived the warmest sympathy of friendship. Yet her own situation could not help finding its place in her thoughts. She felt no concern for the death of young Conrad, except commiseration; and she was not sorry to be delivered from a marriage, which had promised her little felicity, either from her destined bridegroom, or from the severe temper of Manfred; who, though he had distinguished her by great indulgence, had impressed her mind with terror, from his causeless rigour to such amiable princesses as Hippolita and Matilda.

While the ladies were conveying the wretched mother to her bed, Manfred remained in the court, gazing on the ominous casque, and regardless of the crowd, which the strangeness of the event had now assembled around him. The few words he articulated, tended solely to inquiries, whether any man knew from

whence it could have come? Nobody could give him the least information. However, as it seemed to be the sole object of his curiosity, it soon became so to the rest of the spectators, whose conjectures were as absurd and improbable, as the catastrophe itself was
unprecedented. In the midst of their senseless guesses, a young
peasant, whom rumour had drawn thither from a neighbouring
village, observed, that the miraculous helmet was exactly like that
on the figure in black marble of Alfonso the Good, one of their
former princes, in the church of St. Nicholas. "Villain! what
sayest thou?" cried Manfred, starting from his trance in a tempest
of rage, and seizing the young man by the collar; "how darest thou
utter such treason? thy life shall pay for it." The spectators, who
as little comprehended the cause of the prince's fury as all the
rest they had seen, were at a loss to unravel this new circumstance. The young peasant himself was still more astonished, not
conceiving how he had offended the prince: yet, recollecting himself, with a mixture of grace and humility, he disengaged himself
from Manfred's grip, and then, with an obeisance, which discovered more jealousy of innocence, than dismay, he asked, with respect, of what he was guilty? Manfred, more enraged at the vigour,
however decently exerted, with which the young man had shaken
off his hold, than appeased by his submission, ordered his attendants to seize him; and, if he had not been withheld by his friends,
whom he had invited to the nuptials, would have poignarded the
peasant in their arms.

During this altercation, some of the vulgar spectators had run
to the great church, which stood near the castle, and came back
open-mouthed, declaring, that the helmet was missing from Alfonso's statue. Manfred, at this news, grew perfectly frantic; and,
as if he sought a subject on which to vent the tempest within him,
he rushed again on the young peasant, crying, "Villain! monster!
sorcerer! 'tis thou hast done this! 'tis thou hast slain my son!"
The mob, who wanted some object within the scope of their ca-
pacities, on whom they might discharge their bewildered reason-
ings, caught the words from the mouth of their lord, and re-
echoed, "Aye, aye; 'tis he! 'tis he! He has stolen the helmet from
good Alfonso's tomb, and dashed out the brains of our young
prince with it!" never reflecting, how enormous the disproportion
was between the marble helmet that had been in the church, and
that of steel before their eyes; nor, how impossible it was for a

youth, seemingly not twenty, to wield a piece of armour of so prodigious a weight.

The folly of these ejaculations brought Manfred to himself: yet, whether provoked at the peasant having observed the resemblance between the two helmets, and thereby led to the farther discovery of the absence of that in the church; or wishing to bury any fresh rumour under so impertinent a supposition; he gravely pronounced that the young man was certainly a necromancer, and that, till the church could take cognizance of the affair, he would have the magician, whom they had thus detected, kept prisoner under the helmet itself, which he ordered his attendants to raise, and place the young man under it; declaring, he should be kept there without food, with which his own infernal art might furnish him.

It was in vain for the youth to represent against this preposterous sentence: in vain did Manfred's friends endeavour to divert him from this savage and ill-grounded resolution. The generality were charmed with their lord's decision, which, to their apprehensions, carried great appearance of justice; as the magician was to be punished by the very instrument with which he had offended: nor were they struck with the least compunction at the probability of the youth being starved; for they firmly believed, that, by his diabolical skill, he could easily supply himself with nutriment.

Manfred thus saw his commands even cheerfully obeyed; and, appointing a guard, with strict orders to prevent any food being conveyed to the prisoner, he dismissed his friends and attendants, and retired to his own chamber, after locking the gates of the castle, in which he suffered none but his domestics to remain.

In the mean time, the care and zeal of the young ladies had brought the princess Hippolita to herself, who, amidst the transports of her own sorrow, frequently demanded news of her lord; would have dismissed her attendants to watch over him, and at last enjoined Matilda to leave her, and visit and comfort her father. Matilda, who wanted no affectionate duty to Manfred, though she trembled at his austerity, obeyed the orders of Hippolita, whom she tenderly recommended to Isabella; and, enquiring of the domestics for her father, was informed, that he was retired to his chamber, and had commanded that nobody should have admittance to him. Concluding that he was immersed in sorrow for the death of her brother, and fearing to renew his tears by the sight of his sole remaining child, she hesitated whether she should break in upon his affliction; yet, solicitude for him, backed by the commands of her mother, encouraged her to venture disobeying the orders he had given; a fault she had never been guilty of before. The gentle timidity of her nature made her pause for some minutes at his door. She heard him traverse his chamber, backwards and forwards, with disordered steps; a mood which increased her apprehensions. She was, however, just going to beg admittance, when Manfred suddenly opened the door; and, as it was now twilight, concurring with the disorder of his mind, he did not distinguish the person, but asked angrily, who it was? Matilda replied, trembling, "My dearest father, it is I, your daughter." Manfred, stepping back hastily, cried, "Begone! I do not want a daughter"; and, flinging back abruptly, clapped the door against the terrified Matilda.

She was too well acquainted with her father's impetuosity, to venture a second intrusion. When she had a little recovered the shock of so bitter a reception, she wiped away her tears, to prevent the additional stab that the knowledge of it would give to Hippolita, who questioned her, in the most anxious terms, on the health of Manfred, and how he bore his loss. Matilda assured her he was well, and supported his misfortune with manly fortitude. "But, will he not let me see him?" said Hippolita, mournfully; "will he not permit me to blend my tears with his, and shed a mother's sorrows in the bosom of her lord? or do you deceive me, Matilda? I know how Manfred doted on his son: is not the stroke too heavy for him? has he not sunk under it? You do not answer me; alas! I dread the worst! Raise me, my maidens; I will, I will, see my lord. Bear me to him instantly: he is dearer to me even than my children!" Matilda made signs to Isabella to prevent Hippolita's rising; and both those lovely young women were using their gentle violence to stop and calm the princess, when a servant, on the part of Manfred, arrived, and told Isabella, that his lord demanded to speak with her.

"With me!" cried Isabella. "Go," said Hippolita, relieved by a message from her lord. "Manfred cannot support the sight of his own family. He thinks you less disordered than we are, and dreads the shock of my grief. Console him, dear Isabella; and tell him, I will smother my own anguish rather than add to his."

As it was now evening, the servant, who conducted Isabella, bore a torch before her. When they came to Manfred, who was walking impatiently about the gallery, he started, and said hastily, "Take away that light, and begone!" Then, shutting the door impetuously, he flung himself upon a bench against the wall, and bade Isabella sit by him. She obeyed, trembling. "I sent for you, lady—" said he, and then stopped, under great appearance of confusion. "My lord!" "Yes, I sent for you on a matter of great moment," resumed he; "dry your tears, young lady. You have lost your bridegroom—yes, cruel fate! and I have lost the hopes of my race! but Conrad was not worthy of your beauty." "How! my lord!" said Isabella; "sure you do not suspect me of not feeling the concern I ought! my duty and affection would have always"— "Think no more of him," interrupted Manfred; "he was a sickly, puny child; and heaven has perhaps taken him away, that I might not trust the honours of my house on so frail a foundation. The line of Manfred calls for numerous supports. My foolish fondness for that boy blinded the eyes of my prudence; but it is better as it is. I hope, in a few years, to have reason to rejoice at the death of Conrad."

Words cannot paint the astonishment of Isabella. At first, she apprehended that grief had disordered Manfred's understanding. Her next thought suggested, that this strange discourse was designed to ensnare her: she feared that Manfred had perceived her indifference for his son; and, in consequence of that idea, she replied, "Good my lord, do not doubt my tenderness! my heart would have accompanied my hand. Conrad would have engrossed all my care; and wherever fate shall dispose of me, I shall always cherish his memory, and regard your highness, and the virtuous Hippolita, as my parents." "Curse on Hippolita!" cried Manfred. "Forget her from this moment, as I do. In short, lady, you have missed a husband undeserving of your charms: they shall now be better disposed of. Instead of a sickly boy, you shall have a husband in the prime of his age, who will know how to value your beauties, and who may expect a numerous offspring." "Alas! my lord," said Isabella, "my mind is too sadly engrossed, by the recent catastrophe in your family, to think of another marriage. If ever my father returns, and it shall be his pleasure, I shall obey, as I did when I consented to give my hand to your son: but until his return, permit me to remain under your hospitable roof, and employ the melancholy hours in assuaging yours, Hippolita's, and the fair Matilda's affliction."

"I desired you once before," said Manfred, angrily, "not to name that woman: from this hour she must be a stranger to you, as she must be to me; in short, Isabella, since I cannot give you my son, I offer you myself." "Heavens!" cried Isabella, waking from her delusion, "what do I hear! you, my lord! you! my father-in-law! the father of Conrad! the husband of the virtuous and tender Hippolita!"—"I tell you," said Manfred, imperiously, "Hippolita is no longer my wife; I divorce her from this hour. Too long has she cursed me by her unfruitfulness. My fate depends on having sons; and this night, I trust, will give a new date to my hopes." At these words he seized the cold hand of Isabella, who was half dead with fright and horror. She shrieked, and started from him. Manfred rose to pursue her; when the moon, which was now up, and gleamed in at the opposite casement, presented to his sight the plumes of the fatal helmet, which rose to the height of the windows, waving backwards and forwards in a tempestuous manner, and accompanied with a hollow and rustling sound. Isabella, who gathered courage from her situation, and who dreaded nothing so much as Manfred's pursuit of his declaration, cried, "Look! my lord! see! Heaven itself declares against your impious intentions!"—"Heaven nor hell shall impede my designs!" said Manfred, advancing again to seize the princess. At that instant, the portrait of his grandfather, which hung over the bench where they had been sitting, uttered a deep sigh, and heaved its breast. Isabella, whose back was turned to the picture, saw not the motion, nor whence the sound came; but started, and said, "Hark, my lord! what sound was that?" and, at the same time, made towards the door. Manfred, distracted between the flight of Isabella, who had now reached the stairs, and yet unable to keep his eyes from the picture, which began to move, had, however, advanced some steps after her, still looking backwards on the portrait, when he saw it quit its panel, and descend on the floor, with a grave and melancholy air. "Do I dream?" cried Manfred, returning; "or are the devils themselves in league against me? Speak, infernal spectre! or, if thou art my grandsire, why dost thou too conspire against thy wretched descendant, who too dearly pays for"—ere he could finish the sentence, the vision sighed again, and made a sign to Manfred to follow him. "Lead on!" cried Manfred; "I will follow thee to the gulf of perdition!" The spectre marched sedately, but dejected, to the end of the gallery, and turned into a chamber on the right hand. Manfred accompanied him at a little distance, full of anxiety and horror, but resolved. As he would have entered the chamber, the door was clapped to with violence by an invisible hand. The prince, collecting courage from this delay, would have forcibly burst open the door with his foot, but found that it resisted his utmost efforts. "Since hell will not satisfy my curiosity," said Manfred, "I will use the human means in my power for preserving my race; Isabella shall not escape me."

That lady, whose resolution had given way to terror the moment she had quitted Manfred, continued her flight to the bottom of the principal stair-case. There she stopped, not knowing whither to direct her steps, nor how to escape from the impetuosity of the prince. The gates of the castle, she knew, were locked, and guards placed in the court. Should she, as her heart prompted her, go and prepare Hippolita for the cruel destiny that awaited her? she did not doubt but Manfred would seek her there, and that his violence would incite him to double the injury he meditated, without leaving room for them to avoid the impetuosity of his passions. Delay might give him time to reflect on the horrid measures he had conceived, or produce some circumstance in her favour, if she could, for that night at least, avoid his odious purpose. Yet, where conceal herself! how avoid the pursuit he would infallibly make throughout the castle! As these thoughts passed rapidly through her mind, she recollected a subterraneous passage, which led from the vaults of the castle to the church of St. Nicholas. Could she reach the altar before she was overtaken, she knew even Manfred's violence would not dare to profane the sacredness of the place; and she determined, if no other means of deliverance offered, to shut herself up for ever among the holy virgins, whose convent was contiguous to the cathedral. In this resolution, she seized a lamp, that burned at the foot of the stair-case, and hurried towards the secret passage.

The lower part of the castle was hollowed into several intricate cloisters; and it was not easy for one, under so much anxiety, to find the door that opened into the cavern. An awful silence reigned throughout those subterraneous regions, except, now and then, some blasts of wind that shook the doors she had passed, and which, grating on the rusty hinges, were re-echoed through

that long labyrinth of darkness. Every murmur struck her with
new terror; yet more she dreaded to hear the wrathful voice of
Manfred, urging his domestics to pursue her. She trod as softly
as impatience would give her leave, yet frequently stopped, and
listened to hear if she was followed. In one of those moments she
thought she heard a sigh. She shuddered, and recoiled a few paces.
In a moment she thought she heard the step of some person. Her
blood curdled; she concluded it was Manfred. Every suggestion,
that horror could inspire, rushed into her mind. She condemned
her rash flight, which had thus exposed her to his rage, in a place
where her cries were not likely to draw anybody to her assistance.
Yet the sound seemed not to come from behind; if Manfred knew
where she was, he must have followed her: she was still in one of
the cloisters, and the steps she had heard were too distinct to proceed from the way she had come. Cheered with this reflection,
and hoping to find a friend in whoever was not the prince, she was
going to advance, when a door, that stood a-jar, at some distance
to the left, was opened gently; but, e'er her lamp, which she held
up, could discover who opened it, the person retreated precipitately, on seeing the light.

Isabella, whom every incident was sufficient to dismay, hesitated whether she should proceed. Her dread of Manfred soon
outweighed every other terror. The very circumstance of the person avoiding her, gave her a sort of courage. It could only be,
she thought, some domestic belonging to the castle. Her gentleness had never raised her an enemy, and conscious innocence
made her hope, that, unless sent by the prince's order to seek her,
his servants would rather assist than prevent her flight. Fortifying
herself with these reflections, and believing, by what she could
observe, that she was near the mouth of the subterraneous cavern,
she approached the door that had been opened; but a sudden gust
of wind, that met her at the door, extinguished her lamp, and
left her in total darkness.

Words cannot paint the horror of the princess's situation.
Alone, in so dismal a place, her mind impressed with all the terrible events of the day, hopeless of escaping, expecting every moment the arrival of Manfred, and far from tranquil on knowing
she was within reach of somebody, she knew not whom, who for
some cause seemed concealed thereabouts; all these thoughts
crowded on her distracted mind, and she was ready to sink under

her apprehensions. She addressed herself to every saint in heaven, and inwardly implored their assistance. For a considerable time she remained in an agony of despair. At last, as softly as was possible, she felt for the door; and, having found it, entered trembling into the vault, from whence she had heard the sigh and steps. It gave her a kind of momentary joy to perceive an imperfect ray of clouded moonshine gleam from the roof of the vault, which seemed to be fallen in, and from whence hung a fragment of earth or building, she could not distinguish which, that appeared to have been crushed inwards. She advanced eagerly towards this chasm, when she discerned a human form, standing close against the wall.

She shrieked, believing it the ghost of her betrothed Conrad. The figure, advancing, said in a submissive voice, "Be not alarmed, lady: I will not injure you." Isabella, a little encouraged by the words, and tone of voice, of the stranger, and recollecting that this must be the person who had opened the door, recovered her spirits enough to reply, "Sir, whoever you are, take pity on a wretched princess, standing on the brink of destruction! Assist me to escape from this fatal castle, or in a few moments I may be made miserable for ever!" "Alas!" said the stranger, "what can I do to assist you? I will die in your defence; but I am unacquainted with the castle, and want——" "Oh!" said Isabella, hastily interrupting him, "help me but to find a trap-door, that must be hereabout, and it is the greatest service you can do me, for I have not a minute to lose." Saying these words, she felt about on the pavement, and directed the stranger to search likewise, for a smooth piece of brass, inclosed in one of the stones. "That," said she, "is the lock, which opens with a spring, of which I know the secret. If we can find that, I may escape; if not, alas! courteous stranger, I fear I shall have involved you in my misfortunes: Manfred will suspect you for the accomplice of my flight, and you will fall a victim to his resentment." "I value not my life," said the stranger, "and it will be some comfort to lose it in trying to deliver you from his tyranny." "Generous youth!" said Isabella, "how shall I ever requite"—as she uttered these words, a ray of moonshine, streaming through a cranny of the ruin above, shone directly on the lock they sought. "Oh! transport!" said Isabella, "here is the trap-door!" and, taking out a key, she touched the spring, which, starting aside, discovered an iron ring. "Lift up the

door," said the princess. The stranger obeyed; and beneath appeared some stone steps, descending into a vault totally dark.
"We must go down here," said Isabella: "follow me; dark and
dismal as it is, we cannot miss our way; it leads directly to the
church of St. Nicholas. But perhaps," added the princess, modestly, "you have no reason to leave the castle, nor have I further
occasion for your service; in a few minutes I shall be safe from
Manfred's rage—only let me know, to whom I am so much
obliged?" "I will never quit you," said the stranger, eagerly, "until I have placed you in safety—nor think me, princess, more generous than I am; though you are my principal care"—the
stranger was interrupted by a sudden noise of voices, that seemed
approaching, and they soon distinguished these words: "Talk not
to me of necromancers! I tell you she must be in the castle; I will
find her in spite of enchantment." "Oh! heavens!" cried Isabella,
"it is the voice of Manfred! make haste, or we are ruined! and
shut the trap-door after you." Saying this, she descended the steps
precipitately, and, as the stranger hastened to follow her, he let
the door slip out of his hands; it fell, and the spring closed over
it. He tried in vain to open it, not having observed Isabella's
method of touching the spring; nor had he many moments to
make an essay.—The noise of the falling door had been heard by
Manfred, who, directed by the sound, hastened thither, attended
by his servants with torches. "It must be Isabella," cried Manfred,
before he entered the vault; "she is escaping by the subterraneous
passage, but she cannot have got far." What was the astonishment
of the prince, when, instead of Isabella, the light of the torches
discovered to him the young peasant, whom he thought confined
under the fatal helmet! "Traitor!" said Manfred, "how camest
thou here? I thought thee in durance above in the court." "I am
no traitor," replied the young man, boldly, "nor am I answerable
for your thoughts."—"Presumptuous villain!" cried Manfred,
"dost thou provoke my wrath? tell me; how hast thou escaped
from above? thou hast corrupted thy guards, and their lives shall
answer it."—"My poverty," said the peasant calmly, "will discul-
pate them: though the ministers of a tyrant's wrath, to thee they
are faithful, and but too willing to execute the orders which you
unjustly imposed upon them." "Art thou so hardy as to dare my
vengeance?" said the prince; "but tortures shall force the truth
from thee. Tell me! I will know thy accomplices." "There was

my accomplice!" said the youth, smiling, and pointing to the roof. Manfred ordered the torches to be held up, and perceived that one of the cheeks of the enchanted casque had forced its way through the pavement of the court, as his servants had let it fall over the peasant, and had broken through into the vault, leaving a gap, through which the peasant had pressed himself some minutes before he was found by Isabella. "Was that the way by which thou didst descend?" said Manfred. "It was," said the youth.— "But what noise was that," said Manfred, "which I heard as I entered the cloister?"—"A door clapped," said the peasant; "I heard it as well as you." "What door?" said Manfred, hastily. "I am not acquainted with your castle," said the peasant; "this is the first time I ever entered it; and this vault the only part of it within which I ever was." "But I tell thee," said Manfred (wishing to find out if the youth had discovered the trap-door), "it was this way I heard the noise: my servants heard it too." "My lord," interrupted one of them, officiously, "to be sure it was the trap-door, and he was going to make his escape." "Peace! blockhead!" said the prince, angrily; "if he was going to escape, how should he come on this side? I will know from his own mouth what noise it was I heard. Tell me truly! thy life depends on thy veracity." "My veracity is dearer to me than my life," said the peasant, "nor would I purchase the one by forfeiting the other." "Indeed! young philosopher!" said Manfred, contemptuously; "tell me, then, what was the noise I heard?" "Ask me what I can answer," said he, "and put me to death instantly if I tell you a lie." Manfred, growing impatient at the steady valour and indifference of the youth, cried, "Well then, thou man of truth! answer; was it the fall of the trap-door that I heard?" "It was," said the youth. "It was!" said the prince, "and how didst thou come to know there was a trap-door here?" "I saw the plate of brass by a gleam of moonshine," replied he. "But what told thee it was a lock?" said Manfred; "how didst thou discover the secret of opening it?" "Providence, that delivered me from the helmet, was able to direct me to the spring of a lock," said he. "Providence should have gone a little farther, and have placed thee out of the reach of my resentment," said Manfred; "when Providence had taught thee to open the lock, it abandoned thee for a fool, who did not know how to make use of its favours. Why didst thou not pursue the path pointed out for thy escape? why didst thou shut the trap-door, before thou hadst descended the steps?" "I might ask you, my lord," said the peasant, "how I, totally unacquainted with your castle, was to know that those steps led to any outlet? but I scorn to evade your questions. Wherever those steps led to, perhaps I should have explored the way—I could not be in a worse situation than I was. But the truth is, I let the trap-door fall: your immediate arrival followed. I had given the alarm—what imported it to me whether I was seized a minute sooner or a minute later?" "Thou art a resolute villain, for thy years," said Manfred; "yet, on reflection, I suspect thou dost but trifle with me: thou has not yet told me how thou didst open the lock?" "That I will show you, my lord," said the peasant; and, taking up a fragment of stone that had fallen from above, he laid himself on the trapdoor, and began to beat on the piece of brass that covered it; meaning to gain time for the escape of the princess. This presence of mind, joined to the frankness of the youth, staggered Manfred. He even felt a disposition towards pardoning one, who had been guilty of no crime. Manfred was not one of those savage tyrants, who wanton in cruelty unprovoked. The circumstances of his fortune had given an asperity to his temper, which was naturally humane; and his virtues were always ready to operate, when his passions did not obscure his reason.

While the prince was in this suspense, a confused noise of voices echoed through the distant vaults. As the sound approached, he distinguished the clamours of some of his domestics, whom he had dispersed through the castle in search of Isabella, calling out, "Where is my lord? where is the prince?" "Here I am," said Manfred, as they came nearer; "have you found the princess?" the first that arrived, replied, "Oh! my lord! I am glad we have found you!" "Found me!" said Manfred, "have you found the princess?" "We thought we had, my lord," said the fellow, looking terrified, "but"—"But what?" cried the prince; "has she escaped?" "Jaquez, and I, my lord"—"Yes, I and Diego," interrupted the second, who came up in still greater consternation—"Speak one of you at a time!" said Manfred; "I ask you where is the princess?" "We do not know," said they, both together, "but we are frightened out of our wits!"—"So I think, blockheads," said Manfred; "what is it has scared you thus?" "Oh! my lord," said Jaquez, "Diego has seen such a sight! your highness would not believe your eyes"—"What new absurdity is this?" cried Manfred; "give me a direct answer, or by heaven"—"Why, my lord, if it please your highness to hear me," said the poor fellow, "Diego and I"—"Yes, I and Jaquez," cried his comrade—"Did not I forbid you to speak both at a time?" said the prince; "You, Jaquez, answer; for the other fool seems more distracted than thou art. What is the matter?" "My gracious lord," said Jaquez, "if it please your highness to hear me. Diego and I, according to your highness's orders, went to search for the young lady; but, being apprehensive that we might meet the ghost of my young lord, your highness's son, God rest his soul, as he has not received christian burial"—"Sot!" cried Manfred, in a rage, "is it only a ghost, then, that thou hast seen?" "Oh! worse! worse! my lord," cried Diego; "I had rather have seen ten whole ghosts." "Grant me patience!" said Manfred, "these blockheads distract me. Out of my sight, Diego! and thou, Jaquez, tell me, in one word, art thou sober? art thou raving? thou wast wont to have some sense; has the other sot frightened himself and thee too? speak, what is it he fancies he has seen?" "Why, my lord," replied Jaquez, trembling, "I was going to tell your highness, that since the calamitous misfortune of my young lord, God rest his precious soul! not one of us, your highness's faithful servants—indeed we are, my lord, though poor men—I say, not one of us has dared to set a foot about the castle, but two together: so, Diego and I, thinking that my young lady might be in the great gallery, went up there to look for her, and tell her your highness wanted something to impart to her." "O blundering fools!" cried Manfred, "and, in the mean time, she has made her escape, because you were afraid of goblins! Why, thou knave! she left me in the gallery; I came from thence myself." "For all that, she may be there still, for aught I know," said Jaquez, "but the devil shall have me before I seek her there again—poor Diego! I do not believe he will ever recover it!" "Recover what?" said Manfred; "am I never to learn what it is has terrified these rascals? but I lose my time: follow me, slave; I will see if she is in the gallery." "For heaven's sake, my dear good lord," cried Jaquez, "do not go to the gallery! Satan himself, I believe, is in the chamber next to the gallery." Manfred, who hitherto had treated the terror of his servants as an idle panic, was struck at this new circumstance. He recollected the apparition of the portrait, and the sudden closing of the door at the end of the gallery—his voice faltered, and he asked with disorder, "What is in the great chamber?" "My lord," said

Jaquez, "when Diego and I came into the gallery—he went first, for he said he had more courage than I—So, when we came into the gallery, we found nobody. We looked under every bench and stool; and still we found nobody." "Were all the pictures in their places?" said Manfred. "Yes, my lord," answered Jaquez, "but we did not think of looking behind them." "Well, well," said Manfred, "proceed." "When we came to the door of the great chamber," continued Jaquez, "we found it shut." "And could not you open it?" said Manfred. "Oh yes, my lord; would to heaven we had not," replied he. "Nay, it was not I neither, it was Diego: he was grown fool-hardy, and would go on, though I advised him not—if ever I open a door that is shut again!" "Trifle not," said Manfred, shuddering, "but tell me what you saw in the great chamber, on opening the door." "I, my lord!" said Jaquez, "I saw nothing; I was behind Diego; but I heard the noise." "Jaquez," said Manfred, in a solemn tone of voice, "tell me, I adjure thee by the souls of my ancestors, what was it thou sawest? what was it thou heardest?" "It was Diego saw it, my lord, it was not I," replied Jaquez; "I only heard the noise. Diego had no sooner opened the door, than he cried out, and ran back—I ran back too, and said, 'Is it the ghost?' 'The ghost! no, no,' said Diego, and his hair stood on end—'It is a giant, I believe; he is all clad in armour, for I saw his foot and part of his leg, and they are as large as the helmet, below in the court.' As he said these words, my lord, we heard a violent motion, and the rattling of armour, as if the giant was rising; for Diego has told me since, that he believes the giant was lying down, for the foot and leg were stretched at length on the floor. Before we could get to the end of the gallery, we heard the door of the great chamber clap behind us, but we did not dare turn back to see if the giant was following us—yet, now I think on it, we must have heard him if he had pursued us. But, for heaven's sake, good my lord, send for the chaplain, and have the castle exorcised! for, for certain, it is enchanted." "Aye, pray do, my lord," cried all the servants at once, "or we must leave your highness's service." "Peace, dotards!" said Manfred, "and follow me; I will know what all this means."—"We, my lord!" cried they, with one voice, "we would not go up to the gallery for your highness's revenue." The young peasant, who had stood silent, now spoke. "Will your highness," said he, "permit me to try this adventure? my life is of consequence to nobody: I fear no bad angel, and have offended no good one." "Your behaviour is above your seeming;" said Manfred, viewing him with surprise and admiration—"hereafter I will reward your bravery—but now," continued he, with a sigh, "I am so circumstanced, that I dare trust no eyes but my own—however, I give you leave to accompany me."

Manfred, when he first followed Isabella from the gallery, had gone directly to the apartment of his wife, concluding the princess had retired thither. Hippolita, who knew his step, rose with anxious fondness to meet her lord, whom she had not seen since the death of their son. She would have flown in a transport, mixed of joy and grief, to his bosom; but he pushed her rudely off, and said, "Where is Isabella?"—"Isabella, my lord!" said the astonished Hippolita. "Yes! Isabella;" cried Manfred, imperiously; "I want Isabella."—"My lord," replied Matilda, who perceived how much his behaviour had shocked her mother, "she has not been with us since your highness summoned her to your apartment." "Tell me where she is," said the prince; "I do not want to know where she has been." "My good lord," said Hippolita, "your daughter tells you the truth: Isabella left us by your command, and has not returned since; but, my good lord, compose yourself; retire to your rest: this dismal day has disordered you. Isabella shall wait your orders in the morning." "What then, you know where she is!" cried Manfred: "Tell me directly, for I will not lose an instant— and you, woman," speaking to his wife, "order your chaplain to attend me forthwith." "Isabella," said Hippolita, calmly, "is retired, I suppose, to her chamber: she is not accustomed to watch at this late hour. Gracious my lord," continued she, "let me know what has disturbed you. Has Isabella offended you?" "Trouble me not with questions," said Manfred, "but tell me where she is." "Matilda shall call her," said the princess—"Sit down, my lord, and resume your wonted fortitude." "What! art thou jealous of Isabella," replied he, "that you wish to be present at our interview?" "Good heavens! my lord," said Hippolita, "what is it your highness means?"—"Thou wilt know ere many minutes are past," said the cruel prince. "Send your chaplain to me, and wait my pleasure here." At these words he flung out of the room in search of Isabella; leaving the amazed ladies thunderstruck with his words and frantic deportment, and lost in vain conjectures on what he was meditating.

Manfred was now returning from the vault, attended by the peasant, and a few of his servants, whom he had obliged to accompany him. He ascended the stair-case without stopping, till he arrived at the gallery, at the door of which he met Hippolita and her chaplain. When Diego had been dismissed by Manfred, he had gone directly to the princess's apartment with the alarm of what he had seen. That excellent lady, who no more than Manfred doubted of the reality of the vision, yet affected to treat it as a delirium of the servant. Willing, however, to save her lord from any additional shock, and prepared by a series of grief not to tremble at any accession to it, she determined to make herself the first sacrifice, if fate had marked the present hour for their destruction. Dismissing the reluctant Matilda to her rest, who in vain sued for leave to accompany her mother, and attended only by her chaplain, Hippolita had visited the gallery and great chamber; and now, with more serenity of soul than she had felt for many hours, she met her lord, and assured him that the vision of the gigantic leg and foot was all a fable; and, no doubt, an impression made by fear, and the dark and dismal hour of the night, on the minds of his servants. She and the chaplain had examined the chamber, and found everything in the usual order.

Manfred, though persuaded, like his wife, that the vision had been no work of fancy, recovered a little from the tempest of mind into which so many strange events had thrown him. Ashamed, too, of his inhuman treatment of a princess, who returned every injury with new marks of tenderness and duty; he felt returning love forcing itself into his eyes—but not less ashamed of feeling remorse towards one, against whom he was inwardly meditating a yet more bitter outrage, he curbed the yearnings of his heart, and did not dare to lean even towards pity. The next transition of his soul was to exquisite villainy. Presuming on the unshaken submission of Hippolita, he flattered himself that she would not only acquiesce with patience to a divorce, but would obey, if it was his pleasure, in endeavouring to persuade Isabella to give him her hand; but, ere he could indulge this horrid hope, he reflected that Isabella was not to be found. Coming to himself, he gave orders that every avenue to the castle should be strictly guarded, and charged his domestics, on pain of their lives, to suffer nobody to pass out. The young peasant, to whom he spoke favourably, he ordered to remain in a small chamber on the stairs, in which there was a pallet-bed, and the key of which he took away himself, telling the youth he would talk with him in the morning. Then, dismissing his attendants, and bestowing a sullen kind of half-nod on Hippolita, he retired to his own chamber.

CHAPTER II

Matilda, who, by Hippolita's order, had retired to her apartment, was ill-disposed to take any rest. The shocking fate of her brother had deeply affected her. She was surprised at not seeing Isabella; but the strange words which had fallen from her father, and his obscure menace to the princess, his wife, accompanied by the most furious behaviour, had filled her gentle mind with terror and alarm. She waited anxiously for the return of Bianca, a young damsel that attended her, whom she had sent to learn what was become of Isabella. Bianca soon appeared, and informed her mistress of what she had gathered from the servants, that Isabella was nowhere to be found. She related the adventure of the young peasant, who had been discovered in the vault, though with many simple additions from the incoherent account of the domestics; and she dwelled principally on the gigantic leg and foot, which had been seen in the gallery chamber. This last circumstance had terrified Bianca so much, that she was rejoiced when Matilda told her that she should not go to rest, but would watch till the princess should rise.

The young princess wearied herself in conjectures on the flight of Isabella, and on the threats of Manfred to her mother. "But what business could he have so urgent with the chaplain," said Matilda; "does he intend to have my brother's body interred privately in the chapel?" "Oh! madam," said Bianca, "now I guess. As you are become his heiress, he is impatient to have you married; he has always been raving for more sons; I warrant he is now impatient for grandsons. As sure as I live, madam, I shall see you a bride at last—Good madam, you won't cast off your faithful Bianca! you won't put Donna Rosara over me, now you are a great princess!" "My poor Bianca," said Matilda, "how fast your thoughts amble! I a great princess! What hast thou seen in Manfred's behaviour, since my brother's death, that bespeaks any increase of tenderness to me—but he is my father, and I must not complain. Nay, if heaven shuts my father's heart against me, it over-pays my little merit in the tenderness of my mother. O that dear mother! yes, Bianca, 'tis there I feel the rugged temper of Manfred. I can support his harshness to me with patience; but it wounds my soul when I am witness to his causeless severity towards her." "Oh! madam," said Bianca, "all men use their wives so, when they are weary of them." "And yet you congratulated me but now," said Matilda, "when you fancied my father intended to dispose of me!" "I would have you a great lady," replied Bianca, "come what will. I do not wish to see you moped in a convent, as you would be if you had your will, and if my lady, your mother, who knows that a bad husband is better than no husband at all, did not hinder you—Bless me! what noise is that! St. Nicholas forgive me! I was but in jest." "It is the wind," said Matilda, "whistling through the battlements in the tower above: you have heard it a thousand times." "Nay," said Bianca, "there was no harm in what I said: it is no sin to talk of matrimony—and so, madam, as I was saying, if my lord Manfred should offer you a handsome young prince for a bridegroom, you would drop him a curtsey, and tell him you would rather take the veil?" "Thank heaven! I am in no such danger," said Matilda: "you know how many proposals for me he has rejected." "And you thank him, like a dutiful daughter, do you, madam? but come, madam; suppose, tomorrow morning, he was to send for you to the great council chamber, and there you should find at his elbow a lovely young prince, with large black eyes, a smooth white forehead, and manly curling locks like jet; in short, madam, a young hero resembling the picture of the good Alfonso in the gallery, which you sit and gaze at for hours together." "Do not speak lightly of that picture," interrupted Matilda, sighing: "I know the adoration, with which I look at that picture, is uncommon—but I am not in love with a coloured panel. The character of that virtuous prince, the veneration with which my mother has inspired me for his memory, the orisons which, I know not why, she has enjoined me to pour forth at his tomb, all have concurred to persuade me, that, somehow or other, my destiny is linked with something relating to him." "Lord! madam, how should that be?" said Bianca; "I have always heard that your family was no way related to his; and I am sure I cannot conceive why my lady, the princess, sends you in a cold morning, or a damp evening, to pray at his tomb: he is no saint by the almanack. If you must pray, why does she not bid you address yourself to our great St. Nicholas? I am sure he is the saint I pray to for a husband."—"Perhaps my mind would be less affected," said Matilda, "if my mother would explain her reasons to me: but it is the mystery she observes, that inspires me with this—I know not what to call it. As she never acts from caprice, I am sure there is some fatal secret at bottom—nay, I know there is: in her agony of grief for my brother's death she dropped some words that intimated as much." "Oh! dear madam," cried Bianca, "what were they?" "No," said Matilda; "if a parent lets fall a word, and wishes it recalled, it is not for a child to utter it." "What! was she sorry for what she had said?" asked Bianca; "I am sure, madam, you may trust me." "With my own little secrets, when I have any, I may," said Matilda; "but never with my mother's: a child ought to have no ears or eyes, but as a parent directs." "Well, to be sure, madam, you was born to be a saint," said Bianca, "and there is no resisting one's vocation: you will end in a convent at last. But there is my lady Isabella would not be so reserved to me; she will let me talk to her of young men; and when a handsome cavalier has come to the castle, she has owned to me that she wished your brother Conrad resembled him." "Bianca," said the princess, "I do not allow you to mention my friend disrespectfully. Isabella is of a cheerful disposition, but her soul is as pure as virtue itself. She knows your idle babbling humour, and perhaps has now and then encouraged it, to divert melancholy, and enliven the solitude in which my father keeps us."—"Blessed Mary!" said Bianca, starting, "there it is again! dear madam, do you hear nothing? this castle is certainly haunted!"—"Peace!" said Matilda, "and listen! I did think I heard a voice—but it must be fancy; your terrors, I suppose, have infected me." "Indeed! indeed! madam," said Bianca, half weeping with agony, "I am sure I heard a voice!" "Does anybody lie in the chamber beneath?" said the princess. "Nobody has dared to lie there," answered Bianca, "since the great astrologer, that was your brother's tutor, drowned himself. For certain, madam, his ghost and the young prince's are now met in the chamber below—for heaven's sake let us fly to your mother's apartment!" "I charge you not to stir," said Matilda; "if they are spirits in pain, we may ease their sufferings by questioning them. They can mean no hurt to us, for we have not injured them; and if they should, shall we be more safe in one chamber than another? reach me my beads; we will say a prayer, and then speak to them." "Oh! dear lady, I would not speak to a ghost for the world!" cried Bianca. As she said these words, they heard the casement of the little chamber, below Matilda's, open. They listened attentively, and in a few minutes thought they heard a person sing, but could not distinguish the words. "This can be no evil spirit," said the princess, in a low voice: "it is undoubtedly one of the family—open the window, and we shall know the voice." "I dare not indeed, madam," said Bianca. "Thou art a very fool," said Matilda, opening the window gently herself. The noise the princess made was, however, heard by the person beneath, who stopped; and they concluded had heard the casement open. "Is anybody below?" said the princess: "if there is, speak." "Yes," said an unknown voice. "Who is it?" said Matilda. "A stranger," replied the voice. "What stranger?" said she; "and how didst thou come here at this unusual hour, when all the gates of the castle are locked?" "I am not here willingly," answered the voice—"but pardon me, lady, if I have disturbed your rest: I knew not that I was overheard. Sleep had forsaken me; I left a restless couch, and came to waste the irksome hours with gazing on the fair approach of morning, impatient to be dismissed from this castle." "Thy words and accents," said Matilda, "are of a melancholy cast: if thou art unhappy, I pity thee. If poverty afflicts thee, let me know it: I will mention thee to the princess, whose beneficent soul ever melts for the distressed; and she will relieve thee." "I am indeed unhappy," said the stranger, "and I know not what wealth is: but I do not complain of the lot which heaven has cast for me: I am young and healthy, and am not ashamed of owing my support to myself—yet think me not proud, or that I disdain your generous offers! I will remember you in my orisons, and I will pray for blessings on your gracious self and your noble mistress. If I sigh, lady, it is for others, not for myself." "Now I have it, madam!" said Bianca, whispering the princess; "this is certainly the young peasant; and, by my conscience, he is in love—well this is a charming adventure!—do, madam, let us sift him. He does not know you, but takes you for one of my lady Hippolita's women." "Art thou not ashamed, Bianca!" said the princess: "what right have we to pry into the secrets of this young man's heart? he seems virtuous and frank, and tells us he is unhappy: are those circumstances

that authorise us to make a property of him? how are we entitled
to his confidence?" "Lord! madam, how little you know of love!"
replied Bianca: "why lovers have no pleasure equal to talking of
their mistress!" "And would you have me become a peasant's con-
fidant?" said the princess. "Well, then, let me talk to him," said
Bianca: "though I have the honour of being your highness's maid
of honour, I was not always so great: besides, if love levels ranks,
it raises them too: I have a respect for a young man in love."
"Peace, simpleton!" said the princess; "though he said he was unhappy, it does not follow that he must be in love. Think of all that
has happened to-day, and tell me, if there are no misfortunes but
what love causes!—Stranger," resumed the princess, "if thy misfortunes have not been occasioned by thy own fault, and are
within the compass of the princess Hippolita's power to redress, I
will take upon me to answer that she will be thy protectress. When
thou art dismissed from this castle, repair to holy father Jerome,
at the convent adjoining to the church of St. Nicholas, and make
thy story known to him, as far as thou thinkest meet: he will not
fail to inform the princess, who is the mother of all that want her
assistance. Farewell: it is not seemly for me to hold farther converse with a man, at this unwonted hour." "May the saints guard
thee, gracious lady!" replied the peasant—"but oh! if a poor and
worthless stranger might presume to beg a minute's audience farther—am I so happy? the casement is not shut—might I venture
to ask"—"Speak quickly," said Matilda; "the morning dawns
apace; should the labourers come into the fields and perceive us
—what wouldst thou ask?" "I know not how—I know not if I
dare," said the young stranger, faltering, "yet the humanity with
which you have spoken to me emboldens—lady! dare I trust you?"
"Heavens!" said Matilda, "What dost thou mean? with what
wouldst thou trust me? speak boldly, if thy secret is fit to be entrusted to a virtuous breast." "I would ask," said the peasant, recollecting himself, "whether what I have heard from the domestics
is true, that the princess is missing from the castle?" "What imports it to thee to know?" replied Matilda. "Thy first words
bespoke a prudent and becoming gravity. Dost thou come hither
to pry into the secrets of Manfred? Adieu. I have been mistaken in
thee." Saying these words, she shut the casement hastily, without
giving the young man time to reply. "I had acted more wisely,"
said the princess to Bianca, with some sharpness, "if I had let thee

converse with this peasant: his inquisitiveness seems of a piece with thy own." "It is not fit for me to argue with your highness," replied Bianca; "but perhaps the questions, I should have put to him, would have been more to the purpose than those you have been pleased to ask him." "Oh! no doubt;" said Matilda: "you are a very discreet personage! may I know what you would have asked him?" "A by-stander often sees more of the game than those that play," answered Bianca. "Does your highness think, madam, that his question about my Lady Isabella was the result of mere curiosity? No, no, madam; there is more in it than you great folks are aware of. Lopez told me, that all the servants believe this young fellow contrived my Lady Isabella's escape: now, pray, madam, observe—you and I both know that my Lady Isabella never much fancied the prince your brother—well! he is killed just in the critical minute—I accuse nobody. A helmet falls from the moon—so my lord, your father, says; but Lopez and all the servants say, that this young spark is a magician, and stole it from Alfonso's tomb." "Have done with this rhapsody of impertinence," said Matilda. "Nay, madam, as you please," cried Bianca; "yet it is very particular, though, that my Lady Isabella should be missing the very same day, and that this young sorcerer should be found at the mouth of the trap-door; I accuse nobody; but if my young lord came honestly by his death"—"Dare not, on thy duty," said Matilda, "to breathe a suspicion on the purity of my dear Isabella's fame." "Purity or not purity," said Bianca, "gone she is— a stranger is found that nobody knows: you question him yourself: he tells you he is in love, or unhappy, it is the same thing— nay, he owned he was unhappy about others; and is anybody unhappy about another, unless they are in love with them? And at the very next word, he asks innocently, poor soul! if my Lady Isabella is missing." "To be sure," said Matilda, "thy observations are not totally without foundation—Isabella's flight amazes me: the curiosity of this stranger is very particular—yet Isabella never concealed a thought from me." "So she told you," said Bianca, "to fish out your secrets; but who knows, madam, but this stranger may be some prince in disguise? do, madam, let me open the window, and ask him a few questions!" "No," replied Matilda, "I will ask him myself: if he knows aught of Isabella, he is not worthy that I should converse farther with him." She was going to open the casement, when they heard the bell ring at the postern gate of the castle, which is on the right hand of the tower, where Matilda lay. This prevented the princess from renewing the conversation with the stranger.

After continuing silent for some time, "I am persuaded," said she to Bianca, "that whatever be the cause of Isabella's flight, it had no unworthy motive. If this stranger was accessary to it, she must be satisfied of his fidelity and worth. I observed, did not you, Bianca? that his words were tinctured with an uncommon infusion of piety. It was no ruffian's speech: his phrases were becoming a man of gentle birth." "I told you, madam," said Bianca, "that I was sure he was some prince in disguise." "Yet," said Matilda, "if he was privy to her escape, how will you account for his not accompanying her in her flight? why expose himself unnecessarily and rashly to my father's resentment?" "As for that, madam," replied she, "if he could get from under the helmet, he will find ways of eluding your father's anger. I do not doubt but he has some talisman or other about him." "You resolve everything into magic," said Matilda; "but a man, who has any intercourse with infernal spirits, does not dare to make use of those tremendous and holy words, which he uttered. Didst thou not observe with what fervour he vowed to remember me to heaven in his prayers? yes; Isabella was undoubtedly convinced of his piety." "Commend me to the piety of a young fellow and a damsel, that consult to elope!" said Bianca. "No, no, madam: my Lady Isabella is of another-guess mould than you take her for. She used indeed to sigh and lift up her eyes in your company, because she knows you are a saint—but when your back was turned"—"You wrong her," said Matilda: "Isabella is no hypocrite: she has a due sense of devotion, but never affected a call she has not. On the contrary, she always combated my inclination for the cloister; and, though I own the mystery she has made to me of her flight, confounds me; though it seems inconsistent with the friendship between us; I cannot forget the disinterested warmth with which she always opposed my taking the veil: she wished to see me married, though my dower would have been a loss to her and my brother's children. For her sake I will believe well of this young peasant." "Then you do think there is some liking between them?" said Bianca. While she was speaking, a servant came hastily into the chamber, and told the princess that the Lady Isabella was found. "Where?" said Matilda. "She has taken sanctuary in St. Nicholas's church," replied the servant: "father Jerome has brought the news himself: he is below with his highness." "Where is my mother?" said Matilda. "She is in her own chamber, madam, and has asked for you."

Manfred had risen at the first dawn of light, and gone to Hippolita's apartment, to enquire if she knew aught of Isabella. While he was questioning her, word was brought that Jerome demanded to speak with him. Manfred, little suspecting the cause of the friar's arrival, and knowing he was employed by Hippolita in her charities, ordered him to be admitted, intending to leave them together, while he pursued his search after Isabella. "Is your business with me or the princess?" said Manfred. "With both," replied the holy man. "The Lady Isabella"—"What of her?" interrupted Manfred, eagerly: "Is at St. Nicholas's altar," replied Jerome. "That is no business of Hippolita!" said Manfred, with confusion: "let us retire to my chamber, father; and inform me how she came thither." "No, my lord," replied the good man, with an air of firmness and authority, that daunted even the resolute Manfred, who could not help revering the saint-like virtues of Jerome—"my commission is to both; and, with your highness's good liking, in the presence of both I shall deliver it— but first, my lord, I must interrogate the princess, whether she is acquainted with the cause of the Lady Isabella's retirement from your castle." "No, on my soul;" said Hippolita; "does Isabella charge me with being privy to it?"—"Father," interrupted Manfred, "I pay due reverence to your holy profession; but I am sovereign here, and will allow no meddling priest to interfere in the affairs of my domestic. If you have aught to say, attend me to my chamber—I do not use to let my wife be acquainted with the secret affairs of my state; they are not within a woman's province." "My lord," said the holy man, "I am no intruder into the secrets of families. My office is to promote peace, to heal divisions, to preach repentance, and teach mankind to curb their headstrong passions. I forgive your highness's uncharitable apostrophe: I know my duty, and am the minister of a mightier prince than Manfred. Hearken to him, who speaks through my organs." Manfred trembled with rage and shame. Hippolita's countenance declared her astonishment and impatience, to know where this would end: her silence more strongly spoke her observance of Manfred.

"The Lady Isabella," resumed Jerome, "commends herself to both your highnesses; she thanks both for the kindness with which she has been treated in your castle: she deplores the loss of your son, and her own misfortune in not becoming the daughter of such wise and noble princes, whom she shall always respect as parents; she prays for uninterrupted union and felicity between you: (Manfred's colour changed) but, as it is no longer possible to be allied to you, she entreats your consent to remain in sanctuary, till she can learn news of her father; or, by the certainty of his death, be at liberty, with the approbation of her guardians, to dispose of herself in suitable marriage." "I shall give no such consent," said the prince; "but insist on her return to the castle without delay: I am answerable for her person to her guardians, and will not brook her being in any hands but my own." "Your highness will recollect whether that can any longer be proper," replied the friar. "I want no monitor," said Manfred, colouring; "Isabella's conduct leaves room for strange suspicions—and that young villain, who was at least the accomplice of her flight, if not the cause of it"—"The cause!" interrupted Jerome; "was a young man the cause?"—"This is not to be borne!" cried Manfred. "Am I to be bearded in my own palace by an insolent monk? thou art privy, I guess, to their amours."—"I would pray to heaven to clear up your uncharitable surmises," said Jerome, "if your highness were not satisfied in your conscience how unjustly you accuse me. I do pray to heaven to pardon that uncharitableness: and I implore your highness to leave the princess at peace in that holy place, where she is not liable to be disturbed by such vain and worldly fantasies as discourses of love from any man." "Cant not to me," said Manfred, "but return and bring the princess to her duty." "It is my duty to prevent her return hither;" said Jerome. "She is where orphans and virgins are safest from the snares and wiles of this world; and nothing but a parent's authority shall take her thence." "I am her parent," cried Manfred, "and demand her." "She wished to have you for her parent," said the friar: "but heaven that forbade that connection, has for ever dissolved all ties betwixt you: and I announce to your highness"— "Stop! audacious man," said Manfred, "and dread my displeasure." "Holy father," said Hippolita, "it is your office to be no respecter of persons: you must speak as your duty prescribes—but it is my duty to hear nothing that it pleases not my lord I should hear. Attend the prince to his chamber. I will retire to my oratory, and pray the blessed virgin to inspire you with her holy counsels, and to restore the heart of my gracious lord to its wonted peace and gentleness." "Excellent woman!" said the friar. "My lord, I attend your pleasure."

Manfred, accompanied by the friar, passed to his own apartment, where, shutting the door, "I perceive, father," said he, "that Isabella has acquainted you with my purpose. Now, hear my resolve, and obey. Reasons of state, most urgent reasons, my own and the safety of my people, demand that I should have a son. It is in vain to expect an heir from Hippolita. I have made choice of Isabella. You must bring her back; and you must do more. I know the influence you have with Hippolita: her conscience is in your hands. She is, I allow, a faultless woman: her soul is set on heaven, and scorns the little grandeur of this world: you can withdraw her from it entirely. Persuade her to consent to the dissolution of our marriage, and to retire into a monastery: she shall endow one if she will: and shall have the means of being as liberal to your order, as she or you can wish. Thus you will divert the calamities that are hanging over our heads, and have the merit of saving the principality of Otranto from destruction. You are a prudent man; and, though the warmth of my temper betrayed me into some unbecoming expressions, I honour your virtue, and wish to be indebted to you for the repose of my life and the preservation of my family."

"The will of heaven be done!" said the friar. "I am but its worthless instrument. It makes use of my tongue, to tell thee, prince, of thy unwarrantable designs. The injuries of the virtuous Hippolita have mounted to the throne of pity. By me thou art reprimanded for thy adulterous intention of repudiating her: by me thou art warned not to pursue thine incestuous design on thy contracted daughter. Heaven, that delivered her from thy fury, when the judgments, so recently fallen on thy house, ought to have inspired thee with other thoughts, will continue to watch over her. Even I, a poor and despised friar, am able to protect her from thy violence. I, sinner as I am, and uncharitably reviled by your highness, as an accomplice of I know not what amours, scorn the allurements with which it has pleased thee to tempt my honesty. I love my order; I honour devout souls; I respect the piety of thy princess; but will not betray the confidence she reposes in me,

nor serve even the cause of religion by foul and sinful compli-
ances; but, forsooth! the welfare of the state depends on your
highness having a son! Heaven mocks the shortsighted views of
man. But yester-morn, whose house was so great, so flourishing
as Manfred's? Where is young Conrad now! My lord, I respect your
tears, but I mean not to check them: let them flow, prince: they
will weigh more with heaven, toward the welfare of thy subjects,
than a marriage, which, founded on lust or policy, could never
prosper. The sceptre, which passed from the race of Alfonso to
thine, cannot be preserved by a match which the church will
never allow. If it is the will of the Most High that Manfred's name
must perish, resign yourself, my lord, to its decrees: and thus deserve a crown that can never pass away. Come, my lord; I like this
sorrow; let us return to the princess: she is not apprised of your
cruel intentions; nor did I mean more than to alarm you. You saw
with what gentle patience, with what efforts of love, she heard, she
rejected hearing the extent of your guilt. I know she longs to fold
you in her arms, and assure you of her unalterable affection."
"Father," said the prince, "you mistake my compunction: true; I
honour Hippolita's virtues; I think her a saint; and wish it were
for my soul's health to tie faster the knot that has united us—but
alas! father, you know not the bitterest of my pangs. It is some
time that I have had scruples on the legality of our union: Hippolita is related to me in the fourth degree. It is true, we had a
dispensation; but I have been informed that she had also been
contracted to another. This it is that sits heavy at my heart: to
this state of unlawful wedlock I impute the visitation that has
fallen on me in the death of Conrad! Ease my conscience of this
burden: dissolve our marriage, and accomplish the work of godli-
ness which your divine exhortations have commenced in my soul."

How cutting was the anguish which the good man felt, when
he perceived this turn in the wily prince! He trembled for Hippolita, whose ruin he saw was determined; and he feared if Manfred had no hope of recovering Isabella, that his impatience for
a son would direct him to some other object, who might not be
equally proof against the temptation of Manfred's rank. For some
time the holy man remained absorbed in thought. At length, conceiving some hopes from delay, he thought the wisest conduct
would be to prevent the prince from despairing of recovering
Isabella. Her, the friar knew he could dispose, from her affection

to Hippolita, and from the aversion she had expressed to him for
Manfred's addresses, to second his views, till the censures of the
church could be fulminated against a divorce. With this intention,
as if struck with the prince's scruples, he at length said; "My lord,
I have been pondering on what your highness has said: and if, in
truth, it is delicacy of conscience that is the real motive of your
repugnance to your virtuous lady, far be it from me to endeavour
to harden your heart. The church is an indulgent mother: unfold
your griefs to her: she alone can administer comfort to your soul,
either by satisfying your conscience, or, upon examination of
your scruples, by setting you at liberty, and indulging you in the
lawful means of continuing your lineage. In the latter case, if the
Lady Isabella can be brought to consent"—Manfred, who concluded that he had either overreached the good man, or that his
first warmth had been but a tribute paid to appearance, was over-
joyed at his sudden turn, and repeated the most magnificent promises, if he should succeed by the friar's mediation. The well-mean-
ing priest suffered him to deceive himself, fully determined to
traverse his views, instead of seconding them.

   "Since we now understand one another," resumed the prince,
"I expect, father, that you satisfy me in one point. Who is the
youth that I found in the vault? He must have been privy to Isabella's flight; tell me truly; is he her lover? or is he an agent for
another's passion? I have often suspected Isabella's indifference
to my son: a thousand circumstances crowd on my mind that confirm that suspicion. She herself was so conscious of it, that, while
I discoursed with her, in the gallery, she outran my suspicions,
and endeavoured to justify herself from coolness to Conrad." The
friar, who knew nothing of the youth, but what he had learnt occasionally from the princess, ignorant what was become of him,
and not sufficiently reflecting on the impetuosity of Manfred's
temper, conceived that it might not be amiss to sow the seeds of
jealousy in his mind: they might be turned to some use hereafter,
either by prejudicing the prince against Isabella, if he persisted in
that union; or, by diverting his attention to a wrong scent, and
employing his thoughts on a visionary intrigue, prevent his engaging in any new pursuit. With this unhappy policy, he answered
in a manner to confirm Manfred in the belief of some connection
between Isabella and the youth.

   The prince, whose passions wanted little fuel to throw them

into a blaze, fell into a rage at the idea of what the friar had suggested. "I will fathom to the bottom of this intrigue," cried he; and quitting Jerome abruptly, with a command to remain there till his return, he hastened to the great hall of the castle, and ordered the peasant to be brought before him. "Thou hardened young impostor!" said the prince, as soon as he saw the youth; "what becomes of thy boasted veracity now? it was Providence, was it, and the light of the moon, that discovered the lock of the trap-door to thee? Tell me, audacious boy, who thou art, and how long thou hast been acquainted with the princess—and take care to answer with less equivocation than thou didst last night, or tortures shall wring the truth from thee." The young man, perceiving that his share in the flight of the princess was discovered, and concluding that anything he should say, could no longer be of service or detriment to her, replied, "I am no impostor, my lord, nor have I deserved opprobrious language. I answered to every question, your highness put to me last night, with the same veracity that I shall speak now; and that will not be from fear of your tortures, but because my soul abhors a falsehood. Please to repeat your questions, my lord; I am ready to give you all the satisfaction in my power." "You know my questions," replied the prince, "and only want time to prepare an evasion. Speak directly; who art thou? and how long hast thou been known to the princess?" "I am a labourer at the next village," said the peasant; "my name is Theodore. The princess found me in the vault last night; before that hour I never was in her presence." "I may believe as much, or as little as I please of this," said Manfred; "but I will hear thy own story, before I examine into the truth of it. Tell me what reason did the princess give thee for making her escape? thy life depends on thy answer." "She told me," replied Theodore, "that she was on the brink of destruction, and that if she could not escape from the castle, she was in danger, in a few moments, of being made miserable for ever." "And on this slight foundation, on a silly girl's report," said Manfred, "thou didst hazard my displeasure?" "I fear no man's displeasure," said Theodore, "when a woman in distress puts herself under my protection." During this examination, Matilda was going to the apartment of Hippolita. At the upper end of the hall, where Manfred sat, was a boarded gallery with latticed windows, through which Matilda and Bianca were to pass. Hearing her father's voice, and seeing the servants assembled round him, she stopped to learn the occasion. The prisoner soon drew her attention; the steady and composed manner in which he answered, and the gallantry of his last reply, which were the first words she heard distinctly, interested her in his favour. His person was noble, handsome, and commanding, even in that situation; but his countenance soon engrossed her whole care. "Heavens! Bianca!" said the princess softly, "do I dream? or is not that youth the exact resemblance of Alfonso's picture in the gallery?" She could say no more, for her father's voice grew louder at every word. "This bravado," said he, "surpasses all thy former insolence. Thou shalt experience the wrath with which thou darest to trifle. Seize him," continued Manfred, "and bind him: the first news the princess hears of her champion shall be, that he has lost his head for her sake." "The injustice of which thou art guilty towards me," said Theodore, "convinces me that I have done a good deed, in delivering the princess from thy tyranny. May she be happy, whatever becomes of me!" "This is a lover!" cried Manfred in a rage: "a peasant within sight of death is not animated by such sentiments. Tell me, tell me, rash boy, who thou art, or the rack shall force thy secret from thee." "Thou hast threatened me with death already," saith the youth, "for the truth I have told thee: if that is all the encouragement I am to expect for sincerity, I am not tempted to indulge thy vain curiosity farther." "Then thou wilt not speak?" said Manfred. "I will not," replied he. "Bear him away into the court-yard," said Manfred: "I will see his head this instant severed from his body." Matilda fainted at hearing these words. Bianca shrieked, and cried, "Help! help! the princess is dead!" Manfred started at this ejaculation, and demanded what was the matter? The young peasant, who heard it too, was struck with horror, and asked eagerly the same question; but Manfred ordered him to be hurried into the court, and kept there for execution, till he had informed himself of the cause of Bianca's shrieks. When he learned the meaning, he treated it as a womanish panic, and ordering Matilda to be carried to her apartment, he rushed into the court, and calling for one of his guards, bade Theodore kneel down and prepare to receive the fatal blow.

The undaunted youth received the bitter sentence with a resignation that touched every heart but Manfred's. He wished earnestly to know the meaning of the words he had heard relating to the princess; but fearing to exasperate the tyrant more against her, he desisted. The only boon he deigned to ask, was, that he might be permitted to have a confessor, and make his peace with heaven. Manfred, who hoped, by the confessor's means, to come at the youth's history, readily granted his request: and being convinced that father Jerome was now in his interest, he ordered him to be called and shrieve the prisoner. The holy man, who had little foreseen the catastrophe that his imprudence occasioned, fell on his knees to the prince, and adjured him, in the most solemn manner, not to shed innocent blood. He accused himself, in the bitterest terms, for his indiscretion, endeavoured to exculpate the youth, and left no method untried to soften the tyrant's rage.

Manfred, more incensed than appeased by Jerome's intercession, whose retraction now made him suspect he had been imposed upon by both, commanded the friar to do his duty, telling him he would not allow the prisoner many minutes for confession. "Nor do I ask many, my lord;" said the unhappy young man. "My sins, thank heaven! have not been numerous; nor exceed what might be expected at my years. Dry your tears, good father, and let us dispatch: this is a bad world; nor have I had cause to leave it with regret." "Oh! wretched youth!" said Jerome; "how canst thou bear the sight of me with patience? I am thy murderer! it is I have brought this dismal hour upon thee." "I forgive thee from my soul," said the youth, "as I hope heaven will pardon me. Hear my confession, father; and give me thy blessing." "How can I prepare thee for thy passage, as I ought?" said Jerome. "Thou canst not be saved without pardoning thy foes—and canst thou forgive that impious man there?" "I can," said Theodore; "I do." "And does not this touch thee? cruel prince!" said the friar. "I sent for thee to confess him," said Manfred sternly; "not to plead for him. Thou didst first incense me against him; his blood be upon thy head!" "It will! it will!" said the good man, in an agony of sorrow. "Thou and I must never hope to go where this blessed youth is going!" "Dispatch!" said Manfred: "I am no more to be moved by the whining of priests, than by the shrieks of women." "What!" said the youth; "is it possible that my fate could have occasioned what I heard! is the princess then again in thy power?" "Thou dost but remember me of my wrath," said Manfred: "prepare thee, for this moment is thy last." The youth, who felt his indignation rise, and who was touched with the sorrow which he saw he had

infused into all the spectators, as well as into the friar, suppressed
his emotions, and putting off his doublet, and unbuttoning his
collar, knelt down to his prayers. As he stooped, his shirt slipped
down below his shoulder, and discovered the mark of a bloody
arrow. "Gracious heaven!" cried the holy man, starting, "what
do I see! It is my child! my Theodore!"

The passions that ensued, must be conceived; they cannot be
painted. The tears of the assistants were suspended by wonder,
rather than stopped by joy. They seemed to inquire into the eyes
of their lord what they ought to feel. Surprise, doubt, tenderness,
respect, succeeded each other in the countenance of the youth. He
received, with modest submission, the effusion of the old man's
tears and embraces; yet, afraid of giving a loose to hope, and suspecting, from what had passed, the inflexibility of Manfred's
temper, he cast a glance towards the prince, as if to say, canst
thou be unmoved at such a scene as this?

Manfred's heart was capable of being touched. He forgot his
anger in his astonishment; yet his pride forbade his owning himself affected. He even doubted whether this discovery was not a
contrivance of the friar to save the youth. "What may this mean?"
said he: "how can he be thy son? is it consistent with thy profession, or reputed sanctity, to avow a peasant's offspring for the
fruit of thy irregular amours?" "Oh! God," said the holy man,
"dost thou question his being mine? could I feel the anguish I do,
if I were not his father? Spare him! good prince, spare him! and
revile me as thou pleasest." "Spare him! spare him!" cried the attendants, "for this good man's sake!" "Peace!" said Manfred,
sternly: "I must know more, ere I am disposed to pardon. A saint's
bastard may be no saint himself." "Injurious lord!" said Theodore; "add not insult to cruelty. If I am this venerable man's son,
though no prince, as thou art, know, the blood that flows in my
veins"—"Yes," said the friar, interrupting him, "his blood is noble; nor is he that abject thing, my lord, you speak him. He is my
lawful son; and Sicily can boast of few houses more ancient than
that of Falconara—but alas, my lord, what is blood! what is nobility! we are all reptiles, miserable, sinful creatures. It is piety
alone that can distinguish us from the dust whence we sprung,
and whither we must return." "Truce to your sermon," said Manfred; "you forget, you are no longer friar Jerome, but the Count
of Falconara. Let me know your history; you will have time

enough to moralize hereafter, if you should not happen to obtain the grace of that sturdy criminal there." "Mother of God!" said the friar, "is it possible my lord can refuse a father the life of his only, his long-lost child! Trample me, my lord, scorn, afflict me, accept my life for his, but spare my son!" "Thou canst feel then," said Manfred, "what it is to lose an only son! a little hour ago, thou didst preach up resignation to me: my house, if fate so pleased, must perish—but the Count of Falconara"—"Alas! my lord," said Jerome, "I confess I have offended; but aggravate not an old man's sufferings! I boast not of my family, nor think of such vanities: it is nature that pleads for this boy; it is the memory of the dear woman that bore him. Is she, Theodore, is she dead?" "Her soul has long been with the blessed," said Theodore. "Oh! how?" cried Jerome, "tell me—no—she is happy! Thou art all my care now! Most dread lord! will you—will you grant me my poor boy's life?" "Return to thy convent," answered Manfred; "conduct the princess hither; obey me in what else thou knowest; and I promise thee the life of thy son." "Oh! my lord," said Jerome, "is my honesty the price I must pay for this dear youth's safety?" "For me!" cried Theodore: "let me die a thousand deaths, rather than stain thy conscience. What is it the tyrant would exact of thee? is the princess still safe from his power? protect her, thou venerable old man; and let all the weight of his wrath fall on me." Jerome endeavoured to check the impetuosity of the youth; and ere Manfred could reply, the trampling of horses was heard, and a brazen trumpet, which hung without the gate of the castle, was suddenly sounded. At the same instant, the sable plumes on the enchanted helmet, which still remained at the other end of the court, were tempestuously agitated, and nodded thrice, as if bowed by some invisible wearer.

CHAPTER III

Manfred's heart misgave him, when he beheld the plumage on the miraculous casque shaken in concert with the sounding of the brazen trumpet. "Father!" said he to Jerome, whom he now ceased to treat as Count of Falconara, "what mean these portents? If I have offended"—the plumes were shaken with greater violence than before. "Unhappy prince that I am!" cried Manfred: "Holy father! will you not assist me with your prayers?" "My lord," replied Jerome, "heaven is no doubt displeased with your mockery of its servants. Submit yourself to the church; and cease to persecute her ministers. Dismiss this innocent youth; and learn to respect the holy character I wear: heaven will not be trifled with: you see"—the trumpet sounded again. "I acknowledge I have been too hasty," said Manfred. "Father, do you go to the wicket, and demand who is at the gate." "Do you grant me the life of Theodore?" replied the friar. "I do," said Manfred; "but inquire who is without!"

Jerome, falling on the neck of his son, discharged a flood of tears that spoke the fulness of his soul. "You promised to go to the gate," said Manfred. "I thought," replied the friar, "your highness would excuse my thanking you first in this tribute of my heart." "Go, dearest sir," said Theodore; "obey the prince—I do not deserve that you should delay his satisfaction for me."

Jerome, inquiring who was without, was answered, a herald. "From whom?" said he. "From the knight of the gigantic sabre"; said the herald; "and I must speak with the usurper of Otranto." Jerome returned to the prince, and did not fail to repeat the message, in the very words it had been uttered. The first sounds struck Manfred with terror; but when he heard himself stiled usurper, his rage re-kindled, and all his courage revived. "Usurper! insolent villain!" cried he, "who dares to question my title? Retire, father; this is no business for monks: I will meet this presumptuous man myself. Go to your convent, and prepare the princess's return: your son shall be a hostage for your fidelity: his life depends on your obedience." "Good heaven! my lord," cried Jerome, "your highness did but this instant freely pardon my child —have you so soon forgot the interposition of heaven?" "Heaven," replied Manfred, "does not send heralds to question the title of a lawful prince; I doubt whether it even notifies its will through friars—but that is your affair, not mine. At present you know my pleasure; and it is not a saucy herald that shall save your son, if you do not return with the princess."

It was in vain for the holy man to reply. Manfred commanded him to be conducted to the postern gate, and shut out from the castle: and he ordered some of his attendants to carry Theodore to the top of the black tower, and guard him strictly; scarce permitting the father and son to exchange a hasty embrace at parting. He then withdrew to the hall, and, seating himself in princely state, ordered the herald to be admitted to his presence.

"Well! thou insolent!" said the prince, "what wouldst thou with me?" "I come," replied he, "to thee, Manfred, usurper of the principality of Otranto, from the renowned and invincible knight, the knight of the gigantic sabre: in the name of his lord, Frederic Marquis of Vicenza, he demands the Lady Isabella, daughter of that prince, whom thou hast basely, and traitorously got into thy power, by bribing her false guardians during his absence; and he requires thee to resign the principality of Otranto, which thou hast usurped from the said Lord Frederic, the nearest of blood to the last rightful lord, Alfonso the good. If thou dost not instantly comply with these just demands, he defies thee to single combat to the last extremity." And so saying, the herald cast down his warder.

"And where is this braggart, who sends thee?" said Manfred. "At the distance of a league," said the herald: "he comes to make good his lord's claim against thee, as he is a true knight, and thou an usurper and ravisher."

Injurious as this challenge was, Manfred reflected that it was not his interest to provoke the Marquis. He knew how well founded the claim of Frederic was; nor was this the first time he had heard of it. Frederic's ancestors had assumed the stile of princes of Otranto, from the death of Alfonso the good without issue: but Manfred, his father, and grandfather, had been too powerful for the house of Vicenza to dispossess them. Frederic, a martial and amorous young prince, had married a beautiful young lady of whom he was enamoured, and who had died in childbed of Isabella. Her death affected him so much, that he had taken the cross, and gone to the holy land, where he was wounded in an engagement against the infidels, made prisoner, and reported to be dead. When the news reached Manfred's ears, he bribed the guardians of the Lady Isabella to deliver her up to him, as a bride for his son Conrad, by which alliance he had proposed to unite the claims of the two houses. This motive, on Conrad's death, had co-operated to make him so suddenly resolve on espousing her himself; and the same reflection determined him now to endeavour at obtaining the consent of Frederic to this marriage. A like policy inspired him with the thought of inviting

Frederic's champion into his castle, lest he should be informed of Isabella's flight, which he strictly enjoined his domestics not to disclose to any of the knight's retinue.

"Herald," said Manfred, as soon as he had digested these reflections, "return to thy master, and tell him ere we liquidate our differences by the sword, Manfred would hold some converse with him. Bid him welcome to my castle, where, by my faith, as I am a true knight, he shall have courteous reception, and full security for himself and followers. If we cannot adjust our quarrel by amicable means, I swear he shall depart in safety, and shall have full satisfaction, according to the laws of arms: so help me God, and his holy Trinity!" The herald made three obeisances and retired.

During this interview, Jerome's mind was agitated by a thousand contrary passions. He trembled for the life of his son, and his first thought was to persuade Isabella to return to the castle. Yet he was scarce less alarmed at the thought of her union with Manfred. He dreaded Hippolita's unbounded submission to the will of her lord; and though he did not doubt but he could alarm her piety not to consent to a divorce, if he could get access to her; yet, should Manfred discover that the obstruction came from him, it might be equally fatal to Theodore. He was impatient to know whence came the herald, who, with so little management, had questioned the title of Manfred: yet he did not dare absent himself from the convent, lest Isabella should leave it, and her flight be imputed to him. He returned disconsolately to the monastery, uncertain on what conduct to resolve. A monk, who met him in the porch, and observed his melancholy air, said, "Alas! brother, is it then true that we have lost our excellent princess Hippolita?" The holy man started, and cried, "What meanest thou, brother? I come this instant from the castle, and left her in perfect health." "Martelli," replied the other friar, "passed by the convent, but a quarter of an hour ago, on his way from the castle, and reported that her highness was dead. All our brethren are gone to the chapel to pray for her happy transit to a better life, and willed me to wait thy arrival. They know thy holy attachment to that good lady, and are anxious for the affliction it will cause in thee; indeed we have all reason to weep; she was a mother to our house; but this life is but a pilgrimage; we must not murmur; we shall all follow her! may our end be like hers!" "Good

brother, thou dreamest," said Jerome: "I tell thee I come from
the castle, and left the princess well. Where is the Lady Isabella?"
"Poor gentlewoman!" replied the friar; "I told her the sad news,
and offered her spiritual comfort; I reminded her of the transi-
tory condition of mortality, and advised her to take the veil: I
quoted the example of the holy princess Sanchia of Arragon."
"Thy zeal was laudable," said Jerome, impatiently; "but at present
it was unnecessary: Hippolita is well; at least I trust in the Lord
she is; I heard nothing to the contrary; yet, methinks, the prince's
earnestness—well, brother, but where is the Lady Isabella?" "I
know not," said the friar; "she wept much, and said she would retire to her chamber."

Jerome left his comrade abruptly, and hastened to the princess,
but she was not in her chamber. He enquired of the domestics of
the convent, but could learn no news of her. He searched in vain
throughout the monastery and the church, and dispatched messengers round the neighbourhood, to get intelligence if she had
been seen; but to no purpose. Nothing could equal the good
man's perplexity. He judged that Isabella, suspecting Manfred of
having precipitated his wife's death, had taken the alarm, and
withdrawn herself to some more secret place of concealment. This
new flight would probably carry the prince's fury to the height.
The report of Hippolita's death, though it seemed almost incredible, increased his consternation; and though Isabella's escape
bespoke her aversion of Manfred for a husband, Jerome could feel
no comfort from it, while it endangered the life of his son. He determined to return to the castle, and made several of his brethren
accompany him to attest his innocence to Manfred, and, if necessary, join their intercessions with his for Theodore.

The prince, in the mean time, had passed into the court, and
ordered the gates of the castle to be flung open, for the reception
of the stranger knight and his train. In a few minutes the cavalcade arrived. First came two harbingers with wands. Next a herald, followed by two pages and two trumpeters. Then an hundred
foot guards. These were attended by as many horse. After them
fifty footmen, cloathed in scarlet and black, the colours of the
knight. Then a led horse. Two heralds on each side of a gentleman on horseback, bearing a banner, with the arms of Vicenza
and Otranto quarterly; a circumstance that much offended Manfred, but he stifled his resentment. Two more pages. The knight's

confessor, telling his beads. Fifty more footmen, clad as before. Two knights, habited in complete armour, their beavers down, comrades to the principal knight. The squires of the two knights, carrying their shields and devices. The knight's own squire. An hundred gentlemen, bearing an enormous sword, and seeming to faint under the weight of it. The knight himself on a chestnut steed, in complete armour, his lance in the rest, his face entirely concealed by his vizor, which was surmounted by a large plume of scarlet and black feathers. Fifty foot guards, with drums and trumpets, closed the procession, which wheeled off to the right and left, to make room for the principal knight.

As soon as he approached the gate, he stopped; and the herald advancing, read again the words of the challenge. Manfred's eyes were fixed on the gigantic sword, and he scarce seemed to attend to the cartel: but his attention was soon diverted by a tempest of wind that rose behind him. He turned and beheld the plumes of the enchanted helmet, agitated in the same extraordinary manner as before. It required intrepidity like Manfred's not to sink under a concurrence of circumstances, that seemed to announce his fate. Yet scorning, in the presence of strangers, to betray the courage he had always manifested, he said boldly, "Sir knight, whoever thou art, I bid thee welcome. If thou art of mortal mould, thy valour shall meet its equal: and if thou art a true knight, thou wilt scorn to employ sorcery to carry thy point. Be these omens from heaven or hell, Manfred trusts to the righteousness of his cause, and to the aid of St. Nicholas, who has ever protected his house. Alight, Sir knight, and repose thyself: to-morrow thou shalt have a fair field; and heaven befriend the juster side!"

The knight made no reply, but dismounting, was conducted by Manfred to the great hall of the castle. As they traversed the court, the knight stopped to gaze on the miraculous casque; and, kneeling down, seemed to pray inwardly for some minutes. Rising, he made a sign to the prince to lead on. As soon as they entered the hall, Manfred proposed to the stranger to disarm, but the knight shook his head in token of refusal. "Sir knight," said Manfred, "this is not courteous; but, by my good faith, I will not cross thee; nor shalt thou have cause to complain of the prince of Otranto. No treachery is designed on my part; I hope none is intended on thine; here, take my gage (giving him his ring); your friends and you shall enjoy the laws of hospitality. Rest here, until refreshments are brought: I will but give orders for the accommodation of your train, and return to you." The three knights bowed, as accepting his courtesy. Manfred directed the stranger's retinue to be conducted to an adjacent hospital, founded by the princess Hippolita for the reception of pilgrims. As they made the circuit of the court to return towards the gate, the gigantic sword burst from the supporters, and, falling to the ground opposite to the helmet, remained immoveable. Manfred, almost hardened to preternatural appearances, surmounted the shock of his new prodigy; and returning to the hall, where by this time the feast was ready, he invited his silent guests to take their places. Manfred, however ill his heart was at ease, endeavoured to inspire the company with mirth. He put several questions to them, but was answered only by signs. They raised their vizors but sufficiently to feed themselves, and that but sparingly. "Sirs," said the prince, "ye are the first guests I ever treated within these walls, who scorned to hold intercourse with me; nor has it oft been customary, I ween, for princes to hazard their state and dignity against strangers and mutes. You say you come in the name of Frederic of Vicenza; I have heard that he was a gallant and courteous knight; nor would he, I am bold to say, think it beneath him to mix in social converse with a prince who is his equal, and not unknown by deeds in arms. Still ye are silent—well! be it as it may; by the laws of hospitality and chivalry, ye are masters under this roof; ye shall do your pleasure—but come, give me a goblet of wine; ye will not refuse to pledge me to the healths of your fair mistresses?" The principal knight sighed and crossed himself, and was rising from the board—"Sir knight," said Manfred, "what I said was but in sport: I shall constrain you in nothing; use your good liking. Since mirth is not your mood, let us be sad. Business may hit your fancies better: let us withdraw; and hear if what I have to unfold, may be better relished, than the vain efforts I have made for your pastime."

Manfred, then conducting the three knights into an inner chamber, shut the door, and inviting them to be seated, began thus, addressing himself to the chief personage.

"You come, Sir knight, as I understand, in the name of the Marquis of Vicenza, to re-demand the Lady Isabella, his daughter, who has been contracted, in the face of holy church, to my son,

by the consent of her legal guardians; and to require me to resign
my dominions to your lord, who gives himself for the nearest of
blood to prince Alfonso, whose soul God rest! I shall speak to the
latter article of your demands first. You must know—your lord
knows, that I enjoy the principality of Otranto from my father
Don Manuel, as he received it from his father Don Ricardo. Alfonso, their predecessor, dying childless in the Holy Land, be-
queathed his estates to my grandfather Don Ricardo, in consideration of his faithful services." The stranger shook his head—"Sir
knight," said Manfred, warmly, "Ricardo was a valiant and up-
right man; he was a pious man; witness his munificent foundation
of the adjoining church and two convents. He was peculiarly
patronised by St. Nicholas—my grandfather was incapable—I say,
sir, Don Ricardo was incapable—excuse me, your interruption
has disordered me. I venerate the memory of my grandfather—
well! Sirs, he held this estate; he held it by his good sword, and by
the favour of St. Nicholas—so did my father; and so, sirs, will I,
come what come will—but Frederic, your lord, is nearest in blood
—I have consented to put my title to the issue of the sword—does
that imply a vicious title? I might have asked, where is Frederic
your lord? Report speaks him dead in captivity. You say, your
actions say, he lives—I question it not—I might, sirs, I might, but
I do not. Other princes would bid Frederic take his inheritance
by force, if he can; they would not stake their dignity on a single
combat—they would not submit it to the decision of unknown
mutes—pardon me, gentlemen, I am too warm; but suppose
yourselves in my situation; as ye are stout knights, would it not
move your choler, to have your own, and the honour of your ancestors, called in question? but to the point. Ye require me to deliver up the Lady Isabella—Sirs, I must ask if ye are authorised
to receive her?" The knight nodded. "Receive her," continued
Manfred; "well! you are authorised to receive her; but, gentle
knight, may I ask if you have full powers?" The knight nodded.
"'Tis well," said Manfred; "then hear what I have to offer: ye see,
gentlemen, before you, the most unhappy of men! (he began to
weep) afford me your compassion; I am entitled to it; indeed I
am. Know, I have lost my only hope, my joy, the support of my
house—Conrad died yester-morning." The knights discovered
signs of surprise. "Yes, sirs, fate has disposed of my son; Isabella
is at liberty"—"Do you then restore her?" cried the chief knight,

breaking silence. "Afford me your patience," said Manfred. "I rejoice to find, by this testimony of your good will, that this matter
may be adjusted without blood. It is no interest of mine dictates
what little I have farther to say. Ye behold in me a man disgusted
with the world: the loss of my son has weaned me from earthly
cares. Power and greatness have no longer any charms in my eyes.
I wished to transmit the sceptre I had received from my ancestors
with honour to my son—but that is over! life itself is so indifferent to me, that I accepted your defiance with joy: a good
knight cannot go to the grave with more satisfaction, than when
falling in his vocation: whatever is the will of heaven, I submit;
for, alas! sirs, I am a man of many sorrows. Manfred is no object
of envy—but no doubt you are acquainted with my story." The
knight made signs of ignorance, and seemed curious to have Manfred proceed. "Is it possible, sirs," continued the prince, "that my
story should be a secret to you; have you heard nothing relating to me and the princess Hippolita?" They shook their heads.
"No! thus then, sirs, it is. You think me ambitious: ambition, alas!
is composed of more rugged materials. If I were ambitious, I
should not, for so many years, have been prey to all the hell of
conscientious scruples—but I weary your patience: I will be brief.
Know then, that I have long been troubled in mind on my union
with the princess Hippolita. Oh! sirs, if ye were acquainted with
that excellent woman! if ye knew that I adore her like a mistress,
and cherish her as a friend—but man was not born for perfect
happiness! she shares my scruples, and, with her consent, I have
brought this matter before the church, for we are related within
the forbidden degrees. I expect every hour the definitive sentence
that must separate us for ever—I am sure you feel for me—I see
you do—pardon these tears!" The knights gazed on each other,
wondering where this would end. Manfred continued: "The death
of my son betiding, while my soul was under this anxiety, I
thought of nothing but resigning my dominions, and retiring for
ever from the sight of mankind. My only difficulty was to fix on a
successor, who would be tender of my people, and to dispose of
the Lady Isabella, who is dear to me as my own blood. I was willing to restore the line of Alfonso, even in his most distant kindred: and though, pardon me, I am satisfied it was his will, that
Ricardo's lineage should take place of his own relations; yet where
was I to search for those relations? I knew of none but Frederic

your lord; he was a captive to the infidels, or dead; and were he living, and at home, would he quit the flourishing state of Vicenza, for the inconsiderable principality of Otranto? if he would not, could I bear the thought of seeing a hard, unfeeling viceroy set over my poor faithful people? for, sirs, I love my people, and, thank heaven, am beloved by them: but ye will ask, whither tends this long discourse? briefly then, thus, sirs. Heaven, in your arrival, seems to point out a remedy for those difficulties and my misfortunes. The Lady Isabella is at liberty; I shall soon be so. I would submit to anything for the good of my people—were it not the best, the only way to extinguish the feuds between our families, if I was to take the Lady Isabella to wife—you start— but, though Hippolita's virtues will ever be dear to me, a prince must not consider himself; he is born for his people." A servant at that instant entering the chamber, apprised Manfred that Jerome and several of his brethren demanded immediate access to him.

The prince, provoked at this interruption, and fearing that the friar would discover to the strangers that Isabella had taken sanctuary, was going to forbid Jerome's entrance. But recollecting that he was certainly arrived to notify the princess's return, Manfred began to excuse himself to the knights for leaving them for a few moments, but was prevented by the arrival of the friars. Manfred angrily reprimanded them for their intrusion, and would have forced them back from the chamber; but Jerome was too much agitated to be repulsed. He declared aloud the flight of Isabella, with protestations of his own innocence. Manfred, distracted at the news, and not less at its coming to the knowledge of the strangers, uttered nothing but incoherent sentences; now upbraiding the friar, now apologising to the knights, earnest to know what was become of Isabella, yet equally afraid of their knowing; impatient to pursue her, yet dreading to have them join in the pursuit. He offered to dispatch messengers in quest of her, but the chief knight, no longer keeping silence, reproached Manfred, in bitter terms, for his dark and ambiguous dealing, and demanded the cause of Isabella's first absence from the castle. Manfred, casting a stern look at Jerome, implying a command of silence, pretended that, on Conrad's death, he had placed her in sanctuary, until he could determine how to dispose of her. Jerome, who trembled for his son's life, did not dare to contradict this falsehood, but one of his brethren, not under the same anxiety, declared, frankly, that she had fled to their church in the preceding night. The prince, in vain, endeavoured to stop this discovery, which overwhelmed him with shame and confusion. The principal stranger, amazed at the contradictions he heard, and more than half persuaded that Manfred had secreted the princess, notwithstanding the concern he expressed at her flight, rushing to the door, said, "Thou traitor prince! Isabella shall be found." Manfred endeavoured to hold him, but the other knights assisting their comrade, he broke from the prince, and hastened into the court, demanding his attendants. Manfred, finding it in vain to divert him from the pursuit, offered to accompany him, and summoning his attendants, and taking Jerome and some of the friars to guide them, they issued from the castle; Manfred privately giving orders to have the knight's company secured, while to the knight he affected to dispatch a messenger to require their assistance.

The company had no sooner quitted the castle, than Matilda, who felt herself deeply interested for the young peasant, since she had seen him condemned to death in the hall, and whose thoughts had been taken up with concerting measures to save him, was informed by some of the female attendants, that Manfred had dispatched all his men various ways in pursuit of Isabella. He had, in his hurry, given this order in general terms, not meaning to extend it to the guard he had set upon Theodore, but forgetting it. The domestics, officious to obey so peremptory a prince, and urged by their own curiosity, and love of novelty, to join in any precipitate chase, had, to a man, left the castle. Matilda disengaged herself from her women, stole up to the black tower, and unbolting the door, presented herself to the astonished Theodore. "Young man," said she, "though filial duty and womanly modesty condemn the step I am taking, yet holy charity, surmounting all other ties, justifies this act. Fly, the doors of thy prison are open: my father and his domestics are absent, but they may soon return; be gone in safety, and may the angels of heaven direct thy course!"—"Thou art surely one of those angels!" said the enraptured Theodore: "none but a blessed saint could speak, could act, could look, like thee!—May I not know the name of my divine protectress? Methought thou namedst thy father: is it possible? can Manfred's blood feel holy pity?—Lovely lady, thou answerest not—but how art thou here thyself? why dost thou neg-

lect thy own safety, and waste a thought on a wretch like Theodore? Let us fly together: the life thou bestowest shall be dedicated
to thy defence."—"Alas! thou mistakest," said Matilda, sighing;
"I am Manfred's daughter, but no dangers await me."—"Amazement!" said Theodore; "but last night I blessed myself for yielding
thee the service thy gracious compassion so charitably returns me
now."—"Still thou art in an error," said the princess; "but this is
no time for explanation. Fly, virtuous youth, while it is in my
power to save thee: should my father return, thou and I both
should, indeed, have cause to tremble."—"How," said Theodore,
"thinkest thou, charming maid, that I will accept of life at the
hazard of aught calamitous to thee? better I endured a thousand
deaths."—"I run no risk," said Matilda, "but by thy delay. Depart, it cannot be known that I assisted thy flight."—"Swear by
the saints above," said Theodore, "that thou canst not be suspected; else here I vow to await whatever can befal me"—"Oh!
thou art too generous," said Matilda, "but rest assured that no
suspicion can alight on me."—"Give me thy beauteous hand, in
token that thou dost not deceive me," said Theodore, "and let me
bathe it with the warm tears of gratitude."—"Forbear," said the
princess, "this must not be."—"Alas!" said Theodore, "I have
never known but calamity until this hour—perhaps shall never
know other fortune again: suffer the chaste raptures of holy gratitude: 'tis my soul would print its effusions on thy hand."—"Forbear and be gone," said Matilda: "how would Isabella approve
of seeing thee at my feet?"—"Who is Isabella?" said the young
man, with surprise.—"Ah me! I fear," said the princess, "I am
serving a deceitful one!—hast thou forgot thy curiosity this morning?"—"Thy looks, thy actions, all thy beauteous self, seems an
emanation of divinity," said Theodore, "but thy words are dark
and mysterious,—speak, lady; speak to thy servant's comprehen-
sion."—"Thou understandest but too well!" said Matilda: "but
once more I command thee to be gone: thy blood, which I may
preserve, will be on my head, if I waste the time in vain discourse."—"I go, lady," said Theodore, "because it is thy will, and
because I would not bring the grey hairs of my father with sorrow
to the grave. Say but, adored lady, that I have thy gentle pity."—
"Stay," said Matilda, "I will conduct thee to the subterraneous
vault by which Isabella escaped; it will lead thee to the church of
St. Nicholas, where thou mayest take sanctuary."—"What," said

Theodore, "was it another, and not thy lovely self, that I assisted to find the subterraneous passage?"—"It was," said Matilda, "but ask no more: I tremble to see thee still abide here: fly to the sanctuary."—"To sanctuary," said Theodore, "no, princess, sanctuaries are for helpless damsels, or for criminals. Theodore's soul is free from guilt, nor will wear the appearance of it. Give me a sword, lady, and thy father shall learn that Theodore scorns an ignominious flight."—"Rash youth!" said Matilda, "thou wouldst not dare to lift thy presumptuous arm against the Prince of Otranto?"—"Not against thy father, indeed, I dare not;" said Theodore, "excuse me, lady, I had forgotten—but could I gaze on thee, and remember thou art sprung from the tyrant Manfred? —but he is thy father, and, from this moment, my injuries are buried in oblivion." A deep and hollow groan, which seemed to come from above, startled the princess and Theodore. "Good heaven! we are overheard!" said the princess. They listened, but perceiving no further noise, they both concluded it the effect of pent-up vapours; and the princess, preceding Theodore softly, carried him to her father's armoury, where, equipping him with a complete suit, he was conducted by Matilda to the postern gate. "Avoid the town," said the princess, "and all the western side of the castle: 'tis there the search must be making by Manfred and the strangers: but hie thee to the opposite quarter. Yonder, behind that forest, to the east, is a chain of rocks, hollowed into a labyrinth of caverns, that reach to the sea-coast. There thou mayest lie concealed, till thou canst make signs to some vessel to put on shore and take thee off. Go; heaven be thy guide!—and sometimes in thy prayers remember—Matilda!" Theodore flung himself at her feet, and seizing her lily hand, which with struggles she suffered him to kiss, he vowed, on the earliest opportunity, to get himself knighted, and fervently entreated her permission to swear himself eternally her knight.—Ere the princess could reply, a clap of thunder was suddenly heard, that shook the battlements. Theodore, regardless of the tempest, would have urged his suit; but the princess, dismayed, retreated hastily into the castle, and commanded the youth to be gone, with an air that would not be disobeyed. He sighed, and retired, but with eyes fixed on the gate, until Matilda, closing it, put an end to an interview, in which the hearts of both had drunk so deeply of a passion, which both now tasted for the first time.

Theodore went pensively to the convent, to acquaint his father with his deliverance. There he learned the absence of Jerome, and the pursuit that was making after the Lady Isabella, with some particulars of whose story he now first became acquainted. The generous gallantry of his nature prompted him to wish to assist her; but the monks could lend him no lights to guess at the route she had taken. He was not tempted to wander far in search of her, for the idea of Matilda had imprinted itself so strongly on his heart, that he could not bear to absent himself at much distance from her abode. The tenderness Jerome had expressed for him concurred to confirm this reluctance; and he even persuaded himself that filial affection was the chief cause of his hovering between the castle and monastery. Until Jerome should return at night, Theodore at length determined to repair to the forest that Matilda had pointed out to him. Arriving there, he sought the gloomiest shades, as best suited to the pleasing melancholy that reigned in his mind. In this mood he roved insensibly to the caves which had formerly served as a retreat to hermits, and were now reported round the country to be haunted by evil spirits. He recollected to have heard this tradition; and being of a brave and adventurous disposition, he willingly indulged his curiosity in exploring the secret recesses of this labyrinth. He had not penetrated far, before he thought he heard the steps of some person who seemed to retreat before him. Theodore, though firmly grounded in all our holy faith enjoins to be believed, had no apprehension that good men were abandoned, without cause, to the malice of the powers of darkness. He thought the place more likely to be infested by robbers than by those infernal agents who are reported to molest and bewilder travellers. He had long burned with impatience to approve his valour—drawing his sabre, he marched sedately onwards, still directing his steps, as the imperfect rustling sound before him led the way. The armour he wore was a like indication to the person who avoided him. Theodore, now convinced that he was not mistaken, redoubled his pace, and evidently gained on the person that fled, whose haste increasing, Theodore came up just as a woman fell breathless before him. He hastened to raise her, but her terror was so great, that he apprehended she would faint in his arms. He used every gentle word to dispel her alarms, and assured her, that, far from injuring, he would defend her at the peril of his life. The lady, recovering her spirits from his courteous demeanour, and gazing on her protector, said, "Sure I have heard that voice before!"—"Not to my knowledge," replied Theodore, "unless, as I conjecture, thou art the Lady Isabella."—"Merciful heaven!" cried she, "thou art not sent in quest of me, art thou?" and saying those words, she threw herself at his feet, and besought him not to deliver her up to Manfred. "To Manfred!" cried Theodore —"no, lady; I have once already delivered thee from his tyranny, and it shall fare hard with me now, but I place thee out of the reach of his daring."—"Is it possible," said she, "that thou shouldst be the generous unknown whom I met last night in the vault of the castle? Sure thou art not a mortal, but my guardian angel. On my knees let me thank"—"Hold, gentle princess," said Theodore, "nor demean thyself before a poor and friendless young man. If heaven has selected me for thy deliverer, it will accomplish its work, and strengthen my arm in thy cause—but come, lady, we are too near the mouth of the cavern; let us seek its inmost recesses: I can have no tranquillity till I have placed thee beyond the reach of danger."—"Alas! what mean you, sir?" said she. "Though all your actions are noble, though your sentiments speak the purity of your soul, is it fitting that I should accompany you alone into these perplexed retreats? should we be found together, what would a censorious world think of my conduct?"— "I respect your virtuous delicacy," said Theodore; "nor do you harbour a suspicion that wounds my honour. I meant to conduct you into the most private cavity of these rocks, and then, at the hazard of my life, to guard their entrance against every living thing. Besides, lady," continued he, drawing a deep sigh, "beauteous and all-perfect as your form is, and though my wishes are not guiltless of aspiring, know, my soul is dedicated to another; and although"——a sudden noise prevented Theodore from proceeding. They soon distinguished these sounds, "Isabella! what ho! Isabella!"—the trembling princess relapsed into her former agony of fear. Theodore endeavoured to encourage her, but in vain. He assured her he would die rather than suffer her to return under Manfred's power; and, begging her to remain concealed, he went forth to prevent the person in search of her from approaching.

At the mouth of the cavern he found an armed knight, discoursing with a peasant, who assured him he had seen a lady enter the passes of the rock. The knight was preparing to seek her, when Theodore, placing himself in his way, with his sword drawn, sternly forbade him, at his peril, to advance. "And who art thou, who darest to cross my way?" said the knight, haughtily. "One who does not dare more than he will perform," said Theodore. "I seek the Lady Isabella," said the knight, "and understand she has taken refuge among these rocks. Impede me not, or thou wilt repent having provoked my resentment." "Thy purpose is as odious as thy resentment is contemptible," said Theodore. "Return whence thou camest, or we shall soon know whose resentment is most terrible." The stranger, who was the principal knight that had arrived from the Marquis of Vicenza, had galloped from Manfred as he was busied in getting information of the princess, and giving various orders to prevent her falling into the power of the three knights. Their chief had suspected Manfred of being privy to the princess's absconding; and this insult from a man, who, he concluded, was stationed by that prince to secrete her, confirming his suspicions, he made no reply, but discharging a blow with his sabre at Theodore, would soon have removed all obstruction, if Theodore, who took him for one of Manfred's captains, and who had no sooner given the provocation than prepared to support it, had not received the stroke on his shield. The valour that had so long been smothered in his breast, broke forth at once; he rushed impetuously on the knight, whose pride and wrath were not less powerful incentives to hardy deeds. The combat was furious, but not long: Theodore wounded the knight in three several places, and at last disarmed him, as he fainted by the loss of blood. The peasant, who had fled on the first onset, had given the alarm to some of Manfred's domestics, who, by his orders, were dispersed through the forest, in pursuit of Isabella. They came up as the knight fell, whom they soon discovered to be the noble stranger. Theodore, notwithstanding his hatred to Manfred, could not behold the victory he had gained, without emotions of pity and generosity: but he was more touched when he learned the quality of his adversary, and was informed that he was no retainer, but an enemy of Manfred. He assisted the servants of the latter in disarming the knight, and in endeavouring to staunch the blood that flowed from his wounds. The knight, recovering his speech, said, in a faint and faltering voice, "Generous foe, we have both been in an error: I took thee for an instrument of the tyrant; I perceive thou hast made the like mistake—

it is too late for excuses—I faint—if Isabella is at hand—call her —I have important secrets to"—"He is dying!" said one of the attendants; "has nobody a crucifix about them? Andrea, do thou pray over him."—"Fetch some water," said Theodore, "and pour it down his throat, while I hasten to the princess."—Saying this, he flew to Isabella, and, in few words, told her, modestly, that he had been so unfortunate, by mistake, as to wound a gentleman from her father's court, who wished, ere he died, to impart something of consequence to her.—The princess, who had been transported at hearing the voice of Theodore, as he called her to come forth, was astonished at what she heard. Suffering herself to be conducted by Theodore, the new proof of whose valour recalled her dispersed spirits, she came where the bleeding knight lay speechless on the ground—but her fears returned, when she beheld the domestics of Manfred. She would again have fled, if Theodore had not made her observe that they were unarmed, and had not threatened them with instant death, if they should dare to seize the princess. The stranger opening his eyes, and beholding a woman, said,—"Art thou—pray, tell me truly—art thou Isabella of Vicenza?"—"I am," said she; "Good heaven restore thee!" —"Then thou—then thou"—said the knight, struggling for utterance—"seest—thy father—give me one"—"Oh! amazement! horror! what do I hear! what do I see!" cried Isabella. "My father! you my father! how came you here, sir? for heaven's sake speak!— oh! run for help, or he will expire!"—"'Tis most true," said the wounded knight, exerting all his force; "I am Frederic, thy father —yes, I came to deliver thee—It will not be—give me a parting kiss, and take"—"Sir," said Theodore, "do not exhaust yourself: suffer us to convey you to the castle."—"To the castle!" said Isabella; "is there no help nearer than the castle? would you expose my father to the tyrant? if he goes thither, I dare not accompany him—and yet can I leave him!" "My child," said Frederic, "it matters not for me whither I am carried: a few minutes will place me beyond danger—but while I have eyes to doat on thee, forsake me not, dear Isabella! This brave knight—I know not who he is, will protect thy innocence—Sir, you will not abandon my child, will you?"—Theodore, shedding tears over his victim, and vowing to guard the princess at the expense of his life, persuaded Frederic to suffer himself to be conducted to the castle. They placed him on a horse belonging to one of the domestics, after binding up his wounds as well as they were able. Theodore marched by his side, and the afflicted Isabella, who could not bear to quit him, followed mournfully behind.

CHAPTER IV

The sorrowful troop no sooner arrived at the castle, than they were met by Hippolita and Matilda, whom Isabella had sent one of the domestics before to advertise of their approach. The ladies, causing Frederic to be conveyed into the nearest chamber, retired, while the surgeons examined his wounds. Matilda blushed at seeing Theodore and Isabella together; but endeavoured to conceal it by embracing the latter, and condoling with her on her father's mischance. The surgeons soon came to acquaint Hippolita that none of the marquis's wounds were dangerous; and that he was desirous of seeing his daughter and the princesses. Theodore, under pretence of expressing his joy at being freed from his apprehensions of the combat being fatal to Frederic, could not resist the impulse of following Matilda. Her eyes were so often cast down, on meeting his, that Isabella, who regarded Theodore as attentively as he gazed on Matilda, soon divined who the object was that he had told her, in the cave, engaged his affections. While this mute scene passed, Hippolita demanded of Frederic the cause of his having taken that mysterious course for reclaiming his daughter; and threw in various apologies to excuse her lord for the match contracted between their children. Frederic, however incensed against Manfred, was not insensible to the courtesy and benevolence of Hippolita: but he was still more struck with the lovely form of Matilda. Wishing to detain them by his bedside, he informed Hippolita of his story. He told her, that, while prisoner to the infidels, he had dreamed that his daughter, of whom he had learned no news since his captivity, was detained in a castle, where she was in danger of the most dreadful misfortunes: and that if he obtained his liberty, and repaired to a wood near Joppa, he would learn more. Alarmed at this dream, and incapable of obeying the direction given by it, his chains became more grievous than ever. But while his thoughts were occupied on the means of obtaining his liberty, he received the agreeable news, that the confederate princes, who were warring in Palestine, had paid his ransom. He instantly set out for the wood that had been marked in his dream. For three days he and his attendants had wandered in the forest, without seeing a human form; but, on the evening of the third, they came to a cell, in which they found a venerable hermit in the agonies of death. Applying rich cordials, they brought the saint-like man to his speech. "My sons," said he, "I am bounden to your charity—but it is in vain—I am going to my eternal rest—yet I die with the satisfaction of performing the will of heaven. When first I repaired to this solitude, after seeing my country become a prey to unbelievers—it is, alas! above fifty years since I was witness to that dreadful scene!—St. Nicholas appeared to me, and revealed a secret, which he bade me never disclose to mortal man, but on my death-bed. This is that tremendous hour, and ye are, no doubt, the chosen warriors to whom I was ordered to reveal my trust. As soon as ye have done the last offices to this wretched corse, dig under the seventh tree on the left hand of this poor cave, and your pains will—Oh! good heaven receive my soul!" With those words, the devout man breathed his last. "By break of day," continued Frederic, "when we had committed the holy relics to earth, we dug according to direction—but what was our astonishment, when, about the depth of six feet, we discovered an enormous sabre—the very weapon yonder in the court. On the blade, which was then partly out of the scabbard, though since closed by our efforts in removing it, were written the following lines—no; excuse me, madam," added the marquis, turning to Hippolita, "if I forbear to repeat them: I respect your sex and rank, and would not be guilty of offending your ear with sounds injurious to aught that is dear to you." —He paused: Hippolita trembled. She did not doubt but Frederic was destined by heaven to accomplish the fate that seemed to threaten her house. Looking with anxious fondness at Matilda, a silent tear stole down her cheek; but recollecting herself, she said, "Proceed, my lord; heaven does nothing in vain; mortals must receive its divine behests with lowliness and submission. It is our part to deprecate its wrath, or bow to its decrees. Repeat the sentence, my lord, we listen resigned." Frederic was grieved that he had proceeded so far. The dignity and patient firmness of Hippolita penetrated him with respect, and the tender silent affection with which the princess and her daughter regarded each other,

melted him almost to tears. Yet, apprehensive that his forbear-
ance to obey would be more alarming, he repeated, in a faltering
and low voice, the following lines:—

> "Where'er a casque that suits this sword is found,
> With perils is thy daughter compass'd round;
> Alfonso's blood alone can save the maid,
> And quiet a long restless prince's shade."

"What is there in these lines," said Theodore impatiently, "that
affects these princesses? why were they to be shocked by a mysterious delicacy, that has so little foundation?"—"Your words are
rude, young man," said the marquis; "and though fortune has
favoured you once"—"My honoured lord," said Isabella, who
resented Theodore's warmth, which she perceived was dictated
by his sentiments for Matilda, "discompose not yourself for the
glosing of a peasant's son: he forgets the reverence he owes you;
but he is not accustomed"—Hippolita, concerned at the heat that
had arisen, checked Theodore for his boldness, but with an air
acknowledging his zeal; and, changing the conversation, demanded of Frederic where he had left her lord? As the marquis
was going to reply, they heard a noise without, and rising to inquire the cause, Manfred, Jerome, and part of the troop, who had
met an imperfect rumour of what had happened, entered the
chamber. Manfred advanced hastily towards Frederic's bed, to
condole with him on his misfortune, and to learn the circumstances of the combat, when, starting in an agony of terror and
amazement, he cried, "Ha! what art thou? thou dreadful spectre!
is my hour come?"—"My dearest, gracious lord," cried Hippolita,
clasping him in her arms, "what is it you see? why do you fix
your eye-balls thus?"—"What!" cried Manfred, breathless, "dost
thou see nothing, Hippolita? is this ghastly phantom sent to me
alone—to me, who did not"—"For mercy's sweetest self, my
lord," said Hippolita, "resume your soul, command your reason.
There is none here but we, your friends."—"What! is not that
Alfonso?" cried Manfred: "Dost thou not see him? can it be my
brain's delirium?"—"This! my lord," said Hippolita; "this is
Theodore, the youth who has been so unfortunate"—"Theodore!"
said Manfred, mournfully, and striking his forehead—"Theodore,
or a phantom, he has unhinged the soul of Manfred—but how
comes he here? and how comes he in armour?"—"I believe
he went in search of Isabella," said Hippolita. "Of Isabella!"

said Manfred, relapsing into rage—"yes, yes, that is not doubtful—but how did he escape from durance in which I left
him? was it Isabella, or this hypocritical old friar, that procured his enlargement?"—"And would a parent be criminal, my
lord," said Theodore, "if he meditated the deliverance of his
child?" Jerome, amazed to hear himself, in a manner, accused by
his son, and without foundation, knew not what to think. He
could not comprehend how Theodore had escaped; how he came
to be armed, and to encounter Frederic. Still he would not venture
to ask any questions that might tend to inflame Manfred's wrath
against his son. Jerome's silence convinced Manfred that he had
contrived Theodore's release—"And is it thus, thou ungrateful
old man," said the prince, addressing himself to the friar, "that
thou repayest mine and Hippolita's bounties? And, not content
with traversing my heart's nearest wishes, thou armest thy bastard,
and bringest him into my own castle to insult me!"—"My lord,"
said Theodore, "you wrong my father: nor he nor I are capable
of harbouring a thought against your peace. Is it insolence thus
to surrender myself to your highness's pleasure?" added he, laying his sword respectfully at Manfred's feet. "Behold my bosom;
strike, my lord, if you suspect that a disloyal thought is lodged
there. There is not a sentiment engraven on my heart, that does
not venerate you and yours." The grace and fervour with which
Theodore uttered these words, interested every person present in
his favour.—Even Manfred was touched—yet still possessed with
his resemblance to Alfonso, his admiration was dashed with secret
horror. "Rise," said he; "thy life is not my present purpose. But
tell me thy history, and how thou camest connected with this old
traitor here."—"My lord," said Jerome, eagerly—"Peace, impostor," said Manfred; "I will not have him prompted."—"My
lord," said Theodore, "I want no assistance. My story is very brief.
I was carried, at five years of age, to Algiers, with my mother, who
had been taken by corsairs from the coast of Sicily. She died of
grief in less than a twelvemonth." The tears gushed from Jerome's
eyes, on whose countenance a thousand anxious passions stood
expressed. "Before she died," continued Theodore, "she bound a
writing about my arm under my garments, which told me I was
the son of the Count Falconara."—"It is most true," said Jerome;
"I am that wretched father."—"Again I enjoin thee silence," said
Manfred; "proceed."—"I remained in slavery," said Theodore,

"until within these two years, when attending on my master in his cruises, I was delivered by a Christian vessel, which overpowered the pirate; and discovering myself to the captain, he generously put me on shore in Sicily—but alas! instead of finding a father, I learned that his estate, which was situated on the coast, had, during his absence, been laid waste by the Rover, who had carried my mother and me into captivity; that his castle had been burnt to the ground, and that my father, on his return, had sold what remained, and was retired into religion in the kingdom of Naples, but where no man could inform me. Destitute and friendless, hopeless almost of attaining the transport of a parent's embrace, I took the first opportunity of setting sail for Naples, from whence, within these six days, I wandered into this province, still supporting myself by the labour of my hands; nor until yestermorn did I believe that heaven had reserved any lot for me but peace of mind and contented poverty. This, my lord, is Theodore's story. I am blessed, beyond my hope, in finding a father: I am unfortunate, beyond my desert, in having incurred your highness's displeasure." He ceased. A murmur of approbation gently arose from the audience. "This is not all," said Frederic: "I am bound in honour to add what he suppresses. Though he is modest, I must be generous—he is one of the bravest youths on Christian ground. He is warm too; and, from the short knowledge I have of him, I will pledge myself for his veracity: if what he reports of himself were not true, he would not utter it—and for me, youth, I honour a frankness which becomes thy birth. But now, and thou didst offend me: yet the noble blood, which flows in thy veins, may well be allowed to boil out, when it has so recently traced itself to its source. Come, my lord," turning to Manfred, "if I can pardon him, surely you may. It is not the youth's fault, if you took him for a spectre." This bitter taunt galled the soul of Manfred. "If beings from another world," replied he, haughtily, "have power to impress my mind with awe, it is more than living man can do; nor could a stripling's arm"—"My lord," interrupted Hippolita, "your guest has occasion for repose: shall we not leave him to rest?" Saying this, and taking Manfred by the hand, she took leave of Frederic, and led the company forth. The prince, not sorry to quit a conversation, which recalled to mind the discovery he had made of his most secret sensations, suffered himself to be conducted to his own apartment, after permitting

Theodore, though under engagement to return to the castle on the morrow—a condition the young man gladly accepted—to retire with his father to the convent. Matilda and Isabella were too much occupied with their own reflections, and too little content with each other, to wish for farther converse that night. They separated each to her chamber, with more expressions of ceremony, and fewer of affection, than had passed between them since their childhood.

If they parted with small cordiality, they did but meet with greater impatience as soon as the sun was risen. Their minds were in a situation that excluded sleep, and each recollected a thousand questions which she wished she had put to the other overnight. Matilda reflected that Isabella had been twice delivered by Theodore in very critical situations, which she could not believe accidental. His eyes, it was true, had been fixed on her in Frederic's chamber; but that might have been to disguise his passion for Isabella from the fathers of both. It were better to clear this up. She wished to know the truth, lest she should wrong her friend, by entertaining a passion for Isabella's lover. Thus jealousy prompted, and, at the same time, borrowed an excuse from friendship to justify its curiosity.

Isabella, not less restless, had better foundation for her suspicions. Both Theodore's tongue and eyes had told her his heart was engaged—it was true—yet, perhaps, Matilda might not correspond to his passion—she had ever appeared insensible to love: all her thoughts were set on heaven.—"Why did I dissuade her?" said Isabella to herself: "I am punished for my generosity—but when did they meet? where? It cannot be: I have deceived myself—perhaps last night was the first time they ever beheld each other; it must be some other object that has prepossessed his affections; if it is, I am not so unhappy as I thought; if it is not my friend Matilda—how! can I stoop to wish for the affection of a man, who rudely and unnecessarily acquainted me with his indifference! and that, at the very moment in which common courtesy demanded at least expressions of civility. I will go to my dear Matilda, who will confirm me in this becoming pride—man is false— I will advise with her on taking the veil: she will rejoice to find me in this disposition; and I will acquaint her that I no longer oppose her inclination for the cloister." In this frame of mind, and determined to open her heart entirely to Matilda, she went to that

princess's chamber, whom she found already dressed, and leaning
pensively on her arm. This attitude, so correspondent to what she
felt herself, revived Isabella's suspicions, and detroyed the confidence she had purposed to place in her friend. They blushed at
meeting, and were too much novices to disguise their sensations
with address. After some unmeaning questions and replies, Matilda demanded of Isabella the cause of her flight? The latter, who
had almost forgotten Manfred's passion, so entirely was she occupied by her own, concluding that Matilda referred to her last
escape from the convent, which had occasioned the events of the
preceding evening, replied, "Martelli brought word to the convent that your mother was dead." "Oh!" said Matilda, interrupting her, "Bianca has explained that mistake to me: on seeing me
faint, she cried out, 'The princess is dead!' and Martelli, who had
come for the usual dole to the castle"—"And what made you
faint?" said Isabella, indifferent to the rest.—Matilda blushed,
and stammered—"My father—he was sitting in judgment on a
criminal."—"What criminal?" said Isabella, eagerly. "A young
man," said Matilda; "I believe—I think it was that young man
that"—"What, Theodore?" said Isabella. "Yes!" answered she;
"I never saw him before; I do not know how he had offended my
father—but as he has been of service to you, I am glad my lord
has pardoned him."—"Served me!" replied Isabella, "do you term
it serving me, to wound my father, and almost occasion his death?
Though it is but since yesterday that I am blessed with knowing
a parent, I hope Matilda does not think I am such a stranger to
filial tenderness as not to resent the boldness of that audacious
youth, and that it is impossible for me ever to feel any affection
for one who dared to lift his arm against the author of my being.
No, Matilda, my heart abhors him; and if you still retain the
friendship for me that you have vowed from your infancy, you
will detest a man who has been on the point of making me miserable for ever." Matilda held down her head, and replied, "I
hope my dearest Isabella does not doubt her Matilda's friendship: I never beheld that youth until yesterday; he is almost a
stranger to me: but, as the surgeons have pronounced your father
out of danger, you ought not to harbour uncharitable resentment
against one, who, I am persuaded, did not know the marquis was
related to you." "You plead his cause very pathetically," said Isabella, "considering he is so much a stranger to you! I am mistaken,

or he returns your charity."—"What mean you?" said Matilda. "Nothing," said Isabella: repenting that she had given Matilda a hint of Theodore's inclination for her. Then, changing the discourse, she asked Matilda what occasioned Manfred to take Theodore for a spectre? "Bless me," said Matilda, "did not you observe his extreme resemblance to the portrait of Alfonso in the gallery? I took notice of it to Bianca even before I saw him in armour; but with the helmet on, he is the very image of that picture." "I do not much observe pictures," said Isabella; "much less have I examined this young man so attentively as you seem to have done —ah! Matilda, your heart is in danger—but let me warn you as a friend—he has owned to me that he is in love; it cannot be with you, for yesterday was the first time you ever met—was it not?" "Certainly," replied Matilda; "but why does my dearest Isabella conclude from anything I have said, that"—she paused—then continuing; "he saw you first, and I am far from having the vanity to think that my little portion of charms could engage a heart devoted to you—may you be happy, Isabella, whatever is the fate of Matilda!"—"My lovely friend," said Isabella, whose heart was too honest to resist a kind expression, "it is you that Theodore admires; I saw it; I am persuaded of it; nor shall a thought of my own happiness suffer me to interfere with yours." This frankness drew tears from the gentle Matilda; and jealousy, that, for a moment, had raised a coolness between these amiable maidens, soon gave way to the natural sincerity and candour of their souls. Each confessed to the other the impression that Theodore had made on her; and this confidence was followed by a struggle of generosity, each insisting on yielding her claim to her friend. At length, the dignity of Isabella's virtue reminding her of the preference which Theodore had almost declared for her rival, made her determine to conquer her passion, and cede the beloved object to her friend.

During this contest of amity, Hippolita entered her daughter's chamber. "Madam," said she to Isabella, "you have so much tenderness for Matilda, and interest yourself so kindly in whatever affects our wretched house, that I can have no secrets with my child which are not proper for you to hear." The princesses were all attention and anxiety. "Know then, madam," continued Hippolita, "and you, my dearest Matilda, that, being convinced, by all the events of these two last ominous days, that Heaven purposes the sceptre of Otranto should pass from Manfred's hands into those of the Marquis Frederic, I have been, perhaps, inspired with the thought of averting our total destruction by the union of our rival houses. With this view I have been proposing to Manfred, my lord, to tender this dear, dear child, to Frederic, your father"—"Me to Lord Frederic!" cried Matilda—"good heavens! my gracious mother—and have you named it to my father?"—"I have," said Hippolita; "he listened benignly to my proposal, and is gone to break it to the marquis."—"Ah! wretched princess!" cried Isabella; "what hast thou done! what ruin has thy inadvertent goodness been preparing for thyself, for me, and for Matilda!"—"Ruin from me to you and to my child!" said Hippolita, "what can this mean?"—"Alas!" said Isabella, "the purity of your own heart prevents your seeing the depravity of others. Manfred, your lord, that impious man"—"Hold," said Hippolita; "you must not, in my presence, young lady, mention Manfred with disrespect; he is my lord and husband, and"— "Will not long be so," said Isabella, "if his wicked purposes can be carried into execution."—"This language amazes me!" said Hippolita. "Your feeling, Isabella, is warm; but, until this hour, I never knew it betray you into intemperance. What deed of Manfred authorises you to treat him as a murderer, an assassin?" —"Thou virtuous, and too credulous princess!" replied Isabella; "it is not thy life he aims at—it is to separate himself from thee! to divorce thee! to"—"To divorce me!"—"To divorce my mother!" cried Hippolita and Matilda at once. "Yes," said Isabella; "and to complete his crime he meditates—I cannot speak it!"—"What can surpass what thou hast already uttered!" said Matilda. Hippolita was silent. Grief choked her speech; and the recollection of Manfred's late ambiguous discourses confirmed what she heard. "Excellent, dear lady! madam! mother!" cried Isabella, flinging herself at Hippolita's feet in a transport of passion; "trust me, believe me, I will die a thousand deaths sooner than consent to injure you, than yield to so odious—oh!"— "This is too much!" cried Hippolita: "What crimes does one crime suggest! Rise, dear Isabella; I do not doubt your virtue. Oh! Matilda, this stroke is too heavy for thee! weep not, my child! and not a murmur, I charge thee. Remember, he is thy father still!"—"But you are my mother too," said Matilda, fervently; "and you are virtuous, you are guiltless!—Oh! must not I, must not I complain?"—"You must not," said Hippolita; "come, all will yet be well. Manfred, in the agony for the loss of thy brother, knew not what he said: perhaps Isabella misunderstood him: his heart is good—and, my child, thou knowest not all! There is a destiny hangs over us; the hand of Providence is stretched out—Oh! could I but save thee from the wreck!—Yes," continued she, in a firmer tone; "perhaps the sacrifice of myself may atone for all—I will go and offer myself to this divorce—it boots not what becomes of me. I will withdraw into the neighbouring monastery, and waste the remainder of life in prayers and tears for my child and—the prince!"—"Thou art as much too good for this world," said Isabella, "as Manfred is execrable—but think not, lady, that thy weakness shall determine for me. I swear, hear me all ye angels"—"Stop, I adjure thee," cried Hippolita; "remember thou dost not depend on thyself; thou hast a father," —"My father is too pious, too noble," interrupted Isabella, "to command an impious deed. But should he command it; can a father enjoin a cursed act? I was contracted to the son, can I wed the father?—No, madam, no; force should not drag me to Manfred's hated bed. I loathe him, I abhor him: divine and human laws forbid—and my friend, my dearest Matilda! would I wound her tender soul by injuring her adored mother? my own mother— I never have known another."—"Oh! she is the mother of both!" cried Matilda: "Can we, can we, Isabella, adore her too much?"— "My lovely children," said the touched Hippolita, "your tenderness overpowers me—but I must not give way to it. It is not ours to make election for ourselves: heaven, our fathers, and our husbands, must decide for us. Have patience until you hear what Manfred and Frederic have determined. If the marquis accepts Matilda's hand, I know she will readily obey. Heaven may interpose and prevent the rest.—What means my child?" continued she, seeing Matilda fall at her feet with a flood of speechless tears —"But no; answer me not, my daughter: I must not hear a word against the pleasure of thy father."—"Oh! doubt not my obedience, my dreadful obedience to him and to you!" said Matilda. "But can I, most respected of women, can I experience all this tenderness, this world of goodness, and conceal a thought from the best of mothers?"—"What art thou going to utter?" said Isabella, trembling. "Recollect thyself, Matilda."—"No, Isabella," said the princess, "I should not deserve this incomparable parent, if the inmost recesses of my soul harboured a thought without her permission—nay, I have offended her; I have suffered a passion to enter my heart without her avowal—but here I disclaim it; here I vow to heaven and her"—"My child! my child!" said Hippolita, "what words are these! what new calamities has fate in store for us! Thou, a passion! Thou, in this hour of destruction!" —"Oh! I see all my guilt!" said Matilda.—"I abhor myself, if I cost my mother a pang. She is the dearest thing I have on earth— Oh! I will never, never behold him more!"—"Isabella!" said Hippolita, "thou art conscious to this unhappy secret; whatever it is, speak!"—"What!" cried Matilda, "have I so forfeited my mother's love, that she will not permit me even to speak my own guilt? oh! wretched, wretched Matilda!"—"Thou art too cruel," said Isabella to Hippolita: "canst thou behold this anguish of a virtuous mind, and not commiserate it?"—"Not pity my child!" said Hippolita, catching Matilda in her arms—"Oh! I know she is good, she is all virtue, all tenderness, and duty; I do forgive thee, my excellent, my only hope!" The princesses then revealed to Hippolita their mutual inclination for Theodore, and the purpose of Isabella to resign him to Matilda.—Hippolita blamed their imprudence, and shewed them the improbability that either father would consent to bestow his heiress on so poor a man, though nobly born. Some comfort it gave her to find their passion of so recent a date, and that Theodore had but little cause to suspect it in either. She strictly enjoined them to avoid all correspondence with him. This Matilda fervently promised; but Isabella, who flattered herself that she meant no more than to promote his union with her friend, could not determine to avoid him; and made no reply. "I will go to the convent," said Hippolita, "and order new masses to be said for a deliverance from these calamities."—"Oh! my mother," said Matilda, "you mean to quit us: you mean to take sanctuary, and to give my father an opportunity of pursuing his fatal intention. Alas! on my knees I supplicate you to forbear—will you leave me a prey to Frederic? I will follow you to the convent."—"Be at peace, my child," said Hippolita; "I will return instantly.—I will never abandon thee, until I know it is the will of heaven, and for thy benefit."—"Do not deceive me," said Matilda. "I will not marry Frederic until thou commandest it.—Alas! what will become of me?"—"Why that exclamation?" said Hippolita.—"I have promised thee to return."—"Ah! my mother," replied Matilda, "stay and save me from myself. A frown from thee can do more than all my father's severity. I have given away my heart, and you alone can make me recal it."—"No more," said Hippolita; "thou must not relapse, Matilda."—"I can quit Theodore," said she, "but must I wed another? let me attend thee to the altar, and shut myself from the world for ever."—"Thy fate depends on thy father," said Hippolita; "I have ill bestowed my tenderness, if it has taught thee to revere aught beyond him. Adieu! my child: I go to pray for thee."

Hippolita's real purpose was to demand of Jerome, whether in conscience she might not consent to the divorce. She had oft urged Manfred to resign the principality, which the delicacy of her conscience rendered an hourly burden to her. These scruples concurred to make the separation from her husband appear less dreadful to her, than it would have seemed in any other situation.

Jerome, at quitting the castle over-night, had questioned Theodore severely why he had accused him to Manfred of being privy to his escape. Theodore owned it had been with the design to prevent Manfred's suspicion from alighting on Matilda; and added, the holiness of Jerome's life and character secured him from the tyrant's wrath. Jerome was heartily grieved to discover his son's inclination for that princess; and leaving him to his rest, promised in the morning to acquaint him with important reasons for conquering his passion. Theodore, like Isabella, was too recently acquainted with parental authority, to submit to its decisions against the impulse of his heart. He had little curiosity to learn the friar's reasons, and less disposition to obey them. The lovely Matilda had made stronger impressions on him than filial affection. All night he pleased himself with visions of love; and it was not till late after the morning-office, that he recollected the friar's commands to attend him at Alfonso's tomb.

"Young man," said Jerome, when he saw him, "this tardiness does not please me. Have a father's commands already so little weight?" Theodore made awkward excuses, and attributed his delay to having overslept himself. "And on whom were thy dreams employed?" said the friar, sternly. His son blushed.—"Come, come," resumed the friar, "inconsiderate youth, this must not be; eradicate this guilty passion from thy breast."—"Guilty passion!" cried Theodore, "Can guilt dwell with innocent beauty and virtuous modesty?"—"It is sinful," replied the friar, "to cherish those whom heaven has doomed to destruction. A tyrant's

race must be swept from the earth to the third and fourth generation."—"Will heaven visit the innocent for the crimes of the
guilty?" said Theodore. "The fair Matilda has virtues enough"—
"To undo thee," interrupted Jerome. "Hast thou so soon forgotten that twice the savage Manfred has pronounced thy sentence?"
—"Nor have I forgotten, sir," said Theodore, "that the charity of
his daughter delivered me from his power. I can forget injuries,
but never benefits."—"The injuries thou hast received from Manfred's race," said the friar, "are beyond what thou canst conceive.
Reply not, but view this holy image! Beneath this marble monument rest the ashes of the good Alfonso; a prince adorned with
every virtue! the father of his people! the delight of mankind!
kneel, headstrong boy, and list, while a father unfolds a tale of
horror, that will expel every sentiment from thy soul, but sensations of sacred vengeance.—Alfonso! much-injured prince! let thy
unsatisfied shade sit awful on the troubled air, while these trembling lips—Ha! who comes there?"—"The most wretched of
women!" said Hippolita, entering the choir. "Good father, art
thou at leisure?—but why this kneeling youth? what means the
horror imprinted on each countenance? why at this venerable
tomb—alas! hast thou seen aught?"—"We were pouring forth
our orisons to heaven," replied the friar, with some confusion,
"to put an end to the woes of this deplorable province. Join with
us, lady! thy spotless soul may obtain an exemption from the
judgments which the portents of these days but too speakingly
denounce against thy house."—"I pray fervently to heaven to divert them," said the pious princess. "Thou knowest it has been
the occupation of my life to wrest a blessing for my lord and my
harmless children—One, alas! is taken from me! would heaven
but hear me for my poor Matilda! Father! intercede for her!"—
"Every heart will bless her," cried Theodore, with rapture. "Be
dumb, rash youth!" said Jerome. "And thou, fond princess, contend not with the powers above! the Lord giveth, and the Lord
taketh away: bless his holy name, and submit to his decrees."—
"I do most devoutly," said Hippolita: "but will he not spare my
only comfort? must Matilda perish too? Ah! father, I came—but
dismiss thy son. No ear but thine must hear what I have to utter."
—"May heaven grant thy every wish, most excellent princess!"
said Theodore, retiring. Jerome frowned.

Hippolita then acquainted the friar with the proposal she had suggested to Manfred, his approbation of it, and the tender of Matilda that he was gone to make to Frederic. Jerome could not conceal his dislike of the motion, which he covered under the pretence of the improbability that Frederic, the nearest of blood to Alfonso, and who was come to claim his succession, would yield to an alliance with the usurper of his right. But nothing could equal the perplexity of the friar, when Hippolita confessed her readiness not to oppose the separation, and demanded his opinion on the legality of her acquiescence. The friar catched eagerly at her request of his advice, and, without explaining his aversion to the proposed marriage of Manfred and Isabella, he painted to Hippolita, in the most alarming colours, the sinfulness of her consent, denounced judgments against her if she complied, and enjoined her, in the severest terms, to treat any such proposition with every mark of indignation and refusal.

Manfred, in the mean time, had broken his purpose to Frederic, and proposed the double marriage. That weak prince, who had been struck with the charms of Matilda, listened but too eagerly to the offer. He forgot his enmity to Manfred, whom he saw but little hope of dispossessing by force; and flattering himself that no issue might succeed from the union of his daughter with the tyrant, he looked upon his own succession to the principality as facilitated by wedding Matilda. He made faint opposition to the proposal; affecting, for form only, not to acquiesce unless Hippolita should consent to the divorce.—Manfred took that upon himself. Transported with his success, and impatient to see himself in a situation to expect sons, he hastened to his wife's apartment, determined to extort her compliance. He learned with indignation that she was absent at the convent. His guilt suggested to him that she had probably been informed by Isabella of his purpose. He doubted whether her retirement to the convent did not import an intention of remaining there, until she could raise obstacles to their divorce; and the suspicions he had already entertained of Jerome, made him apprehend that the friar would not only traverse his views, but might have inspired Hippolita with the resolution of taking sanctuary. Impatient to unravel this clue, and to defeat its success, Manfred hastened to the convent, and arrived there as the friar was earnestly exhorting the princess never to yield to the divorce.

"Madam," said Manfred, "what business drew you hither?

why did you not await my return from the marquis?"—"I came to implore a blessing on your councils," replied Hippolita. "My councils do not need a friar's intervention:" said Manfred—"and of all men living is that hoary traitor the only one whom you delight to confer with?"—"Profane prince!" said Jerome; "is it at the altar that thou choosest to insult the servants of the altar?—but, Manfred, thy impious schemes are known. Heaven and this virtuous lady know them—nay, frown not, prince. The church despises thy menaces. Her thunders will be heard above thy wrath. Dare to proceed in thy curst purpose of a divorce, until her sentence be known, and here I lance her anathema at thy head."—"Audacious rebel!" said Manfred, endeavouring to conceal the awe with which the friar's words inspired him; "dost thou presume to threaten thy lawful prince?"—"Thou art no lawful prince," said Jerome; "thou art no prince—go, discuss thy claim with Frederic: and when that is done"—"It is done," replied Manfred; "Frederic accepts Matilda's hand, and is content to wave his claim, unless I have no male issue"—as he spoke those words, three drops of blood fell from the nose of Alfonso's statue. Manfred turned pale, and the princess sunk on her knees. "Behold!" said the friar; "mark this miraculous indication that the blood of Alfonso will never mix with that of Manfred!"—"My gracious lord," said Hippolita, "let us submit ourselves to heaven.—Think not thy ever obedient wife rebels against thy authority. I have no will but that of my lord and the church. To that revered tribunal let us appeal. It does not depend on us to burst the bonds that unite us. If the church shall approve the dissolution of our marriage, be it so—I have but few years, and those of sorrow, to pass. Where can they be worn away so well as at the foot of this altar, in prayers for thine and Matilda's safety?"—"But thou shalt not remain here until then," said Manfred. "Repair with me to the castle, and there I will advise on the proper measures for a divorce; but this meddling friar comes not thither: my hospitable roof shall never more harbour a traitor—and for thy reverence's offspring," continued he, "I banish him from my dominions. He, I ween, is no sacred personage, nor under the protection of the church. Whoever weds Isabella, it shall not be Father Falconara's started-up son."—"They start up," said the friar, "who are suddenly beheld in the seat of lawful princes; but they wither away like the grass, and their place knows them no more." Manfred, casting a look of scorn at the friar, led Hippolita forth; but, at the door of the church, whispered one of his attendants to remain concealed about the convent, and bring him instant notice, if any one from the castle should repair thither.

CHAPTER V

Every reflection which Manfred made on the friar's behaviour, conspired to persuade him that Jerome was privy to an amour between Isabella and Theodore. But Jerome's new presumption, so dissonant from his former meekness, suggested still deeper apprehensions. The prince even suspected that the friar depended on some secret support from Frederic, whose arrival coinciding with the novel appearance of Theodore, seemed to bespeak a correspondence. Still more was he troubled with the resemblance of Theodore to Alfonso's portrait. The latter he knew had unquestionably died without issue. Frederic had consented to bestow Isabella on him.—These contradictions agitated his mind with numberless pangs. He saw but two methods of extricating himself from his difficulties. The one was to resign his dominions to the marquis—pride, ambition, and his reliance on ancient prophecies, which had pointed out a possibility of preserving them to his posterity, combated that thought. The other was to press his marriage with Isabella. After long ruminating on these anxious thoughts, as he marched silently with Hippolita to the castle, he at last discoursed with that princess on the subject of his disquiet, and used every insinuating and plausible argument to extract her consent to, even her promise of promoting the divorce. Hippolita needed little persuasion to bend her to his pleasure. She endeavoured to win him over to the measure of resigning his dominions; but, finding her exhortations fruitless, she assured him, that, as far as her conscience would allow, she would raise no opposition to a separation, though, without better-founded scruples than what he yet alleged, she would not engage to be active in demanding it.

This compliance, though inadequate, was sufficient to raise Manfred's hopes. He trusted that his power and wealth would easily advance his suit at the court of Rome, whither he resolved to engage Frederic to take a journey on purpose. That prince had discovered so much passion for Matilda, that Manfred hoped to obtain all he wished, by holding out or withdrawing his daughter's charms, according as the marquis should appear more or less disposed to co-operate in his views. Even the absence of Frederic would be a material point gained, until he could take farther measures for his security.

Dismissing Hippolita to her apartment, he repaired to that of the marquis, but crossing the great hall, through which he was to pass, he met Bianca. That damsel he knew was in the confidence of both the young ladies. It immediately occurred to him to sift her on the subject of Isabella and Theodore. Calling her aside into the recess of the oriel window of the hall, and soothing her with many fair words and promises, he demanded of her, whether she knew aught of the state of Isabella's affections. "I! my lord! no, my lord—yes, my lord—poor lady! she is wonderfully alarmed about her father's wounds; but I tell her he will do well, don't your highness think so?"—"I do not ask you," replied Manfred, "what she thinks about her father: but you are in her secrets: come, be a good girl, and tell me; is there any young man—ha! you understand me."—"Lord bless me! understand your highness? no, not I: I told her a few vulnerary herbs and repose."—"I am not talking," replied the prince, impatiently, "about her father: I know he will do well."—"Bless me, I rejoice to hear your highness say so; for though I thought it right not to let my young lady despond, methought his greatness had a wan look, and a something—I remember when young Ferdinand was wounded by the Venetian"—"Thou answerest from the point," interrupted Manfred; "but here, take this jewel; perhaps that may fix thy attention—nay, no reverences; my favour shall not stop here—come, tell me truly; how stands Isabella's heart?"—"Well! your highness has such a way!" said Bianca, "to be sure—but can your highness keep a secret?—if it should ever come out of your lips" —"It shall not, it shall not," cried Manfred. "Nay, but swear, your highness:—by my halidame, if it should ever be known that I said it!—Why, truth is truth, I do not think my Lady Isabella ever much affectioned my young lord, your son—yet he was a sweet youth as one should see—I am sure, if I had been a princess —but bless me! I must attend my Lady Matilda; she will marvel what is become of me."—"Stay," cried Manfred; "thou hast not satisfied my question. Hast thou ever carried any message, any letter?"—"I! good gracious!" cried Bianca; "I carry a letter? I would not, to be a queen. I hope your highness thinks, though I am poor, I am honest;—did your highness never hear what Count Marsigli offered me, when he came a wooing to my Lady Matilda?"—"I have not leisure," said Manfred, "to listen to thy tales. I do not question thy honesty; but it is thy duty to conceal nothing from me. How long has Isabella been acquainted with Theodore?"—"Nay, there is nothing can escape your highness!" said Bianca—"not that I know anything of the matter—Theodore, to be sure, is a proper young man, and, as my Lady Matilda says, the very image of good Alfonso: has not your highness remarked it?" —"Yes, yes,—No—thou torturest me," said Manfred. "Where did they meet?—when?"—"Who! my Lady Matilda?" said Bianca. "No, no, not Matilda; Isabella. When did Isabella first become acquainted with this Theodore?"—"Virgin Mary!" said Bianca, "how should I know?"—"Thou dost know," said Manfred, "and I must know; I will."—"Lord! your highness is not jealous of young Theodore!" said Bianca. "Jealous! no, no: why should I be jealous?—perhaps I mean to unite them. If I were sure Isabella would have no repugnance"—"Repugnance! no, I'll warrant her," said Bianca: "he is as comely a youth as ever trod on Christian ground. We are all in love with him; there is not a soul in the castle but would be rejoiced to have him for our prince—I mean, when it shall please Heaven to call your highness to itself." —"Indeed!" said Manfred; "has it gone so far! oh! this cursed friar!—but I must not lose time:—go, Bianca, attend Isabella; but, I charge thee, not a word of what has passed. Find out how she is affected towards Theodore: bring me good news, and that ring has a companion. Wait at the foot of the winding staircase: I am going to visit the marquis, and will talk farther with thee at my return."

Manfred, after some general conversation, desired Frederic to dismiss the two knights, his companions, having to talk with him on urgent affairs. As soon as they were alone, he began, in artful guise, to sound the marquis on the subject of Matilda; and, finding him disposed to his wish, he let drop hints on the difficulties that would attend the celebration of their marriage, unless—at that instant Bianca burst into the room, with a wildness in her look and gestures that spoke the utmost terror. "Oh! my lord, my lord!" cried she, "we are all undone! it is come again! it is come again!"—"What is come again?" cried Manfred, amazed. "Oh! the hand! the giant! the hand!—support me! I am terrified out of my senses," cried Bianca. "I will not sleep in the castle to-night. Where shall I go?—my things may come after me to-morrow— would I had been content to wed Francisco!—this comes of am- bition!"—"What has terrified thee thus, young woman?" said the marquis; "thou art safe here; be not alarmed."—"Oh! your great- ness is wonderfully good," said Bianca, "but I dare not—no, pray let me go—I had rather leave everything behind me, than stay another hour under this roof."—"Go to—thou hast lost thy senses," said Manfred. "Interrupt us not; we were communing on important matters. My lord, this wench is subject to fits. Come with me, Bianca."—"Oh! the saints! no," said Bianca; "for cer- tain it comes to warn your highness: why should it appear to me else? I say my prayers morning and evening—oh! if your highness had believed Diego! 'tis the same hand that he saw the foot to in the gallery-chamber—Father Jerome has often told us the prophecy would be out one of these days. 'Bianca,' said he, 'mark my words' "—"Thou ravest," said Manfred, in a rage; "be gone, and keep these fooleries to frighten thy companions."—"What! my lord," cried Bianca, "do you think I have seen nothing? go to the foot of the great stairs yourself—as I live, I saw it."—"Saw what? tell us, fair maid, what thou hast seen," said Frederic. "Can your highness listen," said Manfred, "to the delirium of a silly wench, who has heard stories of apparitions until she believes them?"—"This is more than fancy," said the marquis; "her terror is too natural, and too strongly impressed, to be the work of imag- ination. Tell us, fair maiden, what it is has moved thee thus."— "Yes, my lord; thank your greatness," said Bianca; "I believe I look very pale; I shall be better when I have recovered myself. I was going to my Lady Isabella's chamber, by his highness's or- der"—"We do not want the circumstances," interrupted Man- fred: "since his highness will have it so, proceed; but be brief." —"Lord! your highness thwarts one so!" replied Bianca: "I fear my hair—I am sure I never in my life—well! as I was telling your greatness, I was going, by his highness's order, to my Lady Isa- bella's chamber: she lies in the watchet-coloured chamber, on the right hand, one pair of stairs: so when I came to the great stairs, I was looking on his highness's present here"—"Grant me patience," said Manfred: "will this wench never come to the point? what imports it to the marquis, that I gave thee a bauble for thy faithful attendance on my daughter? we want to know what thou sawest."—"I was going to tell your highness," said Bianca, "if you would permit me.—So as I was rubbing the ring—I am sure I had not gone up three steps, but I heard the rattling of armour; for all the world such a clatter, as Diego says he heard when the giant turned him about in the gallery-chamber."— "What does she mean, my lord!" said the marquis: "is your castle haunted by giants and goblins?" "Lord! what, has not your greatness heard the story of the giant in the gallery-chamber?" cried Bianca. "I marvel his highness has not told you—mayhap you do not know there is a prophecy"—"This trifling is intolerable," interrupted Manfred. "Let us dismiss this silly wench, my lord! we have more important affairs to discuss."—"By your favour," said Frederic, "these are no trifles: the enormous sabre I was directed to in the wood, yon casque, its fellow—are these visions of this poor maiden's brain?"—"So Jaquez thinks, may it please your greatness," said Bianca. "He says this moon will not be out without our seeing some strange revolution. For my part I should not be surprised if it was to happen to-morrow; for, as I was saying, when I heard the clattering of armour, I was all in a cold sweat— I looked up, and if your greatness will believe me, I saw upon the uppermost bannister of the great stairs a hand in armour as big, as big—I thought I should have swooned—I never stopped until I came hither—would I were well out of this castle! My Lady Matilda told me but yester-morning that her highness Hippolita knows something"—"Thou art an insolent!" cried Manfred.— "Lord Marquis, it much misgives me that this scene is concerted to affront me. Are my own domestics suborned to spread tales injurious to my honour? Pursue your claim by manly daring; or let us bury our feuds, as was proposed, by the intermarriage of our children: but trust me, it ill becomes a prince of your bearing to practise on mercenary wenches."—"I scorn your imputation," said Frederic; "until this hour I never set eyes on this damsel: I have given her no jewel! my lord, my lord, your conscience, your guilt accuses you, and you would throw the suspicion on me— but keep your daughter, and think no more of Isabella: the judgments already fallen on your house forbid me matching into it."

Manfred, alarmed at the resolute tone in which Frederic delivered these words, endeavoured to pacify him. Dismissing Bianca, he made such submissions to the marquis, and threw in such artful encomiums on Matilda, that Frederic was once more staggered. However, as his passion was of so recent a date, it could not, at once, surmount the scruples he had conceived. He had gathered enough from Bianca's discourse to persuade him that Heaven declared itself against Manfred. The proposed marriages too removed his claim to a distance; and the principality of Otranto was a stronger temptation, than the contingent reversion of it with Matilda. Still he would not absolutely recede from his engagements; but purposing to gain time, he demanded of Manfred if it was true in fact that Hippolita consented to the divorce. The prince, transported to find no other obstacle, and depending on his influence over his wife, assured the marquis it was so, and that he might satisfy himself of the truth from her own mouth.

As they were thus discoursing, word was brought that the banquet was prepared. Manfred conducted Frederic to the great hall, where they were received by Hippolita and the young princesses. Manfred placed the marquis next to Matilda, and seated himself between his wife and Isabella. Hippolita comported herself with an easy gravity; but the young ladies were silent and melancholy. Manfred, who was determined to pursue his point with the marquis in the remainder of the evening, pushed on the feast until it waxed late; affecting unrestrained gaiety, and plying Frederic with repeated goblets of wine. The latter, more upon his guard than Manfred wished, declined his frequent challenges, on pretence of his late loss of blood; while the prince, to raise his own disordered spirits, and to counterfeit unconcern, indulged himself in plentiful draughts, though not to the intoxication of his senses.

The evening being far advanced, the banquet concluded. Manfred would have withdrawn with Frederic; but the latter pleading weakness, and want of repose, retired to his chamber, gallantly telling the prince, that his daughter should amuse his highness until himself could attend him. Manfred accepted the party, and, to the no small grief of Isabella, accompanied her to her apartment. Matilda waited on her mother to enjoy the freshness of the evening on the ramparts of the castle.

Soon as the company were dispersed their several ways, Frederic, quitting his chamber, inquired if Hippolita was alone, and was told by one of her attendants, who had not noticed her going forth, that, at that hour, she generally withdrew to her oratory, where he probably would find her. The marquis, during the repast, had beheld Matilda with increase of passion. He now wished to find Hippolita in the disposition her lord had promised. The portents that had alarmed him were forgotten in his desires. Stealing softly and unobserved to the apartment of Hippolita, he entered it with a resolution to encourage her acquiescence to the divorce, having perceived that Manfred was resolved to make the possession of Isabella an unalterable condition, before he would grant Matilda to his wishes.

The marquis was not surprised at the silence that reigned in the princess's apartment. Concluding her, as he had been advertised, in her oratory, he passed on. The door was ajar; the evening gloomy and overcast. Pushing open the door gently, he saw a person kneeling before the altar. As he approached nearer, it seemed not a woman, but one in a long woollen weed, whose back was towards him. The person seemed absorbed in prayer. The marquis was about to return, when the figure, rising, stood some moments fixed in meditation, without regarding him. The marquis, expecting the holy person to come forth, and meaning to excuse his uncivil interruption, said, "Reverend father, I sought the Lady Hippolita."—"Hippolita!" replied a hollow voice, "camest thou to this castle to seek Hippolita?" and then the figure, turning slowly round, discovered to Frederic the fleshless jaws and empty sockets of a skeleton, wrapt in a hermit's cowl. "Angels of grace, protect me!" cried Frederic, recoiling. "Deserve their protection!" said the spectre. Frederic, falling on his knees, adjured the phantom to take pity on him. "Dost thou not remember me?" said the apparition: "Remember the wood of Joppa!"—"Art thou that holy hermit?" cried Frederic, trembling; "Can I do aught for thy eternal peace?"—"Wast thou delivered from bondage," said the spectre, "to pursue carnal delights?—Hast thou forgotten the buried sabre, and the behest of heaven engraven on it?"—"I have not, I have not," said Frederic; "but say, blest spirit, what is thy errand to me?—what remains to be done?"—"To forget Matilda!" said the apparition—and vanished.

Frederic's blood froze in his veins. For some minutes he remained motionless. Then, falling prostrate on his face before the altar, he besought the intercession of every saint for pardon. A flood of tears succeeded to this transport; and the image of the beauteous Matilda, rushing, in spite of him, on his thoughts, he lay on the ground in a conflict of penitence and passion. Ere he could recover from this agony of his spirits, the Princess Hippolita, with a taper in her hand, entered the oratory alone. Seeing a man, without motion, on the floor, she gave a shriek, concluding him dead. Her fright brought Frederic to himself. Rising suddenly, his face bedewed with tears, he would have rushed from her presence; but Hippolita, stopping him, conjured him, in the most plaintive accents, to explain the cause of his disorder, and by what strange chance she had found him there in that posture. "Ah! virtuous princess," said the marquis, penetrated with grief—and stopped. "For the love of Heaven, my lord," said Hippolita, "disclose the cause of this transport! what mean these doleful sounds, this alarming exclamation on my name? What woes has Heaven still in store for the wretched Hippolita?—Yet silent!—By every pitying angel, I adjure thee, noble prince," continued she, falling at his feet, "to disclose the purport of what lies at thy heart—I see thou feelest for me; thou feelest the sharp pangs that thou inflictest—speak, for pity!—does aught thou knowest concern my child?"—"I cannot speak," cried Frederic, bursting from her —"Oh! Matilda!"

Quitting the princess thus abruptly, he hastened to his own apartment. At the door of it he was accosted by Manfred, who, flushed by wine and love, had come to seek him, and to propose to waste some hours of the night in music and revelling. Frederic, offended at an invitation so dissonant from the mood of his soul, pushed him rudely aside, and, entering his chamber, flung the door intemperately against Manfred, and bolted it inwards. The haughty prince, enraged at this unaccountable behaviour, withdrew in a frame of mind capable of the most fatal excesses. As he crossed the court, he was met by the domestic whom he had planted at the convent, as a spy on Jerome and Theodore. This man, almost breathless with the haste he had made, informed his lord, that Theodore and some lady from the castle, were, at that instant, in private conference at the tomb of Alfonso, in St. Nicholas's church. He had dogged Theodore thither, but the gloominess of the night had prevented his discovering who the woman was.

Manfred, whose spirits were inflamed, and whom Isabella had driven from her on his urging his passion with too little reserve, did not doubt but the inquietude she had expressed had been occasioned by her impatience to meet Theodore. Provoked by this conjecture, and enraged at her father, he hastened secretly to the great church. Gliding softly between the aisles, and guided by an imperfect gleam of moonshine that shone faintly through the illuminated windows, he stole towards the tomb of Alfonso, to which he was directed by indistinct whispers of the persons he sought.—The first sounds he could distinguish were—"Does it, alas! depend on me? Manfred will never permit our union."— "No, this shall prevent it!" cried the tyrant, drawing his dagger, and plunging it over her shoulder into the bosom of the person that spoke—"Ah, me! I am slain!" cried Matilda, sinking; "good Heaven, receive my soul!"—"Savage, inhuman monster! what hast thou done?" cried Theodore, rushing on him, and wrenching his dagger from him—"Stop, stop thy impious hand!" cried Matilda: "it is my father!" Manfred, waking as from a trance, beat his breast, twisted his hands in his locks, and endeavoured to recover his dagger from Theodore, to dispatch himself. Theodore, scarce less distracted, and only mastering the transports of his grief to assist Matilda, had now, by his cries, drawn some of the monks to his aid. While part of them endeavoured, in concert with the afflicted Theodore, to stop the blood of the dying princess, the rest prevented Manfred from laying violent hands on himself.

Matilda, resigning herself patiently to her fate, acknowledged, with looks of grateful love, the zeal of Theodore. Yet, oft as her faintness would permit her speech its way, she begged the assistants to comfort her father. Jerome, by this time, had learnt the fatal news, and reached the church. His looks seemed to reproach Theodore: but, turning to Manfred, he said, "Now, tyrant! behold the completion of woe fulfilled on thy impious and devoted head! The blood of Alfonso cried to Heaven for vengeance, and Heaven has permitted its altar to be polluted by assassination, that thou mightest shed thy own blood at the foot of that prince's sepulchre!"—"Cruel man!" cried Matilda, "to aggravate the woes of a parent! may Heaven bless my father, and forgive him as I do! My lord, my gracious sire, dost thou forgive thy child? Indeed, I came not hither to meet Theodore! I found him praying at this tomb, whither my mother sent me to intercede for thee, for her— dearest father, bless your child, and say you forgive her."—"Forgive thee! murderous monster!" cried Manfred—"can assassins forgive! I took thee for Isabella; but Heaven directed my bloody hand to the heart of my child—oh! Matilda—I cannot utter it—canst thou forgive the blindness of my rage?"—"I can, I do! and may Heaven confirm it!" said Matilda—"but, while I have life to ask it—Oh! my mother! what will she feel!—will you comfort her, my lord; will you not put her away? indeed she loves you—oh! I am faint! bear me to the castle—can I live to have her close my eyes?"

Theodore and the monks besought her earnestly to suffer herself to be borne into the convent; but her instances were so pressing to be carried to the castle, that, placing her on a litter, they conveyed her thither as she requested; Theodore supporting her head with his arm, and hanging over her in an agony of despairing love, still endeavoured to inspire her with hopes of life. Jerome, on the other side, comforted her with discourses of Heaven, and, holding a crucifix before her, which she bathed with innocent tears, prepared her for her passage to immortality. Manfred, plunged in the deepest affliction, followed the litter in despair.

Ere they reached the castle, Hippolita, informed of the dreadful catastrophe, had flown to meet her murdered child: but when she saw the afflicted procession, the mightiness of her grief deprived her of her senses, and she fell lifeless to the earth in a swoon. Isabella and Frederic, who attended her, were overwhelmed in almost equal sorrow. Matilda alone seemed insensible to her own situation: every thought was lost in tenderness for her mother. Ordering the litter to stop, as soon as Hippolita was brought to herself, she asked for her father. He approached, unable to speak. Matilda, seizing his hand and her mother's, locked them in her own, and then clasped them to her heart. Manfred could not support this act of pathetic piety. He dashed himself on the ground, and cursed the day he was born. Isabella, apprehensive that these struggles of passion were more than Matilda could support, took upon herself to order Manfred to be borne to his apartment, while she caused Matilda to be conveyed to the nearest chamber. Hippolita, scarce more alive than her daughter, was regardless of everything but her: but when the tender Isabella's care would have likewise removed her, while the surgeons examined Matilda's wound, she cried, "Remove me! never! never! I lived but in her, and will expire with her." Matilda raised her eyes, at her moth-

er's voice, but closed them again without speaking. Her sinking
pulse, and the damp coldness of her hand, soon dispelled all hopes
of recovery. Theodore followed the surgeons into the outer chamber, and heard them pronounce the fatal sentence, with a transport equal to frenzy—"Since she cannot live mine," cried he, "at
least she shall be mine in death! Father! Jerome! will you not join
our hands!" cried he to the friar, who, with the marquis, had accompanied the surgeons. "What means thy distracted rashness?"
said Jerome: "Is this an hour for marriage?"—"It is, it is," cried
Theodore; "alas! there is no other!"—"Young man, thou art too
unadvised," said Frederic:—"Dost thou think we are to listen to
thy fond transports in this hour of fate?—what pretensions hast
thou to the princess?"—"Those of a prince," said Theodore—"of
the sovereign of Otranto. This reverend man, my father, has informed me who I am."—"Thou ravest," said the marquis: "there
is no Prince of Otranto but myself, now Manfred, by murder, by
sacrilegious murder, has forfeited all pretensions."—"My lord,"
said Jerome, assuming an air of command, "he tells you true.
It was not my purpose the secret should have been divulged so
soon; but fate presses onward to its work. What his hot-headed
passion has revealed, my tongue confirms. Know, prince, that
when Alfonso set sail for the Holy Land"—"Is this a season for
explanations?" cried Theodore:—"Father, come and unite me to
the princess; she shall be mine—in every other thing I will duti-
fully obey you. My life, my adored Matilda!" continued Theodore, rushing back into the inner chamber, "will you not be mine?
will you not bless your"—Isabella made signs to him to be silent,
apprehending the princess was near her end. "What! is she dead?"
cried Theodore: "is it possible!"—The violence of his exclamations brought Matilda to herself. Lifting up her eyes, she looked
round for her mother—"Life of my soul! I am here," cried Hippolita; "think not I will quit thee!"—"Oh! you are too good," said
Matilda—"but weep not for me, my mother! I am going where
sorrow never dwells—Isabella, thou hast loved me; wo't thou not
supply my fondness to this dear, dear woman?—indeed I am
faint!"—"Oh! my child! my child!" said Hippolita, in a flood of
tears; "can I not withhold thee a moment?"—"It will not be,"
said Matilda—"commend me to Heaven:—where is my father?—
forgive him, dearest mother—forgive him my death; it was an
error—Oh! I had forgotten—dearest mother, I vowed never to see

Theodore more—perhaps that has drawn down this calamity—
but it was not intentional—can you pardon me?"—"Oh! wound
not my agonizing soul!" said Hippolita; "thou never could'st offend me—Alas! she faints! help! help!"—"I would say something
more," said Matilda, struggling; "but it wonnot be—Isabella—
Theodore—for my sake—Oh!"—she expired. Isabella and her
women tore Hippolita from the corse; but Theodore threatened
destruction to all who attempted to remove him from it. He
printed a thousand kisses on her clay-cold hands, and uttered
every expression that despairing love could dictate.

Isabella, in the mean time, was accompanying the afflicted
Hippolita to her apartment; but, in the middle of the court, they
were met by Manfred, who, distracted with his own thoughts,
and anxious once more to behold his daughter, was advancing to
the chamber where she lay. As the moon was now at its height, he
read in the countenances of this unhappy company, the event he
dreaded. "What? is she dead?" cried he, in wild confusion—a
clap of thunder, at that instant, shook the castle to its foundations; the earth rocked, and the clank of more than mortal armour was heard behind. Frederic and Jerome thought the last
day was at hand. The latter, forcing Theodore along with them,
rushed into the court. The moment Theodore appeared, the walls
of the castle behind Manfred were thrown down with a mighty
force, and the form of Alfonso, dilated to an immense magnitude,
appeared in the centre of the ruins. "Behold in Theodore the true
heir of Alfonso!" said the vision: and having pronounced these
words, accompanied by a clap of thunder, it ascended solemnly
towards Heaven, where, the clouds parting asunder, the form of
St. Nicholas was seen, and, receiving Alfonso's shade, they were
soon wrapt from mortal eyes in a blaze of glory.

The beholders fell prostrate on their faces, acknowledging the
divine will. The first that broke silence was Hippolita. "My lord,"
said she, to the desponding Manfred, "behold the vanity of human greatness! Conrad is gone! Matilda is no more! in Theodore
we view the true Prince of Otranto. By what miracle he is so, I
know not—suffice it to us, our doom is pronounced! shall we not,
—can we do other than dedicate the few deplorable hours we
have to live, in deprecating the farther wrath of heaven? Heaven
ejects us—whither can we fly, but to yon holy cells that yet offer
us a retreat?"—"Thou guiltless, but unhappy woman! unhappy

by my crimes!" replied Manfred, "my heart, at last, is open to thy devout admonitions. Oh! could—but it cannot be—ye are lost in wonder—let me at last do justice on myself! To heap shame on my own head is all the satisfaction I have left to offer to offended Heaven. My story has drawn down these judgments: let my confession atone—but ah! what can atone for usurpation, and a murdered child! a child murdered in a consecrated place!—List, sirs, and may this bloody record be a warning to future tyrants!

"Alfonso, ye all know, died in the Holy Land—ye would interrupt me; ye would say he came not fairly to his end—it is most true—why else this bitter cup which Manfred must drink to the dregs? Ricardo, my grandfather, was his chamberlain—I would draw a veil over my ancestor's crimes—but it is in vain! Alfonso died by poison. A fictitious will declared Ricardo his heir. His crimes pursued him—yet he lost no Conrad, no Matilda! I pay the price of usurpation for all! A storm overtook him. Haunted by his guilt, he vowed to St. Nicholas to found a church and two convents, if he lived to reach Otranto. The sacrifice was accepted: the saint appeared to him in a dream, and promised that Ricardo's posterity should reign in Otranto, until the rightful owner should be grown too large to inhabit the castle, and as long as issue male from Ricardo's loins should remain to enjoy it—Alas! alas! nor male nor female, except myself, remains of all his wretched race!—I have done—the woes of these three days speak the rest. How this young man can be Alfonso's heir, I know not—yet I do not doubt it. His are these dominions; I resign them—yet I knew not Alfonso had an heir—I question not the will of Heaven—poverty and prayer must fill up the woeful space until Manfred shall be summoned to Ricardo."

"What remains, is my part to declare," said Jerome. "When Alfonso set sail for the Holy Land, he was driven by a storm on the coast of Sicily. The other vessel, which bore Ricardo and his train, as your lordship must have heard, was separated from him."—"It is most true," said Manfred; "and the title you give me is more than an outcast can claim—well! be it so—proceed." Jerome blushed, and continued. "For three months, Lord Alfonso was wind-bound in Sicily. There he became enamoured of a fair virgin, named Victoria. He was too pious to tempt her to forbidden pleasures. They were married.—Yet, deeming this amour incongruous with the holy vow of arms by which he was bound, he determined to conceal their nuptials, until his return from the Crusade, when he purposed to seek and acknowledge her for his lawful wife. He left her pregnant. During his absence, she was delivered of a daughter: but scarce had she felt a mother's pangs, ere she heard the fatal rumour of her lord's death, and the succession of Ricardo. What could a friendless, helpless woman do? Would her testimony avail?—yet, my lord, I have an authentic writing"—"It needs not," said Manfred; "the horrors of these days, the vision we have but now seen, all corroborate thy evidence beyond a thousand parchments. Matilda's death, and my expulsion"—"Be composed, my lord," said Hippolita; "this holy man did not mean to recal your griefs." Jerome proceeded.

"I shall not dwell on what is needless.—The daughter of which Victoria was delivered, was, at her maturity, bestowed in marriage on me. Victoria died; and the secret remained locked in my breast. Theodore's narrative has told the rest."

The friar ceased. The disconsolate company retired to the remaining part of the castle. In the morning, Manfred signed his abdication of the principality, with the approbation of Hippolita, and each took on them the habit of religion, in the neighbouring convents. Frederic offered his daughter to the new prince, which Hippolita's tenderness for Isabella concurred to promote: but Theodore's grief was too fresh to admit the thought of another love; and it was not until after frequent discourses with Isabella of his dear Matilda, that he was persuaded he could know no happiness but in the society of one, with whom he could for ever indulge the melancholy that had taken possession of his soul.

VATHEK

An Arabian Tale

VATHEK

An Arabian Tale

Vathek, ninth caliph* of the race of the Abassides, was the son of Motassem, and the grandson of Haroun al Raschid. From an early accession to the throne, and the talents he possessed to adorn it, his subjects were induced to expect that his reign would be long and happy. His figure was pleasing and majestic: but when he was angry, one of his eyes became so terrible, that no person could bear to behold it; and the wretch upon whom it was fixed instantly fell backward, and sometimes expired. For fear, however, of depopulating his dominions and making his palace desolate, he but rarely gave way to his anger.

Being much addicted to women and the pleasures of the table, he sought by his affability to procure agreeable companions; and he succeeded the better as his generosity was unbounded and his indulgences unrestrained: for he did not think, with the Caliph Omar Ben Abdalaziz, that it was necessary to make a hell of this world to enjoy paradise in the next.

He surpassed in magnificence all his predecessors. The palace of Alkoremi, which his father, Motassem, had erected on the hill of Pied Horses, and which commanded the whole city of Samarah, was, in his idea, far too scanty: he added, therefore, five wings, or rather other palaces, which he destined for the particular gratification of each of the senses.

In the first of these were tables continually covered with the most exquisite dainties; which were supplied both by night and by day, according to their constant consumption; whilst the most delicious wines and the choicest cordials flowed forth from a hundred fountains that were never exhausted. This palace was called *The Eternal or Unsatiating Banquet.*

[* A section of explanatory notes begins on p. 195.]

The second was styled *The Temple of Melody, or the Nectar of the Soul.* It was inhabited by the most skilful musicians and admired poets of the time; who not only displayed their talents within, but dispersing in bands without, caused every surrounding scene to reverberate their songs, which were continually varied in the most delightful succession.

The palace named *The Delight of the Eyes, or the Support of Memory,* was one entire enchantment. Rarities, collected from every corner of the earth, were there found in such profusion as to dazzle and confound, but for the order in which they were arranged. One gallery exhibited the pictures of the celebrated Mani, and statues that seemed to be alive. Here a well-managed perspective attracted the sight; there the magic of optics agreeably deceived it: whilst the naturalist, on his part, exhibited in their several classes the various gifts that Heaven had bestowed on our globe. In a word, Vathek omitted nothing in this palace that might gratify the curiosity of those who resorted to it, although he was not able to satisfy his own; for, of all men, he was the most curious.

The Palace of Perfumes, which was termed likewise *The Incentive to Pleasure,* consisted of various halls, where the different perfumes which the earth produces were kept perpetually burning in censers of gold. Flambeaux and aromatic lamps were here lighted in open day. But the too powerful effects of this agreeable delirium might be alleviated by descending into an immense garden, where an assemblage of every fragrant flower diffused through the air the purest odours.

The fifth palace, denominated *The Retreat of Mirth, or the Dangerous,* was frequented by troops of young females, beautiful as the Houris, and not less seducing; who never failed to receive, with caresses, all whom the caliph allowed to approach them and enjoy a few hours of their company.

Notwithstanding the sensuality in which Vathek indulged, he experienced no abatement in the love of his people, who thought that a sovereign giving himself up to pleasure was as able to govern as one who declared himself an enemy to it. But the unquiet and impetuous disposition of the caliph would not allow him to rest there. He had studied so much for his amusement in the lifetime of his father, as to acquire a great deal of knowledge, though not a sufficiency to satisfy himself; for he wished to know everything; even sciences that did not exist. He was fond of engaging in disputes with the learned, but did not allow them to push their opposition with warmth. He stopped with presents the mouths of those whose mouths could be stopped; whilst others, whom his liberality was unable to subdue, he sent to prison to cool their blood, a remedy that often succeeded.

Vathek discovered also a predilection for theological controversy; but it was not with the orthodox that he usually held. By this means he induced the zealots to oppose him, and then persecuted them in return; for he resolved, at any rate, to have reason on his side.

The great prophet, Mahomet, whose vicars the caliphs are, beheld with indignation from his abode in the seventh heaven the irreligious conduct of such a vicegerent. "Let us leave him to himself," said he to the Genii, who are always ready to receive his commands: "let us see to what lengths his folly and impiety will carry him: if he run into excess, we shall know how to chastise him. Assist him, therefore, to complete the tower which, in imitation of Nimrod, he hath begun; not, like that great warrior, to escape being drowned, but from the insolent curiosity of penetrating the secrets of heaven:—he will not divine the fate that awaits him."

The Genii obeyed; and, when the workmen had raised their structure a cubit in the daytime, two cubits more were added in the night. The expedition with which the fabric arose was not a little flattering to the vanity of Vathek: he fancied that even insensible matter showed a forwardness to subserve his designs; not considering that the successes of the foolish and wicked form the first rod of their chastisement.

His pride arrived at its height when, having ascended, for the first time, the fifteen hundred stairs of his tower, he cast his eyes below, and beheld men not larger than pismires; mountains, than shells; and cities, than bee-hives. The idea which such an elevation inspired of his own grandeur completely bewildered him: he was almost ready to adore himself; till, lifting his eyes upward, he saw the stars as high above him as they appeared when he stood on the surface of the earth.

He consoled himself, however, for this intruding and unwelcome perception of his littleness, with the thought of being great in the eyes of others; and flattered himself that the light of his mind would extend beyond the reach of his sight, and extort from the stars the decrees of his destiny.

With this view, the inquisitive prince passed most of his nights on the summit of his tower, till becoming an adept in the mysteries of astrology, he imagined that the planets had disclosed to him the most marvellous adventures, which were to be accomplished by an extraordinary personage, from a country altogether unknown. Prompted by motives of curiosity, he had always been courteous to strangers; but, from this instant, he redoubled his attention, and ordered it to be announced, by sound of trumpet, through all the streets of Samarah, that no one of his subjects, on peril of his displeasure, should either lodge or detain a traveller, but forthwith bring him to the palace.

Not long after this proclamation, arrived in his metropolis a man so abominably hideous, that the very guards who arrested him were forced to shut their eyes as they led him along: the caliph himself appeared startled at so horrible a visage; but joy succeeded to this emotion of terror, when the stranger displayed to his view such rarities as he had never before seen, and of which he had no conception.

In reality, nothing was ever so extraordinary as the merchandise this stranger produced; most of his curiosities, which were not less admirable for their workmanship than splendour, had, besides, their several virtues described on a parchment fastened to each. There were slippers, which, by spontaneous springs, enabled the feet to walk; knives, that cut without motion of the hand; sabres, that dealt the blow at the person they were wished to strike; and the whole enriched with gems that were hitherto unknown.

The sabres especially, the blades of which emitted a dazzling radiance, fixed, more than all the rest, the caliph's attention; who promised himself to decipher, at his leisure, the uncouth characters engraven on their sides. Without, therefore, demanding their price, he ordered all the coined gold to be brought from his treasury, and commanded the merchant to take what he pleased. The stranger obeyed, took little, and remained silent.

Vathek, imagining that the merchant's taciturnity was occasioned by the awe which his presence inspired, encouraged him to advance, and asked him, with an air of condescension, who he was? whence he came? and where he obtained such beautiful commodities? The man, or rather monster, instead of making a reply, thrice rubbed his forehead, which, as well as his body, was blacker than ebony; four times clapped his paunch, the projection of which was enormous; opened wide his huge eyes, which glowed like firebrands; began to laugh with a hideous noise, and discovered his long amber-coloured teeth, bestreaked with green.

The caliph, though a little startled, renewed his inquiries, but without being able to procure a reply. At which, beginning to be ruffled, he exclaimed, "Knowest thou, wretch, who I am, and at whom thou art aiming thy gibes?"—Then, addressing his guards, "Have ye heard him speak?—is he dumb?"—"He hath spoken," they replied, "but to no purpose."—"Let him speak then again," said Vathek, "and tell me who he is, from whence he came, and where he procured these singular curiosities; or I swear, by the ass of Balaam, that I will make him rue his pertinacity."

This menace was accompanied by one of the caliph's angry and perilous glances, which the stranger sustained without the slightest emotion; although his eyes were fixed on the terrible eye of the prince.

No words can describe the amazement of the courtiers, when they beheld this rude merchant withstand the encounter unshocked. They all fell prostrate with their faces on the ground, to avoid the risk of their lives; and would have continued in the same abject posture, had not the caliph exclaimed, in a furious tone, "Up, cowards! seize the miscreant! see that he be committed to prison, and guarded by the best of my soldiers! Let him, however, retain the money I gave him; it is not my intent to take from him his property; I only want him to speak."

No sooner had he uttered these words, than the stranger was surrounded, pinioned, and bound with strong fetters, and hurried away to the prison of the great tower, which was encompassed by seven empalements of iron bars, and armed with spikes in every direction, longer and sharper than spits. The caliph, nevertheless, remained in the most violent agitation. He sat down indeed to eat; but, of the three hundred dishes that were daily placed before him, he could taste of no more than thirty-two.

A diet to which he had been so little accustomed was sufficient of itself to prevent him from sleeping; what then must be its effect when joined to the anxiety that preyed upon his spirits? At the first glimpse of dawn he hastened to the prison, again to importune this intractable stranger; but the rage of Vathek exceeded all bounds on finding the prison empty, the grates burst asunder, and his guards lying lifeless around him. In the paroxysm of his passion he fell furiously on the poor carcasses, and kicked them till evening without intermission. His courtiers and viziers exerted their efforts to soothe his extravagance; but, finding every expedient ineffectual, they all united in one vociferation, "The caliph is gone mad! the caliph is out of his senses!"

This outcry, which soon resounded through the streets of Samarah, at length reached the ears of Carathis, his mother, who flew in the utmost consternation to try her ascendency on the mind of her son. Her tears and caresses called off his attention; and he was prevailed upon, by her entreaties, to be brought back to the palace.

Carathis, apprehensive of leaving Vathek to himself, had him put to bed; and, seating herself by him, endeavoured by her conversation to appease and compose him. Nor could any one have attempted it with better success; for the caliph not only loved her as a mother, but respected her as a person of superior genius. It was she who had induced him, being a Greek herself, to adopt the sciences and systems of her country, which all good Mussulmans hold in such thorough abhorrence.

Judicial astrology was one of those sciences in which Carathis was a perfect adept. She began, therefore, with reminding her son of the promise which the stars had made him; and intimated an attention of consulting them again. "Alas!" said the caliph as soon as he could speak, "what a fool I have been! not for having bestowed forty thousand kicks on my guards, who so tamely submitted to death; but for never considering that this extraordinary man was the same that the planets had foretold; whom, instead of ill-treating, I should have conciliated by all the arts of persuasion."

"The past," said Carathis, "cannot be recalled; but it behoves us to think of the future: perhaps you may again see the object you so much regret: it is possible the inscriptions on the sabres will afford information. Eat, therefore, and take thy repose, my dear son. We will consider, to-morrow, in what manner to act."

Vathek yielded to her counsel as well as he could, and arose in the morning with a mind more at ease. The sabres he commanded to be instantly brought; and, poring upon them, through a coloured glass, that their glittering might not dazzle, he set himself in earnest to decipher the inscriptions; but his reiterated attempts were all of them nugatory: in vain did he beat his head, and bite his nails; not a letter of the whole was he able to ascertain. So unlucky a disappointment would have undone him again, had not Carathis, by good fortune, entered the apartment.

"Have patience, my son!" said she: "you certainly are possessed of every important science; but the knowledge of languages is a trifle at best, and the accomplishment of none but a pedant. Issue a proclamation, that you will confer such rewards as become your greatness upon any one that shall interpret what you do not understand, and what is beneath you to learn; you will soon find your curiosity gratified."

"That may be," said the caliph; "but, in the meantime, I shall be horribly disgusted by a crowd of smatterers, who will come to the trial as much for the pleasure of retailing their jargon as from the hope of gaining the reward. To avoid this evil, it will be proper to add, that I will put every candidate to death, who shall fail to give satisfaction; for, thank Heaven! I have skill enough to distinguish, whether one translates or invents."

"Of that I have no doubt," replied Carathis; "but to put the ignorant to death is somewhat severe, and may be productive of dangerous effects. Content yourself with commanding their beards to be burnt: beards in a state are not quite so essential as men."

The caliph submitted to the reasons of his mother; and, sending for Morakanabad, his prime vizier, said, "Let the common criers proclaim, not only in Samarah, but throughout every city in my empire, that whosoever will repair hither and decipher certain characters which appear to be inexplicable, shall experience that liberality for which I am renowned; but that all who fail upon trial shall have their beards burnt off to the last hair. Let them add, also, that I will bestow fifty beautiful slaves, and as many jars of apricots from the Isle of Kirmith, upon any man that shall bring me intelligence of the stranger."

The subjects of the caliph, like their sovereign, being great admirers of women and apricots from Kirmith, felt their mouths water at these promises, but were totally unable to gratify their hankering; for no one knew what had become of the stranger.

As to the caliph's other requisition, the result was different. The learned, the half-learned, and those who were neither, but fancied themselves equal to both, came boldly to hazard their beards, and all shamefully lost them. The exaction of these forfeitures, which found sufficient employment for the eunuchs, gave them such a smell of singed hair as greatly to disgust the ladies of the seraglio, and to make it necessary that this new occupation of their guardians should be transferred to other hands.

At length, however, an old man presented himself, whose beard was a cubit and a half longer than any that had appeared before him. The officers of the palace whispered to each other, as they ushered him in, "What a pity, oh! what a great pity that such a beard should be burnt!" Even the caliph, when he saw it, concurred with them in opinion; but his concern was entirely needless. This venerable personage read the characters with facility, and explained them verbatim as follows: "We were made where everything is well made: we are the least of the wonders of a place where all is wonderful, and deserving the sight of the first potentate on earth."

"You translate admirably!" cried Vathek; "I know to what these marvellous characters allude. Let him receive as many robes of honour and thousands of sequins of gold as he hath spoken words. I am in some measure relieved from the perplexity that embarrassed me!" Vathek invited the old man to dine, and even to remain some days in the palace.

Unluckily for him, he accepted the offer; for the caliph, having ordered him next morning to be called, said: "Read again to me what you have read already; I cannot hear too often the promise that is made me—the completion of which I languish to obtain." The old man forthwith put on his green spectacles, but they instantly dropped from his nose, on perceiving that the characters he had read the day preceding had given place to others of different import. "What ails you?" asked the caliph; "and why these symptoms of wonder?"—"Sovereign of the world!" replied the old man, "these sabres hold another language to-day from that they yesterday held."—"How say you?" returned Vathek:—"but it matters not; tell me, if you can, what they mean."—"It is this, my lord," rejoined the old man: " 'Woe to the rash mortal who seeks to know that of which he should remain ignorant; and to undertake that which surpasseth his power!' "—"And woe to thee!" cried the caliph, in a burst of indignation: "to-day thou art void of understanding: begone from my presence, they shall burn but the half of thy beard, because thou wert yesterday fortunate in guessing:—my gifts I never resume." The old man, wise enough to perceive he had luckily escaped, considering the folly of disclosing so disgusting a truth, immediately withdrew and appeared not again.

But it was not long before Vathek discovered abundant reason to regret his precipitation; for, though he could not decipher the characters himself, yet, by constantly poring upon them, he plainly perceived that they every day changed; and, unfortunately, no other candidate offered to explain them. This perplexing occupation inflamed his blood, dazzled his sight, and brought on such a giddiness and debility that he could hardly support himself. He failed not, however, though in so reduced a condition, to be often carried to his tower, as he flattered himself that he might there read in the stars, which he went to consult, something more congruous to his wishes: but in this his hopes were deluded; for his eyes, dimmed by the vapours of his head, began to subserve his curiosity so ill, that he beheld nothing but a thick, dun cloud, which he took for the most direful of omens.

Agitated with so much anxiety, Vathek entirely lost all firmness; a fever seized him, and his appetite failed. Instead of being one of the greatest eaters, he became as distinguished for drinking. So insatiable was the thirst which tormented him, that his mouth, like a funnel, was always open to receive the various liquors that might be poured into it, and especially cold water, which calmed him more than any other.

This unhappy prince, being thus incapacitated for the enjoyment of any pleasure, commanded the palaces of the five senses to be shut up; forbore to appear in public, either to display his magnificence or administer justice, and retired to the inmost apartment of his harem. As he had ever been an excellent husband, his wives, overwhelmed with grief at his deplorable situation, incessantly supplied him with prayers for his health, and water for his thirst.

In the mean time the Princess Carathis, whose affliction no words can describe, instead of confining herself to sobbing and tears, was closeted daily with the vizier Morakanabad, to find out some cure, or mitigation, of the caliph's disease. Under the persuasion that it was caused by enchantment, they turned over together, leaf by leaf, all the books of magic that might point out a remedy; and caused the horrible stranger, whom they accused as the enchanter, to be everywhere sought for with the strictest diligence.

At the distance of a few miles from Samarah stood a high mountain, whose sides were swarded with wild thyme and basil, and its summit overspread with so delightful a plain, that it might have been taken for the paradise destined for the faithful. Upon it grew a hundred thickets of eglantine and other fragrant shrubs; a hundred arbours of roses, entwined with jessamine and honeysuckle; as many clumps of orange trees, cedar, and citron; whose branches, interwoven with the palm, the pomegranate, and the vine, presented every luxury that could regale the eye or the taste. The ground was strewed with violets, harebells, and pansies; in the midst of which numerous tufts of jonquils, hyacinths, and carnations perfumed the air. Four fountains, not less clear than deep, and so abundant as to slake the thirst of ten armies, seemed purposely placed here to make the scene more resemble the garden of Eden watered by four sacred rivers. Here, the nightingale sang the birth of the rose, her well-beloved, and, at the same time, lamented its short-lived beauty: whilst the dove deplored the loss of more substantial pleasures; and the wakeful lark hailed the rising light that reanimates the whole creation. Here, more than anywhere, the mingled melodies of birds expressed the various passions which inspired them; and the exquisite fruits which they pecked at pleasure seemed to have given them a double energy.

To this mountain Vathek was sometimes brought, for the sake of breathing a purer air; and, especially, to drink at will of the four fountains. His attendants were his mother, his wives, and some eunuchs, who assiduously employed themselves in filling capacious bowls of rock crystal, and emulously presenting them to him. But it frequently happened that his avidity exceeded their zeal, insomuch that he would prostrate himself upon the ground to lap the water, of which he could never have enough.

One day, when this unhappy prince had been long lying in so debasing a posture, a voice, hoarse but strong, thus addressed him: "Why dost thou assimilate thyself to a dog, O caliph, proud as thou art of thy dignity and power?" At this apostrophe, he raised up his head, and beheld the stranger that had caused him so much affliction. Inflamed with anger at the sight, he exclaimed, "Accursed Giaour! what comest thou hither to do?—is it not enough to have transformed a prince remarkable for his agility into a water budget? Perceivest thou not, that I may perish by drinking to excess, as well as by thirst?"

"Drink, then, this draught," said the stranger, as he presented to him a phial of a red and yellow mixture: "and, to satiate the thirst of thy soul as well as of thy body, know that I am an Indian, but from a region of India which is wholly unknown."

The caliph, delighted to see his desires accomplished in part, and flattering himself with the hope of obtaining their entire fulfilment, without a moment's hesitation swallowed the potion, and instantaneously found his health restored, his thirst appeased, and his limbs as agile as ever. In the transports of his joy, Vathek leaped upon the neck of the frightful Indian, and kissed his horrid mouth and hollow cheeks, as though they had been the coral lips and the lilies and roses of his most beautiful wives.

Nor would these transports have ceased had not the eloquence of Carathis repressed them. Having prevailed upon him to return to Samarah, she caused a herald to proclaim as loudly as possible: "The wonderful stranger hath appeared again; he hath healed the caliph; he hath spoken! he hath spoken!"

Forthwith, all the inhabitants of this vast city quitted their habitations, and ran together in crowds to see the procession of Vathek and the Indian, whom they now blessed as much as they had before execrated, incessantly shouting, "He hath healed our sovereign; he hath spoken! he hath spoken!" Nor were these words forgotten in the public festivals which were celebrated the same evening, to testify the general joy; for the poets applied them as a chorus to all the songs they composed on this interesting subject.

The caliph, in the meanwhile, caused the palaces of the senses to be again set open; and, as he found himself naturally prompted to visit that of taste in preference to the rest, immediately ordered a splendid entertainment, to which his great officers and favourite courtiers were all invited. The Indian, who was placed near the prince, seemed to think that, as a proper acknowledgment of so distinguished a privilege, he could neither eat, drink, nor talk too much. The various dainties were no sooner served up than they vanished, to the great mortification of Vathek, who piqued himself on being the greatest eater alive, and at this time in particular was blessed with an excellent appetite.

The rest of the company looked round at each other in amaze-

ment; but the Indian, without appearing to observe it, quaffed
large bumpers to the health of each of them; sung in a style altogether extravagant; related stories, at which he laughed immoderately, and poured forth extemporaneous verses, which
would not have been thought bad, but for the strange grimaces
with which they were uttered. In a word, his loquacity was equal
to that of a hundred astrologers; he ate as much as a hundred por-
ters, and caroused in proportion.

The caliph, notwithstanding the table had been thirty-two
times covered, found himself incommoded by the voraciousness of
his guest, who was now considerably declined in the prince's esteem. Vathek, however, being unwilling to betray the chagrin he
could hardly disguise, said in a whisper to Bababalouk, the chief
of his eunuchs: "You see how enormous his performances are in
every way; what would be the consequence should he get at my
wives!—Go! redouble your vigilance, and be sure look well to my
Circassians, who would be more to his taste than all of the rest."

The bird of the morning had thrice renewed his song, when the
hour of the divan was announced. Vathek, in gratitude to his subjects having promised to attend, immediately arose from table
and repaired thither, leaning upon his vizier, who could scarce
support him; so disordered was the poor prince by the wine he
had drunk, and still more by the extravagant vagaries of his boisterous guest.

The viziers, the officers of the crown and of the law, arranged
themselves in a semicircle about their sovereign, and preserved a
respectful silence; whilst the Indian, who looked as cool as if he
had been fasting, sat down without ceremony on one of the steps
of the throne, laughing in his sleeve at the indignation with which
his temerity had filled the spectators.

The caliph, however, whose ideas were confused, and whose
head was embarrassed, went on administering justice at hap-
hazard; till at length the prime vizier, perceiving his situation,
hit upon a sudden expedient to interrupt the audience and rescue the honour of his master, to whom he said in a whisper, "My
lord, the Princess Carathis, who hath passed the night in consulting the planets, informs you that they portend you evil, and the
danger is urgent. Beware lest this stranger, whom you have so
lavishly recompensed for his magical gewgaws, should make some
attempt on your life: his liquor, which at first had the appear-

ance of effecting your cure, may be no more than a poison, the operation of which will be sudden. Slight not this surmise; ask him, at least, of what it was compounded, whence he procured it; and mention the sabres which you seem to have forgotten."

Vathek, to whom the insolent airs of the stranger became every moment less supportable, intimated to his vizier, by a wink of acquiescence, that he would adopt his advice; and, at once turning towards the Indian, said, "Get up, and declare in full divan of what drugs was compounded the liquor you enjoined me to take, for it is suspected to be poison: give also that explanation I have so earnestly desired concerning the sabres you sold me, and thus show your gratitude for the favours heaped on you."

Having pronounced these words in as moderate a tone as he well could, he waited in silent expectation for an answer. But the Indian, still keeping his seat, began to renew his loud shouts of laughter, and exhibit the same horrid grimaces he had shown them before, without vouchsafing a word in reply. Vathek, no longer able to brook such insolence, immediately kicked him from the steps; instantly descending, repeated his blow; and persisted, with such assiduity, as incited all who were present to follow his example. Every foot was up and aimed at the Indian, and no sooner had any one given him a kick, than he felt himself constrained to reiterate the stroke.

The stranger afforded them no small entertainment; for, being both short and plump, he collected himself into a ball, and rolled on all sides at the blows of his assailants, who pressed after him, wherever he turned, with an eagerness beyond conception, whilst their numbers were every moment increasing. The ball, indeed, in passing from one apartment to another, drew every person after it that came in its way: insomuch that the whole palace was thrown into confusion, and resounded with a tremendous clamour. The women of the harem, amazed at the uproar, flew to their blinds to discover the cause; but no sooner did they catch a glimpse of the ball than, feeling themselves unable to refrain, they broke from the clutches of their eunuchs, who, to stop their flight, pinched them till they bled; but in vain: whilst themselves, though trembling with terror at the escape of their charge, were as incapable of resisting the attraction.

After having traversed the halls, galleries, chambers, kitchens, gardens, and stables of the palace, the Indian at last took his course through the courts; whilst the caliph, pursuing him closer than the rest, bestowed as many kicks as he possibly could; yet not without receiving now and then a few which his competitors, in their eagerness, designed for the ball.

Carathis, Morakanabad, and two or three old viziers, whose wisdom had hitherto withstood the attraction, wishing to prevent Vathek from exposing himself in the presence of his subjects, fell down in his way to impede the pursuit: but he, regardless of their obstruction, leaped over their heads, and went on as before. They then ordered the muezzins to call the people to prayers; both for the sake of getting them out of the way, and of endeavouring, by their petitions, to avert the calamity: but neither of these expedients was a whit more successful. The sight of this fatal ball was alone sufficient to draw after it every beholder. The muezzins themselves, though they saw it but at a distance, hastened down from their minarets, and mixed with the crowd; which continued to increase in so surprising a manner that scarce an inhabitant was left in Samarah except the aged; the sick, confined to their beds; and infants at the breast, whose nurses could run more nimbly without them. Even Carathis, Morakanabad, and the rest, were all become of the party. The shrill screams of the females, who had broken from their apartments and were unable to extricate themselves from the pressure of the crowd, together with those of the eunuchs jostling after them, and terrified lest their charge should escape from their sight; the execrations of husbands, urging forward and menacing each other; kicks given and received; stumblings and overthrows at every step; in a word, the confusion that universally prevailed, rendered Samarah like a city taken by storm, and devoted to absolute plunder. At last, the cursed Indian, who still preserved his rotundity of figure, after passing through all the streets and public places, and leaving them empty, rolled onwards to the plain of Catoul, and entered the valley at the foot of the mountain of the four fountains.

As a continual fall of water had excavated an immense gulf in the valley, whose opposite side was closed in by a steep acclivity, the caliph and his attendants were apprehensive lest the ball should bound into the chasm, and, to prevent it, redoubled their efforts, but in vain. The Indian persevered in his onward direction; and, as had been apprehended, glancing from the precipice with the rapidity of lightning, was lost in the gulf below.

Vathek would have followed the perfidious Giaour, had not an invisible agency arrested his progress. The multitude that pressed after him were at once checked in the same manner, and a calm instantaneously ensued. They all gazed at each other with an air of astonishment; and notwithstanding that the loss of veils and turbans, together with torn habits, and dust blended with sweat, presented a most laughable spectacle, yet there was not one smile to be seen. On the contrary, all with looks of confusion and sadness returned in silence to Samarah, and retired to their inmost apartments, without ever reflecting, that they had been impelled by an invisible power into the extravagance for which they reproached themselves; for it is but just that men, who so often arrogate to their own merit the good of which they are but instruments, should also attribute to themselves absurdities which they could not prevent.

The caliph was the only person who refused to leave the valley. He commanded his tents to be pitched there, and stationed himself on the very edge of the precipice, in spite of the representations of Carathis and Morakanabad, who pointed out the hazard of its brink giving way, and the vicinity to the magician that had so cruelly tormented him. Vathek derided all their remonstances; and having ordered a thousand flambeaux to be lighted, and directed his attendants to proceed in lighting more, lay down on the slippery margin, and attempted, by the help of this artificial splendour, to look through that gloom, which all the fires of the empyrean had been insufficient to pervade. One while he fancied to himself voices arising from the depth of the gulf; at another, he seemed to distinguish the accents of the Indian; but all was no more than the hollow murmur of waters, and the din of the cataracts that rushed from steep to steep down the sides of the mountain.

Having passed the night in this cruel perturbation, the caliph at daybreak retired to his tent; where, without taking the least sustenance, he continued to doze till the dusk of evening began again to come on. He then resumed his vigils as before, and persevered in observing them for many nights together. At length, fatigued with so fruitless an employment, he sought relief from change. To this end, he sometimes paced with hasty strides across the plain; and as he wildly gazed at the stars, reproached them with having deceived him; but, lo! on a sudden, the clear blue sky appeared streaked over with streams of blood, which reached from the valley even to the city of Samarah. As this awful phenomenon seemed to touch his tower, Vathek at first thought of repairing thither to view it more distinctly; but, feeling himself unable to advance, and being overcome with apprehension, he muffled up his face in the folds of his robe.

Terrifying as these prodigies were, this impression upon him was no more than momentary, and served only to stimulate his love of the marvellous. Instead, therefore, of returning to his palace, he persisted in the resolution of abiding where the Indian had vanished from his view. One night, however, while he was walking as usual on the plain, the moon and stars were eclipsed at once, and a total darkness ensued. The earth trembled beneath him, and a voice came forth, the voice of the Giaour, who, in accents more sonorous than thunder, thus addressed him: "Wouldest thou devote thyself to me? adore the terrestrial influences, and abjure Mahomet? On these conditions I will bring thee to the Palace of Subterranean Fire. There shalt thou behold, in immense depositories, the treasures which the stars have promised thee; and which will be conferred by those Intelligences whom thou shalt thus render propitious. It was from thence I brought my sabres, and it is there that Soliman Ben Daoud reposes, surrounded by the talismans that control the world."

The astonished caliph trembled as he answered, yet he answered in a style that showed him to be no novice in preternatural adventures: "Where art thou? be present to my eyes; dissipate the gloom that perplexes me, and of which I deem thee the cause. After the many flambeaux I have burnt to discover thee, thou mayest at least grant a glimpse of thy horrible visage."—"Abjure then Mahomet!" replied the Indian, "and promise me full proofs of thy sincerity: otherwise, thou shalt never behold me again."

The unhappy caliph, instigated by insatiable curiosity, lavished his promises in the utmost profusion. The sky immediately brightened; and, by the light of the planets which seemed almost to blaze, Vathek beheld the earth open; and, at the extremity of a vast black chasm, a portal of ebony, before which stood the Indian, holding in his hand a golden key which he sounded against the lock.

"How," cried Vathek, "can I descend to thee? Come, take me,

and instantly open the portal."—"Not so fast," replied the Indian, "impatient caliph! Know that I am parched with thirst, and cannot open this door, till my thirst be thoroughly appeased; I require the blood of fifty children. Take them from among the most beautiful sons of thy viziers and great men; or neither can my thirst nor thy curiosity be satisfied. Return to Samarah; procure for me this necessary libation; come back hither; throw it thyself into this chasm, and then shalt thou see!"

Having thus spoken, the Indian turned his back on the caliph, who, incited by the suggestions of demons, resolved on the direful sacrifice. He now pretended to have regained his tranquillity, and set out for Samarah amidst the acclamations of a people who still loved him, and forbore not to rejoice when they believed him to have recovered his reason. So successfully did he conceal the emotion of his heart, that even Carathis and Morakanabad were equally deceived with the rest. Nothing was heard of but festivals and rejoicings. The fatal ball, which no tongue had hitherto ventured to mention, was brought on the tapis. A general laugh went round, though many, still smarting under the hands of the surgeon from the hurts received in that memorable adventure, had no great reason for mirth.

The prevalence of this gay humour was not a little grateful to Vathek, who perceived how much it conduced to his project. He put on the appearance of affability to every one; but especially to his viziers and the grandees of his court, whom he failed not to regale with a sumptuous banquet; during which he insensibly directed the conversation to the children of his guests. Having asked, with a good-natured air, which of them were blessed with the handsomest boys, every father at once asserted the pretensions of his own; and the contest imperceptibly grew so warm, that nothing could have withholden them from coming to blows but their profound reverence for the person of the caliph. Under the pretence, therefore, of reconciling the disputants, Vathek took upon him to decide; and, with this view, commanded the boys to be brought.

It was not long before a troop of these poor children made their appearance, all equipped by their fond mothers with such ornaments as might give the greatest relief to their beauty, or most advantageously display the graces of their age. But, whilst this brilliant assemblage attracted the eyes and hearts of every one besides, the caliph scrutinized each, in his turn, with a malignant avidity that passed for attention, and selected from their number the fifty whom he judged the Giaour would prefer.

With an equal show of kindness as before, he proposed to celebrate a festival on the plain, for the entertainment of his young favourites, who, he said, ought to rejoice still more than all at the restoration of his health, on account of the favours he intended for them.

The caliph's proposal was received with the greatest delight, and soon published through Samarah. Litters, camels, and horses were prepared. Women and children, old men and young, every one placed himself as he chose. The cavalcade set forward, attended by all the confectioners in the city and its precincts; the populace, following on foot, composed an amazing crowd, and occasioned no little noise. All was joy; nor did any one call to mind what most of them had suffered when they lately travelled the road they were now passing so gaily.

The evening was serene, the air refreshing, the sky clear, and the flowers exhaled their fragrance. The beams of the declining sun, whose mild splendour reposed on the summit of the mountain, shed a glow of ruddy light over its green declivity, and the white flocks sporting upon it. No sounds were heard, save the murmurs of the four fountains, and the reeds and voices of shepherds, calling to each other from different eminences.

The lovely innocents, destined for the sacrifice, added not a little to the hilarity of the scene. They approached the plain full of sportiveness, some coursing butterflies, others culling flowers, or picking up the shining little pebbles that attracted their notice. At intervals they nimbly started from each other for the sake of being caught again and mutually imparting a thousand caresses.

The dreadful chasm, at whose bottom the portal of ebony was placed, began to appear at a distance. It looked like a black streak that divided the plain. Morakanabad and his companions took it for some work which the caliph had ordered. Unhappy men! little did they surmise for what it was destined. Vathek, unwilling that they should examine it too nearly, stopped the procession, and ordered a spacious circle to be formed on this side, at some distance from the accursed chasm. The body-guard of eunuchs was detached, to measure out the lists intended for the games, and prepare the rings for the arrows of the young archers.

The fifty competitors were soon stripped, and presented to the admiration of the spectators the suppleness and grace of their delicate limbs. Their eyes sparkled with a joy, which those of their fond parents reflected. Every one offered wishes for the little candidate nearest his heart, and doubted not of his being victorious. A breathless suspense awaited the contests of these amiable and innocent victims.

The caliph, availing himself of the first moment to retire from the crowd, advanced towards the chasm; and there heard, yet not without shuddering, the voice of the Indian; who, gnashing his teeth, eagerly demanded, "Where are they?—where are they?—perceivest thou not how my mouth waters?"—"Relentless Giaour!" answered Vathek, with emotion; "can nothing content thee but the massacre of these lovely victims? Ah! wert thou to behold their beauty, it must certainly move thy compassion."—"Perdition on thy compassion, babbler!" cried the Indian: "give them me; instantly give them, or my portal shall be closed against thee for ever!"—"Not so loudly," replied the caliph, blushing.—"I understand thee," returned the Giaour with the grin of an ogre; "thou wantest no presence of mind: I will for a moment forbear."

During this exquisite dialogue, the games went forward with all alacrity, and at length concluded, just as the twilight began to overcast the mountains. Vathek, who was still standing on the edge of the chasm, called out, with all his might, "Let my fifty little favourites approach me, separately; and let them come in the order of their success. To the first, I will give my diamond bracelet; to the second, my collar of emeralds; to the third, my aigret of rubies; to the fourth, my girdle of topazes; and to the rest, each a part of my dress, even down to my slippers."

This declaration was received with reiterated acclamations; and all extolled the liberality of a prince who would thus strip himself for the amusement of his subjects and the encouragement of the rising generation. The caliph in the meanwhile, undressed himself by degrees, and, raising his arm as high as he was able, made each of the prizes glitter in the air; but whilst he delivered it with one hand to the child who sprung forward to receive it, he with the other pushed the poor innocent into the gulf, where the Giaour, with a sullen muttering, incessantly repeated, "More! more!"

This dreadful device was excuted with so much dexterity, that the boy who was approaching him remained unconscious of the fate of his forerunner; and, as to the spectators, the shades of evening, together with their distance, precluded them from perceiving any object distinctly. Vathek, having in this manner thrown in the last of the fifty, and, expecting that the Giaour, on receiving him, would have presented the key, already fancied himself as great as Soliman, and consequently above being amenable for what he had done; when, to his utter amazement, the chasm closed, and the ground became as entire as the rest of the plain.

No language could express his rage and despair. He execrated the perfidy of the Indian; loaded him with the most infamous invectives; and stamped with his foot, as resolving to be heard. He persisted in this till his strength failed him, and then fell on the earth like one void of sense. His viziers and grandees, who were nearer than the rest, supposed him at first to be sitting on the grass, at play with their amiable children; but at length, prompted by doubt, they advanced towards the spot, and found the caliph alone, who wildly demanded what they wanted? "Our children! our children!" cried they. "It is assuredly pleasant," said he, "to make me accountable for accidents. Your children, while at play, fell from the precipice, and I should have experienced their fate, had I not suddenly started back."

At these words, the fathers of the fifty boys cried out aloud; the mothers repeated their exclamations an octave higher; whilst the rest, without knowing the cause, soon drowned the voices of both with still louder lamentations of their own. "Our caliph," said they, and the report soon circulated, "our caliph has played us this trick, to gratify his accursed Giaour. Let us punish him for perfidy! let us avenge ourselves! let us avenge the blood of the innocent! let us throw this cruel prince into the gulf that is near, and let his name be mentioned no more!"

At this rumour and these menaces, Carathis, full of consternation, hastened to Morakanabad, and said: "Vizier, you have lost two beautiful boys, and must necessarily be the most afflicted of fathers; but you are virtuous, save your master."—"I will brave every hazard," replied the vizier, "to rescue him from his present danger, but afterwards will abandon him to his fate. Bababalouk," continued he, "put yourself at the head of your eunuchs: disperse the mob, and, if possible, bring back this unhappy prince to his palace." Bababalouk and his fraternity, felicitating each other in a low voice on their having been spared the cares as well as the honour of paternity, obeyed the mandate of the vizier; who, seconding their exertions to the utmost of his power, at length accomplished his generous enterprise; and retired, as he resolved, to lament at his leisure.

No sooner had the caliph re-entered his palace than Carathis commanded the doors to be fastened; but perceiving the tumult to be still violent, and hearing the imprecations which resounded from all quarters, she said to her son, "Whether the populace be right or wrong, it behoves you to provide for your safety; let us retire to your own apartment, and from thence through the subterranean passage, known only to ourselves, into your tower: there, with the assistance of the mutes who never leave it, we may be able to make a powerful resistance. Bababalouk, supposing us to be still in the palace, will guard its avenues for his own sake; and we shall soon find, without the counsels of that blubberer Morakanabad, what expedient may be the best to adopt."

Vathek, without making the least reply, acquiesced in his mother's proposal, and repeated as he went, "Nefarious Giaour! where art thou? hast thou not yet devoured those poor children? where are thy sabres? thy golden key? thy talismans?" Carathis, who guessed from these interrogations a part of the truth, had no difficulty to apprehend in getting at the whole as soon as he should be a little composed in his tower. This princess was so far from being influenced by scruples, that she was as wicked as woman could be, which is not saying a little; for the sex pique themselves on their superiority in every competition. The recital of the caliph, therefore, occasioned neither terror nor surprise to his mother: she felt no emotion but from the promises of the Giaour, and said to her son, "This Giaour, it must be confessed, is somewhat sanguinary in his taste; but the terrestrial powers are always terrible; nevertheless, what the one hath promised, and the others can confer, will prove a sufficient indemnification. No crimes should be thought too dear for such a reward: forbear, then, to revile the Indian; you have not fulfilled the conditions to which his services are annexed: for instance, is not a sacrifice to the subterranean Genii required? and should we not be prepared to offer it as soon as the tumult is subsided? This charge I will take on myself, and have no doubt of succeeding, by means of your treasures, which, as there are now so many others in store, may without fear be exhausted." Accordingly, the princess, who possessed the most consummate skill in the art of persuasion, went immediately back through the subterranean passage; and, presenting herself to the populace from a window of the palace, began to harangue them with all the address of which she was mistress; whilst Bababalouk showered money from both hands amongst the crowd, who by these united means were soon appeased. Every person retired to his home, and Carathis returned to the tower.

Prayer at break of day was announced, when Carathis and Vathek ascended the steps which led to the summit of the tower, where they remained for some time, though the weather was lowering and wet. This impending gloom corresponded with their malignant dispositions; but when the sun began to break through the clouds, they ordered a pavilion to be raised, as a screen against the intrusion of his beams. The caliph, overcome with fatigue, sought refreshment from repose, at the same time hoping that significant dreams might attend on his slumbers; whilst the indefatigable Carathis, followed by a party of her mutes, descended to prepare whatever she judged proper for the oblation of the approaching night.

By secret stairs, contrived within the thickness of the wall, and known only to herself and her son, she first repaired to the mysterious recesses in which were deposited the mummies that had been wrested from the catacombs of the ancient Pharaohs. Of these she ordered several to be taken. From thence she resorted to a gallery where, under the guard of fifty female negroes, mute, and blind of the right eye, were preserved the oil of the most venomous serpents, rhinoceros' horns, and woods of a subtile and penetrating odour procured from the interior of the Indies, together with a thousand other horrible rarities. This collection had been formed for a purpose like the present, by Carathis herself, from a presentiment that she might one day enjoy some intercourse with the infernal powers, to whom she had ever been passionately attached, and to whose taste she was no stranger.

To familiarize herself the better with the horrors in view, the princess remained in the company of her negresses, who squinted in the most amiable manner from the only eye they had, and leered, with exquisite delight, at the skulls and skeletons which Carathis had drawn forth from her cabinets; all of them making the most frightful contortions, and uttering such shrill chatterings, that the princess, stunned by them and suffocated by the potency of the exhalations, was forced to quit the gallery, after stripping it of a part of its abominable treasures.

Whilst she was thus occupied, the caliph, who, instead of the visions he expected, had acquired in these unsubstantial regions a voracious appetite, was greatly provoked at the mutes. For having totally forgotten their deafness, he had impatiently asked them for food; and seeing them regardless of his demand, he began to cuff, pinch, and bite them, till Carathis arrived to terminate a scene so indecent, to the great content of these miserable creatures. "Son! what means all this?" said she, panting for breath. "I thought I heard as I came up the shrieks of a thousand bats, torn from their crannies in the recesses of a cavern; and it was the outcry only of these poor mutes, whom you were so unmercifully abusing. In truth, you but ill deserve the admirable provision I have brought you."—"Give it me instantly," exclaimed the caliph; "I am perishing for hunger!"—"As to that," answered she, "you must have an excellent stomach if it can digest what I have brought."—"Be quick," replied the caliph;—"but, oh heavens! what horrors! what do you intend?"—"Come, come," returned Carathis, "be not so squeamish; but help me to arrange everything properly; and you shall see that what you reject with such symptoms of disgust will soon complete your felicity. Let us get ready the pile for the sacrifice of to-night; and think not of eating till that is performed: know you not, that all solemn rites ought to be preceded by a rigorous abstinence?"

The caliph, not daring to object, abandoned himself to grief and the wind that ravaged his entrails, whilst his mother went forward with the requisite operations. Phials of serpents' oil, mummies, and bones, were soon set in order on the balustrade of the tower. The pile began to rise, and in three hours was twenty cubits high. At length darkness approached, and Carathis, having stripped herself to her inmost garment, clapped her hands in an impulse of ecstasy; the mutes followed her example; but Vathek, extenuated with hunger and impatience, was unable to support himself, and fell down in a swoon. The sparks had already kindled the dry wood; the venomous oil burst into a thousand blue flames; the mummies, dissolving, emitted a thick dun vapour; and the rhinoceros' horns, beginning to consume, all together diffused such a stench, that the caliph, recovering, started from his trance, and gazed wildly on the scene in full blaze around him. The oil gushed forth in a plenitude of streams; and the negresses, who supplied it without intermission, united their cries to those of the princess. At last the fire became so violent, and the flames reflected from the polished marble so dazzling, that the caliph, unable to withstand the heat and the blaze, effected his escape, and took shelter under the imperial standard.

In the meantime, the inhabitants of Samarah, scared at the light which shone over the city, arose in haste, ascended their roofs, beheld the tower on fire, and hurried, half naked, to the square. Their love for their sovereign immediately awoke; and, apprehending him in danger of perishing in his tower, their whole thoughts were occupied with the means of his safety. Morakanabad flew from his retirement, wiped away his tears, and cried out for water like the rest. Bababalouk, whose olfactory nerves were more familiarized to magical odours, readily conjecturing that Carathis was engaged in her favourite amusements, strenuously exhorted them not to be alarmed. Him, however, they treated as an old poltroon, and styled him a rascally traitor. The camels and dromedaries were advancing with water; but no one knew by which way to enter the tower. Whilst the populace was obstinate in forcing the doors, a violent north-east wind drove an immense volume of flame against them. At first they recoiled, but soon came back with redoubled zeal. At the same time, the stench of the horns and mummies increasing, most of the crowd fell backwards in a state of suffocation. Those that kept their feet mutually wondered at the cause of the smell, and admonished each other to retire. Morakanabad, more sick than the rest, remained in a piteous condition. Holding his nose with one hand, every one persisted in his efforts with the other to burst open the doors and obtain admission. A hundred and forty of the strongest and most resolute at length accomplished their purpose. Having gained the staircase, by their violent exertions, they attained a great height in a quarter of an hour.

Carathis, alarmed at the signs of her mutes, advanced to the staircase, went down a few steps, and heard several voices calling out from below, "You shall in a moment have water!" Being rather alert, considering her age, she presently regained the top of the tower, and bade her son suspend the sacrifice for some minutes; adding, "We shall soon be enabled to render it more grateful. Certain dolts of your subjects, imagining, no doubt, that we were on fire, have been rash enough to break through those doors which had hitherto remained inviolate, for the sake of bringing up water. They are very kind, you must allow, so soon to forget the wrongs you have done them; but that is of little moment. Let us offer them to the Giaour; let them come up; our mutes, who neither want strength nor experience, will soon dispatch them, exhausted as they are with fatigue."—"Be it so," answered the caliph, "provided we finish, and I dine." In fact, these good people, out of breath from ascending fifteen hundred stairs in such haste, and chagrined at having spilt by the way the water they had taken, were no sooner arrived at the top, than the blaze of the flames and the fumes of the mummies at once overpowered their senses. It was a pity! for they beheld not the agreeable smile with which the mutes and negresses adjusted the cord to their necks: these amiable personages rejoiced, however, no less at the scene. Never before had the ceremony of strangling been performed with so much facility. They all fell, without the least resistance or struggle: so that Vathek, in the space of a few moments, found himself surrounded by the dead bodies of the most faithful of his subjects; all which were thrown on the top of the pile. Carathis, whose presence of mind never forsook her, perceiving that she had carcasses sufficient to complete her oblation, commanded the chains to be stretched across the staircase, and the iron doors barricadoed, that no more might come up.

No sooner were these orders obeyed, than the tower shook; the dead bodies vanished in the flames, which at once changed from a swarthy crimson to a bright rose colour; an ambient vapour emitted the most exquisite fragrance; the marble columns rang with harmonious sounds, and the liquefied horns diffused a delicious perfume. Carathis, in transports, anticipated the success of her enterprise; whilst her mutes and negresses, to whom these sweets had given the colic, retired grumbling to their cells.

Scarcely were they gone, when, instead of the pile, horns, mummies, and ashes, the caliph both saw and felt, with a degree of pleasure which he could not express, a table covered with the most magnificent repast: flagons of wine and vases of exquisite sherbet reposing on snow. He availed himself, without scruple, of such an entertainment; and had already laid hands on a lamb stuffed with pistachios, whilst Carathis was privately drawing from a filigree urn a parchment that seemed to be endless, and which had escaped the notice of her son. Totally occupied in gratifying an importunate appetite, he left her to peruse it without interruption; which having finished, she said to him, in an authoritative tone, "Put an end to your gluttony, and hear the splendid promises with which you are favoured!" She then read as follows: "Vathek, my well-beloved, thou hast surpassed my hopes: my nostrils have been regaled by the savour of thy mummies, thy horns, and, still more, by the lives devoted on the pile. At the full of the moon, cause the bands of thy musicians, and thy timbals, to be heard; depart from thy palace, surrounded by all the pageants of majesty—thy most faithful slaves, thy best beloved wives, thy most magnificent litters, thy richest loaden camels —and set forward on thy way to Istakhar. There I await thy coming: that is the region of wonders: there shalt thou receive the diadem of Gian Ben Gian, the talismans of Soliman, and the treasures of the pre-Adamite sultans: there shalt thou be solaced with all kinds of delight.—But beware how thou enterest any dwelling on thy route; or thou shalt feel the effects of my anger."

The caliph, notwithstanding his habitual luxury, had never before dined with so much satisfaction. He gave full scope to the joy of these golden tidings, and betook himself to drinking anew. Carathis, whose antipathy to wine was by no means insuperable, failed not to pledge him at every bumper he ironically quaffed to the health of Mahomet. This infernal liquor completed their impious temerity, and prompted them to utter a profusion of blasphemies. They gave a loose to their wit, at the expense of the ass of Balaam, the dog of the seven sleepers, and the other animals admitted into the paradise of Mahomet. In this sprightly humour, they descended the fifteen hundred stairs, diverting themselves, as they went, at the anxious faces they saw on the square, through the barbacans and loopholes of the tower; and at length arrived at the royal apartments, by the subterranean passage. Bababalouk was parading to and fro, and issuing his mandates with great pomp to the eunuchs, who were snuffing the lights and painting the eyes of the Circassians. No sooner did he catch sight of the caliph and his mother, than he exclaimed, "Hah! you have then, I perceive, escaped from the flames; I was not, however, altogether out of doubt."—"Of what moment is it to us what you thought or think?" cried Carathis: "go, speed, tell Morakanabad that we immediately want him; and take care not to stop by the way to make your insipid reflections."

Morakanabad delayed not to obey the summons, and was received by Vathek and his mother with great solemnity. They told him, with an air of composure and commiseration, that the fire at the top of the tower was extinguished; but that it had cost the lives of the brave people who sought to assist them.

"Still more misfortunes!" cried Morakanabad, with a sigh. "Ah, commander of the faithful, our holy Prophet is certainly irritated against us! it behoves you to appease him." "We will appease him hereafter," replied the caliph, with a smile that augured nothing of good. "You will have leisure sufficient for your supplications during my absence, for this country is the bane of my health. I am disgusted with the mountain of the four fountains, and am resolved to go and drink of the stream of Rocnabad. I long to refresh myself in the delightful valleys which it waters. Do you, with the advice of my mother, govern my dominions, and take care to supply whatever her experiments may demand; for you well know that our tower abounds in materials for the advancement of science."

The tower but ill suited Morakanabad's taste. Immense treasures had been lavished upon it; and nothing had he ever seen carried thither but female negroes, mutes, and abominable drugs. Nor did he know well what to think of Carathis, who, like a chameleon, could assume all possible colours. Her cursed eloquence had often driven the poor Mussulman to his last shifts. He considered, however, that if she possessed but few good qualities, her son had still fewer; and that the alternative, on the whole, would be in her favour. Consoled, therefore, with this reflection, he went, in good spirits, to soothe the populace, and make the proper arrangements for his master's journey.

Vathek, to conciliate the spirits of the subterranean palace, resolved that his expedition should be uncommonly splendid. With this view he confiscated, on all sides, the property of his subjects; whilst his worthy mother stripped the seraglios she visited of the gems they contained. She collected all the sempstresses and embroiderers of Samarah and other cities, to the distance of sixty leagues, to prepare pavilions, palanquins, sofas, canopies, and litters for the train of the monarch. There was not left, in Masulipatan, a single piece of chintz; and so much muslin had been brought up to dress out Bababalouk and the other black eunuchs, that there remained not an ell of it in the whole Irak of Babylon.

During these preparations, Carathis, who never lost sight of her great object, which was to obtain favour with the powers of darkness, made select parties of the fairest and most delicate ladies of the city; but in the midst of their gaiety, she contrived to introduce vipers amongst them, and to break pots of scorpions under the table. They all bit to a wonder; and Carathis would have left her friends to die, were it not that, to fill up the time, she now and then amused herself in curing their wounds, with an excellent anodyne of her own invention; for this good princess abhorred being indolent.

Vathek, who was not altogether so active as his mother, devoted his time to the sole gratification of his senses, in the palaces which were severally dedicated to them. He disgusted himself no more with the divan, or the mosque. One half of Samarah followed his example, whilst the other lamented the progress of corruption.

In the midst of these transactions, the embassy returned, which had been sent, in pious times, to Mecca. It consisted of the most reverend mullahs, who had fulfilled their commission and brought back one of those precious besoms which are used to sweep the sacred Caaba; a present truly worthy of the greatest potentate on earth!

The caliph happened at this instant to be engaged in an apartment by no means adapted to the reception of embassies. He heard the voice of Bababalouk, calling out from between the door and the tapestry that hung before it, "Here are the excellent Edris al Shafei, and the seraphic Al Mouhateddin, who have brought the besom from Mecca, and, with tears of joy, entreat they may present it to your majesty in person."—"Let them bring the besom hither; it may be of use," said Vathek.—"How!" answered Bababalouk, half aloud and amazed.—"Obey," replied the caliph, "for it is my sovereign will; go instantly, vanish! for here will I receive the good folk who have thus filled thee with joy."

The eunuch departed muttering, and bade the venerable train attend him. A sacred rapture was diffused amongst these reverend old men. Though fatigued with the length of their expedition, they followed Bababalouk with an alertness almost miraculous, and felt themselves highly flattered, as they swept along the stately porticoes, that the caliph would not receive them like ambassadors in ordinary in his hall of audience. Soon reaching the interior of the harem (where, through blinds of Persian, they perceived large soft eyes, dark and blue, that came and went like lightning), penetrated with respect and wonder, and full of their celestial mission, they advanced in procession towards the small corridors that appeared to terminate in nothing, but, nevertheless, led to the cell where the caliph expected their coming.

"What! is the commander of the faithful sick?" said Edris al Shafei in a low voice to his companion.—"I rather think he is in his oratory," answered Al Mouhateddin. Vathek, who heard the dialogue, cried out, "What imports it you, how I am employed? approach without delay." They advanced, whilst the caliph, without showing himself, put forth his hand from behind the tapestry that hung before the door, and demanded of them the besom. Having prostrated themselves as well as the corridor would permit, and even in a tolerable semicircle, the venerable Al Shafei, drawing forth the besom from the embroidered and perfumed scarves in which it had been enveloped and secured from the profane gaze of vulgar eyes, arose from his associates, and advanced, with an air of the most awful solemnity, towards the supposed oratory; but with what astonishment! with what horror was he seized! Vathek, bursting out into a villainous laugh, snatched the besom from his trembling hand, and, fixing upon some cobwebs, that hung from the ceiling, gravely brushed them away till not a single one remained. The old men, overpowered with amazement, were unable to lift their beards from the ground; for, as Vathek had carelessly left the tapestry between them half drawn, they were witnesses of the whole transaction. Their tears bedewed the marble. Al Mouhateddin swooned through mortification and fatigue, whilst the caliph, throwing himself backward on his seat, shouted and clapped his hands without mercy. At last, addressing himself to Bababalouk, "My dear black," said he, "go, regale these pious poor souls with my good wine from Schiraz, since they can boast of having seen more of my palace than any one besides." Having said this, he threw the besom in their face, and went to enjoy the laugh with Carathis. Bababalouk did all in his power to console the ambassadors; but the two most infirm expired on the spot: the rest were carried to their beds, from whence, being heartbroken with sorrow and shame, they never arose.

The succeeding night, Vathek, attended by his mother, ascended the tower to see if everything were ready for his journey; for he had great faith in the influence of the stars. The planets appeared in their most favourable aspects. The caliph, to enjoy so flattering a sight, supped gaily on the roof; and fancied that he heard, during his repast, loud shouts of laughter resound through the sky, in a manner that inspired the fullest assurance.

All was in motion at the palace; lights were kept burning through the whole of the night: the sound of implements, and of artisans finishing their work; the voices of women, and their guardians, who sung at their embroidery; all conspired to interrupt the stillness of nature, and infinitely delighted the heart of Vathek, who imagined himself going in triumph to sit upon the throne of Soliman. The people were not less satisfied than himself: all assisted to accelerate the moment which should rescue them from the wayward caprices of so extravagant a master.

The day preceding the departure of this infatuated prince was employed by Carathis in repeating to him the decrees of the mysterious parchment, which she had thoroughly gotten by heart; and in recommending him not to enter the habitation of any one by the way:—"For well thou knowest," added she, "how liquorish thy taste is after good dishes and young damsels: let me, therefore, enjoin thee to be content with thy old cooks, who are the best in the world; and not to forget that, in thy ambulatory seraglio, there are at least three dozen of pretty faces which Bababalouk has not yet unveiled. I myself have a great desire to watch over thy conduct, and visit the subterranean palace, which, no doubt, contains whatever can interest persons like us. There is nothing so pleasing as retiring to caverns: my taste for dead bodies, and everything like mummy, is decided; and, I am confident, thou wilt see the most exquisite of their kind. Forget me not then, but the moment thou art in possession of the talismans which are to open the way to the mineral kingdoms and the centre of the earth itself, fail not to dispatch some trusty genius to take me and my cabinet; for the oil of the serpents I have pinched to death will be a pretty present to the Giaour, who cannot but be charmed with such dainties."

Scarcely had Carathis ended this edifying discourse, when the sun, setting behind the mountain of the four fountains, gave place to the rising moon. This planet, being that evening at full, appeared of unusual beauty and magnitude in the eyes of the women, the eunuchs, and the pages, who were all impatient to set forward. The city re-echoed with shouts of joy and flourishing of trumpets. Nothing was visible but plumes nodding on pavilions, and aigrets shining in the mild lustre of the moon. The spacious square resembled an immense parterre variegated with the most stately tulips of the East.

Arrayed in the robes which were only worn at the most distinguished ceremonials, and supported by his vizier and Bababalouk, the caliph descended the great staircase of the tower in the sight of all his people. He could not forbear pausing, at intervals, to admire the superb appearance which everywhere courted his view; whilst the whole multitude, even to the camels with their sumptuous burdens, knelt down before him. For some time a general stillness prevailed, which nothing happened to disturb but the shrill screams of some eunuchs in the rear. These vigilant guards, having remarked certain cages of the ladies swagging somewhat awry, and discovered that a few adventurous gallants had contrived to get in, soon dislodged the enraptured culprits, and consigned them, with good commendations, to the surgeons of the serail. The majesty of so magnificent a spectacle was not, however, violated by incidents like these. Vathek, meanwhile, saluted the moon with an idolatrous air, that neither pleased Morakanabad, nor the doctors of the law, any more than the viziers and grandees of his court, who were all assembled to enjoy the last view of their sovereign.

At length, the clarions and trumpets from the top of the tower announced the prelude of departure. Though the instruments were in unison with each other, yet a singular dissonance was blended with their sounds. This proceeded from Carathis, who was singing her direful orisons to the Giaour, whilst the negresses and mutes supplied thorough-bass, without articulating a word. The good Mussulmans fancied that they heard the sullen hum of those nocturnal insects which presage evil, and importuned Vathek to beware how he ventured his sacred person.

On a given signal, the great standard of the Califat was displayed: twenty thousand lances shone around it; and the caliph, treading royally on the cloth of gold which had been spread for his feet, ascended his litter amidst the general acclamations of his subjects.

The expedition commenced with the utmost order, and so entire a silence, that even the locusts were heard from the thickets on the plain of Catoul. Gaiety and good humour prevailing, they made full six leagues before the dawn; and the morning star was still glittering in the firmament, when the whole of this numerous train had halted on the banks of the Tigris, where they encamped to repose for the rest of the day.

The three days that followed were spent in the same manner; but on the fourth the heavens looked angry: lightnings broke forth in frequent flashes; re-echoing peals of thunder succeeded; and the trembling Circassians clung with all their might to their ugly guardians. The caliph himself was greatly inclined to take shelter in the large town of Ghulchissar, the governor of which came forth to meet him, and tendered every kind of refreshment the place could supply. But, having examined his tablets, he suffered the rain to soak him almost to the bone, notwithstanding the importunity of his first favourites. Though he began to regret the palace of the senses, yet he lost not sight of his enterprise, and his sanguine expectation confirmed his resolution. His geographers were ordered to attend him; but the weather proved so terrible that these poor people exhibited a lamentable appearance: and their maps of the different countries, spoiled by the rain, were in a still worse plight than themselves. As no long journey had been undertaken since the time of Haroun al Raschid, every one was ignorant which way to turn; and Vathek, though well versed in the course of the heavens, no longer knew his situation on earth. He thundered even louder than the elements; and muttered forth certain hints of the bow-string, which were not very soothing to literary ears. Disgusted at the toilsome weariness of the way, he determined to cross over the craggy heights and follow the guidance of a peasant, who undertook to bring him in four days to Rocnabad. Remonstrances were all to no purpose: his resolution was fixed.

The females and eunuchs uttered shrill wailings at the sight of the precipices below them, and the dreary prospects that opened in the vast gorges of the mountains. Before they could reach the ascent of the steepest rock, night overtook them, and a boisterous tempest arose, which, having rent the awnings of the palanquins and cages, exposed to the raw gusts the poor ladies within, who had never before felt so piercing a cold. The dark clouds that overcast the face of the sky deepened the horrors of this disastrous night, insomuch that nothing could be heard distinctly but the mewling of pages and lamentations of sultanas.

To increase the general misfortune, the frightful uproar of wild beasts resounded at a distance; and there were soon perceived in the forest they were skirting the glaring of eyes, which could belong only to devils or tigers. The pioneers, who, as well as they could, had marked out a track, and a part of the advanced guard, were devoured before they had been in the least apprised of their danger. The confusion that prevailed was extreme. Wolves, tigers, and other carnivorous animals, invited by the howling of their companions, flocked together from every quarter. The crashing of bones was heard on all sides, and a fearful rush of wings overhead; for now vultures also began to be of the party.

The terror at length reached the main body of the troops which surrounded the monarch and his harem at the distance of two leagues from the scene. Vathek (voluptuously reposed in his capacious litter upon cushions of silk, with two little pages beside him of complexions more fair than the enamel of Franguestan, who were occupied in keeping off flies) was soundly asleep, and contemplating in his dreams the treasures of Soliman. The shrieks, however, of his wives awoke him with a start; and, instead of the Giaour with his key of gold, he beheld Bababalouk full of consternation. "Sire," exclaimed this good servant of the most potent of monarchs, "misfortune is arrived at its height; wild beasts, who entertain no more reverence for your sacred person than for a dead ass, have beset your camels and their drivers; thirty of the most richly laden are already become their prey, as well as your confectioners, your cooks, and purveyors; and unless our holy Prophet should protect us, we shall have all eaten our last meal." At the mention of eating, the caliph lost all patience. He began to bellow, and even beat himself (for there was no seeing in the dark). The rumour every instant increased; and Bababalouk, finding no good could be done with his master, stopped both his ears against the hurlyburly of the harem, and called out aloud, "Come, ladies and brothers! all hands to work: strike light in a moment! never shall it be said, that the commander of the faithful served to regale these infidel brutes." Though there wanted not, in this bevy of beauties, a sufficient number of capricious and wayward, yet, on the present occasion, they were all compliance.

Fires were visible, in a twinkling, in all their cages. Ten thousand torches were lighted at once. The caliph himself seized a large one of wax; every person followed his example; and by kindling ropes' ends, dipped in oil and fastened on poles, an amazing blaze was spread. The rocks were covered with the splendour of sunshine. The trails of sparks, wafted by the wind, communicated to the dry fern, of which there was plenty. Serpents were observed to crawl forth from their retreats, with amazement and hissings; whilst the horses snorted, stamped the ground, tossed their noses in the air, and plunged about without mercy.

One of the forests of cedar that bordered their way took fire; and the branches that overhung the path, extending their flames to the muslins and chintzes which covered the cages of the ladies, obliged them to jump out, at the peril of their necks. Vathek, who vented on the occasion a thousand blasphemies, was himself compelled to touch, with his sacred feet, the naked earth.

Never had such an incident happened before. Full of mortification, shame, and despondence, and not knowing how to walk, the ladies fell into the dirt. "Must I go on foot?" said one. "Must I wet my feet?" cried another. "Must I soil my dress?" asked a third. "Execrable Bababalouk!" exclaimed all. "Outcast of hell! what hast thou to do with torches? Better were it to be eaten by tigers, than to fall into our present condition! we are for ever undone! Not a porter is there in the army, nor a currier of camels, but hath seen some part of our bodies; and, what is worse, our very faces!" On saying this the most bashful amongst them hid their foreheads on the ground, whilst such as had more boldness flew at Bababalouk; but he, well apprised of their humour, and not wanting in shrewdness, betook himself to his heels along with his comrades, all dropping their torches and striking their timbals.

It was not less light than in the brightest of the dog-days, and the weather was hot in proportion; but how degrading was the spectacle, to behold the caliph bespattered, like an ordinary mortal! As the exercise of his faculties seemed to be suspended, one of his Ethiopian wives (for he delighted in variety) clasped him in her arms, threw him upon her shoulder like a sack of dates, and, finding that the fire was hemming them in, set off with no small expedition, considering the weight of her burden. The other ladies, who had just learned the use of their feet, followed her; their guards galloped after; and the camel-drivers brought up the rear, as fast as their charge would permit.

They soon reached the spot where the wild beasts had commenced the carnage, but which they had too much good sense not to leave at the approaching of the tumult, having made besides a most luxurious supper. Bababalouk, nevertheless, seized on a few of the plumpest, which were unable to budge from the place, and began to flay them with admirable adroitness. The cavalcade having proceeded so far from the conflagration that the heat felt rather grateful than violent, it was immediately resolved on to halt. The tattered chintzes were picked up; the scraps, left by the wolves and tigers, interred; and vengeance was taken on some dozens of vultures, that were too much glutted to rise on the wing. The camels, which had been left unmolested to make sal ammoniac, being numbered, and the ladies once more enclosed in their cages, the imperial tent was pitched on the levellest ground they could find.

Vathek, reposing upon a mattress of down, and tolerably recovered from the jolting of the Ethiopian, who, to his feelings, seemed the roughest trotting jade he had hitherto mounted, called out for something to eat. But, alas! those delicate cakes which had been baked in silver ovens for his royal mouth, those rich manchets, amber comfits, flagons of Schiraz wine, porcelain vases of snow, and grapes from the banks of the Tigris, were all irremediably lost! And nothing had Bababalouk to present in their stead but a roasted wolf, vultures *à la daube,* aromatic herbs of the most acrid poignancy, rotten truffles, boiled thistles, and such other wild plants as much ulcerate the throat and parch up the tongue. Nor was he better provided in the article of drink; for he could procure nothing to accompany these irritating viands but a few phials of abominable brandy which had been secreted by the scullions in their slippers. Vathek made wry faces at so savage a repast, and Bababalouk answered them with shrugs and contortions. The caliph, however, ate with tolerable appetite, and fell into a nap that lasted six hours.

The splendour of the sun, reflected from the white cliffs of the mountains, in spite of the curtains that enclosed Vathek, at length disturbed his respose. He awoke terrified, and stung to the quick by wormwood-colour flies, which emitted from their wings a suffocating stench. The miserable monarch was perplexed how to act, though his wits were not idle in seeking expedients; whilst Bababalouk lay snoring amidst a swarm of those insects that busily thronged to pay court to his nose. The little pages, famished with hunger, had dropped their fans on the ground, and exerted their dying voices in bitter reproaches on the caliph, who now, for the first time, heard the language of truth.

Thus stimulated, he renewed his imprecations against the Giaour, and bestowed upon Mahomet some soothing expressions. "Where am I?" cried he: "what are these dreadful rocks—these valleys of darkness? Are we arrived at the horrible Kaf? Is the Simurgh coming to pluck out my eyes, as a punishment for undertaking this impious enterprise?" Having said this he turned himself towards an outlet in the side of his pavilion; but, alas! what objects occurred to his view? on one side a plain of black sand that appeared to be unbounded; and, on the other, perpendicular crags, bristled over with those abominable thistles which had so severely lacerated his tongue. He fancied, however, that he perceived amongst the brambles and briars some gigantic flowers, but was mistaken; for these were only the dangling palampores and variegated tatters of his gay retinue. As there were several clefts in the rock from whence water seemed to have flowed, Vathek applied his ear with the hope of catching the sound of some latent torrent; but could only distinguish the low murmurs of his people, who were repining at their journey, and complaining for the want of water. "To what purpose," asked they, "have we been brought hither? hath our caliph another tower to build? or have the relentless afrits, whom Carathis so much loves, fixed their abode in this place?"

At the name of Carathis, Vathek recollected the tablets he had received from his mother, who assured him they were fraught with preternatural qualities, and advised him to consult them as emergencies might require. Whilst he was engaged in turning them over, he heard a shout of joy and a loud clapping of hands. The curtains of his pavilion were soon drawn back, and he beheld Bababalouk, followed by a troop of his favourites, conducting two dwarfs, each a cubit high; who had brought between them a large basket of melons, oranges, and pomegranates. They were singing in the sweetest tones the words that follow: "We dwell on the top of these rocks, in a cabin of rushes and canes; the eagles envy us our nest: a small spring supplies us with water for the Abdest, and we daily repeat prayers, which the Prophet approves. We love you, O commander of the faithful! our master, the good Emir Fakreddin, loves you also: he reveres, in your person, the vicegerent of Mahomet. Little as we are, in us he confides: he knows our hearts to be as good as our bodies are contemptible; and hath placed us here to aid those who are bewildered on these dreary mountains. Last night, whilst we were occupied within our cell in reading the holy Koran, a sudden hurricane blew out our lights, and rocked our habitation. For two whole hours a palpable darkness prevailed; but we heard sounds at a distance, which we conjectured to proceed from the bells of a cafila, passing over the rocks. Our ears were soon filled with deplorable shrieks, frightful roarings, and the sound of timbals. Chilled with terror, we concluded that the Deggial, with his exterminating angels, had sent forth his plagues on the earth. In the midst of these melancholy reflections, we perceived flames of the deepest red glow in the horizon; and found ourselves, in a few moments, covered with flakes of fire. Amazed at so strange an appearance, we took up the volume dictated by the blessed Intelligence, and, kneeling, by the light of the fire that surrounded us, we recited the verse which says, 'Put no trust in any thing but the mercy of Heaven: there is no help, save in the holy Prophet: the mountain of Kaf itself may tremble; it is the power of Allah only that cannot be moved.' After having pronounced these words, we felt consolation, and our minds were hushed into a sacred repose. Silence ensued, and our ears clearly distinguished a voice in the air, saying: 'Servants of my faithful servant! go down to the happy valley of Fakreddin: tell him that an illustrious opportunity now offers to satiate the thirst of his hospitable heart. The commander of true believers is, this day, bewildered amongst these mountains, and stands in need of thy aid.'—We obeyed with joy the angelic mission; and our master, filled with pious zeal, hath culled with his own hands these melons, oranges, and pomegranates. He is following us, with a hundred dromedaries, laden with the purest waters of his fountains; and is coming to kiss the fringe of your consecrated robe, and implore you to enter his humble habitation, which, placed amidst these barren wilds, resembles an emerald set in lead." The dwarfs, having ended their address, remained still standing, and, with hands crossed upon their bosoms, preserved a respectful silence.

Vathek, in the midst of this curious harangue, seized the basket; and, long before it was finished, the fruits had dissolved in his mouth. As he continued to eat, his piety increased; and, in the same breath, he recited his prayers and called for the Koran and sugar.

Such was the state of his mind when the tablets, which were thrown by at the approach of the dwarfs, again attracted his eye. He took them up; but was ready to drop on the ground when he beheld, in large red characters, inscribed by Carathis, these words —which were, indeed, enough to make him tremble: "Beware of old doctors and their puny messengers of but one cubit high: distrust their pious frauds; and, instead of eating their melons, impale on a spit the bearers of them. Shouldest thou be such a fool as to visit them, the portal of the subterranean palace will shut in thy face, with such force as shall shake thee asunder: thy body shall be spit upon, and bats will nestle in thy belly."

"To what tends this ominous rhapsody?" cries the caliph; "and must I, then, perish in these deserts with thirst, whilst I may refresh myself in the delicious valley of melons and cucumbers? Accursed be the Giaour with his portal of ebony! he hath made me dance attendance too long already. Besides, who shall prescribe laws to me? I, forsooth, must not enter any one's habitation! Be it so; but what one can I enter that is not my own?" Bababalouk, who lost not a syllable of this soliloquy, applauded it with all his heart; and the ladies, for the first time, agreed with him in opinion.

The dwarfs were entertained, caressed, and seated, with great ceremony, on little cushions of satin. The symmetry of their persons was a subject of admiration; not an inch of them was suffered to pass unexamined. Knick-knacks and dainties were offered in profusion; but all were declined with respectful gravity. They climbed up the sides of the caliph's seat, and, placing themselves each on one of his shoulders, began to whisper prayers in his ears. Their tongues quivered like aspen leaves; and the patience of Vathek was almost exhausted, when the acclamations of the troops announced the approach of Fakreddin, who was come with a hundred old grey-beards, and as many Korans and dromedaries. They instantly set about their ablutions, and began to repeat the Bismillah. Vathek, to get rid of these officious monitors, followed their example, for his hands were burning.

The good emir, who was punctiliously religious, and likewise a great dealer in compliments, made an harangue five times more prolix and insipid than his little harbingers had already delivered. The caliph, unable any longer to refrain, exclaimed, "For the love of Mahomet, my dear Fakreddin, have done! let us proceed to your valley, and enjoy the fruits that Heaven hath vouchsafed you." The hint of proceeding put all into motion. The venerable attendants of the emir set forward somewhat slowly, but Vathek having ordered his little pages, in private, to goad on the dromedaries, loud fits of laughter broke forth from the cages; for the unwieldy curvetting of these poor beasts, and the ridiculous distress of their superannuated riders, afforded the ladies no small entertainment.

They descended, however, unhurt into the valley, by the easy slopes which the emir had ordered to be cut in the rock; and already the murmuring of streams and the rustling of leaves began to catch their attention. The cavalcade soon entered a path, which was skirted by flowering shrubs, and extended to a vast wood of palm trees, whose branches overspread a vast building of freestone. This edifice was crowned with nine domes, and adorned with as many portals of bronze, on which was engraven the following inscription: "This is the asylum of pilgrims, the refuge of travellers, and the depository of secrets from all parts of the world."

Nine pages, beautiful as the day, and decently clothed in robes of Egyptian linen, were standing at each door. They received the whole retinue with an easy and inviting air. Four of the most amiable placed the caliph on a magnificent tecthtrevan; four others, somewhat less graceful, took charge of Bababalouk, who capered for joy at the snug little cabin that fell to his share: the pages that remained waited on the rest of the train.

Every man being gone out of sight, the gate of a large enclosure on the right turned on its harmonious hinges; and a young female, of a slender form, came forth. Her light brown hair floated in the hazy breeze of the twilight. A troop of young maidens, like the Pleiades, attended her on tiptoe. They hastened to the pavilions that contained the sultanas; and the young lady, gracefully bending, said to them, "Charming princesses! everything is ready; we have prepared beds for your repose, and strewed your apartments with jasmine. No insects will keep off slumber from visiting your eyelids; we will dispel them with a thousand plumes. Come, then, amiable ladies! refresh your delicate feet and your ivory limbs in baths of rosewater; and, by the light of perfumed lamps, your servants will amuse you with tales." The sultanas accepted with pleasure these obliging offers, and followed the young lady to the emir's harem; where we must, for a moment, leave them and return to the caliph.

Vathek found himself beneath a vast dome, illuminated by a thousand lamps of rock crystal: as many vases of the same material, filled with excellent sherbet, sparkled on a large table, where a profusion of viands were spread. Amongst others, were rice boiled in milk of almonds, saffron soups, and lamb *à la crême;* of all which the caliph was amazingly fond. He took of each as much as he was able; testified his sense of the emir's friendship by the gaiety of his heart; and made the dwarfs dance against their will, for these little devotees durst not refuse the commander of the faithful. At last, he spread himself on the sofa, and slept sounder than he ever had before.

Beneath this dome a general silence prevailed; for there was nothing to disturb it but the jaws of Bababalouk, who had untrussed himself to eat with greater advantage, being anxious to make amends for his fast in the mountains. As his spirits were too high to admit of his sleeping, and hating to be idle, he proposed with himself to visit the harem, and repair to his charge of the ladies: to examine if they had been properly lubricated with the balm of Mecca; if their eyebrows and tresses were in order; and, in a word, to perform all the little offices they might need. He sought for a long time together, but without being able to find out the door. He durst not speak aloud, for fear of disturbing the caliph; and not a soul was stirring in the precincts of the palace. He almost despaired of effecting his purpose, when a low whispering just reached his ear. It came from the dwarfs, who were returned to their old occupation, and, for the nine hundred and ninety-ninth time in their lives, were reading over the Koran. They very politely invited Bababalouk to be of their party; but his head was full of other concerns. The dwarfs, though not a little scandalized at his dissolute morals, directed him to the apartments he wanted to find. His way thither lay through a hundred dark corridors, along which he groped as he went, and at last began to catch, from the extremity of a passage, the charming gossiping of the women, which not a little delighted his heart. "Ah, ha! what, not yet asleep?" cried he; and, taking long strides as he spoke, "did you not suspect me of abjuring my charge?"

Two of the black eunuchs, on hearing a voice so loud, left their party in haste, sabre in hand, to discover the cause; but presently was repeated on all sides, " 'Tis only Bababalouk! no one but Bababalouk!" This circumspect guardian, having gone up to a thin veil of carnation-colour silk that hung before the doorway, distinguished, by means of the softened splendour that shone through it, an oval bath of dark porphyry, surrounded by curtains, festooned in large folds. Through the apertures between them, as they were not drawn close, groups of young slaves were visible; amongst whom Bababalouk perceived his pupils, indulgingly expanding their arms, as if to embrace the perfumed water and refresh themselves after their fatigues. The looks of tender languor; their confidential whispers, and the enchanting smiles with which they were imparted; the exquisite fragrance of the roses: all combined to inspire a voluptuousness, which even Bababalouk himself was scarce able to withstand.

He summoned up, however, his usual solemnity; and, in the peremptory tone of authority, commanded the ladies instantly to leave the bath. Whilst he was issuing these mandates, the young Nouronihar, daughter of the emir, who was as sprightly as an antelope, and full of wanton gaiety, beckoned one of her slaves to let down the great swing which was suspended to the ceiling by cords of silk; and whilst this was doing, winked to her companions in the bath, who, chagrined to be forced from so soothing a state of indolence, began to twist and entangle their hair to plague and detain Bababalouk, and teased him, besides, with a thousand vagaries.

Nouronihar, perceiving that he was nearly out of patience, accosted him, with an arch air of respectful concern, and said, "My lord! it is not by any means decent that the chief eunuch of the caliph, our sovereign, should thus continue standing; deign but to recline your graceful person upon this sofa, which will burst with vexation if it have not the honour to receive you." Caught by these flattering accents, Bababalouk gallantly replied, "Delight of the apple of my eye! I accept the invitation of your honeyed lips; and, to say truth, my senses are dazzled with the radiance that beams from your charms."—"Repose, then, at your ease," replied the beauty, as she placed him on the pretended sofa, which, quicker than lightning, flew up all at once. The rest of the women, having aptly conceived her design, sprang naked from the bath, and plied the swing with such unmerciful jerks that it swept through the whole compass of a very lofty dome, and took from the poor victim all power of respiration. Sometimes his feet razed the surface of the water; and, at others, the skylight almost flattened his nose. In vain did he fill the air with the cries of a voice that resembled the ringing of a cracked jar; the peals of laughter were still predominant.

Nouronihar, in the inebriety of youthful spirits, being used only to eunuchs of ordinary harems, and having never seen anything so eminently disgusting, was far more diverted than all the rest. She began to parody some Persian verses, and sang, with an accent most demurely piquant, "Oh, gentle white dove! as thou soar'st through the air, vouchsafe one kind glance on the mate of thy love: melodious Philomel, I am thy rose; warble some couplet to ravish my heart!"

The sultanas and their slaves, stimulated by these pleasantries, persevered at the swing with such unremitted assiduity, that at length the cord which had secured it snapped suddenly asunder; and Bababalouk fell, floundering like a turtle, to the bottom of the bath. This accident occasioned an universal shout. Twelve little doors, till now unobserved, flew open at once; and the ladies, in an instant, made their escape; but not before having heaped all the towels on his head, and put out the lights that remained.

The deplorable animal, in water to the chin, overwhelmed with darkness, and unable to extricate himself from the wrappers that embarrassed him, was still doomed to hear, for his further consolation, the fresh bursts of merriment his disaster occasioned. He bustled, but in vain, to get from the bath; for the margin was become so slippery with the oil spilt in breaking the lamps, that, at every effort, he slid back with a plunge which resounded aloud through the hollow of the dome. These cursed peals of laughter were redoubled at every relapse, and he, who thought the place infested rather by devils than women, resolved to cease groping, and abide in the bath; where he amused himself with soliloquies, interspersed with imprecations, of which his malicious neighbours, reclining on down, suffered not an accent to escape. In this delectable plight the morning surprised him. The caliph, wondering at his absence, had caused him to be sought for everywhere. At last he was drawn forth almost smothered from under the wisp of linen, and wet even to the marrow. Limping, and his teeth chattering with cold, he approached his master, who inquired what was the matter, and how he came soused in so strange a pickle.—"And why did you enter this cursed lodge?" answered Bababalouk gruffly. "Ought a monarch like you to visit with his harem the abode of a grey-bearded emir, who knows nothing of life?—And with what gracious damsels doth the place too abound! Fancy to yourself how they have soaked me like a burnt crust; and made me dance like a jack-pudding, the livelong night through, on their damnable swing. What an excellent lesson for your sultanas, into whom I had instilled such reserve and decorum!" Vathek, comprehending not a syllable of all this invective, obliged him to relate minutely the transaction: but, instead of sympathizing with the miserable sufferer, he laughed immoderately at the device of the swing and the figure of Bababalouk mounted upon it. The stung eunuch could scarcely preserve the semblance of respect. "Ay, laugh, my lord! laugh," said he; "but I wish this Nouronihar would play some trick on you; she is too wicked to spare even majesty itself." These words made, for the present, but a slight impression on the caliph; but they not long after recurred to his mind.

This conversation was cut short by Fakreddin, who came to request that Vathek would join in the prayers and ablutions, to be solemnized on a spacious meadow watered by innumerable streams. The caliph found the waters refreshing, but the prayers abominably irksome. He diverted himself, however, with the multitude of calenders, santons, and dervishes, who were continually coming and going; but especially with the Brahmins, fakirs, and other enthusiasts, who had travelled from the heart of India, and halted on their way with the emir. These latter had each of them some mummery peculiar to himself. One dragged a huge chain wherever he went; another an orang-outang; whilst a third was furnished with scourges; and all performed to a charm. Some would climb up trees, holding one foot in the air; others poise themselves over a fire, and without mercy fillip their noses. There were some amongst them that cherished vermin, which were not ungrateful in requiting their caresses. These rambling fanatics revolted the hearts of the dervishes, the calenders, and santons; however, the vehemence of their aversion soon subsided, under the hope that the presence of the caliph would cure their folly, and convert them to the Mussulman faith. But, alas! how great was their disappointment! for Vathek, instead of preaching to them, treated them as buffoons, bade them present his compliments to Visnow and Ixhora, and discovered a predilection for a squat old man from the Isle of Serendib, who was more ridiculous than any of the rest. "Come!" said he, "for the love of your gods, bestow a few slaps on your chops to amuse me." The old fellow, offended at such an address, began loudly to weep; but, as he betrayed a villainous drivelling in shedding tears, the caliph turned his back and listened to Bababalouk, who whispered, whilst he held the umbrella over him, "Your majesty should be cautious of this odd assembly, which hath been collected I know not for what. Is it necessary to exhibit such spectacles to a mighty potentate, with interludes of talapoins more mangy than dogs? Were I you, I would command a fire to be kindled, and at once rid the estates of the emir, of his harem, and all his menagerie." —"Tush, dolt," answered Vathek, "and know that all this infinitely charms me. Nor shall I leave the meadow till I have visited every hive of these pious mendicants."

Wherever the caliph directed his course, objects of pity were sure to swarm round him; the blind, the purblind, smarts without noses, damsels without ears, each to extol the munificence of Fakreddin, who, as well as his attendant grey-beards, dealt about, gratis, plasters and cataplasms to all that applied. At noon, a superb corps of cripples made its appearance; and soon after advanced, by platoons, on the plain, the completest association of invalids that had ever been embodied till then. The blind went groping with the blind, the lame limped on together, and the maimed made gestures to each other with the only arm that remained. The sides of a considerable waterfall were crowded by the deaf; amongst whom were some from Pegû, with ears uncommonly handsome and large, but who were still less able to hear than the rest. Nor were there wanting others in abundance with hump-backs, wenny necks, and even horns of an exquisite polish.

The emir, to aggrandize the solemnity of the festival, in honour of his illustrious visitant, ordered the turf to be spread on all sides with skins and table-cloths; upon which were served up for the good Mussulmans pilaus of every hue, with other orthodox dishes; and, by the express order of Vathek, who was shamefully tolerant, small plates of abominations were prepared, to the great scandal of the faithful. The holy assembly began to fall to. The caliph, inspite of every remonstrance from the chief of his eunuchs, resolved to have a dinner dressed on the spot. The complaisant emir immediately gave orders for a table to be placed in the shade of the willows. The first service consisted of fish, which they drew from a river, flowing over sands of gold at the foot of a lofty hill. These were broiled as fast as taken, and served up with a sauce of vinegar and small herbs that grew on Mount Sinai; for everything with the emir was excellent and pious.

The dessert was not quite set on, when the sound of lutes from the hill was repeated by the echoes of the neighbouring mountains. The caliph, with an emotion of pleasure and surprise, had no sooner raised up his head, than a handful of jasmine dropped on his face. An abundance of tittering succeeded the frolic, and instantly appeared, through the bushes, the elegant forms of several young females, skipping and bounding like roes. The fragrance diffused from their hair struck the sense of Vathek, who, in an ecstasy, suspending his repast, said to Bababalouk, "Are the peris come down from their spheres? Note her, in particular, whose form is so perfect; venturously running on the brink of the precipice, and turning back her head, as regardless of nothing but the graceful flow of her robe. With what captivating impatience doth she contend with the bushes for her veil? could it be she who threw the jasmine at me?"—"Ay! she it was; and you too would she throw, from the top of the rock," answered Bababalouk, "for that is my good friend Nouronihar, who so kindly lent me her swing. My dear lord and master," added he, wresting a twig from a willow, "let me correct her for her want of respect: the emir will have no reason to complain; since (bating what I owe to his piety) he is much to be blamed for keeping a troop of girls on the mountains, where the sharpness of the air gives their blood too brisk a circulation."

"Peace! blasphemer," said the caliph; "speak not thus of her, who, over these mountains, leads my heart a willing captive. Contrive, rather, that my eyes may be fixed upon hers; that I may respire her sweet breath as she bounds panting along these delightful wilds!" On saying these words, Vathek extended his arms towards the hill; and directing his eyes with an anxiety unknown to him before, endeavoured to keep within view the object that enthralled his soul; but her course was as difficult to follow as the flight of one of those beautiful blue butterflies of Cash-mere which are at once, so volatile and rare.

The caliph, not satisfied with seeing, wished also to hear Nou-ronihar, and eagerly turned to catch the sound of her voice. At last, he distinguished her whispering to one of her companions behind the thicket from whence she had thrown the jasmine: "A caliph, it must be owned, is a fine thing to see; but my little Gul-chenrouz is much more amiable: one lock of his hair is of more value to me than the richest embroidery of the Indies. I had rather that his teeth should mischievously press my finger, than the richest ring of the imperial treasure. Where have you left him, Sutlememe? and why is he not here?"

The agitated caliph still wished to hear more; but she imme-diately retired with all her attendants. The fond monarch pur-sued her with his eyes till she was gone out of sight; and then continued like a bewildered and benighted traveller, from whom the clouds had obscured the constellation that guided his way. The curtain of night seemed dropped before him: everything ap-peared discoloured. The falling waters filled his soul with dejec-tion, and his tears trickled down the jasmines he had caught from Nouronihar, and placed in his inflamed bosom. He snatched up a few shining pebbles, to remind him of the scene where he felt the first tumults of love. Two hours were elapsed, and evening drew on, before he could resolve to depart from the place. He often, but in vain, attempted to go: a soft languor enervated the powers of his mind. Extending himself on the brink of the stream, he turned his eyes towards the blue summits of the mountain, and ex-claimed, "What concealest thou behind thee, pitiless rock? what is passing in thy solitudes? Whither is she gone? O heaven! per-haps she is now wandering in thy grottoes with her happy Gul-chenrouz!"

In the meantime, the damps began to descend; and the emir, solicitous for the health of the caliph, ordered the imperial litter to be brought. Vathek, absorbed in his reveries, was impercep-tibly removed and conveyed back to the saloon that received him the evening before. But let us leave the caliph immersed in his new passion, and attend Nouronihar beyond the rocks, where she had again joined her beloved Gulchenrouz.

This Gulchenrouz was the son of Ali Hassan, brother to the emir; and the most delicate and lovely creature in the world. Ali

Hassan, who had been absent ten years on a voyage to the un-known seas, committed, at his departure, this child, the only sur-vivor of many, to the care and protection of his brother. Gulchen-rouz could write in various characters with precision, and paint upon vellum the most elegant arabesques that fancy could devise. His sweet voice accompanied the lute in the most enchanting manner; and when he sang the loves of Megnoun and Leilah, or some unfortunate lovers of ancient days, tears insensibly over-flowed the cheeks of his auditors. The verses he composed (for, like Megnoun, he, too, was a poet) inspired that unresisting languor, so frequently fatal to the female heart. The women all doted upon him; and, though he had passed his thirteenth year, they still detained him in the harem. His dancing was light as the gossamer waved by the zephyrs of spring; but his arms, which twined so gracefully with those of the young girls in the dance, could neither dart the lance in the chase, nor curb the steeds that pastured in his uncle's domains. The bow, however, he drew with a certain aim, and would have excelled his competitors in the race, could he have broken the ties that bound him to Nouronihar.

The two brothers had mutually engaged their children to each other; and Nouronihar loved her cousin more than her own beautiful eyes. Both had the same tastes and amusements; the same long, languishing looks; the same tresses; the same fair com-plexions; and, when Gulchenrouz appeared in the dress of his cousin, he seemed to be more feminine than even herself. If, at any time, he left the harem to visit Fakreddin, it was with all the bashfulness of a fawn, that consciously ventures from the lair of its dam: he was, however, wanton enough to mock the solemn old grey-beards, though sure to be rated without mercy in return. Whenever this happened, he would hastily plunge into the re-cesses of the harem; and, sobbing, take refuge in the fond arms of Nouronihar, who loved even his faults beyond the virtues of others.

It fell out this evening, that, after leaving the caliph in the meadow, she ran with Gulchenrouz over the green sward of the mountain that sheltered the vale where Fakreddin had chosen to reside. The sun was dilated on the edge of the horizon; and the young people, whose fancies were lively and inventive, imagined they beheld, in the gorgeous clouds of the west, the domes of Shaddukian and Amberabad, where the Peries have fixed their abode. Nouronihar, sitting on the slope of the hill, supported on her knees the perfumed head of Gulchenrouz. The unexpected arrival of the caliph, and the splendour that marked his appearance, had already filled with emotion the ardent soul of Nouronihar. Her vanity irresistibly prompted her to pique the prince's attention; and this she before took good care to effect, whilst he picked up the jasmine she had thrown upon him. But when Gulchenrouz asked after the flowers he had culled for her bosom, Nouronihar was all in confusion. She hastily kissed his forehead, arose in a flutter, and walked with unequal steps on the border of the precipice. Night advanced, and the pure gold of the setting sun had yielded to a sanguine red, the glow of which, like the reflection of a burning furnace, flushed Nouronihar's animated countenance. Gulchenrouz, alarmed at the agitation of his cousin, said to her, with a supplicating accent, "Let us be gone; the sky looks portentous, the tamarisks tremble more than common, and the raw wind chills my very heart. Come! let us be gone; 'tis a melancholy night!" Then taking hold of her hand, he drew it towards the path he besought her to go. Nouronihar unconsciously followed the attraction; for a thousand strange imaginations occupied her spirits. She passed the large round of honeysuckles, her favourite resort, without ever vouchsafing it a glance; yet Gulchenrouz could not help snatching off a few shoots in his way, though he ran as if a wild beast were behind.

The young females seeing them approach in such haste, and, according to custom, expecting a dance, instantly assembled in a circle and took each other by the hand; but Gulchenrouz, coming up out of breath, fell down at once on the grass. This accident struck with consternation the whole of this frolicsome party; whilst Nouronihar, half distracted and overcome, both by the violence of her exercise and the tumult of her thoughts, sunk feebly down at his side, cherished his cold hands in her bosom, and chafed his temples with a fragrant perfume. At length he came to himself, and wrapping up his head in the robe of his cousin, entreated that she would not return to the harem. He was afraid of being snapped at by Shaban his tutor, a wrinkled old eunuch of a surly disposition; for, having interrupted the wonted walk of Nouronihar, he dreaded lest the churl should take it amiss. The whole of this sprightly group, sitting round upon a mossy knoll, began to entertain themselves with various pastimes, whilst their superintendents, the eunuchs, were gravely conversing at a distance. The nurse of the emir's daughter, observing her pupil sit ruminating with her eyes on the ground, endeavoured to amuse her with diverting tales; to which Gulchenrouz, who had already forgotten his inquietudes, listened with a breathless attention. He laughed, he clapped his hands, and passed a hundred little tricks on the whole of the company, without omitting the eunuchs, whom he provoked to run after him, in spite of their age and decrepitude.

During these occurrences, the moon arose, the wind subsided, and the evening became so serene and inviting, that a resolution was taken to sup on the spot. One of the eunuchs ran to fetch melons, whilst others were employed in showering down almonds from the branches that overhung this amiable party. Sutlememe, who excelled in dressing a salad, having filled large bowls of porcelain with eggs of small birds, curds turned with citron juice, slices of cucumber, and the inmost leaves of delicate herbs, handed it round from one to another, and gave each their shares with a large spoon of cocknos. Gulchenrouz, nestling, as usual, in the bosom of Nouronihar, pouted out his vermilion little lips against the offer of Sutlememe; and would take it only from the hand of his cousin, on whose mouth he hung, like a bee inebriated with the nectar of flowers.

In the midst of this festive scene, there appeared a light on the top of the highest mountain, which attracted the notice of every eye. This light was not less bright than the moon when at full, and might have been taken for her, had not the moon already risen. The phenomenon occasioned a general surprise, and no one could conjecture the cause. It could not be a fire, for the light was clear and bluish; nor had meteors ever been seen of that magnitude or splendour. This strange light faded for a moment, and immediately renewed its brightness. It first appeared motionless, at the foot of the rock; whence it darted in an instant, to sparkle in a thicket of palm-trees: from thence it glided along the torrent; and at last fixed in a glen that was narrow and dark. The moment it had taken its direction, Gulchenrouz, whose heart always trembled at anything sudden or rare, drew Nouronihar by the robe, and anxiously requested her to return to the harem. The women were importunate in seconding the entreaty; but the curiosity of the emir's daughter prevailed. She not only refused to go back, but resolved, at all hazards, to pursue the appearance.

Whilst they were debating what was best to be done, the light shot forth so dazzling a blaze that they all fled away shrieking. Nouronihar followed them a few steps; but, coming to the turn of a little by-path, stopped, and went back alone. As she ran with an alertness peculiar to herself, it was not long before she came to the place where they had just been supping. The globe of fire now appeared stationary in the glen, and burned in majestic stillness. Nouronihar, pressing her hands upon her bosom, hesitated, for some moments, to advance. The solitude of her situation was new, the silence of the night awful, and every object inspired sensations which, till then, she never had felt. The affright of Gulchenrouz recurred to her mind, and she a thousand times turned to go back; but this luminous appearance was always before her. Urged on by an irresistible impulse, she continued to approach it, in defiance of every obstacle that opposed her progress.

At length she arrived at the opening of the glen; but, instead of coming up to the light, she found herself surrounded by darkness; excepting that, at a considerable distance, a faint spark glimmered by fits. She stopped a second time: the sound of waterfalls mingling their murmurs, the hollow rustlings among the palm-branches and the funereal screams of the birds from their rifted trunks, all conspired to fill her soul with terror. She imagined, every moment, that she trod on some venomous reptile. All the stories of malignant dives and dismal ghouls thronged into her memory; but her curiosity was, notwithstanding, more predominant than her fears. She therefore firmly entered a winding track that led towards the spark; but, being a stranger to the path, she had not gone far, till she began to repent of her rashness. "Alas!" said she, "that I were but in those secure and illuminated apartments, where my evenings glided on with Gulchenrouz! Dear child! how would thy heart flutter with terror, wert thou wandering in these wild solitudes, like me!" Thus speaking, she advanced, and coming up to steps hewn in the rock, ascended them undismayed. The light, which was now gradually enlarging, appeared above her on the summit of the mountain, and as if proceeding from a cavern. At length, she distinguished a plaintive and melodious union of voices, that resembled the dirges which are sung over tombs. A sound like that which arises from the filling of baths struck her ear at the same time. She continued ascending, and discovered large wax torches in full blaze, planted here and there in the fissures of the rock. This appearance filled her with fear, whilst the subtle and potent odour which the torches exhaled caused her to sink, almost lifeless, at the entrance of the grot.

Casting her eyes within in this kind of trance, she beheld a large cistern of gold, filled with a water, the vapour of which distilled on her face a dew of the essence of roses. A soft symphony resounded through the grot. On the sides of the cistern she noticed appendages of royalty, diadems and feathers of the heron, all sparkling with carbuncles. Whilst her attention was fixed on this display of magnificence, the music ceased, and a voice instantly demanded, "For what monarch are these torches kindled, this bath prepared, and these habiliments which belong not only to the sovereigns of the earth, but even to the talismanic powers?" To which a second voice answered, "They are for the charming daughter of the Emir Fakreddin."—"What," replied the first, "for that trifler, who consumes her time with a giddy child, immersed in softness, and who, at best, can make but a pitiful husband?"— "And can she," rejoined the other voice, "be amused with such empty toys, whilst the caliph, the sovereign of the world, he who is destined to enjoy the treasures of the pre-Adamite sultans, a prince six feet high, and whose eyes pervade the inmost soul of a female, is inflamed with love for her? No! she will be wise enough to answer that passion alone that can aggrandize her glory. No doubt she will, and despise the puppet of her fancy. Then all the riches this place contains, as well as the carbuncle of Giamschid, shall be hers."—"You judge right," returned the first voice; "and I haste to Istakhar to prepare the palace of subterranean fire for the reception of the bridal pair."

The voices ceased; the torches were extinguished; the most entire darkness succeeded; and Nouronihar, recovering with a start, found herself reclined on a sofa in the harem of her father. She clapped her hands, and immediately came together Gulchenrouz and her women, who, in despair at having lost her, had dispatched eunuchs to seek her in every direction. Shaban appeared with the rest, and began to reprimand her, with an air of consequence: "Little impertinent," said he, "have you false keys, or are you beloved of some genius that hath given you a picklock? I will try the extent of your power: come to the dark chamber, and expect not the company of Gulchenrouz: be expeditious! I will shut you up, and turn the key twice upon you!" At these menaces, Nouronihar indignantly raised her head, opened on Shaban her black eyes, which, since the important dialogue of the enchanted grot, were considerably enlarged, and said, "Go, speak thus to slaves; but learn to reverence her who is born to give laws, and subject all to her power."

Proceeding in the same style, she was interrupted by a sudden exclamation of "The caliph! the caliph!" All the curtains were thrown open, the slaves prostrated themselves in double rows, and poor little Gulchenrouz went to hide beneath the couch of a sofa. At first appeared a file of black eunuchs trailing after them long trains of muslin embroidered with gold, and holding in their hands censers, which dispensed, as they passed, the grateful perfume of the wood of aloes. Next marched Bababalouk with a solemn strut, and tossing his head, as not overpleased at the visit. Vathek came close after, superbly robed: his gait was unembarrassed and noble; and his presence would have engaged admiration, though he had not been the sovereign of the world. He approached Nouronihar with a throbbing heart, and seemed enraptured at the full effulgence of her radiant eyes, of which he had before caught but a few glimpses; but she instantly depressed them, and her confusion augmented her beauty.

Bababalouk, who was a thorough adept in coincidences of this nature, and knew that the worst game should be played with the best face, immediately made a signal for all to retire; and no sooner did he perceive beneath the sofa the little one's feet, than he drew him forth without ceremony, set him upon his shoulders, and lavished him, as he went off, a thousand unwelcome caresses. Gulchenrouz cried out, and resisted till his cheeks became the colour of the blossom of pomegranates, and his tearful eyes sparkled with indignation. He cast a significant glance at Nouronihar, which the caliph noticing, asked, "Is that, then, your Gulchenrouz?"—"Sovereign of the world!" answered she, "spare my cousin, whose innocence and gentleness deserve not your anger!"—"Take comfort," said Vathek, with a smile: "he is in good hands. Bababalouk is fond of children, and never goes without sweetmeats and comfits." The daughter of Fakreddin was abashed, and suffered Gulchenrouz to be borne away without adding a word. The tumult of her bosom betrayed her confusion, and Vathek, becoming still more impassioned, gave a loose to his frenzy; which had only not subdued the last faint strugglings of reluctance, when the emir, suddenly bursting in, threw his face upon the ground at the feet of the caliph, and said, "Commander of the faithful! abase not yourself to the meanness of your slave." —"No, emir," replied Vathek, "I raise her to an equality with myself: I declare her my wife; and the glory of your race shall extend from one generation to another."—"Alas! my lord," said Fakreddin, as he plucked off a few grey hairs of his beard, "cut short the days of your faithful servant, rather than force him to depart from his word. Nouronihar is solemnly promised to Gulchenrouz, the son of my brother Ali Hassan: they are united, also, in heart; their faith is mutually plighted; and affiances, so sacred, cannot be broken."—"What then!" replied the caliph bluntly; "would you surrender this divine beauty to a husband more womanish than herself? and can you imagine that I will suffer her charms to decay in hands so inefficient and nerveless? No! she is destined to live out her life within my embraces: such is my will; retire, and disturb not the night I devote to the worship of her charms."

The irritated emir drew forth his sabre, presented it to Vathek, and stretching out his neck, said, in a firm tone of voice, "Strike your unhappy host, my lord: he has lived long enough, since he hath seen the Prophet's vicegerent violate the rights of hospitality." At his uttering these words, Nouronihar, unable to support any longer the conflict of her passions, sunk down into a swoon. Vathek, both terrified for her life and furious at an opposition to his will, bade Fakreddin assist his daughter, and withdrew; darting his terrible look at the unfortunate emir, who suddenly fell backward, bathed in a sweat as cold as the damp of death.

Gulchenrouz, who had escaped from the hands of Bababalouk, and was at that instant returned, called out for help as loudly as he could, not having strength to afford it himself. Pale and panting, the poor child attempted to revive Nouronihar by caresses; and it happened, that the thrilling warmth of his lips restored her to life. Fakreddin, beginning also to recover from the look of the caliph, with difficulty tottered to a seat; and, after warily casting round his eye, to see if this dangerous prince were gone, sent for Shaban and Sutlememe; and said to them apart, "My friends!

violent evils require violent remedies; the caliph has brought desolation and horror into my family; and how shall we resist his power? Another of his looks will send me to the grave. Fetch, then, that narcotic powder which a dervish brought me from Aracan. A dose of it, the effect of which will continue three days, must be administered to each of these children. The caliph will believe them to be dead; for they will have all the appearance of death. We shall go as if to inter them in the cave of Meimouné, at the entrance of the great desert of sand, and near the bower of my dwarfs. When all the spectators shall be withdrawn, you, Shaban, and four select eunuchs, shall convey them to the lake; where provision shall be ready to support them a month: for one day allotted to the surprise this event will occasion, five to the tears, a fortnight to reflection, and the rest to prepare for renewing his progress, will, according to my calculation, fill up the whole time that Vathek will tarry; and I shall then be freed from his intrusion."

"Your plan is good," said Sutlememe, "if it can but be effected. I have remarked, that Nouronihar is well able to support the glances of the caliph, and that he is far from being sparing of them to her; be assured, therefore, that, notwithstanding her fondness for Gulchenrouz, she will never remain quiet, while she knows him to be here. Let us persuade her that both herself and Gulchenrouz are really dead, and that they were conveyed to those rocks, for a limited season, to expiate the little faults of which their love was the cause. We will add, that we killed ourselves in despair; and that your dwarfs, whom they never yet saw, will preach to them delectable sermons. I will engage that everything shall succeed to the bent of your wishes."—"Be it so!" said Fakreddin: "I approve your proposal: let us lose not a moment to give it effect."

They hastened to seek for the powder, which, being mixed in a sherbet was immediately administered to Gulchenrouz and Nouronihar. Within the space of an hour, both were seized with violent palpitations, and a general numbness gradually ensued. They arose from the floor where they had remained ever since the caliph's departure, and, ascending to the sofa, reclined themselves upon it, clasped in each other's embraces. "Cherish me, my dear Nouronihar!" said Gulchenrouz: "put thy hand upon my heart; it feels as if it were frozen. Alas! thou art as cold as myself! hath the caliph murdered us both, with his terrible look?"—"I am dying!" cried she, in a faltering voice: "press me closer; I am ready to expire!"—"Let us die, then, together," answered the little Gulchenrouz, whilst his breast laboured with a convulsive sigh; "let me, at least, breathe forth my soul on thy lips!" They spoke no more, and became as dead.

Immediately the most piercing cries were heard through the harem; whilst Shaban and Sutlememe personated, with great adroitness, the parts of persons in despair. The emir, who was sufficiently mortified to be forced into such untoward expedients, and had now, for the first time, made a trial of his powder, was under no necessity of counterfeiting grief. The slaves, who had flocked together from all quarters, stood motionless at the spectacle before them. All lights were extinguished, save two lamps, which shed a wan glimmering over the faces of these lovely flowers, that seemed to be faded in the spring-time of life. Funeral vestments were prepared; their bodies were washed with rose-water; their beautiful tresses were braided and incensed; and they were wrapped in cymars whiter than alabaster.

At the moment that their attendants were placing two wreaths of their favourite jasmines on their brows, the caliph, who had just heard the tragical catastrophe, arrived. He looked not less pale and haggard than the ghouls that wander at night among the graves. Forgetful of himself and every one else, he broke through the midst of the slaves; fell prostrate at the foot of the sofa; beat his bosom; called himself "atrocious murderer!" and invoked upon his head a thousand imprecations. With a trembling hand he raised the veil that covered the countenance of Nouronihar, and uttering a loud shriek, fell lifeless on the floor. The chief of the eunuchs dragged him off, with horrible grimaces, and repeated as he went, "Ay, I foresaw she would play you some ungracious turn!"

No sooner was the caliph gone, than the emir commanded biers to be brought, and forbade that any one should enter the harem. Every window was fastened; all instruments of music were broken; and the imans began to recite their prayers. Towards the close of this melancholy day, Vathek sobbed in silence; for they had been forced to compose with anodynes his convulsions of rage and desperation.

At the dawn of the succeeding morning, the wide folding

doors of the palace were set open, and the funeral procession moved forward for the mountain. The wailful cries of "La Ilah illa Alla!" reached the caliph, who was eager to cicatrize himself and attend the ceremonial; nor could he have been dissuaded, had not his excessive weakness disabled him from walking. At the few first steps he fell on the ground, and his people were obliged to lay him on a bed, where he remained many days in such a state of insensibility as excited compassion in the emir himself.

When the procession was arrived at the grot of Meimouné, Shaban and Sutlememe dismissed the whole of the train, excepting the four confidential eunuchs who were appointed to remain. After resting some moments near the biers, which had been left in the open air, they caused them to be carried to the brink of a small lake, whose banks were overgrown with a hoary moss. This was the great resort of herons and storks, which preyed continually on little blue fishes. The dwarfs, instructed by the emir, soon repaired thither, and, with the help of the eunuchs, began to construct cabins of rushes and reeds, a work in which they had admirable skill. A magazine also was contrived for provisions, with a small oratory for themselves, and a pyramid of wood, neatly piled, to furnish the necessary fuel, for the air was bleak in the hollows of the mountains.

At evening two fires were kindled on the brink of the lake, and the two lovely bodies, taken from their biers, were carefully deposited upon a bed of dried leaves within the same cabin. The dwarfs began to recite the Koran, with their clear shrill voices; and Shaban and Sutlememe stood at some distance, anxiously waiting the effects of the powder. At length Nouronihar and Gulchenrouz faintly stretched out their arms; and, gradually opening their eyes, began to survey, with looks of increasing amazement, every object around them. They even attempted to rise; but, for want of strength, fell back again. Sutlememe, on this, administered a cordial, which the emir had taken care to provide.

Gulchenrouz, thoroughly aroused, sneezed out aloud; and, raising himself with an effort that expressed his surprise, left the cabin and inhaled the fresh air with the greatest avidity. "Yes," said he, "I breathe again! again do I exist! I hear sounds! I behold a firmament, spangled over with stars!" Nouronihar, catching these beloved accents, extricated herself from the leaves and

ran to clasp Gulchenrouz to her bosom. The first objects she remarked were their long cymars, their garlands of flowers, and
their naked feet: she hid her face in her hands to reflect. The
vision of the enchanted bath, the despair of her father, and,
more vividly than both, the majestic figure of Vathek, recurred to
her memory. She recollected, also, that herself and Gulchenrouz
had been sick and dying; but all these images bewildered her
mind. Not knowing where she was, she turned her eyes on all
sides, as if to recognize the surrounding scene. This singular lake,
those flames reflected from its glassy surface, the pale hues of its
banks, the romantic cabins, the bulrushes that sadly waved their
drooping heads, the storks whose melancholy cries blended with
the shrill voices of the dwarfs—everything conspired to persuade
her that the angel of death had opened the portal of some other
world.

Gulchenrouz on his part, lost in wonder, clung to the neck of
his cousin. He believed himself in the region of phantoms, and
was terrified at the silence she preserved. At length addressing her:
"Speak," said he; "where are we? Do you not see those spectres
that are stirring the burning coals? Are they Monker and Nekir
who are come to throw us into them? Does the fatal bridge across
this lake, whose solemn stillness perhaps conceals from us an
abyss, in which for whole ages we shall be doomed incessantly to
sink?"

"No, my children," said Sutlememe, going towards them; "take
comfort! the exterminating angel, who conducted our souls hither
after yours, hath assured us, that the chastisement of your indolent and voluptuous life shall be restricted to a certain series of
years, which you must pass in this dreary abode; where the sun is
scarcely visible, and where the soil yields neither fruits nor flowers. These," continued she, pointing to the dwarfs, "will provide
for our wants; for souls so mundane as ours retain too strong a
tincture of their earthly extraction. Instead of meats, your food
will be nothing but rice; and your bread shall be moistened in the
fogs that brood over the surface of the lake."

At this desolating prospect, the poor children burst into tears,
and prostrated themselves before the dwarfs; who perfectly supported their characters, and delivered an excellent discourse, of a
customary length, upon the sacred camel which, after a thousand
years, was to convey them to the paradise of the faithful.

The sermon being ended, and ablutions performed, they praised Alla and the Prophet, supped very indifferently, and retired to their withered leaves. Nouronihar and her little cousin consoled themselves on finding that the dead might lie in one cabin. Having slept well before, the remainder of the night was spent in conversation on what had befallen them; and both, from a dread of apparitions, betook themselves for protection to one another's arms.

In the morning, which was lowering and rainy, the dwarfs mounted high poles, like minarets, and called them to prayers. The whole congregation, which consisted of Sutlememe, Shaban, the four eunuchs, and a few storks that were tired of fishing, was already assembled. The two children came forth from their cabin with a slow and dejected pace. As their minds were in a tender and melancholy mood, their devotions were performed with fervour. No sooner were they finished than Gulchenrouz demanded of Sutlememe and the rest, "how they happened to die so opportunely for his cousin and himself?"—"We killed ourselves," returned Sutlememe, "in despair at your death." On this, Nouronihar, who, notwithstanding what had passed, had not yet forgotten her vision, said, "And the caliph! is he also dead of his grief? and will he likewise come hither?" The dwarfs, who were prepared with an answer, most demurely replied, "Vathek is damned beyond all redemption!"—"I readily believe so," said Gulchenrouz; "and am glad, from my heart, to hear it; for I am convinced it was his horrible look that sent us hither, to listen to sermons, and mess upon rice." One week passed away on the side of the lake unmarked by any variety; Nouronihar ruminating on the grandeur of which death had deprived her, and Gulchenrouz applying to prayers and basket-making with the dwarfs, who infinitely pleased him.

Whilst this scene of innocence was exhibiting in the mountains, the caliph presented himself to the emir in a new light. The instant he recovered the use of his senses, with a voice that made Bababalouk quake, he thundered out, "Perfidious Giaour! I renounce thee for ever! it is thou who hast slain my beloved Nouronihar! and I supplicate the pardon of Mahomet, who would have preserved her to me had I been more wise. Let water be brought to perform my ablutions, and let the pious Fakreddin be called to offer up his prayers with mine, and reconcile me to him. Afterwards, we will go together and visit the sepulchre of the unfortunate Nouronihar. I am resolved to become a hermit, and consume the residue of my days on this mountain, in hope of expiating my crimes."—"And what do you intend to live upon there?" inquired Bababalouk.—"I hardly know," replied Vathek; "but I will tell you when I feel hungry—which, I believe, will not soon be the case."

The arrival of Fakreddin put a stop to this conversation. As soon as Vathek saw him, he threw his arms around his neck, bedewed his face with a torrent of tears, and uttered things so affecting, so pious, that the emir, crying for joy, congratulated himself in his heart upon having performed so admirable and unexpected a conversion. As for the pilgrimage to the mountain, Fakreddin had his reasons not to oppose it; therefore, each ascending his own litter, they started.

Notwithstanding the vigilance with which his attendants watched the caliph, they could not prevent his harrowing his cheeks with a few scratches, when on the place where he was told Nouronihar had been buried; they were even obliged to drag him away, by force of hands, from the melancholy spot. However, he swore, with a solemn oath, that he would return thither every day. This resolution did not exactly please the emir—yet he flattered himself that the caliph might not proceed farther, and would merely perform his devotions in the cavern of Meimouné. Besides, the lake was so completely concealed within the solitary bosom of those tremendous rocks, that he thought it utterly impossible any one could ever find it. This security of Fakreddin was also considerably strengthened by the conduct of Vathek, who performed his vow most scrupulously, and returned daily from the hill so devout, and so contrite, that all the grey-beards were in a state of ecstasy on account of it.

Nouronihar was not altogether so content; for though she felt a fondness for Gulchenrouz, who, to augment the attachment, had been left at full liberty with her, yet she still regarded him as but a bauble that bore no competition with the carbuncle of Giamschid. At times, she indulged doubts on the mode of her being; and scarcely could believe that the dead had all the wants and the whims of the living. To gain satisfaction, however, on so perplexing a topic, one morning, whilst all were asleep, she arose with a breathless caution from the side of Gulchenrouz; and, after having given him a soft kiss, began to follow the windings of the lake, till it terminated with a rock, the top of which was accessible, though lofty. This she climbed with considerable toil; and having reached the summit, set forward in a run, like a doe before the hunter. Though she skipped with the alertness of an antelope, yet, at intervals, she was forced to desist, and rest beneath the tamarisks to recover her breath. Whilst she, thus reclined, was occupied with her little reflections on the apprehension that she had some knowledge of the place, Vathek, who, finding himself that morning but ill at ease, had gone forth before the dawn, presented himself on a sudden to her view. Motionless with surprise, he durst not approach the figure before him trembling and pale, but yet lovely to behold. At length Nouronihar, with a mixture of pleasure and affliction, raising her fine eyes to him, said, "My lord! are you then come hither to eat rice and hear sermons with me?"—"Beloved phantom!" cried Vathek, "thou dost speak; thou hast the same graceful form; the same radiant features; art thou palpable likewise?" and, eagerly embracing her, added, "Here are limbs and a bosom animated with a gentle warmth!—What can such a prodigy mean?"

Nouronihar, with indifference, answered,—"You know, my lord, that I died on the very night you honoured me with your visit. My cousin maintains it was from one of your glances; but I cannot believe him; for to me they seem not so dreadful. Gulchenrouz died with me, and we were both brought into a region of desolation, where we are fed with a wretched diet. If you be dead also, and are come hither to join us, I pity your lot; for you will be stunned with the clang of the dwarfs and the storks. Besides, it is mortifying in the extreme, that you, as well as myself, should have lost the treasures of the subterranean palace."

At the mention of the subterranean palace, the caliph suspended his caresses (which, indeed, had proceeded pretty far), to seek from Nouronihar an explanation of her meaning. She then recapitulated her vision, what immediately followed, and the history of her pretended death; adding, also, a description of the place of expiation from whence she had fled; and all in a manner that would have extorted his laughter, had not the thoughts of Vathek been too deeply engaged. No sooner, however, had she ended, than he again clasped her to his bosom and said, "Light of my eyes, the mystery is unravelled; we both are alive! Your father is a cheat, who, for the sake of dividing us, hath deluded us both; and the Giaour, whose design, as far as I can discover, is that we shall proceed together, seems scarce a whit better. It shall be some time at least before he finds us in his palace of fire. Your lovely little person in my estimation is far more precious than all the treasures of the pre-Adamite sultans; and I wish to possess it at pleasure, and in open day, for many a moon, before I go to burrow underground, like a mole. Forget this little trifler, Gulchenrouz; and——"—"Ah, my lord!" interposed Nouronihar, "let me entreat that you do him no evil."—"No, no!" replied Vathek; "I have already bid you forbear to alarm yourself for him. He has been brought up too much on milk and sugar to stimulate my jealousy. We will leave him with the dwarfs; who, by the by, are my old acquaintants: their company will suit him far better than yours. As to other matters, I will return no more to your father's. I want not to have my ears dinned by him and his dotards with the violation of the rights of hospitality, as if it were less an honour for you to espouse the sovereign of the world than a girl dressed up like a boy."

Nouronihar could find nothing to oppose in a discourse so eloquent. She only wished the amorous monarch had discovered more ardour for the carbuncle of Giamschid; but flattered herself it would gradually increase, and therefore yielded to his will with the most bewitching submission.

When the caliph judged it proper, he called for Bababalouk, who was asleep in the cave of Meimouné, and dreaming that the phantom of Nouronihar, having mounted him once more on her swing, had just given him such a jerk, that he one moment soared above the mountains, and the next sunk into the abyss. Starting from his sleep at the sound of his master, he ran, gasping for breath, and had nearly fallen backward at the sight, as he believed, of the spectre by whom he had so lately been haunted in his dream. "Ah, my lord!" cried he, recoiling ten steps, and covering his eyes with both hands, "do you then perform the office of a ghoul? have you dug up the dead? Yet hope not to make her your prey; for, after all she hath caused me to suffer, she is wicked enough to prey even upon you."

"Cease to play the fool," said Vathek, "and thou shalt soon be convinced that it is Nouronihar herself, alive and well, whom I clasp to my breast. Go and pitch my tents in the neighbouring valley. There will I fix my abode, with this beautiful tulip, whose colours I soon shall restore. There exert thy best endeavours to procure whatever can augment the enjoyments of life, till I shall disclose to thee more of my will."

The news of so unlucky an event soon reached the ears of the emir, who abandoned himself to grief and despair, and began, as did his old grey-beards, to begrime his visage with ashes. A total supineness ensued; travellers were no longer entertained; no more plasters were spread; and, instead of the charitable activity that had distinguished this asylum, the whole of its inhabitants exhibited only faces of half a cubit long, and uttered groans that accorded with their forlorn situation.

Though Fakreddin bewailed his daughter as lost to him for ever, yet Gulchenrouz was not forgotten. He dispatched immediate instructions to Sutlememe, Shaban, and the dwarfs, enjoining them not to undeceive the child in respect to his state, but, under some pretence, to convey him far from the lofty rock at the extremity of the lake, to a place which he should appoint, as safer from danger, for he suspected that Vathek intended him evil.

Gulchenrouz, in the meanwhile, was filled with amazement at not finding his cousin; nor were the dwarfs less surprised: but Sutlememe, who had more penetration, immediately guessed what had happened. Gulchenrouz was amused with the delusive hope of once more embracing Nouronihar in the interior recesses of the mountains, where the ground, strewed over with orange blossoms and jasmines, offered beds much more inviting than the withered leaves in their cabin; where they might accompany with their voices the sounds of their lutes, and chase butterflies. Sutlememe was far gone in this sort of description, when one of the four eunuchs beckoned her aside, to apprise her of the arrival of a messenger from their fraternity, who had explained the secret of the flight of Nouronihar, and brought the commands of the emir. A council with Shaban and the dwarfs was immediately held. Their baggage being stowed in consequence of it, they embarked in a shallop, and quietly sailed with the little one, who acquiesced in all their proposals. Their voyage proceeded in the same manner, till they came to the place where the lake sinks beneath the hollow of a rock: but as soon as the bark had entered it, and Gulchenrouz found himself surrounded with darkness, he was seized with a dreadful consternation, and incessantly uttered the most piercing outcries; for he now was persuaded he should actually be damned for having taken too many little freedoms in his lifetime with his cousin.

But let us return to the caliph, and her who ruled over his heart. Bababalouk had pitched the tents, and closed up the extremities of the valley with magnificent screens of India cloth, which were guarded by Ethiopian slaves with their drawn sabres. To preserve the verdure of this beautiful enclosure in its natural freshness, white eunuchs went continually round it with gilt water vessels. The waving of fans was heard near the imperial pavilion; where, by the voluptuous light that glowed through the muslins, the caliph enjoyed, at full view, all the attractions of Nouronihar. Inebriated with delight, he was all ear to her charming voice, which accompanied the lute; while she was not less captivated with his descriptions of Samarah, and the tower full of wonders, but especially with his relation of the adventure of the ball, and the chasm of the Giaour, with its ebony portal.

In this manner they conversed the whole day, and at night they bathed together in a basin of black marble, which admirably set off the fairness of Nouronihar. Bababalouk, whose good graces this beauty had regained, spared no attention, that their repasts might be served up with the minutest exactness: some exquisite rarity was ever placed before them; and he sent even to Schiraz, for that fragrant and delicious wine which had been hoarded up in bottles, prior to the birth of Mahomet. He had excavated little ovens in the rock, to bake the nice manchets which were prepared by the hands of Nouronihar, from whence they had derived a flavour so grateful to Vathek, that he regarded the ragouts of his other wives as entirely mawkish: whilst they would have died of chagrin at the emir's, at finding themselves so neglected, if Fakreddin, notwithstanding his resentment, had not taken pity upon them.

The Sultana Dilara, who, till then, had been the favourite, took this dereliction of the caliph to heart, with a vehemence natural to her character; for, during her continuance in favour, she had imbibed from Vathek many of his extravagant fancies, and was fired with impatience to behold the superb tombs of Istakhar, and the palace of forty columns; besides, having been brought up amongst the magi, she had fondly cherished the idea of the caliph's devoting himself to the worship of fire: thus his voluptuous and desultory life with her rival was to her a double source of affliction. The transient piety of Vathek had occasioned her some serious alarms; but the present was an evil of far greater magnitude. She resolved, therefore, without hesitation, to write to Carathis, and acquaint her that all things went ill; that they had eaten, slept, and revelled at an old emir's, whose sanctity was very formidable; and that, after all, the prospect of possessing the treasures of the pre-Adamite sultans was no less remote than before. This letter was entrusted to the care of two woodmen, who were at work in one of the great forests of the mountains, and who, being acquainted with the shortest cuts, arrived in ten days at Samarah.

The Princess Carathis was engaged at chess with Morakanabad, when the arrival of these woodfellers was announced. She, after some weeks of Vathek's absence, had forsaken the upper regions of her tower, because everything appeared in confusion among the stars, which she consulted relative to the fate of her son. In vain did she renew her fumigations, and extend herself on the roof, to obtain mystic visions; nothing more could she see in her dreams, than pieces of brocade, nosegays of flowers, and other unmeaning gewgaws. These disappointments had thrown her into a state of dejection, which no drug in her power was sufficient to remove. Her only resource was in Morakanabad, who was a good man, and endowed with a decent share of confidence; yet whilst in her company he never thought himself on roses.

No person knew aught of Vathek, and, of course, a thousand ridiculous stories were propagated at his expense. The eagerness of Carathis may be easily guessed at receiving the letter, as well as her rage at reading the dissolute conduct of her son. "Is it so?" said she; "either I will perish, or Vathek shall enter the palace of fire. Let me expire in flames, provided he may reign on the throne of Soliman!" Having said this, and whirled herself round in a magical manner, which struck Morakanabad with such terror as caused him to recoil, she ordered her great camel Alboufaki to be brought, and the hideous Nerkes, with the unrelenting Cafour, to attend. "I require no other retinue," said she to Morakanabad; "I am going on affairs of emergency; a truce, therefore, to parade! Take you care of the people: fleece them well in my absence; for we shall expend large sums, and one knows not what may betide."

The night was uncommonly dark, and a pestilential blast blew from the plain of Catoul, that would have deterred any other traveller, however urgent the call: but Carathis enjoyed most whatever filled others with dread. Nerkes concurred in opinion with her; and Cafour had a particular predilection for a pestilence. In the morning this accomplished caravan, with the woodfellers, who directed their route, halted on the edge of an extensive marsh, from whence so noxious a vapour arose as would have destroyed any animal but Alboufaki, who naturally inhaled these malignant fogs with delight. The peasants entreated their convoy not to sleep in this place. "To sleep," cried Carathis, "what an excellent thought! I never sleep, but for visions; and, as to my attendants, their occupations are too many to close the only eye they have." The poor peasants, who were not overpleased with their party, remained open-mouthed with surprise.

Carathis alighted, as well as her negresses; and, severally stripping off their outer garments, they all ran to cull from those spots where the sun shone fiercest the venomous plants that grew on the marsh. This provision was made for the family of the emir, and whoever might retard the expedition to Istakhar. The woodmen were overcome with fear, when they beheld these three horrible phantoms run; and, not much relishing the company of Alboufaki, stood aghast at the command of Carathis to set forward, notwithstanding it was noon, and the heat fierce enough to calcine even rocks. In spite, however, of every remonstrance, they were forced implicitly to submit.

Alboufaki, who delighted in solitude, constantly snorted whenever he perceived himself near a habitation; and Carathis, who was apt to spoil him with indulgence, as constantly turned him aside: so that the peasants were precluded from procuring subsistence; for the milch goats and ewes, which Providence had sent towards the district they traversed to refresh travellers with their milk, all fled at the sight of the hideous animal and his strange riders. As to Carathis, she needed no common aliment; for her invention had previously furnished her with an opiate to stay her stomach, some of which she imparted to her mutes.

At dusk Alboufaki, making a sudden stop, stamped with his foot; which, to Carathis, who knew his ways, was a certain indication that she was near the confines of some cemetery. The moon shed a bright light on the spot, which served to discover a long wall with a large door in it, standing ajar, and so high that Al-

boufaki might easily enter. The miserable guides, who perceived
their end approaching, humbly implored Carathis, as she had
now so good an opportunity, to inter them, and immediately gave
up the ghost. Nerkes and Cafour, whose wit was of a style peculiar
to themselves, were by no means parsimonious of it on the folly of
these poor people; nor could anything have been found more
suited to their taste than the site of the burying-ground, and the
sepulchres which its precincts contained. There were at least two
thousand of them on the declivity of a hill. Carathis was too
eager to execute her plan to stop at the view, charming as it appeared in her eyes. Pondering the advantages that might accrue
from her present situation, she said to herself, "So beautiful a
cemetery must be haunted by ghouls! they never want for intelligence: having heedlessly suffered my stupid guides to expire, I
will apply for directions to them; and, as an inducement, will in-
vite them to regale on these fresh corpses." After this wise soliloquy, she beckoned to Nerkes and Cafour, and made signs with her
fingers, as much as to say, "Go; knock against the sides of the
tombs, and strike up your delightful warblings."

The negresses, full of joy at the behests of their mistress, and
promising themselves much pleasure from the society of the
ghouls, went with an air of conquest, and began their knockings
at the tombs. As their strokes were repeated, a hollow noise was
made in the earth; the surface hove up into heaps; and the ghouls,
on all sides, protruded their noses to inhale the effluvia which the
carcasses of the woodmen began to emit. They assembled before a
sarcophagus of white marble, where Carathis was seated between
the bodies of her miserable guides. The princess received her
visitants with distinguished politeness; and, supper being ended,
they talked of business. Carathis soon learned from them everything she wanted to discover; and, without loss of time, prepared
to set forward on her journey. Her negresses, who were forming
tender connections with the ghouls, importuned her, with all
their fingers, to wait at least till the dawn. But Carathis, being
chastity in the abstract, and an implacable enemy to love intrigues and sloth, at once rejected their prayer, mounted Alboufaki, and commanded them to take their seats instantly. Four days
and four nights she continued her route without interruption. On
the fifth, she traversed craggy mountains and half-burnt forests;
and arrived on the sixth before the beautiful screens which concealed from all eyes the voluptuous wanderings of her son.

It was daybreak, and the guards were snoring on their posts in careless security, when the rough trot of Alboufaki awoke them in consternation. Imagining that a group of spectres, ascended from the abyss, was approaching, they all, without ceremony, took to their heels. Vathek was at that instant with Nouronihar in the bath, hearing tales, and laughing at Bababalouk who related them; but, no sooner did the outcry of his guards reach him, than he flounced from the water like a carp, and as soon threw himself back at the sight of Carathis; who, advancing with her negresses upon Alboufaki, broke through the muslin awnings and veils of the pavilion. At this sudden apparition, Nouronihar (for she was not at all times free from remorse) fancied that the moment of celestial vengeance was come, and clung about the caliph in amorous despondence.

Carathis, still seated on her camel, foamed with indignation at the spectacle which obtruded itself on her chaste view. She thundered forth without check or mercy, "Thou double-headed and four-legged monster! what means all this winding and writhing? Art thou not ashamed to be seen grasping this limber sapling, in preference to the sceptre of the pre-Adamite sultans? Is it then for this paltry doxy that thou hast violated the conditions in the parchment of our Giaour? Is it on her thou hast lavished thy precious moments? Is this the fruit of the knowledge I have taught thee? Is this the end of thy journey? Tear thyself from the arms of this little simpleton; drown her in the water before me, and instantly follow my guidance."

In the first ebullition of his fury, Vathek had resolved to rip open the body of Alboufaki, and to stuff it with those of the negresses and of Carathis herself; but the remembrance of the Giaour, the palace of Istakhar, the sabres, and the talismans, flashing before his imagination with the simultaneousness of lightning, he became more moderate, and said to his mother in a civil, but decisive tone, "Dread lady, you shall be obeyed; but I will not drown Nouronihar. She is sweeter to me than a Myrabolan comfit; and is enamoured of carbuncles, especially that of Giamschid, which hath also been promised to be conferred upon her: she, therefore, shall go along with us; for I intend to repose with her upon the sofas of Soliman: I can sleep no more without her."—"Be it so," replied Carathis, alighting, and at the same time committing Alboufaki to the charge of her black women.

Nouronihar, who had not yet quitted her hold, began to take

courage; and said, with an accent of fondness to the caliph, "Dear sovereign of my soul! I will follow thee, if it be thy will, beyond the Kaf, in the land of the afrits. I will not hesitate to climb, for thee, the nest of the Simurgh; who, this lady excepted, is the most awful of created beings."—"We have here, then," subjoined Carathis, "a girl both of courage and science!" Nouronihar had certainly both; but, notwithstanding all her firmness, she could not help casting back a thought of regret upon the graces of her little Gulchenrouz, and the days of tender endearments she had participated with him. She even dropped a few tears, which the caliph observed; and inadvertently breathed out with a sigh, "Alas! my gentle cousin, what will become of thee?" Vathek, at this apostrophe, knitted up his brows, and Carathis inquired what it could mean. "She is preposterously sighing after a stripling with languishing eyes and soft hair, who loves her," said the caliph.—"Where is he?" asked Carathis. "I must be acquainted with this pretty child; for," added she, lowering her voice, "I design, before I depart, to regain the favour of the Giaour. There is nothing so delicious, in his estimation, as the heart of a delicate boy palpitating with the first tumults of love."

Vathek, as he came from the bath, commanded Bababalouk to collect the women and other movables of his harem, embody his troops, and hold himself in readiness to march within three days; whilst Carathis retired alone to a tent, where the Giaour solaced her with encouraging visions: but at length waking, she found at her feet Nerkes and Cafour, who informed her, by their signs, that having led Alboufaki to the borders of a lake, to browse on some grey moss that looked tolerably venomous, they had discovered certain blue fishes, of the same kind with those in the reservoir on the top of the tower. "Ah! ha!" said she, "I will go thither to them. These fish are, past doubt, of a species that, by a small operation, I can render oracular. They may tell me where this little Gulchenrouz is, whom I am bent upon sacrificing." Having thus spoken, she immediately set out with her swarthy retinue.

It being but seldom that time is lost in the accomplishment of a wicked enterprise, Carathis and her negresses soon arrived at the lake; where, after burning the magical drugs with which they were always provided, they stripped themselves naked, and waded to their chins; Nerkes and Cafour waving torches around them, and Carathis pronouncing her barbarous incantations. The fishes, with one accord, thrust forth their heads from the water, which was violently rippled by the flutter of their fins; and at length finding themselves constrained by the potency of the charm, they opened their piteous mouths, and said, "From gills to tail, we are yours; what seek ye to know?"—"Fishes," answered she, "I conjure you, by your glittering scales, tell me where now is Gulchenrouz?"—"Beyond the rock," replied the shoal, in full chorus; "will this content you? for we do not delight in expanding our mouths."—"It will," returned the princess; "I am not to learn that you are not used to long conversations; I will leave you therefore to repose, though I had other questions to propound." The instant she had spoken, the water became smooth, and the fishes at once disappeared.

Carathis, inflated with the venom of her projects, strode hastily over the rock, and found the amiable Gulchenrouz asleep in an arbour, whilst the two dwarfs were watching at his side, and ruminating their accustomed prayers. These diminutive personages possessed the gift of divining whenever an enemy to good Mussulmans approached; thus they anticipated the arrival of Carathis, who, stopping short, said to herself, "How placidly doth he recline his lovely little head! how pale and languishing are his looks! it is just the very child of my wishes!" The dwarfs interrupted this delectable soliloquy by leaping instantly upon her, and scratching her face with their utmost zeal. But Nerkes and Cafour, betaking themselves to the succour of their mistress, pinched the dwarfs so severely in return, that they both gave up the ghost, imploring Mahomet to inflict his sorest vengeance upon this wicked woman and all her household.

At the noise which this strange conflict occasioned in the valley, Gulchenrouz awoke, and bewildered with terror, sprung impetuously and climbed an old fig-tree that rose against the acclivity of the rocks; from thence he gained their summits, and ran for two hours without once looking back. At last, exhausted with fatigue, he fell senseless into the arms of a good old genius, whose fondness for the company of children had made it his sole occupation to protect them. Whilst performing his wonted rounds through the air, he had pounced on the cruel Giaour, at the instant of his growling in the horrible chasm, and had rescued the fifty little victims which the impiety of Vathek had devoted to his voracity. These the genius brought up in nests still higher than the clouds, and himself fixed his abode in a nest more capacious than the rest, from which he had expelled the rocs that had built it.

These inviolable asylums were defended against the dives and the afrits by waving streamers; on which were inscribed in characters of gold, that flashed like lightning, the names of Alla and the Prophet. It was there that Gulchenrouz, who as yet remained undeceived with respect to his pretended death, thought himself in the mansions of eternal peace. He admitted without fear the congratulations of his little friends, who were all assembled in the nest of the venerable genius, and vied with each other in kissing his serene forehead and beautiful eyelids. Remote from the inquietudes of the world, the impertinence of harems, the brutality of eunuchs, and the inconstancy of women, there he found a place truly congenial to the delights of his soul. In this peaceable society his days, months, and years glided on; nor was he less happy than the rest of his companions: for the genius, instead of burdening his pupils with perishable riches and vain sciences, conferred upon them the boon of perpetual childhood.

Carathis, unaccustomed to the loss of her prey, vented a thousand execrations on her negresses, for not seizing the child, instead of amusing themselves with pinching to death two insignificant dwarfs from which they could gain no advantage. She returned into the valley murmuring; and, finding that her son was not risen from the arms of Nouronihar, discharged her ill-humour upon both. The idea, however, of departing next day for Istakhar, and of cultivating, through the good offices of the Giaour, an intimacy with Eblis himself, at length consoled her chagrin. But fate had ordained it otherwise.

In the evening, as Carathis was conversing with Dilara, who through her contrivance had become of the party, and whose taste resembled her own, Bababalouk came to acquaint her that the sky towards Samarah looked of a fiery red, and seemed to portend some alarming disaster. Immediately recurring to her astrolabes and instruments of magic, she took the altitude of the planets, and discovered, by her calculations, to her great mortification, that a formidable revolt had taken place at Samarah, that Motavakel, availing himself of the disgust which was inveterate against his brother, had incited commotions amongst the populace, made himself master of the palace, and actually invested the great tower, to which Morakanabad had retired, with a handful of the few that still remained faithful to Vathek.

"What!" exclaimed she; "must I lose, then, my tower! my mutes! my negresses! my mummies! and, worse than all, the laboratory, the favourite resort of my nightly lucubrations, without knowing, at least, if my hare-brained son will complete his adventure? No! I will not be the dupe! immediately will I speed to support Morakanabad. By my formidable art, the clouds shall pour grape-shot in the faces of the assailants, and shafts of red-hot iron on their heads. I will let loose my stores of hungry serpents and torpedoes from beneath them; and we shall soon see the stand they will make against such an explosion!"

Having thus spoken, Carathis hasted to her son, who was tranquilly banqueting with Nouronihar in his superb carnation-coloured tent. "Glutton that thou art!" cried she; "were it not for me, thou wouldst soon find thyself the mere commander of savoury pies. Thy faithful subjects have abjured the faith they swore to thee. Motavakel, thy brother, now reigns on the hill of Pied Horses, and, had I not some slight resources in the tower, would not be easily persuaded to abdicate. But, that time may not be lost, I shall only add a few words: Strike tent to-night; set forward; and beware how thou loiterest again by the way. Though thou hast forfeited the conditions of the parchment, I am not yet without hope; for it cannot be denied that thou hast violated, to admiration, the laws of hospitality by seducing the daughter of the emir, after having partaken of his bread and his salt. Such a conduct cannot but be delightful to the Giaour; and if, on thy march, thou canst signalize thyself by an additional crime, all will still go well, and thou shalt enter the palace of Soliman in triumph. Adieu! Alboufaki and my negresses are waiting at the door."

The caliph had nothing to offer in reply: he wished his mother a prosperous journey, and ate on till he had finished his supper. At midnight the camp broke up, amidst the flourishing of trumpets and other martial instruments; but loud indeed must have been the sound of the timbals, to overpower the blubbering of the emir and his grey-beards; who, by an excessive profusion of tears, had so far exhausted the radical moisture, that their eyes shrivelled up in their sockets, and their hairs dropped off by the roots. Nouronihar, to whom such a symphony was painful, did not grieve to get out of hearing. She accompanied the caliph in the imperial litter, where they amused themselves with imagining the splendour which was soon to surround them. The other women, overcome with dejection, were dolefully rocked in their cages; whilst Dilara consoled herself with anticipating the joy of celebrating the rites of fire on the stately terraces of Istakhar.

In four days they reached the spacious valley of Rocnabad. The season of spring was in all its vigour; and the grotesque branches of the almond trees in full blossom, fantastically chequered with hyacinths and jonquils, breathed forth a delightful fragrance. Myriads of bees, and scarce fewer of santons, had there taken up their abode. On the banks of the stream, hives and oratories were alternately ranged; and their neatness and whiteness were set off by the deep green of the cypresses that spired up amongst them. These pious personages amused themselves with cultivating little gardens, that abounded with flowers and fruits; especially musk-melons of the best flavour that Persia could boast. Sometimes dispersed over the meadow, they entertained themselves with feeding peacocks whiter than snow, and turtles more blue than the sapphire. In this manner were they occupied when the harbingers of the imperial procession began to proclaim, "Inhabitants of Rocnabad! prostrate yourselves on the brink of your pure waters; and tender your thanksgivings to Heaven, that vouchsafeth to show you a ray of its glory: for, lo! the commander of the faithful draws near."

The poor santons, filled with holy energy, having bustled to light up wax torches in their oratories, and expand the Koran on their ebony desks, went forth to meet the caliph with baskets of honeycomb, dates, and melons. But, whilst they were advancing in solemn procession and with measured steps, the horses, camels, and guards wantoned over their tulips and other flowers, and made a terrible havoc amongst them. The santons could not help casting from one eye a look of pity on the ravages committing around them; whilst the other was fixed upon the caliph and heaven. Nouronihar, enraptured with the scenery of a place which brought back to her remembrance the pleasing solitudes where her infancy had passed, entreated Vathek to stop: but he, suspecting that these oratories might be deemed by the Giaour an habitation, commanded his pioneers to level them all. The santons stood motionless with horror at the barbarous mandate, and

at last broke out into lamentations; but these were uttered with
so ill a grace, that Vathek bade his eunuchs to kick them from his
presence. He then descended from the litter with Nouronihar.
They sauntered together in the meadow; and amused themselves
with culling flowers, and passing a thousand pleasantries on each
other. But the bees, who were staunch Mussulmans, thinking it
their duty to revenge the insult offered to their dear masters the
santons, assembled so zealously to do it with good effect, that the
caliph and Nouronihar were glad to find their tents prepared to
receive them.

Bababalouk, who, in capacity of purveyor, had acquitted himself with applause as to peacocks and turtles, lost no time in con-
signing some dozens to the spit, and as many more to be fricasseed.
Whilst they were feasting, laughing, carousing, and blaspheming
at pleasure on the banquet so liberally furnished, the moullahs,
the sheiks, the cadis, and imans of Schiraz (who seemed not to
have met the santons) arrived; leading by bridles of riband,
inscribed from the Koran, a train of asses which were loaded
with the choicest fruits the country could boast. Having presented their offerings to the caliph, they petitioned him to honour
their city and mosques with his presence. "Fancy not," said
Vathek, "that you can detain me. Your presence I condescend to
accept, but beg you will let me be quiet, for I am not over-fond
of resisting temptation. Retire, then; yet, as it is not decent for
personages so reverend to return on foot, and as you have not the
appearance of expert riders, my eunuchs shall tie you on your
asses, with the precaution that your backs be not turned towards
me; for they understand etiquette."—In this deputation were some
high-stomached sheiks, who, taking Vathek for a fool, scrupled
not to speak their opinion. These Bababalouk girded with double
cords; and having well disciplined their asses with nettles behind,
they all started, with a preternatural alertness, plunging, kicking,
and running foul of one another, in the most ludicrous manner
imaginable.

Nouronihar and the caliph mutually contended who should
most enjoy so degrading a sight. They burst out in peals of
laughter to see the old men and their asses fall into the stream.
The leg of one was fractured; the shoulder of another dislo-
cated; the teeth of a third dashed out; and the rest suffered still
worse.

Two days more undisturbed by fresh embassies, having been

devoted to the pleasures of Rocnabad, the expedition proceeded; leaving Schiraz on the right, and verging towards a large plain; from whence were discernible, on the edge of the horizon, the dark summits of the mountains of Istakhar.

At this prospect the caliph and Nouronihar were unable to repress their transports. They bounded from their litter to the ground, and broke forth into such wild exclamations, as amazed all within hearing. Interrogating each other, they shouted, "Are we not approaching the radiant palace of light? or gardens, more delightful than those of Sheddad?"—Infatuated mortals! they thus indulged delusive conjecture, unable to fathom the decrees of the Most High!

The good genii, who had not totally relinquished the superintendence of Vathek, repairing to Mahomet in the seventh heaven, said, "Merciful Prophet! stretch forth thy propitious arms towards thy vicegerent; who is ready to fall, irretrievably, into the snare which his enemies, the dives, have prepared to destroy him. The Giaour is awaiting his arrival, in the abominable palace of fire; where, if he once set his foot, his perdition will be inevitable." Mahomet answered, with an air of indignation, "He hath too well deserved to be resigned to himself; but I permit you to try if one effort more will be effectual to divert him from pursuing his ruin."

One of these beneficent genii, assuming, without delay, the exterior of a shepherd, more renowned for his piety than all the dervishes and santons of the region, took his station near a flock of white sheep, on the slope of a hill; and began to pour forth from his flute such airs of pathetic melody, as subdued the very soul, and, wakening remorse, drove far from it every frivolous fancy. At these energetic sounds, the sun hid himself beneath a gloomy cloud; and the waters of two little lakes, that were naturally clearer than crystal, became of a colour like blood. The whole of this superb assembly was involuntarily drawn towards the declivity of the hill. With downcast eyes, they all stood abashed; each upbraiding himself with the evil he had done. The heart of Dilara palpitated; and the chief of the eunuchs, with a sigh of contrition, implored pardon of the women, whom, for his own satisfaction, he had so often tormented.

Vathek and Nouronihar turned pale in their litter; and, regarding each other with haggard looks, reproached themselves—

the one with a thousand of the blackest crimes, a thousand projects of impious ambition; the other with the desolation of her family, and the perdition of the amiable Gulchenrouz. Nouronihar persuaded herself that she heard, in the fatal music, the groans of her dying father; and Vathek, the sobs of the fifty children he had sacrificed to the Giaour. Amidst these complicated pangs of anguish, they perceived themselves impelled towards the shepherd, whose countenance was so commanding that Vathek, for the first time, felt overawed; whilst Nouronihar concealed her face with her hands. The music paused; and the genius, addressing the caliph, said, "Deluded prince! to whom Providence hath confided the care of innumerable subjects, is it thus that thou fulfillest thy mission? Thy crimes are already completed; and art thou now listening towards thy punishment? Thou knowest that, beyond these mountains, Eblis and his accursed dives hold their infernal empire; and, seduced by a malignant phantom, thou art proceeding to surrender thyself to them! This moment is the last of grace allowed thee: abandon thy atrocious purpose: return: give back Nouronihar to her father, who still retains a few sparks of life: destroy thy tower with all its abominations: drive Carathis from thy councils: be just to thy subjects: respect the ministers of the Prophet: compensate for thy impieties by an exemplary life; and, instead of squandering thy days in voluptuous indulgence, lament thy crimes on the sepulchres of thy ancestors. Thou beholdest the clouds that obscure the sun: at the instant he recovers his splendour, if thy heart be not changed, the time of mercy assigned thee will be past for ever."

Vathek, depressed with fear, was on the point of prostrating himself at the feet of the shepherd, whom he perceived to be of a nature superior to man: but, his pride prevailing, he audaciously lifted his head, and, glancing at him one of his terrible looks, said, "Whoever thou art, withhold thy useless admonitions: thou wouldst either delude me, or art thyself deceived. If what I have done be so criminal as thou pretendest, there remains not for me a moment of grace. I have traversed a sea of blood to acquire a power which will make thy equals tremble; deem not that I shall retire when in view of the port, or that I will relinquish her who is dearer to me than either my life or thy mercy. Let the sun appear! let him illume my career! it matters not where it may end."
On uttering these words, which made even the genius shudder,

Vathek threw himself into the arms of Nouronihar, and commanded that his horses should be forced back to the road.

There was no difficulty in obeying these orders, for the attraction had ceased: the sun shone forth in all his glory, and the shepherd vanished with a lamentable scream.

The fatal impression of the music of the genius remained, notwithstanding, in the heart of Vathek's attendants. They viewed each other with looks of consternation. At the approach of night almost all of them escaped; and of this numerous assemblage there only remained the chief of the eunuchs, some idolatrous slaves, Dilara, and a few other women who, like herself, were votaries of the religion of the Magi.

The caliph, fired with the ambition of prescribing laws to the powers of darkness, was but little embarrassed at this dereliction. The impetuosity of his blood prevented him from sleeping; nor did he encamp any more as before. Nouronihar, whose impatience, if possible, exceeded his own, importuned him to hasten his march, and lavished on him a thousand caresses, to beguile all reflection. She fancied herself already more potent than Balkis, and pictured to her imagination the genii falling prostrate at the foot of her throne. In this manner they advanced by moonlight till they came within view of the two towering rocks that form a kind of portal to the valley, at the extremity of which rose the vast ruins of Istakhar. Aloft on the mountain glimmered the fronts of various royal mausoleums, the horror of which was deepened by the shadows of night. They passed through two villages almost deserted, the only inhabitants remaining being a few feeble old men, who, at the sight of horses and litters, fell upon their knees, and cried out, "O Heaven! is it then by these phantoms that we have been for six months tormented? Alas! it was from the terror of these spectres, and the noise beneath the mountains, that our people have fled, and left us at the mercy of the maleficent spirits!" The caliph, to whom these complaints were but unpromising auguries, drove over the bodies of these wretched old men, and at length arrived at the foot of the terrace of black marble. There he descended from his litter, handing down Nouronihar. Both with beating hearts stared wildly around them, and expected, with an apprehensive shudder, the approach of the Giaour; but nothing as yet announced his appearance.

A deathlike stillness reigned over the mountain and through

the air; the moon dilated on a vast platform the shades of the lofty columns, which reached from the terrace almost to the clouds; the gloomy watch-towers, whose number could not be counted, were covered by no roof; and their capitals, of an archi-tecture unknown in the records of the earth, served as an asylum for the birds of night, which, alarmed at the approach of such visitants, fled away croaking.

The chief of the eunuchs, trembling with fear, besought Vathek that a fire might be kindled. "No," replied he, "there is no time left to think of such trifles. Abide where thou art, and expect my commands." Having thus spoken, he presented his hand to Nou-ronihar; and ascending the steps of a vast staircase, reached the terrace, which was flagged with squares of marble, and resembled a smooth expanse of water, upon whose surface not a blade of grass ever dared to vegetate. On the right rose the watch-towers, ranged before the ruins of an immense palace, whose walls were embossed with various figures. In front stood forth the colossal forms of four creatures, composed of the leopard and the griffin, and though but of stone, inspired emotions of terror. Near these were distinguished, by the splendour of the moon, which streamed full on the place, characters like those on the sabres of the Giaour, and which possessed the same virtue of changing every moment. These, after vacillating for some time, fixed at last in Arabic let-ters, and prescribed to the caliph the following words: "Vathek, thou hast violated the conditions of my parchment, and deservest to be sent back; but in favour to thy companion, and as the meed for what thou hast done to obtain it, Eblis permitteth that the portal of his palace shall be opened, and the subterranean fire will receive thee into the number of its adorers."

He scarcely had read these words before the mountain, against which the terrace was reared, trembled, and the watch-towers were ready to topple headlong upon them; the rock yawned, and dis-closed within it a staircase of polished marble, that seemed to ap-proach the abyss. Upon each stair were planted two large torches, like those Nouronihar had seen in her vision, the camphorated vapour of which ascended and gathered itself into a cloud under the hollow of the vault.

This appearance, instead of terrifying, gave new courage to the daughter of Fakreddin. Scarcely deigning to bid adieu to the moon and the firmament, she abandoned without hesitation the pure atmosphere, to plunge into these infernal exhalations. The gait of those impious personages was haughty and determined. As they descended, by the effulgence of the torches, they gazed on each other with mutual admiration, and both appeared so resplendent that they already esteemed themselves spiritual intelligences. The only circumstance that perplexed them was their not arriving at the bottom of the stairs: on hastening their descent with an ardent impetuosity, they felt their steps accelerated to such a degree, that they seemed not walking but falling from a precipice. Their progress, however, was at length impeded by a vast portal of ebony, which the caliph without difficulty recognized. Here the Giaour awaited them with the key in his hand. "Ye are welcome!" said he to them, with a ghastly smile, "in spite of Mahomet and all his dependents. I will now usher you into that palace where you have so highly merited a place." Whilst he was uttering these words he touched the enamelled lock with his key, and the doors at once flew open with a noise still louder than the thunder of the dog-days, and as suddenly recoiled the moment they had entered.

The caliph and Nouronihar beheld each other with amazement at finding themselves in a place which, though roofed with a vaulted ceiling, was so spacious and lofty, that at first they took it for an immeasurable plain. But their eyes at length growing familiar to the grandeur of the surrounding objects, they extended their view to those at a distance, and discovered rows of columns and arcades, which gradually diminished, till they terminated in a point radiant as the sun when he darts his last beams athwart the ocean. The pavement, strewed over with gold dust and saffron, exhaled so subtle an odour as almost overpowered them. They, however, went on, and observed an infinity of censers, in which ambergris and the wood of aloes were continually burning. Between the several columns were placed tables, each spread with a profusion of viands, and wines of every species sparkling in vases of crystal. A throng of genii and other fantastic spirits of either sex danced lasciviously at the sound of music which issued from beneath.

In the midst of this immense hall, a vast multitude was incessantly passing, who severally kept their right hands on their hearts, without once regarding anything around them: they had all the livid paleness of death. Their eyes, deep sunk in their sockets, resembled those phosphoric meteors that glimmer by night in places of interment. Some stalked slowly on, absorbed in profound reverie; some, shrieking with agony, ran furiously about like tigers wounded with poisoned arrows; whilst others, grinding their teeth in rage, foamed along more frantic than the wildest maniac. They all avoided each other; and, though surrounded by a multitude that no one could number, each wandered at random unheedful of the rest, as if alone on a desert where no foot had trodden.

Vathek and Nouronihar, frozen with terror at a sight so baleful, demanded of the Giaour what these appearances might mean, and why these ambulating spectres never withdrew their hands from their hearts? "Perplex not yourselves with so much at once," replied he bluntly; "you will soon be acquainted with all: let us haste and present you to Eblis." They continued their way through the multitude: but, notwithstanding their confidence at first, they were not sufficiently composed to examine with attention the various perspectives of halls and of galleries that opened on the right hand and left; which were all illuminated by torches and braziers, whose flames rose in pyramids to the centre of the vault. At length they came to a place where long curtains, brocaded with crimson and gold, fell from all parts in solemn confusion. Here the choirs and dances were heard no longer. The light which glimmered came from afar.

After some time, Vathek and Nouronihar perceived a gleam brightening through the drapery, and entered a vast tabernacle hung round with the skins of leopards. An infinity of elders with streaming beards, and afrits in complete armour, had prostrated themselves before the ascent of a lofty eminence; on the top of which, upon a globe of fire, sat the formidable Eblis. His person was that of a young man, whose noble and regular features seemed to have been tarnished by malignant vapours. In his large eyes appeared both pride and despair: his flowing hair retained some resemblance to that of an angel of light. In his hand, which thunder had blasted, he swayed the iron sceptre that causes the monster Ouranbad, the afrits, and all the powers of the abyss to tremble. At his presence, the heart of the caliph sunk within him; and he fell prostrate on his face. Nouronihar, however, though greatly dismayed, could not help admiring the person of Eblis; for she expected to have seen some stupendous giant. Eblis, with a voice more mild than might be imagined, but such as penetrated the soul and filled it with the deepest melancholy, said, "Creatures of clay, I receive you into mine empire: ye are numbered amongst my adorers: enjoy whatever this palace affords: the treasures of the pre-Adamite sultans, their fulminating sabres, and those talismans that compel the dives to open the subterranean expanses of the mountain of Kaf, which communicate with these. There, insatiable as your curiosity may be, shall you find sufficient objects to gratify it. You shall possess the exclusive privilege of entering the fortresses of Aherman, and the halls of Argenk, where are portrayed all creatures endowed with intelligence; and the various animals that inhabited the earth prior to the creation of that contemptible being whom ye denominate the father of mankind."

Vathek and Nouronihar, feeling themselves revived and encouraged by this harangue, eagerly said to the Giaour, "Bring us instantly to the place which contains these precious talismans."—"Come," answered this wicked dive, with his malignant grin—"come and possess all that my sovereign hath promised, and more." He then conducted them into a long aisle adjoining the tabernacle; preceding them with hasty steps, and followed by his disciples with the utmost alacrity. They reached, at length, a hall of great extent, and covered with a lofty dome; around which appeared fifty portals of bronze, secured with as many fastenings of iron. A funereal gloom prevailed over the whole scene. Here, upon two beds of incorruptible cedar, lay recumbent the fleshless forms of the pre-Adamite kings, who had been monarchs of the whole earth. They still possessed enough of life to be conscious of their deplorable condition. Their eyes retained a melancholy motion; they regarded one another with looks of the deepest dejection, each holding his right hand, motionless, on his heart. At their feet were inscribed the events of their several reigns, their power, their pride, and their crimes; Soliman Raad, Soliman Daki, and Soliman, called Gian Ben Gian, who, after having chained up the dives in the dark caverns of Kaf, became so presumptuous as to doubt of the Supreme Power. All these maintained great state, though not to be compared with the eminence of Soliman Ben Daoud.

This king, so renowned for his wisdom, was on the loftiest elevation, and placed immediately under the dome. He appeared to possess more animation than the rest. Though, from time to time, he laboured with profound sighs; and, like his companions, kept his right hand on his heart, yet his countenance was more composed, and he seemed to be listening to the sullen roar of a cataract visible in part through one of the grated portals. This was the only sound that intruded on the silence of these doleful mansions. A range of brazen cases surrounded the elevation. "Remove the covers from these cabalistic depositories," said the Giaour to Vathek, "and avail thyself of the talismans which will break asunder all these gates of bronze, and not only render thee master of the treasures contained within them, but also of the spirits by which they are guarded."

The caliph, whom this ominious preliminary had entirely disconcerted, approached the vase with faltering footsteps; and was ready to sink with terror when he heard the groans of Soliman. As he proceeded, a voice from the livid lips of the prophet articulated these words: "In my lifetime I filled a magnificent throne; having, on my right hand, twelve thousand seats of gold, where the patriarchs and the prophets heard my doctrines: on my left, the sages and doctors, upon as many thrones of silver, were present at all my decisions. Whilst I thus administered justice to innumerable multitudes, the birds of the air, hovering over me, served as a canopy against the rays of the sun. My people flourished; and my palace rose to the clouds. I erected a temple to the Most High, which was the wonder of the universe; but I basely suffered myself to be seduced by the love of women, and a curiosity that could not be restrained by sublunary things. I listened to the counsels of Aherman and the daughter of Pharaoh; and adored fire and the hosts of heaven. I forsook the holy city, and commanded the genii to rear the stupendous palace of Istakhar, and the terrace of the watch-towers; each of which was consecrated to a star. There, for a while, I enjoyed myself in the zenith of glory and pleasure. Not only men but supernatural beings were subject also to my will. I began to think, as these unhappy monarchs around had already thought, that the vengeance of Heaven was asleep; when, at once, the thunder burst my structures asunder, and precipitated me hither: where, however, I do not remain, like the other inhabitants, totally destitute of hope; for an angel of light hath revealed that in consideration of the piety of my early youth my woes shall come to an end, when this cataract shall

for ever cease to flow. Till then I am in torments, ineffable torments! an unrelenting fire preys on my heart."

Having uttered this exclamation, Soliman raised his hands towards heaven, in token of supplication; and the caliph discerned
through his bosom, which was transparent as crystal, his heart
enveloped in flames. At a sight so full of horror, Nouronihar fell
back, like one petrified, into the arms of Vathek, who cried out
with a convulsive sob, "O Giaour! whither hast thou brought us!
Allow us to depart, and I will relinquish all thou hast promised.
O Mahomet! remains there no more mercy?"—"None! none!" replied the malicious dive. "Know, miserable prince! thou art now
in the abode of vengeance and despair. Thy heart, also, will be
kindled like those of the other votaries of Eblis. A few days are
allotted thee previous to this fatal period: employ them as thou
wilt; recline on these heaps of gold; command the infernal potentates; range, at thy pleasure, through these immense subterranean
domains: no barrier shall be shut against thee. As for me, I have
fulfilled my mission: I now leave thee to thyself." At these words
he vanished.

The caliph and Nouronihar remained in the most abject affliction. Their tears were unable to flow, and scarcely could they support themselves. At length, taking each other despondingly by
the hand, they went faltering from this fatal hall, indifferent
which way they turned their steps. Every portal opened at their
approach. The dives fell prostrate before them. Every reservoir of
riches was disclosed to their view; but they no longer felt the incentives of curiosity, of pride, or avarice. With like apathy they
heard the chorus of genii, and saw the stately banquets prepared
to regale them. They went wandering on, from chamber to
chamber, hall to hall, and gallery to gallery; all without bounds
or limit; all distinguishable by the same lowering gloom; all
adorned with the same awful grandeur; all traversed by persons
in search of repose and consolation, but who sought them in
vain; for every one carried within him a heart tormented in
flames. Shunned by these various sufferers, who seemed by their
looks to be upbraiding the partners of their guilt, they withdrew
from them to wait, in direful suspense, the moment which should
render them to each other the like objects of terror.

"What?" exclaimed Nouronihar; "will the time come when I
shall snatch my hand from thine?"—"Ah!" said Vathek, "and

shall my eyes ever cease to drink from thine long draughts of enjoyment? Shall the moments of our reciprocal ecstasies be reflected
on with horror? It was not thou that broughtest me hither; the
principles by which Carathis perverted my youth have been the
sole cause of my perdition! it is but right she should have her
share of it." Having given vent to these painful expressions, he
called to an afrit, who was stirring up one of the braziers, and
bade him fetch the Princess Carathis from the palace of Samarah.

After issuing these orders, the caliph and Nouronihar continued walking amidst the silent crowd, till they heard voices at the
end of the gallery. Presuming them to proceed from some unhappy beings, who, like themselves, were awaiting their final
doom, they followed the sound, and found it to come from a small
square chamber, where they discovered, sitting on sofas, four
young men of goodly figure, and a lovely female, who were holding a melancholy conversation by the glimmering of a lonely
lamp. Each had a gloomy and forlorn air; and two of them were
embracing each other with great tenderness. On seeing the caliph
and the daughter of Fakreddin enter, they arose, saluted, and
made room for them. Then he who appeared the most considerable of the group, addressed himself thus to Vathek: "Strangers!
who doubtless are in the same state of suspense with ourselves, as
you do not yet bear your hand on your heart, if you come hither
to pass the interval allotted, previous to the infliction of our common punishment, condescend to relate the adventures that have
brought you to this fatal place; and we, in return, will acquaint
you with ours, which deserve but too well to be heard. To trace
back our crimes to their source, though we are not permitted to
repent, is the only employment suited to wretches like us!"

The caliph and Nouronihar assented to the proposal; and
Vathek began, not without tears and lamentations, a sincere recital of every circumstance that had passed. When the afflicting
narrative was closed, the young man entered on his own. Each
person proceeded in order; and, when the third prince had
reached the midst of his adventures, a sudden noise interrupted
him, which caused the vault to tremble and to open.

Immediately a cloud descended, which, gradually dissipating,
discovered Carathis on the back of an afrit, who grievously complained of his burden. She, instantly springing to the ground, advanced towards her son, and said, "What dost thou here, in this

little square chamber? As the dives are become subject to thy beck, I expected to have found thee on the throne of the pre-Adamite kings."

"Execrable woman!" answered the caliph; "cursed be the day thou gavest me birth! Go, follow this afrit; let him conduct thee to the hall of the prophet Soliman: there thou wilt learn to what these palaces are destined, and how much I ought to abhor the impious knowledge thou hast taught me."

"Has the height of power, to which thou art arrived, turned thy brain?" answered Carathis; "but I ask no more than permission to show my respect for Soliman the prophet. It is, however, proper thou shouldst know that (as the afrit has informed me neither of us shall return to Samarah) I requested his permission to arrange my affairs, and he politely consented. Availing myself, therefore, of the few moments allowed me, I set fire to the tower, and consumed in it the mutes, negresses, and serpents, which have rendered me so much good service; nor should I have been less kind to Morakanabad, had he not prevented me, by deserting at last to thy brother. As for Bababalouk, who had the folly to return to Samarah, to provide husbands for thy wives, I undoubtedly would have put him to the torture; but being in a hurry, I only hung him, after having decoyed him in a snare, with thy wives, whom I buried alive by the help of my negresses, who thus spent their last moments greatly to their satisfaction. With respect to Dilara, who ever stood high in my favour, she hath evinced the greatness of her mind, by fixing herself near, in the service of one of the magi; and, I think, will soon be one of our society."

Vathek, too much cast down to express the indignation excited by such a discourse, ordered the afrit to remove Carathis from his presence, and continued immersed in thoughts which his companions durst not disturb.

Carathis, however, eagerly entered the dome of Soliman, and without regarding in the least the groans of the prophet, undauntedly removed the covers of the vases and violently seized on the talismans. Then, with a voice more loud than had hitherto been heard within these mansions, she compelled the dives to disclose to her the most secret treasures, the most profound stores, which the afrit himself had not seen. She passed, by rapid descents, known only to Eblis and his most favoured potentates; and thus penetrated the very entrails of the earth, where breathes the sansar, or the icy wind of death. Nothing appalled her dauntless soul. She perceived, however, in all the inmates who bore their hands on their heart, a little singularity not much to her taste.

As she was emerging from one of the abysses, Eblis stood forth to her view; but notwithstanding he displayed the full effulgence of his infernal majesty, she preserved her countenance unaltered, and even paid her compliments with considerable firmness.

This superb monarch thus answered: "Princess, whose knowledge and whose crimes have merited a conspicuous rank in my empire, thou dost well to avail thyself of the leisure that remains; for the flames and torments, which are ready to seize on thy heart, will not fail to provide thee soon with full employment." He said, and was lost in the curtains of his tabernacle.

Carathis paused for a moment with surprise; but, resolved to follow the advice of Eblis, she assembled all the choirs of genii, and all the dives, to pay her homage. Thus marched she, in triumph, through a vapour of perfumes, amidst the acclamations of all the malignant spirits, with most of whom she had formed a previous acquaintance. She even attempted to dethrone one of the Solimans, for the purpose of usurping his place; when a voice, proceeding from the abyss of death, proclaimed, "All is accomplished!" Instantaneously the haughty forehead of the intrepid princess became corrugated with agony; she uttered a tremendous yell, and fixed, no more to be withdrawn, her right hand upon her heart, which was become a receptacle of eternal fire.

In this delirium, forgetting all ambitious projects, and her thirst for that knowledge which should ever be hidden from mortals, she overturned the offerings of the genii; and, having execrated the hour she was begotten and the womb that had borne her, glanced off in a rapid whirl that rendered her invisible, and continued to revolve without intermission.

Almost at the same instant, the same voice announced to the caliph, Nouronihar, the four princes, and the princess, the awful and irrevocable decree. Their hearts immediately took fire, and they, at once, lost the most precious gift of heaven—HOPE. These unhappy beings recoiled, with looks of the most furious distraction. Vathek beheld in the eyes of Nouronihar nothing but rage and vengeance; nor could she discern aught in his but aversion and despair. The two princes who were friends, and, till that moment, had preserved their attachment, shrunk back, gnashing their teeth with mutual and unchangeable hatred. Kalilah and his sister made reciprocal gestures of imprecation; all testified their horror for each other by the most ghastly convulsions, and screams that could not be smothered. All severally plunged themselves into the accursed multitude, there to wander in an eternity of unabating anguish.

Such was, and such should be, the punishment of unrestrained passions and atrocious deeds! Such shall be the chastisement of that blind curiosity, which would transgress those bounds the wisdom of the Creator has prescribed to human knowledge; and such the dreadful disappointment of that restless ambition, which, aiming at discoveries reserved for beings of a supernatural order, perceives not, through its infatuated pride, that the condition of man upon earth is to be—humble and ignorant.

Thus the caliph Vathek, who, for the sake of empty pomp and forbidden power, had sullied himself with a thousand crimes, became a prey to grief without end, and remorse without mitigation; whilst the humble, the despised Gulchenrouz passed whole ages in undisturbed tranquillity, and in the pure happiness of childhood.

Notes

PAGE 109. *Caliph*

This title, amongst the Mahometans, comprehends the concrete character of Prophet, Priest, and King, and is used to signify *the Vicar of God on Earth*. It is, at this day, one of the titles of the Grand Signior, as successor of Mahomet; and of the Sophi of Persia, as successor of Ali.—HABESCI'S *State of the Ottoman Empire,* p. 9. D'HERBELOT, p. 985.

PAGE 109. *. . . one of his eyes became so terrible*

The author of *Nighiaristan* hath preserved a fact that supports this account; and there is no history of Vathek in which his *terrible eye* is not mentioned.

PAGE 109. *Omar Ben Abdalaziz*

This caliph was eminent above all others for temperance and self-denial, insomuch that he is believed to have been raised to Mahomet's bosom, as a reward for his abstinence in an age of corruption.—D'HERBELOT, p. 690.

PAGE 109. *Samarah*

A city of the Babylonian Irak; supposed to have stood on the site where Nimrod erected his tower. Khondemir relates, in his life of Motassem, that this prince, to terminate the disputes which were perpetually happening between the inhabitants of Bagdat and his Turkish slaves, withdrew from thence, and having fixed on a situation in the plain of Catoul, there founded Samarah. He is said to have had, in the stables of this city, a hundred and thirty thousand *pied horses,* each of which carried, by his order, a sack of earth to a place he had chosen. By this accumulation an elevation was formed that commanded a view of all Samarah, and served for the foundation of his magnificent palace.—D'HERBELOT, pp. 752, 808, 985. *Anecdotes Arabes,* p. 413.

PAGE 110. *. . . in the most delightful succession*

The great men of the East have been always fond of music. Though forbidden by the Mahometan religion, it commonly makes a part of every entertainment. *Nitimur in vetitum semper.* Female slaves are generally kept to amuse them and the ladies of their harems. The Persian Khanyagere seems nearly to have resembled our old English minstrel; as he usually accompanied his barbut, or lute, with heroic songs. Their musicians appear to have known the art of moving the passions, and to have generally directed their music to the heart. Al Farabi, a philosopher, who died about the middle of the tenth century, on his return from the pilgrimage of Mecca, introduced himself, though a stranger, at the court of Seifeddoula, Sultan of Syria. Musicians were accidentally performing, and he joined them. The prince admired him, and wished to hear something of his own. He drew a composition from his pocket, and distributing the parts amongst the band, the first movement threw the prince and his courtiers into violent laughter, the next melted all into tears, and the last lulled even the performers asleep.—RICHARDSON's *Dissertation on the Languages, &c., of Eastern Nations,* p. 211.

PAGE 110. *Mani*

This artist, whom Inatulla of Delhi styles *the far-famed,* lived in the reign of Schabur, or Sapor, the son of Ardschir Babegan, was founder of the sect of Manichaeans, and was, by profession, a painter and sculptor. His pretensions, supported by an uncommon skill in mechanical contrivances, induced the ignorant to believe that his powers were more than human. After having secluded himself from his followers, under the pretence of passing a year in heaven, he produced a wonderful volume, which he affirmed to have brought from thence; containing images and figures of a marvellous nature.—D'HERBELOT, p. 458. It appears, from the *Arabian Nights,* that Haroun al Raschid, Vathek's grandfather, had adorned his palace and furnished his magnificent pavilion with the most capital performances of the Persian artists.

PAGE 110. *Houris*

The virgins of Paradise, called, from their large black eyes,* *Hur al oyun.* An intercourse with these, according to the institution of Mahomet, is to constitute the principal felicity of the faithful. Not formed of clay, like mortal women, they are deemed in the highest degree beautiful, and exempt from every inconvenience incident to the sex.—*Al Koran; passim.*

PAGE 111. *. . . it was not with the orthodox that he usually held*

Vathek persecuted, with extreme rigour, all who defended the eternity of the Koran; which the Sonnites, or orthodox, maintained to be uncreated, and the Motazalites and Schiites as strenuously denied.—D'HERBELOT, p. 85, etc.

* Might not Akenside's expression,

        In the dark Heaven of Mira's eye,

have been suggested by the eyes of the virgins of Paradise?
    The enthusiasm of the acute Winckelmann for the statuary of the ancients was apt to mislead both his judgment and taste. What but such a bias could induce him to maintain—after asserting that Homer meant by the word βοῶπις, to characterize the beauty of Juno's eyes, and citing with approbation ΜΕΛ-ΑΝΟΦΘΑΛΜΟΣ—ΚΑΛΗ ΤΟ ΠΡΟΣΩΠΟΝ as the gloss of the scholiast upon it, that the epithet the poet had selected was designed by him to express, not what it naturally imports, but a sense independent of it, and which it could

PAGE 111.   *Mahomet in the seventh heaven*

In this heaven, the paradise of Mahomet is supposed to be placed, contiguous to the throne of Alla. Hagi Khalfah relates, that Ben Iatmaiah, a celebrated doctor of Damascus, had the temerity to assert that, when the Most High erected his throne, he reserved a vacant place for Mahomet upon it.

PAGE 111.   *Genii*

Genn, or *Ginn,* in the Arabic, signifies a Genius or Demon, a being of a higher order, and formed of more subtile matter than man. According to Oriental mythology, the Genii governed the world long before the creation of Adam. The Mahometans regarded them as an intermediate race between angels and men, and capable of salvation; whence Mahomet pretended a commission to convert them. Consonant to this, we read that, *when the* Servant of God *stood up to invoke him, it wanted little but that the* Genii *had pressed on him in crowds, to hear him rehearse the Koran.*—D'HERBELOT, p. 375. *Al Koran,* ch. 72. It is asserted, and not without plausible reasons, that the words *Genn, Ginn—Genius, Genie, Gian, Gigas, Giant, Géant*—proceed from the same themes, viz. Γῆ, *the earth,* and γάω, *to produce;* as if these supernatural agents had been an early production of the earth, long before Adam was modelled out from a lump of it. The Ὄντες and Ἔωντες of Plato bear a close analogy to these supposed intermediate creatures between God and man. From these premises arose the consequence that, boasting a higher order, formed of more subtile matter, and possessed of much greater knowledge, than man, they lorded over this planet, and invisibly governed it with superior intellect. From this last circumstance they obtained in Greece the title of Δαίμονες, Demons, from δάημων, *sciens,* knowing. The Hebrew word, נפלים, Nephilim (Gen. vi, 4), translated by *Gigantes,* giants, claiming the same etymon with νεφέλη, a cloud, seems also to indicate that these intellectual beings inhabited the void expanse of the terrestrial at-

---

only be supposed to imply from being placed in an absurd connection? The eye of the animal to which the term belongs is, no doubt, large, if referred to the human countenance; but not properly so in its own situation. Had Homer applied βοῶπις to the statue of Juno, βοῶπις (as the Abbé contends) must have been interpreted large-eyed; because in this relation no idea, except that of magnitude [unless we add prominence], could possibly be extorted from it; but it must be allowed, on the same principle, that an epithet taken from the eye of the ass, or any other creature's of equal size, whatever were its colour, would have become the statue of the goddess as well, and signified precisely the same. On such commentators a poet might justly exclaim:

> Pol, me occidistis, amici,
> Non servastis!

In their descriptions of female beauty, the poets of the East frequently use the same image with Homer; and exactly in his sense. Thus, in particular, Lebeid:

"A company of maidens were seated in the vehicles, with black eyes and graceful motions, like the wild heifers of Tudah."

mosphere. Hence the very ancient fable of men of enormous strength and size revolting against the gods, and all the mythological lore relating to that mighty conflict; unless we trace the origin of this important event to the ambition of Satan, his revolt against the Almighty, and his fall with the angels.

PAGE 111.   *Assist him to complete the tower*

The Genii, who were styled by the Persians *Peris* and *Dives,* were famous for their architectural skill. The pyramids of Egypt have been ascribed to them; and we are told of a strange fortress which they constructed in the remote mountains of Spain, whose frontal presented the following inscription:—

> It is no light task to disclose the portal of this asylum:
> The bolt, rash Passenger, is not of iron; but the tooth of a furious Dragon:
> Know thou that no one can break this charm,
> Till Destiny shall have consigned the key to his adventurous hand.

The Koran relates, that the Genii were employed by Solomon in the erection of his magnificent temple.—BAILLY, *Sur l'Atlantide,* p. 146. D'HERBELOT, p. 8. *Al Koran,* ch. 34.

The reign of Gian Ben Gian over the Peris is said to have continued for two thousand years; after which EBLIS was sent by the Deity to exile them, on account of their disorders, and confine them in the remotest region of the earth.—D'HERBELOT, p. 396. BAILLY, *Sur l'Atlantide,* p. 147.

PAGE 112.   *. . . the stranger displayed such rarities as he had never before seen*

In the *Tales of Inatulla,* we meet with a traveller who, like this, was furnished with trinkets and curiosities of an extraordinary kind. That such were much sought after in the days of Vathek, may be concluded from the encouragement which Haroun al Raschid gave to the mechanic arts, and the present he sent by his ambassadors to Charlemagne. This consisted of a clock, which, when put into motion, by means of a clepsydra, not only pointed out the hours in their round, but also, by dropping small balls on a bell, struck them, and, at the same instant, threw open as many little doors, to let out an equal number of horsemen. Besides these, the clock displayed various other contrivances.—*Ann. Reg. Franc. Pip. Caroli, etc.,* ad ann. 807. WEIDLER, p. 205.

PAGE 112.   *. . . characters on the sabres*

Such inscriptions often occur in Eastern romances. We find, in the *Arabian Nights,* a cornelian, on which *unknown characters* were engraven; and, also, a sabre, like those here described. In the French king's library is a curious treatise, entitled *Sefat Alaclam;* containing a variety of alphabets, arranged under different heads; such as the *prophetic,* the *mystical,* the *philosophic,* the *magical,* the *talismanic,* etc., which seems to have escaped the research of the indefatigable Mr. Astle.—*Arabian Nights,* vol. ii, p. 246; vol. i, p. 143. D'HERBELOT, p. 797.

PAGE 114.   ... *endeavoured by her conversation to appease and compose him*

The same sanative quality is ascribed to soothing conversation both by Aeschylus and Milton:—

> Ὀργῆς νοσούσης εἰσὶν ἰατροὶ λόγοι.
> *Prometh.*, v. 378.

> Apt words have power to swage
> The tumours of a troubled mind;
> And are as balm to fester'd wounds.
> *Samson Agon.*, v. 184.

PAGE 115.   ... *beards burnt off*

The loss of the beard, from the earliest ages, was accounted highly disgraceful. An instance occurs, in the *Tales of Inatulla,* of one being *singed off*, as a mulct on the owner, for having failed to explain a question propounded; and, in the *Arabian Nights,* a proclamation may be seen similar to this of Vathek.—Vol. i. p. 268; vol. ii, p. 228.

PAGE 116.   ... *robes of honour and sequins of gold*

Such rewards were common in the East.—See particularly *Arabian Nights,* vol. ii., pp. 72, 125; vol. iii., p. 64.

PAGE 116.   *The old man put on his green spectacles*

This is an apparent anachronism; but such frequently occur in reading the Arabian writers. It should be remembered, the difficulty of ascertaining facts and fixing the dates of inventions must be considerable in a vast extent of country, where books are comparatively few, and the art of printing unpractised. Though the origin of *spectacles* can be traced back, with certainty, no higher than the thirteenth century, yet the observation of Seneca—that letters appeared of an increased magnitude when viewed through the medium of convex glass—might have been noted also by others, and *a sort of spectacles* contrived, in consequence of it. But, however this might have been, the art of staining glass is sufficiently ancient, to have suggested in the days of Vathek the use of *green,* as a protection to the eye from a glare of light.

PAGE 117.   ... *the stars, which he went to consult*

The phrase of the original corresponds with the Greek expression, Ἄστρα ΒΙΑΖΕΣΘΑΙ· which, in another view, will illustrate St. Matthew xi. 12.

PAGE 118.   ... *to drink at will of the four fountains*

Agathocles (cited by Athenaeus, l. xi., p. 515) relates that "there were *certain fountains in these regions,* to the number of seventy, *whose* WATERS *were denominated* GOLDEN; and of which it was death for any one to drink, save *the* KING *and his eldest son.*" In this number, the four fountains were formerly reckoned; whose waters, as Vathek had no son, *were* sacred *to his own use.*

The citation from Agathocles may likewise explain the wish of King David for *water* from the *well* of *Bethlehem;* unless we suppose it to have arisen from a predilection, like that of the *Parthian monarchs,* for the water of Choaspes, which was carried with them wherever they went, and, from that circumstance, styled by Tibullus, *regia lympha,* and by Milton,

> The *drink* of *none* but *kings.*

PAGE 118.   . . . *bowls of rock crystal*

In the *Arabian Nights,* Schemselnihar and Ebn Thaher were served by three of their attendants, each bringing them a *goblet of rock crystal,* filled with curious wine.

PAGE 118.   *Accursed Giaour!*

Dives of this kind are frequently mentioned by Eastern writers. Consult their tales in general; and especially those of the Fishermen, Aladdin, and the Princess of China.

PAGE 119.   . . . *Drink this draught, said the stranger, as he presented a phial*

A phial of a similar potion is ordered to be instantaneously drunk off in one of the *Tales of Inatulla.* These "brewed enchantments" have been used in the East from the days of Homer. Milton, in his *Comus,* describes one of them, which greatly resembles the Indian's:—

> And first behold this cordial julep here,
> That flames, and dances in his crystal bounds,
> With spirits of balm, and fragrant syrups mixed.
> Not that Nepenthes, which the wife of Thone
> In Egypt gave to Jove-born Helena,
> Is of such power *to stir up joy as this:*
> To *life* so *friendly,* or so *cool* to *thirst.*

PAGE 119.   . . . *The poets applied them as a chorus to all the songs they composed*

Sir John Chardin, describing a public entertainment and rejoicing, observes that the most ingenious poets in Persia (as is related of Homer) sung their own works; which, for the most part, are in praise of the king, whom they fail not to extol, let him be never so worthy of blame and oblivion. The songs of this day were adapted to the occasion of the festival, which was the restoration of the prime minister to his office: he adds, I saw one that abounded in fine and witty turns, the burden of which was this:—

> Him set aside, all men but equals are;
> E'en *Sol* survey'd the spacious realms of air,

To see if he could find another star:
A star, that like the *polar star* could reign;
And long he sought it, but he sought in vain.*

The ingenuity of the poet seems to consist in an allusion to the prime minister's title, *Iran Medave,* or the Pole of Persia.

PAGE 120. *Bababalouk, the chief of his eunuchs*

As it was the employment of the *black eunuchs* to wait upon and guard the sultanas; so the general superintendence of the harem was particularly committed to their chief.—HABESCI's *State of the Ottoman Empire,* pp. 155, 156.

PAGE 120. ... *the divan*

This was both the supreme council and court of justice, at which the caliphs of the race of the Abassides assisted in person, to redress the injuries of every appellant.—D'HERBELOT, p. 298.

PAGE 120. *The officers arranged themselves in a semicircle*

Such was the etiquette, constantly observed, on entering the divan.—*Arabian Nights,* vol. iv, p. 36. D'HERBELOT, p. 912.

PAGE 120. ... *the prime vizier*

Vazir, vezir, or, as we express it, vizier, literally signifies a *porter;* and, by metaphor, the minister who bears the principal burden of the state, generally called the Sublime Porte.

PAGE 121. ... *The Indian, being short and plump, collected himself into a ball, &c.*

Happy as Horace has been in his description of the Wise Man, the figurative expressions which finish the character are literally applicable to our author's Indian:—

In seipso totus, teres atque rotundus;
Externi ni quid valeat per leve morari:
In quem manca ruit semper fortuna.

PAGE 122. *The muezzins and their minarets*

Valid, the son of Abdalmalek, was the first who erected a *minaret,* or turret; and this he placed on the grand mosque at Damascus, for the *muezzin,* or crier, to announce from it the hour of prayer. This practice has constantly been kept to this day.—D'HERBELOT, p. 576.

PAGE 124. ... *The Palace of Subterranean Fire*

Of this palace, which is frequently mentioned in Eastern romance, a full description will be found in the sequel.

* See LLOYD's *Introduction to a Collection of Voyages and Travels, never before published in English,* p. 21.

The name of *David* in Hebrew is composed of the letter ו *Vau* between two ד *Daleths* דוד ; and, according to the Masoretic points, ought to be pronounced *David*. Having no v consonant in their tongue, the Septuagint substituted the letter β for v, and wrote Δαβιδ, *Dabid*. The Syriac reads *Dad* or *Dod;* and the Arabs articulate *Daoud*.

PAGE 125.   *I require the blood of fifty of the most beautiful sons of the viziers*

Amongst the infatuated votaries of the powers of darkness, the most acceptable offering was *the blood of their children*. If the parents were not at hand to make an immediate offer, *the magistrates did not fail to select those who were most fair and promising,* that the demon might not be defrauded of his dues. On one occasion, *two hundred of the prime nobility were sacrificed together*.—BRYANT's *Observations*, p. 279, etc.

PAGE 127.   *. . . Give them me, cried the Indian*

In the story of Codadad and his brother, we read of a *Black,* like this, *who fed upon human blood*.—*Arabian Nights,* vol. iii., p. 199.

PAGE 127.   *. . . with the grin of an ogre*

Thus, in the history of the punished vizier:—"The prince heard enough to convince him of his danger, and then perceived that the lady, who called herself the daughter of an *Indian* king, was an *ogress;* wife to one of those *savage demons* called an ogre, who stay in remote places, and make use of a thousand wiles to surprise and devour passengers."—*Arabian Nights,* vol. i., p. 56.

PAGE 127.   *. . . bracelet*

The bracelet, in the East, was an emblem of royalty.—D'HERBELOT, p. 541. For want of a more proper term to denominate the ornament *serkhooj,* the word *aigret* is here used.

PAGE 129.   *. . . mutes*

It has been usual, in Eastern courts, from time immemorial, to retain a number of mutes. These are not only employed to amuse the monarch, but also to instruct his pages in an art to us little known, of communicating everything by signs, lest the sounds of their voices should disturb the sovereign.—HABESCI's *State of the Ottoman Empire*, p. 164. The mutes are also the secret instruments of his private vengeance, in carrying the fatal string.

PAGE 130.   *Prayer announced at break of day*

The stated seasons of public prayer, in the twenty-four hours, were five: daybreak, noon, midtime between noon and sunset, immediately as the sun leaves the horizon, and an hour and a half after it is down.

PAGE 130. ... *mummies*

Moumia (from *moum,* wax and tallow) signifies the flesh of the human body preserved in the sand, after having been embalmed and wrapped in cerements. They are frequently found in the sepulchres of Egypt; but most of the Oriental mummies are brought from a cavern near Abin, in Persia.—D'HERBELOT, p. 647.

PAGE 131. ... *rhinoceros' horns*

Of their extraordinary qualities and application, a curious account may be seen in the *Bibliothèque Orientale,* and the *Supplement* to it.

PAGE 132. ... *skulls and skeletons*

Both were usually added to the ingredients already mentioned. These magic rites sufficiently resemble the witch scenes of Middleton, Shakespeare, etc., to show their Oriental origin. Nor is it to be wondered if, amongst the many systems adopted from the East, this should have been in the number. It may be seen, from the Arabian Tales, that magic was an art publicly taught; and Father Angelo relates of a rich enchanter, whom he knew at Bassora, that his pupils were so numerous as to occupy an entire quarter of the city.

PAGE 133. *Flagons of wine and vases of sherbet reposing on snow*

Sir John Chardin speaks of a wine much admired in the East, and particularly in Persia, called *roubnar;* which is made from the juice of the pomegranate, and sent abroad in large quantities. The Oriental sherbets, styled by St. Jerome, *sorbitiunculae delicatae,* consisted of various syrups (such as lemon, liquorice, capillaire, etc.) mixed with water. To these, Hasselquist adds several others, and observes, that the sweet-scented violet is a flower greatly esteemed, not only for its smell and colour, but, especially, for its use in *sherbet;* which, when the Easterns intend to entertain their guests in an elegant manner, is made of a solution of violet-sugar. Snow, in the *rinfrescos* of a hot climate, is almost a constant ingredient. Thus, in the *Arabian Nights,* Bedreddin Hassan, having filled a large porcelain bowl with sherbet of roses, put snow into it.

PAGE 133. ... *a lamb stuffed with pistachios*

The same dish is mentioned in the tale of the Barber's sixth brother.

PAGE 134. ... *a parchment*

Parchments of the like mysterious import are frequent in the writings of the Easterns. One in particular, amongst the Arabians, is held in high veneration. It was written by Ali, and Giafar Sadek, in mystic characters, and is said to contain the destiny of the Mahometan religion, and the great events which are to happen previous to the end of the world. This parchment is of *camel's skin;* but it was usual with Catherine of

Medicis to carry about her person, a legend, in cabalistic characters, inscribed on the skin of a dead-born infant.—D'HERBELOT, p. 366. WRAX-
ALL's *House of Valois.*

PAGE 134.   *Istakhar*

This city was the ancient Persepolis, and capital of Persia, under the
kings of the three first races. The author of *Lebtarikh* writes, that Kisch-
tab there established his abode, erected several temples to the element
of fire, and hewed out for himself and his successors sepulchres in the
rocks of the mountain contiguous to the city. The ruins of columns and
broken figures which still remain, defaced as they were by Alexander
and mutilated by time, plainly evince that those ancient potentates had
chosen it for the place of their interment. Their monuments, however,
must not be confounded with the superb palace reared by Queen Homai,
in the midst of Istakhar; which the Persians distinguish by the name of
T'chilminar, or the forty watch-towers. The origin of this city is ascribed
by some to Giamschid, and others carry it higher; but the Persian tradition is, that it was built by the *Peris,* or Fairies, when the world was
governed by Gian Ben Gian.—D'HERBELOT, p. 327.

PAGE 134.   *Gian Ben Gian*

By this appellation was distinguished the monarch of that species of
beings, whom the Arabians denominate *Gian* or *Ginn;* that is, *Genii;*
and the Tarikh Thabari, *Peris, Feez,* or *Fairies.* He was renowned for his
warlike expeditions and stupendous structures. According to Oriental
writers, the pyramids of Egypt were amongst the monuments of his
power. The buckler of this mighty sovereign, no less famous than that of
Achilles, was employed by three successive Solimans, to achieve their
marvellous exploits. From them, it descended to Tahamurath, surnamed
Divbend, or *Conqueror of the* GIANTS. This buckler was endowed with
most wonderful qualities, having been fabricated by talismanic art; and
was alone sufficient to destroy all the charms and enchantments of demons or giants; which, on the contrary, were wrought by magic. Hence
we are no longer at a loss for the origin of the wonderful shield of
Atlante.

The reign of Gian Ben Gian over the Peris is said to have continued
for two thousand years; after which, EBLIS was sent by the Deity to exile
them, on account of their disorders, and confine them in the remotest region of the earth.—D'HERBELOT, p. 396. BAILLY, *Sur l'Atlantide,* p. 147.

PAGE 134.   *. . . the talismans of Soliman*

The most famous *talisman* of the East, and which could control even the
arms and magic of the dives or giants, was *Mohur Solimani,* the seal or
ring of Soliman Jared, fifth monarch of the world after Adam. By means
of it the possessor had the entire command, not only of the elements, but
also of demons and every created being.—RICHARDSON's *Dissertation on
the Languages, etc., of Eastern Nations,* p. 272. D'HERBELOT, p. 820.

PAGE 134. . . . *pre-Adamite sultans*

These monarchs, which were seventy-two in number, are said to have governed each a distinct species of rational beings, prior to the existence of Adam. Amongst the most renowned of them were SOLIMAN RAAD, SOLIMAN DAKI, and SOLIMAN DI GIAN BEN GIAN.—D'HERBELOT, p. 820.

PAGE 134. . . . *beware how thou enterest any dwelling*

Strange as this injunction may seem, it is by no means incongruous to the customs of the country. Dr. Pocock mentions his travelling with the train of the governor of Faiume, who, instead of lodging in a village that was near, passed the night in a grove of palm-trees.—*Travels,* vol. i, p. 56.

PAGE 134. . . . *every bumper he ironically quaffed to the health of Mahomet*

There are innumerable proofs that the Grecian custom συμπιεῖν κυαθιζομένους prevailed amongst the Arabs; but, had these been wanted, Carathis could not be supposed a stranger to it. The practice was, to hail the gods in the first place, and then those who were held in the highest veneration. This they repeated as often as they drank. Thus St. Ambrose: "Quid obtestationes potantium loquar? quid memorem sacramenta, quae violare nefas arbitrantur? Bibamus, inquiunt, pro salute imperatorum; et qui non biberit, sit reus indevotionis."

PAGE 134. . . . *the ass of Balaam, the dog of the seven sleepers, and the other animals admitted into the paradise of Mahomet*

It was a tenet of the Mussulman creed, that all animals would be raised again, and many of them honoured with admission to paradise. The story of the seven sleepers, borrowed from Christian legends, was this: In the days of the Emperor Decius, there were certain Ephesian youths of a good family, who, to avoid the flames of persecution, fled to a secret cavern, and there slept for a number of years. In their flight towards the cave, they were followed by a dog, which, when they attempted to drive back, said, *"I love those who are dear unto God; go sleep, therefore, and I will guard you."* For this dog the Mahometans retain so profound a reverence, that their harshest sarcasm against a covetous person is, "He would not throw a bone to the dog of the seven sleepers." It is even said that their superstition induces them to write his name upon the letters they send to a distance, as a kind of talisman, to secure them a safe conveyance.—*Religious Ceremonies,* vol. vii, p. 74 n. SALE'S *Koran,* chap. xviii and notes.

PAGE 134. . . . *painting the eyes of the Circassians*

It was an ancient custom in the East, and still continues, to tinge the eyes of women, particularly those of a fair complexion, with an impalpable powder, prepared chiefly from crude antimony, and called *surmeh.* Ebni'l Motezz, in a passage translated by Sir W. Jones, hath not only ascertained its *purple* colour, but also likened the *violet* to it:—

> Viola collegit folia sua, similia
> Collyrio nigro, quod bibit lachrymas die discessus,
> Velut si esset super vasa in quibus fulgent
> Primae ignis flammulae in sulphuris extremis partibus.[1]

This pigment, when applied to the inner surface of the lids, communicates to the eye (especially if seen by the light of lamps) so tender and fascinating a languor as no language is competent to express.* Hence the epithet, 'Ιοβλέφαρος, violet-colour eyelids, attributed by the Greeks† to the goddess of beauty; and the Arabian comparison of "the *eyelids* of a fine woman bathed in tears, to violets dropping with dew." Perhaps, also, Shakespeare's—

> violets dim,
> But sweeter than the lids of Juno's eyes—

should be ultimately referred to the same origin. But however this may be, it is obvious (though his commentators have overlooked it) that Anacreon alluded to the same cosmetic, when he required of the painter that the *eyelids* of his mistress's portrait should, like her own, exhibit this appearance:—

> 'Εχέτω δ', ὅπως ἐκείνη,
> ΒΛΕΦΑΡΩΝ 'ΙΤΥΝ ΚΕΛΑΙΝΗΝ·

* When Tasso represents love, as ambushed,

> sotto all'ombra
> Delle palpebre—

he allegorically alludes to that appearance in nature which the artifice here was meant to counterfeit.

† Both Homer and Hesiod have applied 'ΕΛΙΚΟΒΛΕΦΑΡΟΣ to Venus, in a synonymous sense, as is evident from Pliny, who, amongst other properties of the *Helix*, minutely specifies its purplish flowers. This ὑπογραφὴ ὀφθαλμῶν will likewise explain 'ΕΛΙΚΩΠΙΣ.

Winckelmann and Graevius have each given different interpretations; but let them both speak for themselves:—'Ελικοβλέφαρος caractérise des yeux dont les paupières ont un mouvement ondoyant que le Poëte compare au jeune ceps de la vigne.—*Hist. de l'Art de l'Antiq.*, tom. ii., p. 135.—'Ελικοβλέφαροι et ἑλικώπιδες puellae Graecis dicuntur, quae sunt mobili oculorum petulantia, ut Petron. loquitur, sive quae habent, ut idem dicit,—

> blandos oculos et inquietos,
> Et quadam propria nota loquaces.

Qui hinc Ovidio dicuntur *arguti*. Aliter plerique sentiunt, et exponunt: *nigros oculos habentes*. Sed ea vera est quam dixi hujus vocis notio, quam facile pluribus confirmarem, nisi res ipsa loqueretur.—*Lectiones Hesiodeae*, cap. i.

[1 So the passage stands in Sir William Jones' *Works*, ii. 454; but the text is probably corrupt.]

and her eye, both the bright citron* of Minerva's, and the dewy radiance† of Cytherea's:—

Τὸ δὲ ΒΛΕΜΜΑ νῦν ἀληθῶς
'Απὸ τοῦ πυρὸς ποίησον·
"Αμα ΓΛΑΥΚΟΝ, ὡς 'ΑΘΗΝΗΣ·
"Αμα δ' ΥΓΡΟΝ, ὡς ΚΥΘΗΡΗΣ.‡

PAGE 135. *Rocnabad*

The stream thus denominated flows near the city of Schiraz. Its waters are uncommonly pure and limpid, and their banks swarded with the finest verdure. Its praises are celebrated by Hafez, in an animated song, which Sir W. Jones has admirably translated:—

Boy, let yon liquid ruby flow,
And bid thy pensive heart be glad,
Whate'er the frowning zealots say:
Tell them, their Eden cannot show
A stream so clear as Rocnabad.
A bower so sweet as Mosellay.§

PAGE 135. *Do you, with the advice of my mother, govern*

Females in the East were not anciently excluded from power. In the Story of Zeyn Alasnam and the King of the Genii, the mother of Zeyn undertakes, with the aid of his viziers, to govern Bassora during his absence on a similar expedition.

PAGE 136. *Chintz and muslin*

For many curious particulars relative to these articles, consult Mr. Delaval's *Inquiry concerning the Changes of Colours, etc.;* to which may be added, LUCRETIUS, lib. iv, 5. PETRONIUS, c. 37. MARTIAL, viii, Ep. 28, 17; xiv, Ep. 150. PLUTARCH, in *Vita Catonis*. PLINY, viii, 48.

PAGE 136. *. . . serpents and scorpions*

Various accounts are given of the magical applications of these animals, and the power of sorcerers over them, to which even Solomon referred. Sir John Chardin relates that at Surat an Armenian, having seen some of

* "Eyen, bright citrin."—Chaucer. No expression can be less exact than blue-eyed, when used as the characteristic of Minerva; nor any, perhaps, more so than Chaucer's:—unless γλαυκῶπις be literally rendered.

† ΥΓΡΟΣ·—ο εὐκατάφορος, εἰς τὰς ἡδονὰς ῥευματιζόμενος.
Gloss, Bibl. Coislin. Tasso, in his *Jerusalem*, has well paraphrased the import of this epithet:—

Qual raggio in onda, le scintilla un riso
Negli umidi occhj tremulo e lascivo.

‡ Ode xxviii. 18.—2 Kings ix. 30. Ezek. xxiii. 40. D'HERBELOT, p. 832. LADY M. W. MONTAGU'S *Letters*, Let. xxix.
§ Mosella was an oratory on the banks of Rocnabad.

these creatures crawl and twine over the naked bodies of children belonging to the charmers, daringly hazarded the same experiment; but it soon proved fatal to him, for he was bitten, and died in the space of two hours.

PAGE 136. *. . . she amused herself in curing their wounds*

Clorin, in the *Faithful Shepherdess* of Fletcher, possessed the like skill:—

> Of all green wounds I know the remedies,
> In men or cattle; be they stung with snakes,
> Or charm'd with powerful words of wicked art;
>
> . . . .
>
> These I can cure.

PAGE 136. *Mullahs*

Those amongst the Mahometans who were bred to the law had this title; and from their order the judges of cities and provinces were taken.

PAGE 136. *. . . the sacred Caaba*

That part of the temple at Mecca which is chiefly revered, and, indeed, gives a sanctity to the rest, is a square stone building called the Caaba, probably from its quadrangular form. The length of this edifice, from north to south, is twenty-four cubits, and its breadth, from east to east, twenty-three. The door is on the east side, and stands about four cubits from the ground, the floor being level with the threshold. The Caaba has a double roof, supported internally by three octangular pillars of aloes wood, between which, on a bar of iron, hangs a row of silver lamps. The outside is covered with rich black damask, adorned with an embroidered band of gold. This hanging, which is changed every year, was formerly sent by the caliphs.—SALE's *Preliminary Discourse*, p. 152.

PAGE 136. *. . . the tapestry that hung before the door*

This kind of curtain, at first restricted to the serail, or palace, was afterwards adopted by the great, and gradually became of general use. The author of *Lebtarikh* relates, that Lohorashb, King of Persia, having granted to the great officers of his household and army the privilege of giving audience on seats of gold, reserved to himself the right of the *seraperdeh,* or curtain; which was hung before the throne to conceal him from the eyes of his subjects, and thereby preserve their reverence for his person. In later times, the daughter of a law professor, who occasionally, in her father's absence, filled his chair, had recourse to the same expedient, lest the charms of her face should distract her pupil's attention.—ABBÉ DE SADE's *Mémoires de Pétrarque,* tom. i., p. 42.

PAGE 137. *. . . the supposed oratory*

The dishonouring such places as had an appearance of being devoted to religious purposes, by converting them to the most abject offices of nature, was an Oriental method of expressing contempt, and hath continued from remote antiquity.—HARMER's *Observations*, vol. ii, p. 493.

PAGE 137. *... regale these pious poor souls with my good wine*
from Schiraz

The prohibition of wine in the Koran is so rigidly observed by the conscientious, especially if they have performed the pilgrimage to Mecca,
that they deem it sinful to press grapes for the purpose of making it, and
even to use the money arising from its sale.—CHARDIN, *Voy. de Perse,*
tom. ii, p. 212. *Schiraz* was famous in the East for its wines of different
sorts, but particularly for its *red,* which was esteemed more highly than
even the white wine of *Kismische.*

PAGE 138. *... The caliph, to enjoy so flattering a sight, supped*
gaily on the roof

Dr. Pococke relates that he was entertained at Galilee by the steward of
the Sheik, with whom he *supped on the top of the house.* From a similar
motive to Vathek's, Nebuchadnezzar is represented by Daniel as contemplating his capital from the summit of his palace, when he uttered
that exulting apostrophe, *"Is not this great Babylon, that I have built?"*

PAGE 139. *... the most stately tulips of the East*

The tulip is a flower of Eastern growth, and there held in great estimation. Thus, in an ode of Mesihi: "The edge of the bower is filled with the
light of Ahmed; among the plants the fortunate *tulips* represent his companions."

PAGE 139. *... eunuchs in the rear*

As the black eunuchs were the inseparable attendants of the ladies, the
rear was, consequently, their post. So, in the argument to the poem of
Amriolkais:— "One day, when her tribe had struck their tents, and were
changing their station, the women, as usual, came behind the rest, with
the servants and baggage, in carriages fixed on the backs of camels."

PAGE 139. *... certain cages of ladies*

There are many passages of the *Moallakat* in which these *cages* are fully
described. Thus, in the poem of Lebeid:

How were thy tender affections raised, when the damsels of the tribe departed; when they hid themselves in carriages of cotton, like antelopes in their
lair, and the tents as they were struck gave a piercing sound!

They were concealed in vehicles, whose sides were well covered with awnings and carpets, with fine-spun curtains and pictured veils.

Again, Zohair:—

—— Look, my friend! dost thou not discern a company of maidens seated on
camels, and advancing over the high ground above the streams of Jortham?

They leave on their right the mountains and rocky plains of Kenaan. Oh;
how many of my bitter foes, and how many of my firm allies, does Kenaan
contain!

They are mounted in carriages covered with costly awnings, and with rose-
coloured veils, the lining of which have the hue of crimson andem-wood.

They now appear by the valley of Subaan, and now they pass through it; the trappings of all their camels are new and large.

When they ascend from the bosom of the vale, they sit forward on the saddlecloths, with every mark of a voluptuous gaiety.—*Moallakat,* by SIR W. JONES, pp. 46, 35. See also LADY M. W. MONTAGU, Let. xxvi.

PAGE 139.   . . . *swagging somewhat awry*

Amriolkais, in the first poem of the *Moallakat,* hath related a similar adventure:—

On that happy day I entered the carriage, the carriage of Onaiza, who said, "Woe to thee! thou wilt compel me to travel on foot."

She added, while the vehicle was bent aside with our weight, "O Amriolkais, descend, or my beast also will be killed!"

I answered, "Proceed, and loosen his rein; nor withhold from me the fruits of thy love, which again and again may be tasted with rapture.

"Many a fair one, like thee, though not like thee a virgin, have I visited by night."

PAGE 139.   . . . *dislodged*

Our language wants a verb, equivalent to the French *dénicher,* to convey, in this instance, the precise sense of the author.

PAGE 139.   . . . *those nocturnal insects which presage evil*

It is observable that, in the fifth verse of the Ninety-first Psalm, "the terror by night," is rendered, in the old English version, "the bugge by night."* In the first settled parts of North America, every nocturnal fly of a noxious quality is still generically named a bug; whence the term bugbear signifies one that carries terror wherever he goes. Beelzebub, or the Lord of Flies, was an Eastern appellative given to the Devil; and the nocturnal sound called by the Arabians *azif* was believed to be the howling of demons. Analogous to this is a passage in *Comus* as it stood in the original copy:—

> But for that damn'd magician, let him be girt
> With all the grisly legions that troop
> Under the sooty flag of Acheron,

* Instances are not wanted, both in the English and Greek versions, where the translators have modified the sense of the original by their own preconceived opinions. To this source may be ascribed the BUGGE of our old Bible, and δαιμόνιον μεσημβρινὸν, the noon-day demon of the Seventy, unless the copies of the latter be supposed to have read, not יָשׁוּד but וְשֵׁד . If the terror by night be taken in connection with the pestilence that walketh in darkness, and both opposed to the arrow that flieth by day, and the destruction that wasteth at noon, it will seem to imply the dread of real evil only, which may be explained, in the language of the poet, by—

> Night and all her sickly dews;

but if the rendering of our old version, adopting that of the Seventy, be founded, it will, also, include the imaginary evils that follow:—

> Her spectres wan, and birds of boding cry.

> Harpies and Hydras, or all the monstrous buggs
> 'Twixt Africa and Inde, I'll find him out.

PAGE 140.   *. . . the locusts were heard from the thickets on the*
plain of Catoul

The insects here mentioned are of the same species with the τέττιξ of the Greeks, and the *cicada* of the Latins. The locusts are mentioned in Pliny, b. xi, 29. They were so called, from *loco usto,* because the havoc they made wherever they passed left behind the appearance of a place desolated by fire. How could then the commentators of Vathek say that they are called *locusts,* from their having been so denominated by the first English settlers in America?

PAGE 140.   *. . . halted on the banks of the Tigris*

It is a practice in the East, and especially when large parties journey together, to halt, if possible, in the vicinity of a stream. Thus, Zohair:—

> They rose at daybreak: they proceeded at early dawn; they are advancing towards the valley of Ras directly and surely, as the hand to the mouth.
>
> Now, when they have reached the brink of yon blue gushing rivulet, they fix the poles of their tents, like the Arab, in a settled mansion.

PAGE 140.   *. . . the heavens looked angry, &c.*

This tempest may be deemed somewhat the more violent from a supposition that Mahomet interfered; which will appear the more probable, if the circumstance of its obliterating the road* be considered. William of Tyre hath recorded one of a similar kind, that visited Baldwin in his expedition against Damascus:—"He, against whose will all projects are vain, suddenly overspread the sky with darkness; poured down such torrents of rain, and so entirely effaced the roads, that scarce any hope of escaping remained. These disasters were indeed portended by a gloominess in the air, lowering clouds, irregular gusts of winds, increasing thunders, and incessant lightnings: but, as the mind of man knows not what may befall him, these admonitions of Heaven were slighted and opposed."—*Gesta Dei per Francos,* p. 849.

PAGE 140.   *. . . he determined to cross over the craggy heights, &c.,*
to Rocnabad

Oriental travellers have sometimes recourse to these expedients, for the sake of abridging the toils of their journeys. Hence, Amgrad, in the *Arabian Nights,* who had himself been about six weeks in travelling from the Isle of Ebene, could not comprehend the possibility of coming in less time; unless by enchantment, or crossing the mountains, which, from the difficulty of the pass, were but seldom traversed.

---

* Exclusive, however, of preternatural interference, it frequently happens that a sudden blast will arise on the vast deserts of the East, and sweep away, in its eddies, the tracks of the last passenger; whose camel, therefore, in vain, for the wanderer that follows,

> Linquit humi pedibus vestigia pressa bisulcis.

PAGE 141.   ... *tigers and vultures*

The ravages of these animals in the East are almost incredible.

> Before them, Death with shrieks directs their way,
> Fills the wild yell, and leads them to their prey.

From the earliest days they have been the constant attendants on scenes of carnage.

In the Sacred Writings, David threatens "to give the host of the Philistines to the fowls of the air and the wild beasts of the earth." Antara boasts, at the close of a conflict, of "having left the father of his foes, like a victim, to be mangled by the lions of the wood, and the eagles* advanced in years." And, in the narrative of the prisoners taken at Bendore, the author relates that many of them were devoured by tigers and vultures.

PAGE 141.   *Vathek ... with two little pages*

"All the pages of the seraglio are sons of Christians made slaves in time of war, in their most tender age. The incursions of robbers in the confines of Circassia afford the means of supplying the seraglio, even in times of peace."—HABESCI's *State of the Ottoman Empire,* p. 157. That the pages here mentioned were *Circassians,* appears from the description of their complexion—*more fair than the enamel of Franguestan.*

PAGE 141.   ... *confectioners and cooks*

What their precise number might have been in Vathek's establishment it is not now easy to determine; but in the household of the present Grand Signior there are not fewer than a hundred and ninety.—HABESCI's *State of the Ottoman Empire,* p. 145.

PAGE 142.   ... *torches were lighted, &c.*

Mr. Marsden relates, in his *History of Sumatra,* that tigers prove most fatal and destructive enemies to the inhabitants, particularly in their journeys; and adds, that the numbers annually slain by those rapacious tyrants of the woods are almost incredible. As these tremendous enemies are alarmed at the appearance of fire, it is usual for the natives to carry a splendid kind of torch, chiefly to frighten them, and also to make a blaze with wood in different parts round their villages.—P. 149.

---

* Finely as Gray conceived the idea of the eagle, awestruck at the corses of the bards, there is a languor in his expression that wants to be removed. Milton, as his best editor judiciously remarks, applied (he might have said confined) the verb *hurry* to preternatural motion or imaginary beings: adopting it, therefore, in a kindred sense, might we not (for passes) advantageously read:—

"The famish'd eagle screams, and hurries by"?

PAGE 142.   . . . *One of the forests of cedar that bordered their way*
took fire

Accidents of this kind in Persia are not unfrequent. "It was an ancient practice with the kings and great men to set fire to large bunches of dry combustibles fastened round wild beasts and birds, which being then let loose the air and earth appeared one great illumination: and as those terrified creatures naturally fled to the woods for shelter, it is easy to conceive that conflagrations, which would often happen, must have been particularly destructive."—RICHARDSON's *Dissertation*, p. 185. In the 83rd Psalm, v. 14, there is a reference to one of those fires, though arising from another cause; and Homer likewise has taken a simile from thence:—

Ἤυτε πῦρ ᾿ΑΙΔΗΛΟΝ ἐπιφλέγει ἄσπετον ὕλην,
Οὔρεος ἐν κορυφῆς· ἔκαθεν δέ τε φαίνεται αὐγή·

Il., β. 455.

PAGE 142.   . . . *hath seen some part of our bodies; and, what is worse,*
our very faces

"I was informed," writes Dr. Cooke, "that the Persian women, in general, would sooner expose to public view any part of their bodies than their faces."—*Voyages and Travels,* vol. ii, p. 443.

PAGE 143.   . . . *cakes baked in silver ovens for his royal mouth*

Portable ovens were a part of the furniture of Eastern travellers. St. Jerome (on Lament. v. 10) hath particularly described them. The caliph's were of the same kind, only substituting silver for brass. Dr. Pococke mentions his having been entertained in an Arabian camp with cakes baked for him. In what the peculiarity of the royal bread consisted it is not easy to determine; but in one of the Arabian Tales a woman, to gratify her utmost desire, wishes to become the wife of the sultan's baker, assigning for the reason that she might have her fill of that bread which is called the sultan's.—Vol. iv., p. 269.

PAGE 143.   . . . *vases of snow, and grapes from the banks of the Tigris*

It was customary in Eastern climates, and especially in the sultry season, to carry, when journeying, supplies of snow. These *aestivae nives* (as Mamertinus styles them) being put into separate vases, were, by that means, better kept from the air, as no more was opened at once than might suffice for immediate use. To preserve the whole from solution, the vessels that contained it were secured in packages of straw.—*Gesta Dei,* p. 1098. Vathek's ancestor, the CALIPH MAHADI, in the pilgrimage to Mecca, which he undertook from ostentation rather than devotion, loaded upon camels so prodigious a quantity, as was not only sufficient for himself and his attendants amidst the burning sands of Arabia, but also to preserve, in their natural freshness, the various fruits he took with him, and to ice all their drink whilst he stayed at Mecca, the greater part of whose inhabitants had never seen snow till then.—*Anecdotes Arabes,* p. 326.

PAGE 143.   *. . . roasted wolf, &c.*

In the poem of Amriolkais a repast is described which in manner of preparation resembles the present:—

He soon brings us up to the foremost of the beasts, and leaves the rest far behind; nor has the herd time to disperse itself.

He runs from wild bulls to wild heifers, and overpowers them in a single heat, without being bathed, or even moistened with sweat.

Then the busy cook dresses the game, roasting part, baking part on hot stones, and quickly boiling the rest in a vessel of iron."

Disgusting as this refection of Vathek may be thought, Atlante boasts to Ruggiero of having fed him from his infancy on a similar diet:—

> Di midolle già d'orsi e di leoni
> Ti porsi io dunque li primi alimenti.

And we read that lion's flesh was prescribed to Vathek, but on a different occasion.—*Anecdotes Arabes,* p. 419.

The vegetables that made part of this entertainment were such as the Koran had ordained to be food for the damned.

PAGE 144.   *. . . dropped their fans on the ground*

Attendants for the same purpose are mentioned in the story of the King of the Black Isles:—"One day, while she was at bath, I found myself sleepy after dinner, and lay down upon a sofa. Two of her ladies, who were then in my chamber, came and sat down, one at my head and the other at my feet, with fans in their hands to moderate the heat and to hinder the flies from disturbing my slumber." The comfort of such an attendant in the hour of repose can be known only in the climes of intolerable day.

PAGE 144.   *. . . horrible Kaf*

This mountain, which, in reality, is no other than Caucasus, was supposed to surround the earth, like a ring encompassing a finger. The sun was believed to rise from one of its eminences (as over Oeta, by the Latin poets), and to set on the opposite; whence, *from Kaf to Kaf*, signified, from one extremity of the earth to the other. The fabulous historians of the East affirm, that this mountain was founded upon a stone, called *sakhrat,* one grain of which, according to Lokman, would enable the possessor to work wonders. This stone is further described as the pivot of the earth, and said to be one vast emerald, from the refraction of whose beams the heavens derive their azure. It is added, that whenever God would excite an earthquake, he commands the stone to move one of its fibres (which supply in it the office of nerves), and, that being moved, the part of the earth connected with it quakes, is convulsed, and sometimes expands. Such is the philosophy of the Koran!

The *Tarikh Tabari,* written in Persian, analogous to the same tradition, relates, that, were it not for this emerald, the earth would be liable to perpetual commotions, and unfit for the abode of mankind.

To arrive at the Kaf, a vast region,

> Far from the sun and summer gale,

must be traversed. Over this dark and cheerless desert, the way is inextricable without the direction of supernatural guidance. Here the dives or giants were confined, after their defeat by the first heroes of the human race; and here, also, the peris, or fairies, are supposed in ordinary to reside. Sukrage, the giant, was king of Kaf, and had Rucail, one of the children of Adam, for his prime minister. The giant Argenk, likewise, from the time that Tahamurath made war upon him, reigned here, and reared a superb palace in the city of Aherman, with galleries, on whose walls were painted the creatures that inhabited the world prior to the formation of Adam.—D'HERBELOT, p. 230, etc.

PAGE 144.   ... *the Simurgh*

This is that wonderful bird of the East, concerning which so many marvels are told: it was not only endowed with reason, but possessed also the knowledge of every language. Hence it may be concluded to have been a dive in a borrowed form. This creature relates of itself that it had seen the great revolution of seven thousand years twelve times commence and close; and that, in its duration, the world had been seven times void of inhabitants, and as often replenished. The Simurgh is represented as a great friend to the race of Adam, and not less inimical to the dives. Tahamurath and Aherman were apprised by its predictions of all that was destined to befall them, and from it they obtained the promise of assistance in every undertaking. Armed with the buckler of Gian Ben Gian, Tahamurath was borne by it through the air, over the dark desert, to Kaf. From its bosom his helmet was crested with plumes, which the most renowned warriors have ever since worn. In every conflict the Simurgh was invulnerable, and the heroes it favoured never failed of success. Though possessed of power sufficient to exterminate its foes, yet the exertion of that power was supposed to be forbidden. Sadi, a serious author, gives it as an instance of the universality of Providence, that the Simurgh, notwithstanding its immense bulk, is at no loss for sustenance on the mountain of Kaf. Inatulla hath described Getiafrose, queen of the Genii, as seated on a golden chariot, drawn by ten simurghs; whose wings extended wide as the earth-shading bir,* and whose talons

---

* —or *Banian,* to which the epithet of Inatulla most emphatically belongs. Milton hath accurately described this extraordinary tree, though by another name:—

> The *fig-tree*—not that kind for fruit renown'd;
> But such as at this day to Indians known,
> In Malabar or Deccan, spreads her arms,
> Branching so broad and long, that in the ground
> The bended twigs take root, and daughters grow

resembled the proboscis of mighty elephants: but it does not appear from any other writer, that there ever was more than *one*, which is frequently called the *marvellous gryphon*, and said to be like that imaginary monster.—D'HERBELOT, p. 1017, 810, etc. *Tales of Inatulla*, vol. ii, pp. 71, 72.

> About the mother tree: a pillar'd shade
> High over-arch'd, and echoing walks between.

Was it not from hence that Warburton framed his hypothesis on the origin of Gothic architecture? At least, here were materials sufficient for a fancy less forgetive than his. Mr. Ives, in his *Journey from Persia*, thus speaks of this vegetable wonder:—"This is the Indians' sacred tree.—It grows to a prodigious height, and its branches spread a great way. The limbs drop down fibres, which take root and become another tree, united by its branches to the first; and so continue to do, until the trees cover a great extent of ground: the arches which those different stocks make are Gothic, like those we see in Westminster Abbey; the stocks not being single, but appearing as if composed of many stocks, are of a great circumference. There is a certain solemnity accompanying those trees; nor do I remember that I was ever under the cover of any of them, but that my mind was at the time impressed with a reverential awe!"—P. 460. From the

> pillar'd shade
> High over-arch'd, and echoing walks between,

as well as the

> highest woods, impenetrable
> To star, or sunlight,

just before mentioned, and the name given to the tree, it is probable that the poet's description was principally founded on the account of Duret, who, in the Chapter "Du figuier d'Inde" of his singular book (entitled *Histoire admirable des plantes et herbes esmerueillables et miraculeuses en nature, &c.*, à Paris, 1605), thus writes:—"Sa grosseur est quelquefois telle, que trois hommes ne le sçauroient embrasser: quelquefois vn ou deux de ces figuiers font *un* BOIS *assez grand, toffu, & ombrageux, dans lequel les rayons du Soleil ne peuuent aucunement* penetrer, *durant les chaleurs d'Este,* & font ces figuiers infinies *tonnes & cabinets si concaues & couuerts de feuilles & de sinuositez* [ailes and recesses, so arched over with foliage and embowed ramifications], *qu'il s'y forme des* Echos *ou reuerberations de voix & sons, jusques à trois fois;* & est telle *la moindre d'vn seul ombre de ses arbres, qu'elle peut contenir soubs soy à couuert huict cens ou mil personnes, & la plus grande ombre, trois mil hommes.*" P. 124. This tree might well be styled the Earth-shading.*

Though the early architecture of our island be confessedly of a doubtful origin, it nevertheless deserves to be noted, that the resemblance between the columns of the ruined chancel at Orford and those of Tauk Kesserah on the banks of the Tigris is much too strict to be merely casual. It may be added, that the arches of this edifice, and their ornaments, are of the style we call the Early Norman.

---

* The following is an account of the dimensions of a remarkable Banyan tree, near Manjee, twenty miles west of Patna, in Bengal. Diameter 363 to 375 feet. Circumference of its shadow at noon, 1,116 feet. Circumference of the several stems (in number 50 or 60), 921 feet.—MARSDEN's *History of Sumatra*, p. 131.

As the *magic shield of Atlante* resembles the *buckler of Gian Ben Gian,* so *his Ippogrif* apparently came from the *Simurgh,* notwithstanding the reference of Ariosto to the veridical Archbishop:

> Non ho veduto mai, nè letto altrove,
> Fuor che in Turpin, d'un si fatto animale.

PAGE 144. ... *palampores, etc.*

These elegant productions, which abound in all parts of the East, were of very remote antiquity. Not only are σινδόνας ΕΤΑΝΘΕΙΣ, *finely flowered linens,* noticed by Strabo; but Herodotus relates, that the nations of Caucasus *adorned* their *garments* with *figures of various creatures,* by means of the sap of certain vegetables; which, when macerated and diluted with water, communicate colours that cannot be washed out, and are no less permanent than the texture itself.—STRABO, l. xv, p. 709. HERODOTUS, l. i, p. 96. The Arabian Tales repeatedly describe these *"fine linens of India, painted in the most lively colours,* and representing *beasts, trees, flowers,* etc."—*Arabian Nights,* vol. iv, p. 217, etc.

PAGE 144. ... *afrits*

These were a kind of Medusae, or Lamiae, supposed to be the most terrible and cruel of all the orders of the dives.—D'HERBELOT, p. 66.

PAGE 144. ... *tablets fraught with preternatural qualities*

Mr. Richardson observes, "that in the East men of rank in general carried with them pocket astronomical tables, which they consulted on every affair of moment." These tablets, however, were of the *magical* kind, and such as often occur in works of romance. Thus, in Boiardo, Orlando receives, from the father of the youth he had rescued, "a book that would solve all doubts"; and, in Ariosto, Logistilla bestows upon Astolpho a similar directory. The books which Carathis turned over with Morakanabad were imagined to have possessed the like virtues.

PAGE 144. ... *dwarfs*

Such unfortunate beings as are thus "curtailed of fair proportion," have been, for ages, an appendage of Eastern grandeur. One part of their office consists in the instruction of the pages; but their principal duty is the amusement of their master. If a dwarf happen to be a mute, he is much esteemed; but if he be also an eunuch, he is regarded as a prodigy, and no pains or expense are spared to obtain him.—HABESCI's *State of the Ottoman Empire,* p. 164, etc.

PAGE 144. ... *a cabin of rushes and canes*

Huts of this sort are mentioned by Ludeke, in his *Expositio brevis Loc. Scrip.,* p. 51:—"Tuguriola seu palis, fruticibus viridibus, vel juncis circumdatis et tectis, amboque quidem facillimè construuntur."

PAGE 144.   ... *a small spring supplies us with water for the*
Abdest, and we daily repeat prayers, etc.

Amongst the indispensable rules of the Mahometan faith, ablution is
one of the chief. This rite is divided into three kinds. The first, performed before prayers, is called *Abdest*. It begins with washing both
hands, and repeating these words: "Praised be Alla, who created clean
water, and gave it the virtue to purify: he also hath rendered our faith
conspicuous." This done, water is taken in the right hand thrice, and
the mouth being washed, the worshipper subjoins: "I pray thee, O Lord,
to let me taste of that water which thou hast given to thy prophet
Mahomet in paradise, more fragrant than musk, whiter than milk,
sweeter than honey; and which has the power to quench for ever the
thirst of him that drinks it." This petition is accompanied with sniffing
a little water into the nose. The face is then three times washed, and
behind the ears; after which water is taken with both hands, beginning
with the right, and thrown to the elbow. The washing of the crown next
follows, and the apertures of the ear with the thumbs; afterward the
neck with all the fingers, and finally, the feet. In this last operation, it
is held sufficient to wet the sandal only. At each ceremonial a suitable
petition is offered, and the whole concludes with this: "Hold me up
firmly, O Lord! and suffer not my foot to slip, that I may not fall from
the bridge into hell." Nothing can be more exemplary than the attention
with which these rites are performed. If an involuntary cough or sneeze
interrupt them, the whole service is begun anew, and that as often as
it happens.—HABESCI, p. 91, etc.

PAGE 145.   ... *reading the holy Koran*

The Mahometans have a book of stops or pauses in reading the Koran,
which divides it into *seventeen* sections, and allows of no more.—
D'HERBELOT, p. 915.

PAGE 145.   ... *the bells of a cafila*

A cafila, or caravan, according to Pitts, is divided into distinct companies,
at the head of which an officer, or person of distinction, is carried in a
kind of horse-litter, and followed by a sumpter camel, loaded with his
treasure. This camel hath a bell fastened to either side, the sound of
which may be heard at a considerable distance. Others have bells on
their necks and their legs, to solace them when drooping with heat and
fatigue. Inatulla also, in his tales, hath a similar reference: "The bells
of the cafila may be rung in the thirsty desert." Vol. ii, p. 15. These small
bells were known at Rome from the earliest times, and called from their
sounds *tintinnabulum*. Phaedrus gives us a lively description of the mule
carrying the fiscal moneys: *clarumque collo jactans tintinnabulum.*—Bk.
ii, fabl. vii.

PAGE 145.   *Deggial*

This word signifies properly a liar and impostor, but is applied by
Mahometan writers to their *Antichrist*. He is described as having but

one eye and eyebrow, and on his forehead the radicals of *cafer* or *infidel* are said to be impressed. According to the traditions of the faithful, his first appearance will be between Irak and Syria, mounted on an ass. Seventy thousand Jews from Ispahan are expected to follow him. His continuance on earth is to be forty days. All places are to be destroyed by him and his emissaries, except *Mecca* or *Medina*, which will be protected by angels from the general overthrow. At last, however, he will be slain by Jesus, who is to encounter him at the gate of Lud.—D'HERBELOT, p. 282. SALE's *Preliminary Discourse*, p. 106.

PAGE 145. *. . . dictated by the blessed Intelligence*

That is, the angel *Gabriel.* The Mahometans deny that the Koran was composed by their prophet: it being their general and orthodox belief, that it is of divine original; nay, even eternal and uncreated, remaining in the very essence of God; that the first transcript has been from everlasting by his throne, written on a table of immense size, called the *preserved table;* on which are also recorded the divine decrees, past and future: that a copy was by the ministry of the angel *Gabriel* sent down to the lowest heaven, in the month of *Ramadan,* on the night of *power:* from whence *Gabriel* revealed it to Mahomet by parcels, some at Mecca, and some at Medina.—*Al Koran,* ch. ii, etc. SALE's *Preliminary Discourse,* p. 85.

PAGE 145. *. . . hath culled with his own hands these melons, &c.*

The great men of the East have ever been, what Herodotus* shrewdly styled them, δωροφάγοι, or *gift-eaters:* for no visitor can approach them with empty hands. In such a climate and situation, what present could be more acceptable to Vathek than this refreshing collation?

PAGE 145. *. . . to kiss the fringe of your consecrated robe*

This observance was an act of the most profound reverence.—*Arabian Nights,* vol. iv, p. 236, etc.

PAGE 145. *. . . and implore you to enter his humble habitation*

It has long been customary for the Arabs to change their habitations with the seasons. Thus Antara:

> Thou hast possessed thyself of my heart; thou hast fixed thy abode, and art settled there, as a beloved and cherished inhabitant.
> Yet how can I visit my fair one, whilst her family have their *vernal mansion* in Oneizatain, and mine are stationed in Ghailem?

Xenophon relates, in his Anabasis, that it was customary for the kings of Persia θερίζειν καὶ ἐαρίζειν, to pass the *summer* and *spring* in Susa and Ecbatana; and Plutarch observes further, that their winters were spent in Babylon, their summers in Media (that is, *Ecbatana*), and the pleas-

* [Or rather Hesiod. The word does not occur in Herodotus.]

antest part of *Spring* in Susa: Καίτοι τούσγε Περσῶν βασιλέας ἐμακάριζον ἐν Βαβυλῶνι τὸν χειμῶνα διάγοντας· ἐν δὲ Μηδίᾳ τὸ θέρος· ἐν δὲ Σούσοις, τὸ ἥδιστον τοῦ ᾽ΕΑΡΟΣ.—*De Exil.*, p. 604. This ΤΟ ᾽ΗΔΙΣΤΟΝ of the *vernal season* is exquisitely described by Solomon:—

Lo, the winter is past, the rain is over; it is gone. The flowers appear on the earth, the season of singing is come, and the voice of the turtle is heard in our land. The fig-tree putteth forth her green figs, and the vines with the tender grape give a good smell. Arise, my love, my fair one, and come away.

PAGE 145.   *. . . an emerald set in lead*

As nothing at the opening of spring can exceed the luxuriant vegetation of these irriguous valleys, so no term could be chosen more expressive of their verdure. The prophet Ezekiel, emblematizing Tyre under the symbol of Paradise, hath described by the different gems of the East the flowers that variegate its surface, and particularly by the *emerald* its green:—"Thou hast been in Eden, the garden of God: כל־אבן יקרה מסכתך—*thy carpet was an assemblage of every precious stone;* the ruby, the topaz, and the diamond; the chrysolite, the onyx, and the jasper; the sapphire, the *emerald*."*—Ch. xxviii. 13. It hath not, perhaps, hitherto been observed that the *Paradise* of Ariosto was copied from hence:—

> Zaffir, rubini, oro, topazj, e perle,
> E diamanti, e chrysoliti, e giacinti
> Potriano i fiori assimigliar, che per le
> Liete piagge v' avea l' aura dipinti.
> Si *verdi l'erbe,* che potendo averle
> Qua giù, ne furon gli *smeraldi* vinti.
>
> Canto xxxiv. st. 49.

When Gray, in his description of Grasmere, spoke of its *"meadows green as an emerald,"* he might have added also the circumstance noted by our author, beset with mountains of the hue of *lead*. Shakespeare, in a similar comparison, hath denominated our *green* England,

This *precious stone* set in the *silver* sea.

PAGE 146.   *. . . sugar*

Dr. Pococke mentions the sugar-cane as a great dessert in Egypt; and adds, that besides coarse loaf-sugar and sugar-candy it yields a third sort,

---

* The same kind of imagery abounds in the Oriental poets. Thus, Abu Nawas:—
"Behold the gardens of the earth, and consider the emblems of those things which Divine power hath formed: *eyes of silver* (daisies) everywhere disclosed, with pupils like molten gold, united to an emerald stalk: these avouch that no one is equal to God."
So, likewise, Sadi:—
"He hath plainted rubies and emeralds on the hard rock: the ruby rose on its emerald stem."
And Ebn Rumi, of the violet:—"It is not a flower, but an emerald bearing a purple gem."

remarkably fine, which is sent to the Grand Seignor, and prepared only for himself.—*Travels,* vol. i., pp. 183, 204. The jeweller's son, in the Story of the Third Calendar, desires the prince to fetch some *melon* and *sugar,* that he might refresh himself with them.—*Arabian Nights,* vol. i., p. 159.

PAGE 146.   . . . *red characters*

The laws of Draco are recorded by Plutarch, in his *Life of Solon,* to have been written in blood. If more were meant by this expression, than that those laws were of a sanguinary nature, they will furnish the earliest instance of the use of *red characters,* which were afterwards considered as appropriate to supreme authority, and employed to denounce some requisition or threatening design to strike terror. According to Suidas, this manner of writing was, likewise, practised in *magic rites.* Hence their application to the instance here mentioned. —TROTZ, *In Herm. Hugonem,* pp. 106, 307. SUIDAS *sub voc.* Θετταλὴ γυνή.

PAGE 146.   . . . *thy body shall be spit upon*

There was no mark of contempt amongst the Easterns so ignominious as this.—*Arabian Nights,* vol. i, p. 115; vol. iv, p. 275. It was the same in the days of Job. Herodotus relates of the Medes, ΠΤΤΕΙΝ ἀντίον 'ΑΙΣΧΡΟΝ ἐστί, and Xenophon relates, 'ΑΙΣΧΡΟΝ ἐστὶ Πέρσαις τὸ 'ΑΠΟΠΤΤΕΙΝ. Hence the reason is evident for spitting on our Saviour.

PAGE 146.   . . . *bats will nestle in thy belly*

Bats in these countries were very abundant, and, both from their numbers and nature, held in abhorrence. See what is related of them by THEVENOT, part i, pp. 132, 133, EGMONT and HAYMAN, vol. ii, p. 87, and other travellers in the East.

PAGE 146.   . . . *the Bismillah*

This word (which is prefixed to every chapter of the Koran except the ninth) signifies, "in the name of the most merciful God." It became not the initiatory formula of prayer till the time of Moez the Fatimite. —D'HERBELOT, p. 326.

Ablution is of an origin long prior to Mahomet. It is mentioned in Homer, and alluded to by the Psalmist:—"I will *wash my hands in innocency,* and so will I compass thine altar, O Lord."

Again:—"Verily have I cleansed my heart in vain, and *washed my hands in innocency.*"

PAGE 147.   . . . *a vast wood of palm-trees*

Perhaps the palm is nowhere more abundant than in this region, *that* only excepted to which Virgil refers, in a passage as yet not explained:—

Primus Idumaeas referam tibi, Mantua, palmas.

If the ingenuousness and delicacy of a right reverend critic (who is said to have owed his present dignity to a note on the context) had not been long known,* an ordinary reader might be startled at the resemblance between his lordship's critique and Catrou's; whilst a fastidious one in a splenetic mood might apply, like another Edwards, *the marks of imitation,* as so many *canons* to annoy their founder. The hypothesis, however, of Hartley, Priestley, and those other physiologists, who have so clearly deduced the phenomena of mind from organization, and traced back the coincidences of thought to predisposing motives and similar associations, will enable us, on the idea of an internal conformity between the critics, to account for their congruity of writing, without leaving room to surmise that the one ever heard of the other. Not a breath, then, of Achan and his wedge of gold!

Catrou, supposing that Virgil meditated the improvement of his writings, after an excursion to Greece and Asia, translates *ego in* patriam *rediens,* by *à mon retour en* ITALIE; but the restricted sense in which the poet delights to apply *patria* (as in his first Eclogue:—

> Nos *patriae* fines, et dulcia linquimus arva,
> Nos *patriam* fugimus),

as well as the mention of *Mantua* and the *Mincius,* precludes this more extended construction. If, therefore, *ego in* patriam *rediens* be literally taken, it will rather mark the design of Virgil to retire from Rome to the sequestered scenes of his *native Mantua;* where he was first smitten with the love of song, and whither he purposes to bring the sisterhood of the Muses. But the clause least understood is that which immediately follows:—

> Primus Idumaeas referam tibi, Mantua, palmas.

Catrou hath inferred from it that Virgil actually projected a voyage to the Levant—to fetch palms, no doubt! The bishop, however, after remarking that the poet, having held himself forth as a conqueror, and declared the object of his conquest to have been bringing the Muses captive from Greece, subjoins "The *palmy* triumphal entry, which was usual to victors on their return from foreign successes, follows—

> Primus Idumaeas referam tibi, Mantua, palmas."

But, with the deference due to so venerable a critic, will this explication suffice? for, may it not be asked, If, to celebrate a triumph for foreign successes, *palms* from Idumaea were requisite; if victors were accustomed to go thither for them, previous to their triumphal entry; or (allowing Idumaeas to be sine mente sonum, a word without meaning†), how it

---

* See the Tract entitled *On the Delicacy of Friendship, a seventh dissertation, addressed to the author of the sixth.*

† Thus, also, Martyn, because Idumaea was famous for palms, interprets Idumaeas palmas, "palms, in general;" and Heyne, *Idumaeas* autem palmas poetico plane epitheto appellabat, a nobili aliquo genere;" yet, he immediately adds, "*Idumen* poetae pro Idumaea ac *tota Judaea* dicunt, quam quidem palmis frequentem fuisse notum est:—arbusto palmarum dives Idume. —*Lucan,* iii. 216."

could happen that the palmy triumphal entry should have been usual to victors, and yet Virgil the first, whose success was to be graced with it?

> Primus Idumaeas referam — palmas.

It is observable that this book of the *Georgics* opens with proposing its subject, the novelty of which induces the author to remark that, as the usual themes of the Roman poets were all become trite, it would be his aim to seek fame from foreign acquisitions, and his purpose to aggrandise the glory of his country by subjecting to its language the poetical beauties of Greece and Judaea.

If it be admitted that, under the allegory of leading the Muses (who were peculiar to Greece) from the summit of the Aonian mount, the poet intended to characterize the loftiest flights of Grecian poetry, or the Epic,* it follows from parity of reason that, under the symbol of their country,† he equally designed the prophetic strains of the Hebrews:—

> Primus ego in patriam mecum, modo vita supersit,
> Aonio rediens deducam vertice Musas:
> Primus Idumaeas referam tibi, Mantua, palmas.

The verb *referam* in connection with *tibi Mantua* implies that Virgil had already brought Idumaean palms to his natal soil; and what these meant is abundantly plain. For, whoever will compare the Fourth Eclogue with the prophecy of Isaiah, must perceive too close an agreement to suppose that the same images, under similar combinations, and both new to a Roman poet, should have occurred to Virgil rather from chance, than a previous perusal of the prophet‡ in Greek.

It only remains, then, to be inquired, whether Virgil, after having introduced in his pastorals some of the prophetic traits of Hebrew poetry, any further availed himself of it in the Epic here projected? For a satisfactory answer to this question, it might suffice to reply, that if there be any characteristic which discriminates the *Aeneid* more than another, it is the prophetic

---

* It was in this light that the *Aeneis* was regarded by Propertius, who exclaims in reference to it (B. II. El. xxxiv. v. 65):—

> Cedite Graii,
> Nescio quid majus nascitur Iliade!

The author of an elegant and masterly pamphlet, entitled *Critical Observations on the Sixth Book of the Aeneid* (published by Elmsly, 1770), supposes Propertius, in the context, to have had his eye on the shield of Aeneas; but, from comparing the passage itself with the sixth elegy of the fourth book, it appears more likely that he alluded to the battle of Actium, as described in *Aen.*, viii. 704. [But the battle of Actium is only described as one of the scenes represented on the shield of Aeneas.]

† It was by this emblem that the Romans, on their coins, represented Judaea; and particularly on the medal, to signalize its reduction:—

> Beneath her Palm here sad Judaea weeps.

‡ Tacitus mentions the ancient scriptures of the Jewish priests as containing the prediction which Virgil is here supposed to have adopted.—*Hist.*, l. v. § 13.

In medio mihi Caesar erit, templumque tenebit.

As in the Pollio, the images employed by the prophet to pre-figure the
birth of the Messiah, and the blessings of his reign, were applied by
the Roman poet to the birth of the expected son of Augustus,* and the
return of the golden age under his auspices; so, in the *Aeneid,* he re-
sumes the prediction, and applies it to Augustus himself:—

> Hic vir, hic est, tibi quem promitti saepius audis
> Augustus Caesar, divi genus; aurea condet
> Saecula qui rursus Latio, regnata per arva
> Saturno quondam; super et Garamantas et Indos
> Proferet Imperium. Jacet extra sidera tellus
> Extra anni solisque vias, &c.
>
> *Aen.,* vi. 792.

PAGE 147. ... *inscription*

Inscriptions of this sort are still retained. Thus Ludeke: "Interni non
solum Divani pluriumque conclavium parietes, sed etiam frontispicia
super portas inscriptiones habent."—*Expositio,* p. 54. In the History of
Amine, we find an inscription over a gate, in letters of gold, analogous
to this of Fakreddin: "Here is the abode of everlasting pleasures and
content."—*Arabian Nights,* vol. i, p. 193.

PAGE 147. ... *a magnificent tecthtrevan*

This kind of *moving throne,* though more common at present than in
the days of Vathek, is still confined to persons of the highest rank.

PAGE 147. ... *her light brown hair floated in the hazy breeze of the twilight*

Literally, hyacinthine. The metaphor taken from this flower, expressed
by the word *Sunbul,* is familiar to the Arabians. Thus, in Sir William
Jones's *Solima,* an eclogue made up of Eastern images:—

> The fragrant hyacinths of Azza's hair,
> That wanton with the laughing summer air.

Nor was it less common to the Greeks. Perhaps Milton, in the following
lines,—

> Hyacinthin locks
> Round from his parted forelock manly hung
> Clust'ring, but not beneath his shoulders broad—

adopted it from Lucian. The term *manly,* with the restriction at the
close, gives full scope for this conjecture; as in Lucian, the descriptions
relate only to *women.* The poet may be further traced upon the snow
of the classics in the use of the term clustering; an equivalent expression
being appropriated by the ancients to that disposition of the curls which
resembles the growth of grapes, and may be observed on gems, coins, and
statues.—PLUTARCH, *Consol. Apoll.,* p. 196.

* By Scribonia, then pregnant of the infamous Julia. See Bishop Chandler's
Vindication, and Masson's *Dissertation* subjoined.

It is singular that both lexicographers and critics should have considered βοτρυοχαίτης and βοτρυόκοσμος as synonymous. This confusion, however, appears to have arisen from both being attributes of Bacchus, whose hair was not only adorned with clusters from the vine, but, like the locks of Apollo (πλοχμοὶ BOTPΥOENTEΣ. Apollon., 'Αργον., B. 677), was itself clustering.*

Sir William Jones acutely conjectures that Solomon alluded to the hair in that elliptical speech of the Shulamite, Song i. 14:—

אשכל הכפר דודי לי בכרמי עין גדי

A cluster of grapes, &c.

The like epithet, though adopted from a different fruit, occurs in the poem of Amriolkais:—

Her long coal-black hair decorated her back, thick and diffused, like bunches of dates, clustering on the palm-tree.

The diffusion of hair here noticed, and its floating as described by our author, are circumstances so frequent in the works of Hafez and Jami that there is scarce a page of them in which the idea of the breeze playing with the tresses of a beautiful girl is not agreeably and variously expressed.† An instance from Petrarch, resembling their manner, may be seen in the lines that follow:—

> Aura, che quelle chiome bionde e crespe
> Circondi, e movi, e se' mossa da loro
> Soavemente, e spargi quel dolce oro,
> E poi l raccogli, e'n bei nodi l rincrespe.
> Son. cxci.

PAGE 147. ... *your ivory limbs*

The Arabians compare the skin of a beautiful woman to the egg of the ostrich, when preserved unsullied.‡ Thus Amriolkais:

* Winckelmann hath strangely fixed upon the reverse of this character as an exclusive property of these divinities; and so infallible a criterion does he make it, as even from it alone to ascertain their mutilated statues.—*Hist. de l'Art d'Antiq.*, tom. ii., p. 146. However, in another part of his work, he refers to Plutarch, as cited above.

† Preface to Jones's Poems, p. xii.

‡ A fair skin is likened by the Italian poets to curd. Thus, Bracciolini:—

> i suoi teneri membri un latte sieno
> Che tremolante, ma non rotto ancora,
> Pose accorto Pastor su i verdi giunchi.
> *Amoroso Sdegno*, iii, 2.

Likewise, Tasso:—

> egli rivolse
> I cupidi occhi in quelle membra belle,
> Che, come suole tremolare, il latte
> Ne giunchi, si parean morbide, e bianche.
> *Aminta*, iii. 1.

Delicate was her shape; fair her skin; and her body well proportioned: her bosom was as smooth as a mirror,—
Or like the pure egg of an ostrich, of a yellowish tint blended with white.

Also the Koran: "Near them shall lie the virgins of Paradise, refraining their looks from beholding any besides their spouses, having large black eyes, and resembling the eggs of an ostrich, covered with feathers from dust."—*Moallakat*, p. 8. *Al Koran*, ch. 27.

But though the Arabian epithet be taken from thence, yet the word ivory is substituted, as more analogous to European ideas, and not foreign from the Eastern. Thus Amru:

And two sweet breasts, smooth and white as vessels of ivory, modestly defended from the hand of those who presume to touch them.—*Moallakat*, p. 77.

PAGE 147.   ... *baths of rosewater*

The use of perfumed waters for the purpose of bathing is of an early origin in the East, where every odoriferous plant sheds a richer fragrance than is known to our more humid climates. The rose which yields this lotion is, according to Hasselquist, of a beautiful pale blush colour, double, large as a man's fist, and more exquisite in scent than any other species. The quantities of this water distilled annually at Fajhum, and carried to distant countries, is immense. The mode of conveying it is in vessels of copper coated with wax.—*Voyag.*, p. 248. Ben Jonson makes Volpone say to Celia:

Their bath shall be the juyce of gillyflowres,
Spirit of roses, and of violets.

PAGE 148.   ... *amuse you with tales*

Thus, in the story of Alraoui:—"There was an emir of Grand Cairo, whose company was no less coveted for his genius than his rank. Being one day in a melancholy mood, he turned towards a courtier, and said: 'Alraoui, my heart is dejected, and I know not the cause; relate to me some pleasant story, to dispel my chagrin.' Alraoui replied: 'The great have with reason regarded tales as the best antidote to care; if you will allow me, I will tell you my own.' "—Translated from an unpublished MS. "The 'Arabian Nights'," saith Colonel Capper, in his *Observations on the Passage to India through Egypt and across the Great Desert,* "are by many people supposed to be a spurious production, and are therefore slighted in a manner they do not deserve. They are written by an Arabian, and are universally read and admired throughout Asia by persons of all ranks, both old and young. Considered, therefore, as an original work, descriptive as they are of the manners and customs of the East in general, and also of the genius and character of the Arabians in particular, they surely must be thought to merit the attention of the curious; nor are they, in my opinion, entirely destitute of merit in other respects; for although the extravagance of some of the stories is carried too far, yet, on the whole, one cannot help admiring the fancy and invention of the author in striking out such a variety of pleasing incidents. Pleasing, I call them, because they have frequently afforded me much amusement; nor do I envy any man his feelings who is above being pleased with them; but, before any person decides on the merit of these books, he should be eye-witness of the effects they produce on those who best understand them. I have, more than once, seen the Arabians on the Desert, sitting round a fire, listening to these stories with such attention and pleasure as totally to forget the fatigue and hardship with which an instant before they were totally overcome. In short, they are held in the same estimation all over Asia as the adventures of Don Quixote are in Spain."

If the observation of the Knight of La Mancha, respecting translation in general, be just—"me parece, que el traducir de una lengua en otra, es como quien mira los tapices flamencos por el reves, que aunque se ven las figuras, son llenas de hilos que las escurecen, y no se ven con la lisura y tez de la haz,"—the wrong side of the tapestry will represent more truly the figures on the right, notwithstanding the floss that blurs them, than any version the coarse surface and smoothness of the Arabian surface. The prospect of a rich country in all the glories of summer is not more different from its November appearance than the original of those tales when opposed to the French translation, of which, it may be added, our version is, at best, but a moonlight view:—

> pallida la luna
> Tingea d'un lume scolorito e incerto
> La vasta solitudine terrena.

PAGE 148. ... *lamb à la crême*

No dish among the Easterns was more generally admired. The caliph Abdolmelek, at a splendid entertainment, to which whoever came was welcome, asked Amrou, the son of Hareth, what kind of meat he preferred to all others. The old man answered, "An ass's neck, well seasoned and roasted."—"But what say you," replied the caliph, "to the leg or shoulder of a LAMB *à la crême?*" and added:

> How sweetly we live if a shadow would last!

—*MS. Laud.* No. 161. S. OCKLEY's *History of the Saracens,* vol. ii, p. 277.

PAGE 148. ... *made the dwarfs dance against their will*

Ali Chelebi al Moufti, in a treatise on the subject, held that dancing after the example of the dervishes, who made it a part of their devotion, was allowable. But in this opinion he was deemed to be heterodox; for Mahometans, in general, place dancing amongst the things that are forbidden.—D'HERBELOT, p. 98.

PAGE 148. ... *durst not refuse the commander of the faithful*

The mandates of Oriental potentates have ever been accounted irre-

sistible. Hence the submission of these devotees to the will of the caliph.
—Esther, i, 19. Daniel, vi, 8. LUDEKE, *Expos. brevis*, p. 60.

PAGE 148.   ... *he spread himself on the sofa*

The idiom of the original occurs in Euripides, and is from him adopted
by Milton:—

> Ἴδετε τὸν Γέροντ' ἀ-
> μαλὸν ἐπὶ πέδῳ
> ΧΥΜΕΝΟΝ· ὦ τάλας.
>> *Heraclidae*, v. 75.

> See how he lies at random, carelessly diffus'd,
> With languish'd head unpropt,
> As one past hope, abandon'd
> And by himself given over.
>> *Samson*, v. 118.

PAGE 148.   ... *properly lubricated with the balm of Mecca*

Unguents, for reasons sufficiently obvious, have been of general use in
hot climates. According to Pliny, "at the time of the Trojan war, they
consisted of oils perfumed with the odours of flowers, and chiefly of
ROSES,"—whence the 'POΔOEN ἔλαιον of Homer. Hasselquist speaks of oil
impregnated with the tuberose and jessamine; but the unguent here
mentioned was preferred to every other. Lady M. W. Montagu, desirous
to try its effects, seems to have suffered materially from having improperly applied it.

PAGE 148.   ... *if their eyebrows and tresses were in order*

As perfuming and decorating the hair of the sultanas was an essential
duty of their attendants, the translator hath ventured to substitute the
term *tresses* for another more exact to the original. In Don Quixote,
indeed, a waiting woman of the duchess mentions the same services with
our author, but as performed by persons of her own sex:—"Hay en
Candaya mugeres que andan de casa en casa á quitar el vello, y á pulir
las cejas, y hacer otros menjurges tocantes á mugeres, nosotras las dueñas
de mi señora por jamas quisímos admitirlas, porque las mas oliscan á
terceras."—Tom. iv., cap. xl., p. 42.

Other offices of the dressing-room and toilet may be seen in Lucian,
vol. ii. *Amor.* 39, p. 441. The Arabians had a preparation of antimony
and galls, with which they tinged the eyebrows of a beautiful black; and
great pains were taken to shape them into regular arches. In combing the
hair, it was customary to sprinkle it with perfumes, and to dispose it in
a variety of becoming forms.—RICHARDSON's *Dissertat.*, p. 481. LADY M.
W. MONTAGU's *Letters*.

PAGE 148.   ... *the nine hundred and ninety-ninth time*

The Mahometans boast of a doctor who is reported to have read over
the Koran not fewer than twenty thousand times.—D'HERBELOT, p. 75.

PAGE 149.   ... *black eunuchs, sabre in hand*

In this manner the apartments of the ladies were constantly guarded. Thus, in the Story of the Enchanted Horse, Firouz Schah, traversing a strange palace by night, entered a room, "and by the light of a lantern saw that the persons he had heard snoring were black eunuchs with naked sabres by them, which was enough to inform him that this was the guard-chamber of some queen or princess."—*Arabian Nights,* vol. iv, p. 189.

PAGE 149.   ... *Nouronihar, daughter of the emir, was sprightly as an antelope, and full of wanton gaiety*

Solomon has compared his bride to "a company of horses in Pharaoh's chariots"; Horace, a sportive young female to an untamed filly; Sophocles, a delicate virgin to a wild heifer; Ariosto, Angelica to a fawn or kid; and Tasso, Erminia to a hind; but the object of resemblance adopted by our author is of superior beauty to them all.

PAGE 149.   ... *to let down the great swing*

The swing was an exercise much used in the apartments of the Eastern ladies, and not only contributed to their health, but also to their amusement.—*Tales of Inatulla,* vol. i, p. 259.

PAGE 149.   ... *I accept the invitation of your honied lips*

Uncommon as this idiom may appear in our language, it was not so either to the Hebrew or the Greek. Compare Proverbs xvi. 24—

צוּף־דְבַשׁ אִמְרֵי־נֹעַם

with Homer, *Iliad* a. 249—

Τοῦ καὶ ἀπὸ γλώσσης ΜΕΛΙΤΟΣ γλυκίων ῥέεν αὐδή.

Theocritus, Idyl. xx. 26

'Εκ ΣΤΟΜΑΤΩΝ δὲ
Ἕρρεέ μοι ΦΩΝΑ γλυκερωτέρα ἢ ΜΕΛΙΚΗΡΩ.

And Solomon's Song iv. 11—

נֹפֶת תִּטֹּפְנָה שִׂפְתוֹתַיִךְ כַּלָּה דְבַשׁ

with Moschus, Idyl. i. 8, 9—

ἁδὺ ΛΑΛΗΜΑ·
ὡς ΜΕΛΙ, φωνά.

An Arabian fabulist, enumerating the charms of a consummate beauty, hath used the identical expression of our author; but, probably, in an extended sense, as—

from her lip
Not words alone pleased him.

PAGE 149.   ... *my senses are dazzled with the radiance that beams from*
your charms

Or (to express an idiom for which we have no substitute), "thy countenance, rayonnante de beautés et de grâces." Descriptions of this kind
are frequent in Arabian writers; thus, Tarafa:—

> Her face appears to be wrapped in a veil of sunbeams.

And in the *Arabian Nights:*—"Schemselnihar came forward amongst her
attendants with a majesty resembling the sun amidst the clouds; which
receive his splendour, without concealing his lustre." To account for
this compliment in the mouth of Bababalouk, we should remember that
he was, *ex officio, elegans formarum Spectator.*

PAGE 150.   ... *melodious Philomel, I am thy rose*

The passion of the nightingale for the rose is celebrated over all the
East. Thus Mesihi, as translated by Sir W. Jones:

> Come, charming maid, and hear thy poet sing,
> Thyself the rose, and he the bird of spring:
> Love bids him sing, and love will be obey'd,
> Be gay: too soon the flowers of spring will fade.

PAGE 150.   ... *oil spilt in breaking the lamps*

It appears from Thevenot that illuminations were usual on the arrival
of a stranger, and he mentions, on an occasion of this sort, two hundred
lamps being lighted. The quantity of oil, therefore, spilt by Bababalouk
may be easily accounted for from this custom.

PAGE 150.   ... *reclining on down*

See LADY M. W. MONTAGU, Let. xxvi.

PAGE 151.   ... *calenders*

These were a sort of men amongst the Mahometans who abandoned
father and mother, wife and children, relations and possessions, to
wander through the world, under a pretence of religion, entirely sub-
sisting on the fortuitous bounty of those they had the address to dupe.—
D'HERBELOT, *Suppl.,* p. 204.

PAGE 151.   ... *santons*

A body of religionists, who were also called *abdals,* and pretended to be
inspired with the most enthusiastic raptures of divine love. They were
regarded by the vulgar as *saints.*—OLEARIUS, tom. i, p. 971. D'HERBELOT,
p. 5.

PAGE 151.   ... *dervishes*

The term *dervish* signifies a *poor man,* and is the general appellation
by which a religious amongst the Mahometans is named. There are, how-

ever, discriminations that distinguish this class from the others already mentioned. They are bound by no vow of poverty, they abstain not from marriage, and, whenever disposed, they may relinquish both their blue shirt and profession.—D'HERBELOT, *Suppl.,* 214. It is observable, that these different orders, though not established till the reign of Nasser al Samani, are notwithstanding mentioned by our author as coeval with Vathek, and by the author of the *Arabian Nights* as existing in the days of Haroun al Raschid; so that the Arabian fabulists appear as inattentive to chronological exactness in points of this sort as our immortal dramatist himself.

PAGE 151. ... *Brahmins*

These constituted the principal caste of the Indians, according to whose doctrine *Brahma,* from whom they are called, is the first of the three created beings by whom the world was made. This Brahma is said to have communicated to the Indians four books, in which all the sciences and ceremonies of their religion are comprised. The word Brahma, in the Indian language, signifies *pervading all things.* The Brahmins lead a life of most rigid abstinence refraining not only from the use, but even the touch, of animal food; and are equally exemplary for their contempt of pleasures and devotion to philosophy and religion.— D'HERBELOT, p. 212. BRUCKERI *Hist. Philosoph.,* tom. i, p. 194.

PAGE 151. ... *fakirs*

This sect were a kind of religious anchorets, who spent their whole lives in the severest austerities and mortification. It is almost impossible for the imagination to form an extravagance that has not been practised by some of them, to torment themselves. As their reputation for sanctity rises in proportion to their sufferings, those amongst them are reverenced the most, who are most ingenious in the invention of tortures, and persevering in enduring them. Hence some have persisted in sitting or standing for years together in one unvaried posture, supporting an almost intolerable burden, dragging the most cumbrous chains, exposing their naked bodies to the scorching sun, and hanging with the head downward before the fiercest fires.—*Relig. Ceremon.,* vol. iii, p. 264, etc. WHITE'S *Sermons,* p. 504.

PAGE 151. ... *some that cherished vermin*

In this attachment they were not singular. The Emperor Julian not only discovered the same partiality, but celebrated, with visible complacency, the shaggy and *populous* beard which he fondly cherished; and even "The Historian of the Roman Empire" affirms, "that the little animal is a beast familiar to man, and signifies love."—Vol. ii., p. 343.

PAGE 152. ... *Visnow and Ixhora*

Two deities of the East Indians, concerning whose history and adventures more nonsense is related than can be found in the whole compass of mythology besides. The traditions of their votaries are, no doubt, allegorical; but without a key to disclose their mystic import, they are little better than senseless jargon.

PAGE 152.   ... *talapoins*

This order, which abounds in Siam, Laos, Pegu, and other countries, consists of different classes, and both sexes, but chiefly of men.—*Relig. Ceremon.*, vol. iv, p. 62, etc.

PAGE 152.   ... *objects of pity were sure to swarm round him*

Ludeke mentions the practice of bringing those who were suffering under any calamity, or had lost the use of their limbs, &c., into public, for the purpose of exciting compassion. On an occasion, therefore, of this sort, when Fakreddin, like a pious Mussulman, was publicly to distribute his alms, and the commander of the faithful to make his appearance, such an assemblage might well be expected. The Eastern custom of regaling a convention of this kind is of great antiquity, as is evident from the parable of the king in the Gospels, who entertained the maimed, the lame, and the blind; nor was it discontinued when Dr. Pococke visited the East.—Vol. i., p. 182.

PAGE 152.   ... *horns of an exquisite polish*

Jacinto Polo de Medina, in one of his epigrams, has as unexpected a turn on the same topic:—

> Cavando un sepulcro un hombre
> Sacó largo, corvo y grueso,
> Entre otros muchos, un hueso,
> Que tiene cuerno por nombre;
>
> Volviólo al sepulcro al punto:
> Y viéndolo un cortesano,
> Dijo: bien haceis, hermano,
> Que es hueso de ese defunto.

PAGE 152.   ... *small plates of abominations*

The Koran hath established several distinctions relative to different kinds of food, in imitation of the Jewish prescriptions; and many Mahometans are so scrupulous as not to touch the flesh of any animal over which, *in articulo mortis,* the butcher had omitted to pronounce the *Bismillah.*—*Relig. Ceremon.*, vol. vii, p. 110.

PAGE 153.   ... *fish which they drew from a river*

According to Le Bruyn, the Oriental method of fishing with a line, is by winding it round the finger, and when the fisherman feels that the bait is taken, he draws in the string with alternate hands: in this way, he adds, a good dish of fish is soon caught. Tom. i, p. 564. It appears, from a circumstance related by Galand, that Vathek was fond of this amusement.—D'HERBELOT, *Suppl.*, p. 210.

PAGE 153. ... *Sinai*

This mountain is deemed by Mahometans the noblest of all others, and even regarded with the highest veneration, because the divine law was promulgated from it.—D'HERBELOT, p. 812.

PAGE 153. ... *Peris*

The word *Peri,* in the Persian language, signifies that beautiful race of creatures which constitutes the link between angels and men. The Arabians call them *Ginn,* or genii, and we (from the Persian, perhaps) *Fairies:* at least, the peris of the Persian romance correspond to that imaginary class of beings in our poetical system. The Italians denominate them *Fata,* in allusion to their power of charming and enchanting; thus the *Manto fatidica* of Virgil is rendered in *Orlando, La Fata Manto.* The term ginn being common to both peris and dives, some have erroneously fancied that the peris were female dives. This appellation, however, served only to discriminate their common nature from the angelic and human, without respect to their qualities, moral or personal. Thus, the dives are hideous and wicked, whilst the peris are beautiful and good. Amongst the Persian poets, the beauty of the peris is proverbial: insomuch that a woman superlatively handsome, is styled by them, *the offspring of a Peri.*

PAGE 154. ... *butterflies of Cashmere*

The same insects are celebrated in an unpublished poem of Mesihi. Sir Anthony Shirley relates, that it was customary in Persia, "to hawke after butterflies with sparrows, made to that use, and stares." It is, perhaps, to this amusement that our author alludes in the context.

PAGE 154. ... *I had rather that his teeth should mischievously press my finger*

These *molles morsiunculae* remind one of Lesbia and her sparrow:—

> Passer, deliciae meae puellae,
> Quicum ludere, quem in sinu tenere,
> Quoi primum digitum dare adpetenti,
> Et acres solet incitare morsus.

In the Story of the Sleeper Awakened (which the induction to *The Taming of the Shrew* greatly resembles), Abon Hassan thus addresses the lady that was brought him: "Come hither, fair one, and bite the end of my finger,* that I may feel whether I am asleep or awake."— *Arabian Nights,* vol. iii., p. 157. Lady Percy, with all the fondness of insinuation, practises on her wayward Hotspur a blandishment similar to that here instanced by Nouronihar:—

> Come, come, you paraquito, answer me
> Directly to this question that I ask.
> In faith, I'll break thy little finger, Harry,
> An if thou wilt not tell me all things true.

* Ἀλλ' ἐπὶ λέκτρον ἰὼν, ἄκρον δάκτυλον καταδάκνω.
HOMER, *Batrach.*, v. 45.

PAGE 155. . . . *Megnoun and Leilah*

These personages are esteemed amongst the Arabians as the most beautiful, chaste, and impassioned of lovers; and their amours have been
celebrated with all the charms of verse, in every Oriental language. The
Mahometans regard them, and the poetical records of their love, in the
same light as the Bridegroom and Spouse, and the Song of Songs, are
regarded by the Jews.—D'HERBELOT, p. 573.

PAGE 155. . . . *they still detained him in the harem*

Noureddin, who was as old as Gulchenrouz, had a similar indulgence of
resorting to the harem, and no less availed himself of it.—*Arabian Nights,*
vol. iii, pp. 9, 10.

PAGE 155. . . . *dart the lance in the chase*

Throwing the lance was a favourite pastime with the young Arabians;
and so expert were they in this practice (which prepared them for the
mightier conflicts, both of the chase and of war), that they could bear
off a ring on the points of their javelins.—RICHARDSON's *Dissertat.,* pp.
198, 281. Though the ancients had various methods of hunting, yet the
two which chiefly prevailed were those described by Virgil,* and

* Dum trepidant ALAE, saltusque indagine cingunt.—*Aen.,* iv. 121.

Notwithstanding the explanations of *alae* which have been given by Servius,
Burman, and others, there can scarce be a doubt but that Virgil referred to the
custom of scaring deer into holts with feathers fastened on lines; a practice so
effectual to the purpose, that Linnaeus characterized the Dama, or Fallow
Deer, from it: *arcetur filo horizontali.* The same stratagem is mentioned in the
Georgics, iii. 371[372]:—

Puniceaeve agitant pavidos formidine Pinnae:

and again in the *Aeneid,* xii. 749:—

Inclusum veluti si quando flumine nactus
Cervum, aut Puniceae septum formidine Pinnae.

It is observable, however, that the poet, in these instances, hath studiously
varied his mode of expression. The sportsmen of Italy, used pinion feathers,
which, the better to answer their purpose, they dyed of a Lybian red;* but, as
Africa abounded in birds whose wings were impregnated with the spontaneous
and glossy tincture of nature, such an expedient in that country must have
been needless. If we advert, then, to the scene of Dido's chase, the reason will
be obvious why Virgil omitted *puniceae,* and for *pinnae* substituted *alae.*

There is a passage in NEMESIANUS which will at once confirm the interpretation here given, and illustrate the judgment of the poet in the choice of his
terms:—

Hinc (*sc.* ex Africa) mage Puniceas nativo munere sumes:
Namque illic sine fine, greges florentibus alis
Invenies avium, suavique rubescere luto.—*Cynegeticon,* v. 317.

* Lybico fucantur sandyce pinnae.—GRATII *Cyneg.* v. 86.

alluded to by Solomon.*—*Prov.* vii. 22.

PAGE 155. . . . *nor curb the steeds*

Though Gulchenrouz was too young to excel in horsemanship, it nevertheless was an essential accomplishment amongst the Arabians. Hence the boast of Amriolkais:—

> Often have I risen at 'early dawn, while the birds were yet in their nests, and mounted a hunter with smooth short hair, of a full height; and so fleet as to make captive the beasts of the forests.

* The wide region of conjectural emendation cannot produce a happier instance of critical skill than was discovered by that accurate and judicious scholar, the late Dr. Hunt;* who, when the sense of the passage referred to had for ages been lost, sagaciously restored it by curtailing a letter. *Proverbs* vii. 22: "As an hart (אייל for אויל) boundeth into the toils, till a dart strike through his liver."

When the game, driven together, were either circumvented, as described by Virgil, or ensnared by the foot (ποδοστράβη), as alluded to by Solomon, the hunters despatched them with their missile weapons. Thus Xenophon (as cited in Dr. Hunt's Dissertation): Χρὴ δ' ἐὰν οὕτως ἔλῃ—ἐὰν μὲν ᾖ ἄρρην μὴ προσίεναι ἐγγύς· τοῖς γὰρ κέρασι παίει, καὶ τοῖς ποσίν· ἄποθεν οὖν 'ΑΚΟΝΤΙΖΕΙΝ.—"When the animal is thus caught, you must not, if it be a male, advance within his reach, for they are apt to strike with their horns and their heels; it will be proper therefore to *pierce* him at a distance."

---

* The correction, with the context, is this:—

> 22 He goeth after her straightway,
>   As an ox goeth to the slaughter;
> 23 Or as an hart boundeth into the toils,
>   Till a dart strike through his liver:
> 24 As a bird hasteth to the snare,
>   And knoweth not that it is for his life.

Dr. Jebb well imagined (though he hath ill rendered הטתו in the 21st verse, *Irretivit illum*) that the heedless haste of the bird towards the snare might be caused by the lure of a female's call; and adduced from Oppian an apposite example:—

> Ὡς δέ τις οἰωνοῖσι μόρον δολόεντα φυτεύων
> Θήλειαν θάμνοισι κατακρύπτει λασίοισιν
> Ὄρνιν, ὁμογλώσσοιο συνέμπορον ἠθάδα θήρης·
> Ἡ δὲ λίγα κλάζει ξουθὸν μέλος, οἳ δ' αἴοντες
> Πάντες ἐπισπέρχουσι, καὶ ἐς βρόχον αὐτοὶ ἵενται
> Θηλυτέρης ἐνοπῇσι παραπλαγχθέντες ἰωῆς.—*Halieut.*, iv. 120.

> "As when the fowler to the fields resorts,
> His caged domestic partner of his sports
> Behind some shade-projecting bush he lays,
> And wreaths the wiry cell with blooming sprays.
> The pretty captive to the groves around
> Warbles her practised care-deluding sound.
> The attentive flocks pursue with ravish'd ear
> The female music of the feather'd fair,
> Forget to see, and rush upon the snare."—JONES.

Ready in turning, quick in pursuing, bold in advancing, firm in backing; and performing the whole with the strength and swiftness of a vast rock which a torrent has pushed from its lofty base.

A bright bay steed, from whose polished back the trappings slide, as drops of rain slide hastily down the slippery marble.

.   .   .   .

He makes the light youth slide from his seat, and violently shakes the skirts of a heavier and more stubborn rider.—*Moallakat*, p. 10.

The stud of Fakreddin consisted, no doubt, of as noble a breed, though sprung neither from "the mighty Tartar horse" (whose gigantic rider was slain by Codadad), nor the size* of Clavileño, "and the wondrous horse of brass." Milton's allusion to the *last* having occasioned much fruitless inquiry concerning his pedigree,† it shall here be made out, with that of his brother:—

The principal qualities of "the Horse of Brass" were that he was brought before the Tartar king after the third course of a feast which was solemnized at the commencement of spring; that he was able, within the compass of a natural day, to carry his rider wherever he might choose; that he could mount into the air as high as an eagle, and with as equable and easy a motion; that by turning one pin, fixed in his ear, his course might be directed to a destined spot, and, by means of another, he might be made to alight, or return to the place from whence he set out.

The particulars of Clavileño are that he was the production of an enchanter; was capable of rising into the air with the velocity of an arrow, and carrying his rider to any distance; was put into motion by the turning of a pin on his neck, and directed in his course by another in his forehead; that he fleeted so steadily through the air as not to spill a drop from a cup full of water in the hand of his rider; that, being lent by his owner, Pierres made a long voyage upon him, and brought off the fair Magalona, who alighted to become a queen; that Don Quixote, when high in the air, knew not the management of the pin, to prevent his rising; and that he, at last, vanished amidst rockets and crackers.

The resemblances here specified are evidently too strong to have resulted from accident; and it will appear, on further inquiry, that "the Enchanted Horse," in the *Arabian Nights,* was not only possessed of those qualities which were common to them both, but also of such as were peculiar to each. Thus:—

He was presented to the king of Persia at the close of a festival which was celebrated on the opening of spring: could transport his rider, and

---

* [Is not this a misprint in the original for "sire"?]

† "Among the MSS. at Oriel College in Oxford is an old Latin treatise, entitled *Fabula de aeneo caballo.* Here I imagined I had discovered the origin of Chaucer's Squier's Tale, so replete with marvellous imagery, and evidently an Arabian fiction of the middle ages. But I was disappointed; for, on examination, it appeared to have not even a distant connection with Chaucer's story. I mention this, that others, on seeing a title in the catalogue, might not be flattered with specious expectations of so curious a discovery, and misled, like myself, by a fruitless inquiry."—*Warton's edit. of Milton's Poems,* p. 82.

in the space of a day, wherever he listed; moved so smoothly as to cause no shock, even on coming on the ground; could soar above the ken of every beholder; might be guided, by turning a pin in the hollow of his neck, to any point his rider should choose, and by means of another behind his right ear, be made to descend, or return whence he came; was the production of an enchanter; passed through the air with the speed of an arrow; having been lent by his owner to Firouz Schah, carried him a considerable distance, and brought back behind him the Princess of Bengal, to whom the prince was afterwards married; that Firouz Schah, when high in the air, was unable to manage the pin so as to prevent him from rising; and, finally, that he made his last exit in an explosion of fire-works and smoke.*

PAGE 155. ... *The bow, however, he drew with a certain aim*

This, as well as the other accomplishments mentioned before, was a constituent part of an Eastern education. Thus, in the Story of the Sisters who envied their Sister:—"When the princes were learning to mount the managed horse and to ride, the princess could not permit them to have that advantage over her, but went through all their exercises with them, learning to ride the great horse, dart the javelin, and bend the bow."—*Arabian Nights*, vol. iv., p. 276.

PAGE 155. ... *The two brothers had mutually engaged their children to each other*

Contracts of this nature were frequent amongst the Arabians. Another instance occurs in the Story of Noureddin Ali and Bedreddin Hassan.

PAGE 155. ... *Nouronihar loved her cousin more than her own beautiful eyes*

This mode of expression occurs not only in the sacred writers, but also in the Greek and Roman. Thus, Moschus:—

Τὸν μὲν ἐγὼ ΤΙΕΣΚΟΝ ᾽ΙΣΟΝ ΦΑΕΕΣΣΙΝ ᾽ΕΜΟΙΣΙΝ.

and Catullus says:—

Quem plus illa oculis suis amabat.

PAGE 155. ... *The same long, languishing looks*

So Ariosto:—

negri occhi, ——
Pietosi a riguardare, a mover parchi.

The lines which follow, from Shakespeare and Spenser, may serve as a comment upon the brief but beautiful description of our author.

* It may not be impertinent to subjoin, on a kindred subject, as no mention has hitherto been made of him, that the author of *The Touchstone, or Paradoxes brought to the test of a rigorous and fair examination*, printed for Noon, 1732, appears to have been the original projector of sailing through the air in a boat appended to a ball. [He merely plagiarised from the Jesuit Lana, who wrote in 1670.]

Winter's Tale:—

> never gaz'd the moon
> Upon the water as he'll stand, and read,
> As 'twere, my daughter's eyes.

Faerie Queen:*—

> Her eyes, sweet smiling in delight,
> Moystened their fierie beames, with which she thrild
> Fraile hearts, yet quenched not; like starry light,
> Which sparkling on the silent waves does seeme more bright.

PAGE 155. ... *with all the bashfulness of a fawn*

The fawn, as better known, is here substituted for the gazal of the Arabians, an animal uncommonly beautiful and shy.

PAGE 155. ... *take refuge in the fond arms of Nouronihar*

Ample scope is here left to the imagination of the reader, and Tasso will assist him to fill up the picture.

> Sovra lui pende: ed ei nel grembo molle
> Le posa il capo, e'l volto al volto attolle.—*La Gerus.*, xvi. 18.

PAGE 155. ... *Shaddukian and Amberabad*

These were two cities of the peris, in the imaginary region of *Ginnistan:* the former signifies *pleasure* and *desire,* the latter, *the city of Ambergris.* —See RICHARDSON's *Dissertation on the Languages, etc., of Eastern Nations,* p. 169.

PAGE 157. ... *a spoon of cocknos*

The cocknos is a bird whose beak is much esteemed for its beautiful polish, and sometimes used as a spoon. Thus, in the *History of Atalmulck and Zelica Begum,* it was employed for a similar purpose: "Zelica having called for refreshment, six old slaves instantly brought in and distributed *Mahramas,* and then served about in a great basin of Martabam, a salad *made of herbs of various kinds, citron juice, and the pith of cucumbers.* They served it first to the Princess in a *cocknos beak:* she took a beak of the salad, ate it, and gave another to the next slave that sat by her on her right hand; which slave did as her mistress had done."

PAGE 158. ... *Ghouls*

Ghoul, or *ghul,* in Arabic, signifies any terrifying object, which deprives people of the use of their senses. Hence it became the appellative of that species of monster which was supposed to haunt forests, cemeteries, and other lonely places; and believed not only to tear in pieces the living, but to dig up and devour the dead.—RICHARDSON's *Dissertation*

---

* Spencer seems to have copied this simile from Tasso:—

> Qual raggio in onda, le scintilla un riso
> Negli umidi occhi tremulo e lascivo.

on the Languages, etc., of Eastern Nations, pp. 174, 274.

That kind of insanity called by the Arabians *Kutrub* (a word signify-
ing not only a *wolf,* but likewise a *male Ghoul*), which incites such as
are afflicted with it to roam howling amidst those melancholy haunts,
may cast some light on the nature of the possession recorded by St. Mark,
ch. v, 1, etc.

PAGE 159. ... *feathers of the heron, all sparkling with carbuncles*

Panaches of this kind are amongst the attributes of Eastern royalty.—
Tales of Inatulla, vol. ii, p. 205.

PAGE 159. ...*whose eyes pervade the inmost soul of a female*

The original in this instance, as in the others already noticed, is more
analogous to the French than the English idiom: *"Dont l'œil pénètre
jusqu'à la moelle des jeunes filles."*

PAGE 159. ... *the carbuncle of Giamschid*

This mighty potentate was the fourth sovereign of the dynasty of the
Pischadians, and brother or nephew to Tahamurath. His proper name
was *Giam* or *Gem,* and *Schid,* which in the language of the ancient
Persians denominated the sun: an addition ascribed by some to the
majesty of his person, and by others to the splendour of his actions. One
of the most magnificent monuments of his reign was the city of
Istakhar, of which Tahamurath had laid the foundations. This city,
at present called *Gihil-,* or *Tchil-minar,* from the forty columns reared
in it by Homai, or (according to our author and others*) by Soliman Ben
Daoud, was known to the Greeks by the name of Persepolis; and there
is still extant in the East a tradition, that, when Alexander burnt the
edifices of the Persian kings, seven stupendous structures of Giamschid
were consumed with his palace. This prince, after having subjected to
his empire seven vast provinces of Upper Asia, and enjoyed in peace a
long reign (which some authors have protracted to 700 years), became
intoxicated with his greatness; and, foolishly fancying it would have no
end, arrogated to himself divine honours. But the Almighty raised up,
even in his own house, a terrible instrument to abase his pride, by whom
he was easily overcome, and driven into exile.

The author of *Giame al tavatikh* mentions the cup, or concave mirror
of Giamschid, formed of a gem, and called the cup of the sun. To this
vessel the Persian poets often refer, and allegorize it in different ways.
They attribute to it the property of exhibiting everything in the compass of nature, and even some things that are preternatural. The gem
it consisted of appears to be the carbuncle or oriental ruby; which, from
its resemblance to a burning coal, and the splendour it was supposed to
emit in the dark, was called Schebgerag, or, the torch of the night.
According to Strabo, it obtained its high estimation amongst the Per-

* *Examen Critique des Anciens Historiens d'Alexandre le Grand,* p. 287.

sians, who were worshippers of fire, from its igneous qualities; and perhaps those virtues for which it hath been styled "the first of stones."

Milton had a learned retrospect to its fabulous powers, in describing the Old Serpent:

> . . . his head
> Crested aloft, and carbuncle his eyes—

D'HERBELOT, pp. 392, 395, 780, etc. BRIGHTE, *On Melancholie*, p. 321. *Paradise Lost*, IX, 499.

PAGE 159.   . . . the torches were extinguished

From the emblems of royalty in the vision, and the closing declaration of the last voice, it is evident that these torches, λαμπάδας 'ΑΝΤΙ ΤΩΝ ΝΤΜΦΙΚΩΝ τοῦ ΔΑΙΜΟΝΟΣ ἄψαντος, were lighted by the dive to prognosticate* the destined union of which the water in the bath was a further omen. Thus Lactantius:—"A veteribus institutum est, ut sacramento ignis et aquae nuptiarum foedera sanciantur, quod foetus animantium calore et humore corporentur atque animentur ad vitam. Unde aqua et igne uxorem accipere dicitur."—OVID, *Fast.* iv. 792. VAR., *De Ling. Lat.,* iv., 10. SERV. *ad Virg., Aen.* iv. 167.

Of the union here prefigured, the sequel will allow to be added:—

> Non *Hymenaeus* adest non illi gratia lecto;
> Eumenides tenuere faces, de funere raptas:
> Eumenides stravere torum.†

PAGE 159.   . . . She clapped her hands

This was the ordinary method in the East of calling the attendants in waiting.—See *Arabian Nights,* vol. i., pp. 5, 106, 193, &c.

PAGE 159.   . . . have you false keys? Come to the dark chamber

It was the office of Shaban, as chief eunuch, to keep the key of the ladies' apartment. In the Story of Ganem, Haroun al Raschid commands Mesrour, the chief of the eunuchs, "to take the perfidious Fetnah, and shut her up in the dark tower." That tower was within the inclosure of the palace, and commonly served as a prison for the favourites who might chance to disgust the caliph.

PAGE 160.   . . . set him upon his shoulders

The same mode of carrying boys is noted by Sandys; and Ludeke has a passage still more to the purpose:—"Liberos dominorum suorum *grandiusculos ita humeris portant* servi, ut illi lacertis suis horum collum, pedibus vero latera amplectantur, sicque illorum facies super horum caput emineat."—*Expositio Brevis,* p. 37.

---

* Mihi deductae fax omen praetulit.— PROPERT., iv. iii. 13.

† See the *History of Vathek,* pp. 148, 165.

PAGE 160. *. . . his cheeks became the colour of the blossom of pomegranates*

The modest blush of an ingenuous youth (which a Grecian lady of admired taste averred to be the finest colour in nature) is denominated by the Arabians from this very flower. Solomon, in his exquisite Idyllium, hath adopted the same comparison.—Ch. iv., 3.

כפלח הרמון רקתך   "Thy cheeks are like the opening bloom* of the pomegranate."

But a more apposite use of this similitude occurs in an ode by a poet of Damascus:—

The blossom of the pomegranate brings back to my mind the blushes of my beloved, when her cheeks are coloured with a modest resentment.

PAGE 161. *. . . their faith is mutually plighted*

When females in the East are betrothed, their palms and fingers are tinged of a crimson colour, with the herb hinnah. This is called "the crimson of consent."—*Tales of Inatulla,* vol. ii, p. 15.

PAGE 161. *. . . violate the rights of hospitality*

So high an idea of these rights prevails amongst the Arabians, that "a bread and salt traitor," is the most opprobrious invective with which one person can reproach another.—RICHARDSON'S *Dissertation on the Languages, etc., of Eastern Nations,* p. 219. See also the Story of Ali Baba and The Forty Thieves, in the *Arabian Nights,* vol. iv, p. 166.

PAGE 162. *. . . narcotic powder*

A drug of the same quality, mixed in lemonade, is given to Zobeide, in the Story of Ganem.

---

* Simon interprets פלח by *eruptio floris,* and Guarini by *balaustium,* senses which the following passage from Pliny will support:—"Primus pomi hujus partus flore incipientis, *Cytinus* vocatur Graecis. In hoc ipso cytino flosculi sunt, antequam scilicet malum ipsum prodeat, erumpentes, quos balaustium vocari diximus."—*Nat. Hist.,* Lib. xxiii. 59, 60. According to Dioscorides, I. 132, the balaustium was the blossom of the wild, and the citynus of the cultivated, pomegranate.

Dr. Durell, justly dissatisfied with the versions before him, hath rendered the hemistich thus:—"Thy cheeks are like a piece of pomegranate;" and adds, "The cheeks are compared to a piece of this fruit, because the pomegranate, when whole, is of a dull colour; but when cut up of a lively beautiful vermilion." But, if this interpretation and reasoning be allowed, Solomon was less pat at a simile than Sancho: for, whether the cheeks of a blooming bride—or the inwards of a man, "just cleft from noddle down to nock,"—be more like a split pomegranate? "let the forest judge."—DURELL'S *Critical Remarks,* p. 293. *Don Quixote,* tom. iii., p. 282.

PAGE 163. ... *funeral vestments were prepared; their bodies were washed, etc.*

The rites here practised had obtained from the earliest ages. Most of them may be found in Homer and the other poets of Greece. Lucian describes the dead in his time as washed, perfumed, vested, and crowned, ὡραίοις ἄνθεσιν, with the flowers most in season; or, according to other writers, those in particular which the deceased were wont to prefer. The elegant editor of the *Ruins of Palmyra* mentions the fragments of a mummy found there, the hair of which was plaited exactly in the manner as worn at present by the women of Arabia.

The burial dress from the days of Homer hath been commonly white, and amongst Mahometans is made without a seam, that it may not impede the ceremonial of kneeling in the grave, when the dead person undergoes examination.—HOMER, EURIPIDES, etc., *passim.* LUCIAN, tom. ii, p. 927. PASCHAL, *De Coron.,* p. 225. *Ruins of Palmyra,* pp. 22, 23. *Iliad,* xviii, 352. *Relig. Cerem.,* vol. vii, p. 117.

PAGE 163. ... *all instruments of music were broken*

Thus, in the *Arabian Nights:* "Haroun al Raschid wept over Schemselnihar, and, before he left the room, ordered all the musical instruments to be broken."—Vol. ii, p. 196.

PAGE 163. ... *imans began to recite their prayers*

An iman is the principal priest of a mosque. It was the office of the imans to precede the bier, praying as the procession moved on.—*Relig. Cerem.,* vol. vii, p. 117.

PAGE 164. ... *the wailful cries of La Ilah illa Alla!*

This exclamation, which contains the leading principle of Mahometan belief, and signifies *there is no God but God,* was commonly uttered under some violent emotion of mind. The Spaniards adopted it from their Moorish neighbours, and Cervantes hath used it in *Don Quixote:* "En esto llegáron corriendo con grita, LILILIES (literally *professions of faith in Alla*), y algazara los de las libreas adonde Don Quixote suspenso y atónito estava"—*Parte segunda,* cap. lxi, tom. iv, p. 241.

The same expression is sometimes written by the Spaniards, *Lilaila,* and *Hila hilahaila.*

PAGE 165. ... *the angel of death had opened the portal of some other world*

The name of this exterminating angel is *Azrael,* and his office is to conduct the dead to the abode assigned them; which is said by some to be near the place of their interment. Such was the office of Mercury in the Grecian mythology.—SALE'S *Preliminary Discourse,* p. 101. HYDE. *in notis ad Bobov.,* p. 19. R. ELIAS, in *Tishbi.* BUXTORF, *Synag. Jud. et Lexic. Talmud.* HOMER, *Odyssey.*

PAGE 165.   . . . *Monker and Nekir*

These are two black angels of a tremendous appearance, who examine the departed on the subject of his faith: by whom, if he give not a satisfactory account, he is sure to be cudgelled with maces of red-hot iron, and tormented more variously than words can describe.—*Religious Ceremonies,* vol. vii, pp. 59, 68–118; vol. v, p. 290. SALE's *Preliminary Discourse,* p. 101.

PAGE 165.   . . . *the fatal bridge*

This bridge, called in Arabic *al Sirat,* and said to extend over the infernal gulf, is represented as narrower than a spider's web, and sharper than the edge of a sword. Though the attempt to cross it be—

> More full of peril, and advent'rous spirit,
> Than to o'erwalk a current, roaring loud,
> On the unsteadfast footing of a spear;

yet the paradise of Mahomet can be entered by no other avenue. Those, indeed, who have behaved well need not be alarmed; mixed characters will find it difficult; but the wicked soon miss their standing, and plunge headlong into the abyss.—POCOCKE in *Port. Mos.,* p. 282, etc. Milton apparently copied from this well-known fiction, and not, as Dr. Warton conjectured, from the poet Sadi, his way—

> Over the dark abyss, whose boiling gulf
> Tamely endured a bridge of wond'rous length,
> From hell continued, reaching the utmost orb
> Of this frail world.

PAGE 165.   . . . *a certain series of years*

According to the tradition from the prophet, not less than nine hundred, nor more than seven thousand.

PAGE 165.   . . . *the sacred camel*

It was an article of Mahometan creed, that all animals would be raised again, and some of them admitted into paradise. The animal here mentioned appears to have been one of those *white-winged* CAMELS* *caparisoned with gold,* which Ali affirmed had been provided to convey the faithful.—*Religious Ceremonies,* vol. vii, p. 70. SALE's *Preliminary Discourse,* p. 112. AL JAUHERI. EBNO'L ATHIR, etc.

PAGE 166.   . . . *basket-making*

This sort of basket work hath been long used in the East, and consists of the leaves of the date-bearing palm. Panniers of this texture are of

---

* Tarafa, amongst other circumstances in the description of his camel, notices her "bushy tail, which appears as if the two wings of a large white eagle were transfixed by an awl to the bone, and hung waving round both her sides."—*Moallakat,* p. 19.

great utility in conveying fruits, bread, etc., whilst heavier articles, or such as require a more compact covering, are carried in bags of leather, or skin.—HASSELQUIST'S *Voyage*, p. 26.

PAGE 166.   . . . *the caliph presented himself to the emir in a new light*

The propensity of a vicious person, in affliction, to seek consolation from the ceremonies of religion, is an exquisite trait in the character of Vathek.

PAGE 171.   . . . *the waving of fans*

These fans consisted of the trains of peacocks or ostriches, whose quills were set in a long stem, so as to imbricate the plumes in the gradations of their natural growth. Fans of this fashion were formerly used in England.

To judge from the language of Burton ("if he get any remnant of hers, a buske-point, a feather of her fanne, a shoo-tye, a lace"), these fans soon after became common. It was, however, to this kind that Milton alluded in a passage of *Paradise Lost,* the collocation of which, though disjointed through the mistake of his amanuensis, may, by transposing a word, be restored:—

> his sleep
> Was aery light, from pure digestion bred,
> And temperate vapours bland, which th' only sound
> Of fuming rills, and leaves, Aurora's fan,
> Lightly dispers'd, and the shrill matin song
> Of birds on ev'ry bough.

Trees, whose branches are well covered with leaves, may be not improperly styled feathering,* and, in the language of Milton, form the fan of Aurora, which when waved by the breeze of the morning, occasions the rustling that constitutes a third in the complex sound referred to.

PAGE 171.   . . . *wine hoarded up in bottles, prior to the birth of Mahomet*

The prohibition of wine by the Prophet materially diminished its consumption within the limits of his own dominions. Hence a reserve of it might be expected of the age here specified. The custom of hoarding wine was not unknown to the Persians, though not so often practised by them as by the Greeks and the Romans.

"I purchase" (says Lebeid) "the old liquor, at a dear rate, in dark leathern bottles, long reposited; or in casks black with pitch, whose seals I break, and then fill the cheerful goblet."—*Moallakat*, p. 53.

* Thus, Mr. Whateley, the first authority in the language of picturesque description:—"Large boughs, feathering down, often intercept the sight."

PAGE 171. ... *excavated ovens in the rock*

As substitutes for the portable ovens, which were lost.

PAGE 171. ... *manchets prepared by Nouronihar*

Herodotus mentions a lady of equal rank performing a similar office:—
ἡ δὲ ΓΥΝΗ τοῦ ΒΑΣΙΛΗΟΣ αὐτὴ τὰ ΣΙΤΙΑ σφι ἔπεσσε· * and the cakes which
Tamar made for Amnon are well known.

PAGE 172. ... *her great camel Alboufaki*

There is a singular and laboured description of a camel in the poem of
TARAFA; but Alboufaki possessed qualities appropriate to himself, and
which rendered him but little less conspicuous than the deformed dun
camel of Aad.

PAGE 173. .... *to set forward, notwithstanding it was noon*

The employment of wood-fellers was accounted of all others the most
toilsome, as those occupied in it were compelled to forgo that mid-day
cessation with which other labourers were indulged. Inatulla speaks
proverbially of "woodmen in the meridian hour, scarce able to raise
the arms of languor." The guides of Carathis being of this occupation,
she adroitly availed herself of it to urge them forward, without allowing
them that repose during the mid-day fervour which travellers in these
climates always enjoyed,† and which was deemed so essential to the
preservation of their health.

PAGE 173. ... *the confines of some cemetery*

Places of interment in the East were commonly situated in scenes of
solitude. We read of one in the History of the First Calender, abounding
with so many monuments, that four days were successively spent in it
without the inquirer being able to find the tomb he looked for; and,
from the story of Ganem, it appears that the doors of these cemeteries
were often left open.—*Arabian Nights,* vol. ii, p. 112; vol. iii, p. 135.

PAGE 175. ... *a Myrabolan comfit*

The invention of this confection is attributed by M. Cardonne to Avi-
cenna, but there is abundant reason, exclusive of our author's authority,

* Lib. viii., p. 685. That σιτία is to be understood in the sense above given,
is certain from what immediately follows.

† Psalm xci. 5. The explanatory iteration of the subsequent verse points out
a congruity between the Hebrew poet and Homer. As the contagion amongst
the Greeks produced by the excessive heat of the sun was assigned in the
Iliad to the arrows of the God of light; so, the destruction that wasteth at
noon is attributed in the Psalm to the arrow that flieth by day. It has been
observed by a nobleman of many accomplishments that this verse should be
added to the other passages of Scripture which have been noted in the writings ascribed to Zoroaster.

to suppose it of a much earlier origin. Both the Latins and Greeks were acquainted with the balsam, and the tree that produced it was indigenous in various parts of Arabia.

PAGE 176. . . . *blue fishes*

Fishes of the same colour are mentioned in the *Arabian Nights;* and, like these, were endowed with the gift of speech.

PAGE 178. . . . *nests still higher than the clouds*

The metaphor of a nest for a secure habitation occurs in the Sacred Writings. Thus Habakkuk:—"Woe to him that coveteth an evil covetousness to his house, that he may set his nest on high, that he may be delivered from the power of evil." And Obadiah:—"Though thou exalt thyself as the eagle, and though thou set thy nest among the stars," &c. The genius here mentioned seems to have been adopted from the Jewish notion of Guardian Angels, to whom the superintendence of children is supposed to be committed, and to which our Saviour himself hath referred (Matt. xviii. 10); whilst the original possessors of the nest may be presumed to have been some of those marvellous birds so frequently mentioned in Eastern romance.

PAGE 178. . . . *waving streamers on which were inscribed the names of Allah and the Prophet*

The position that "there is no God but God, and Mahomet is his Prophet," pervades every part of the Mahometan religion. Banners, like those here described, are preserved in the several mosques; and, on the death of extraordinary persons, are borne before the bier in solemn state.—*Religious Ceremonies,* vol. vii, pp. 119, 120.

PAGE 178. . . . *astrolabes*

The mention of the astrolabe may be deemed incompatible, at first view, with chronological exactness, as there is no instance of any being constructed by a Mussulman, till after the time of Vathek. It may, however, be remarked, to go no higher, that Sinesius, bishop of Ptolemais, invented one in the fifth century; and that Carathis was not only herself a Greek, but also cultivated those sciences which the good Mussulmans of her time all held in abhorrence.—BAILLY, *Hist. de l'Astronom. Moderne,* tom. i, pp. 563, 573.

PAGE 180. . . . *On the banks of the stream, hives and oratories*

The bee is an insect held in high veneration amongst the Mahometans, it being pointed out in the Koran, "for a sign unto the people that understand." It has been said, in the same sense, "Go to the ant, thou sluggard."—*Proverbs,* vi, 6. The santons, therefore, who inhabit the fertile banks of Rocnabad, are not less famous for their hives than their oratories.—D'HERBELOT, p. 717.

PAGE 180.   *. . . harbingers of the imperial procession began to proclaim*

This circumstance of sending heralds to announce the approach of a sovereign reminds us of "the voice of one crying in the wilderness."

PAGE 181.   *. . . sheiks . . . cadis*

Sheiks are the chiefs of the societies of dervishes; cadis are the magistrates of a town or city.

PAGE 181.   *. . . Asses in bridles of riband inscribed from the Koran*

As the judges of Israel in ancient days rode on white asses, so, amongst the Mahometans, those that affect an extraordinary sanctity use the same animal in preference to the horse. Sir John Chardin observed, in various parts of the East, that their reins, as here represented, were of silk, with the name of God, or other inscriptions, upon them.—LUDEKE, *Expos. brevis,* p. 49. CHARDIN's MS. cited by Harmer.

PAGE 182.   *. . . One of these beneficent genii, assuming the exterior of a shepherd, etc., began to pour from his flute, etc.*

The flute was considered as a sacred instrument, which Jacob and other holy shepherds had sanctified by using.—*Religious Ceremonies,* vol. vii, p. 110.

PAGE 182.   *. . . involuntarily drawn towards the declivity of the hill*

A similar instance of attraction may be seen in the Story of Prince Ahmed and the Peri Parabanon.—*Arabian Nights,* vol. iv, p. 243.

PAGE 183.   *. . . Eblis*

D'Herbelot supposes this title to have been a corruption of the Greek Διάβολος, *diabolos.* It was the appellation conferred by the Arabians upon the prince of the apostate angels, whom they represent as exiled to the infernal regions, for refusing to worship Adam at the command of the Supreme, and appears more likely to originate from the Hebrew הבל , *hebel,* vanity, pride.—See below, the note, *"Creatures of clay."*

PAGE 183.   *. . . compensate for thy impieties by an exemplary life*

It is an established article of the Mussulman creed, that the actions of mankind are all weighed in a vast unerring balance, and the future condition of the agents determined according to the preponderance of evil or good. This fiction, which seems to have been borrowed from the Jews, had probably its origin in the figurative language of Scripture. Thus, Psalm lxii, 9: "Surely men of low degree are vanity, and men of high degree are a lie: to be laid in the balance, they are altogether lighter than vanity"; and in Daniel, the sentence against the King of Babylon, inscribed on the wall, "Thou art weighed in the balance, and found wanting."

PAGE 184.   ... *Balkis*

This was the Arabian name of the Queen of Sheba, who went from the south to hear the wisdom and admire the glory of Solomon. The Koran represents her as a worshipper of fire. Solomon is said not only to have entertained her with the greatest magnificence, but also to have raised her to his bed and his throne.—*Al Koran*, ch. xxvii, and SALE's notes. D'HERBELOT, p. 182.

PAGE 185.   ... *of an architecture unknown in the records of the earth—an immense palace, whose walls were embossed with various figures, &c.*

Thus, Pellegrino Gaudenzi, in his description of the palace of sin:—

> Enorme pondo al suolo, immensa mole
> D'aspri macigni intesta e negri marmi
> Per cui serpeggian di sanguigna tinta
> Lugubri vene: l'atterrito sguardo
> Muto s'arresta sull'altera fronte
> Ch'entro le nubi si sospinge, e s'alza
> Superbamente a minacciar le stelle.
> Sotto grand'archi su marmoree basi
> Fan di sè mostra simulacri orrendi
> Che in faccia ad essa i Demon fabbri alzaro.
> > *La Nascita di Cristo*, c. 1.

PAGE 185.   ... *The chief of the eunuchs, trembling with fear, besought Vathek that a fire might be kindled*

ῙΗτορ ΠΑΧΝΟΥΤΑΙ, the very heart of Bababalouk is congealed with apprehension. Where can a more exquisite trait both of nature and character be found than this request of the eunuch presents?

PAGE 186.   ... *they seemed not walking but falling*

A similar kind of progression is described by Milton:—

> by the hand he took me raised;
> And over fields and waters, as in air,
> Smooth-sliding without step last led me.

PAGE 186.   ... *the pavement, strewed over with saffron*

There are several circumstances in the Story of the Third Calender, that resemble those here mentioned; particularly a pavement strewed with saffron, and the burning of ambergris and aloes-wood.

PAGE 186.   ... *A throng of genii and other fantastic spirits danced, &c.*

A dance of the same kind, and by similar performers, occurs in the History of Ahmed and the Peri Parabanon.

PAGE 187.   ... *let us haste, and present you to Eblis*

If our author's description of the arch-apostate be examined by the criterion of Arabian faith, and in reference to the circumstances of the story, there can no difficulty in appreciating its merit. Gaudenzi, in the poem already cited, hath described the appearance of Satan previous to the birth of Christ in a manner that deserves to be noticed though the poem itself were less scarce:—

> Fra questo orror da sue radici scosso
> Trema repente il suolo, e all'Oriente
> Ardua montagna con rimbombo estremo
> S'apre per mezzo: immensa foce oscura
> Mugghia dal fondo, e fumo, e fiamme, e lampi
> Sboccano a un tratto; i sfracellati massi
> Rotando ardenti nel sulfureo flutto
> Stampan la piaggia di profonda traccia.
> Dai neri gorghi del dolente regno
> Con furibondo orribile muggito
> Rimonta per l'aperta ampia vorago
> L'Angiol d'abisso a funestar la terra.
> Come dell'ocean sola tiranna
> Sconcia Balena per gli ondosi campi
> Move animosa, e coll'enorme petto
> L'ampia spezzando rimugghiante massa
> Alzasi al giorno, e nel turbato fondo
> Il muto armento di sua mole adombra.
> Tale Satan per vasto mar di fiamme
> Ergesi a nuoto: immense ali protese
> Alto flagellan con sonoro scroscio
> L'onda infernal, che in rosseggianti righe
> Sbalza stridente, e il ciel veste di foco.
> Sotto grand'archi di vellute ciglia,
> Quasi comete sanguinose erranti
> Per tenebrose vie, di rabbia pregni
> Volvonsi gli occhi, e in cavernoso speco
> Orrida s'apre l'infiammata bocca
> Aure spirante di veleno infette.*
> Egli s'avanza, e il suol guatando e il cielo,
> Impaziente con le negre braccia
> Le rupi afferra, e d'un immenso slancio
> Balza al confin della frapposta arena.
> Mille del suo furor seguaci Spirti
> Ch' erangli sotto per gl'igniti gorghi
> Sfilangli dietro, e coll'intento sguardo

* Several expressions in this passage appear to have been imitated from the following of Tasso:—

> Orrida maestà nel fero aspetto
> Terrore accresce, e più superbo il rende:
> Rosseggian gli occhj, e di veneno infetto,
> Come infausta cometa, il guardo splende:
> Gl'involve il mento, e su l'irsuto petto
> Ispida e folta la gran barba scende:
> E in guisa di voragine profonda,
> S'apre la bocca d'atro sangue immonda.

La Gerus., c. iv., st. 7.

In lui rivolti gli si fanno al fianco.
In sua possanza alteramente fiera
Stassi l'oste d'Averno, e adombra il piano,
Siccome mille e mille annose quercie
Che a' piè d'un'alta ferruginea rupe
Aride e negre al cielo ergon le teste.
S'addoppian l'ombre della notte, e sola
Al folgorar degl'infernali sguardi
Arde da lungi la solinga piaggia,
Come spezzata da funeste vampe
Massa di nembi.

PAGE 187.   . . . *Ouranbad*

This monster is represented as a fierce-flying hydra, and belongs to the same class with the *rakshe,* whose ordinary food was serpents and dragons; the *soham,* which had the head of a horse, with four eyes, and the body of a flame-coloured dragon; the *syl,* a basilisk with a face resembling the human, but so tremendous that no mortal could bear to behold it; the *ejder,* and others. See these respective titles in RICHARDSON'S *Persian, Arabic, and English Dictionary.*

PAGE 187.   . . . *she expected to have seen some stupendous giant*

Such is the representation which Dante hath given of this infernal sovereign:—

Lo 'mperador del doloroso regno
Da mezzo 'l petto uscia fuor della ghiaccia:
E più con un gigante i' mi convegno,
Che i giganti non fan con le sue braccia.

It is more than probable (though it has not been noticed) that Don Quixote's mistake of the windmills for giants was suggested to Cervantes by the following simile, in which the tremendous personage above-mentioned is so compared:—

però dinanzi mira,
Disse 'l maestro mio, se tu 'l discerni.
Come quando una grossa nebbia spira,
O quando l' emisperio nostro annotta
Par da lungi un mulin che 'l vento gira,
Veder mi parve un tal dificio allotta.

What confirms this conjecture is the reply to Sancho's question, "What Giants?" made by Don Quixote, in reference to the two last lines of the preceding citation:—

And nearer to a giant's is my size
Than giants are when to his arms compar'd.

"Those thou seest yonder, with their vast arms; and some of them there are, that reach nearly two leagues."—*Don Quixote,* parte prim., cap. viii., p. 52. DANTE, *dell' Inferno,* canto xxxiv. It may be added, that a rising wind is mentioned in both.

PAGE 188. . . . *Creatures of clay*

Nothing could have been more appositely imagined than this compellation. Eblis, according to Arabian mythology, had suffered a degradation from his primeval rank, and was consigned to these regions, for having refused to worship Adam in obedience to the supreme command; alleging, in justification of his refusal, that himself had been formed of ethereal fire, whilst Adam was only a creature of clay.—*Al Koran,* c. lv, etc.

PAGE 188. . . . *the fortress of Aherman*

In the mythology of the Easterns, Aherman was accounted *the Demon of Discord.* The ancient Persian romances abound in descriptions of this fortress, in which the inferior demons assemble, to receive the behests of their prince; and from whom they proceed to exercise their malice in every part of the world.—D'HERBELOT, p. 71.

PAGE 188. . . . *the halls of Argenk*

The halls of this mighty dive, who reigned in the mountains of Kaf, contained the statues of the seventy-two Solimans, and the portraits of the various creatures subject to them; not one of which bore the slightest similitude to man. Some had many heads, others many arms, and some consisted of many bodies. Their heads were all very extraordinary, some resembling the elephant's, the buffalo's, and the boar's; whilst others were still more monstrous.—D'HERBELOT, p. 820. Some of the idols worshipped to this day in Hindostan answer to this description.

Ariosto, who owes more to Arabian fable than his commentators have hitherto supposed, seems to have been no stranger to the halls of Argenk, when he described one of the fountains of Merlin:—

> Era una della fonti di Merlino
> Delle quattro di Francia da lui fatte;
> D'intorno cinta di bel marmo fino,
> Lucido, e terso, e bianco più che latte.
> Quivi d'intaglio con lavor divino
> Avea Merlino immagini ritratte.
> Direste che spiravano, e se prive
> Non fossero di voce, ch'eran vive.
>
> Quivi una Bestia uscir della foresta
> Parea di crudel vista, odiosa, e brutta,
> Che avea le orecchie d'asino, e la testa
> Di lupo, e i denti, e per gran fame asciutta;
> Branche avea di leon; l'altro, che resta,
> Tutto era volpe.

PAGE 188. . . . *holding his right hand, motionless, on his heart*

Sandys observes that the application of the right hand to the heart is the customary mode of Eastern salutation; but the perseverance of the votaries of Eblis in this attitude was intended to express their devotion to him both heart and hand.

PAGE 189.   *. . . In my lifetime I filled, etc.*

This recital agrees perfectly with those in the Koran, and other Arabian legends.

PAGE 190.   *. . . an unrelenting fire preys on my heart*

Hariri, to convey the most forcible idea of extreme anxiety, represents the heart as tormented by fierce burning coals. This form of speech, it is observed, is *proverbial;* but do we not see whence the proverb arose?—CHAPPELOW's *Six Assemblies*, p. 106.

PAGE 190.   *. . . in the abode of vengeance and despair*

Thus, Dante's inscription over the gate of hell:—

> Per me si va nella città dolente:
>   Per me si va nell'eterno dolore:
>   Per me si va tra la perduta gente.
> Giustizia mosse 'l mio alto fattore:
>   Fecemi la divina potestate,
>   La somma sapienza, e 'l primo amore.
> Dinanzi a me non fur cose create,
>   Se non eterne, ed io eterno duro:
>   Lasciate ogne speranza, voi che 'ntrate.
>   Canto iii.

> "Through me you pass to Mourning's dark domain;
>   Through me to scenes where Grief must ever pine;
>   Through me to Misery's devoted train.
> Justice and power in my Great Founder join,
>   And love and wisdom all his fabrics rear;
>   Wisdom above control, and love divine!
> Before me Nature saw no works appear,
>   Save works eternal: such was I ordained.
>   Quit every hope, all ye who enter here."

(How much have the public to regret, after the specimen given, that Mr. Hayley did not complete the *Inferno!*)

PAGE 191.   *. . . Carathis on the back of an afrit*

The expedition of the afrit in fetching Carathis is characteristic of this order of dives. We read in the Koran that another of the fraternity offered to bring the Queen of Sheba's throne to Solomon before he could rise from his place.—Ch. xxvii.

PAGE 193.   *. . . glanced off in a rapid whirl that rendered her invisible*

It was not ill conceived to punish Carathis by a rite, and one of the principal characteristics of that science in which she so much delighted, and which was the primary cause of Vathek's perdition and of her own. The circle, the emblem of eternity, and the symbol of the sun, was held sacred in the most ancient ceremonies of incantations; and the whirling round deemed as a necessary operation in magical mysteries. Was not the name of the greatest enchantress in fabulous antiquity, Circe, derived from κιρχος, a circle, on account of her magical revolutions, and of the circular appearance and motion of the sun, her father? The fairies and elves used to arrange themselves in a ring on the grass; and even the augur, in the liturgy of the Romans, whirled round to encompass the four cardinal points of the world. It is remarkable, that a derivative of the verb, rendered, *to whirl in a magical manner* (see page 202), which corresponds to the Hebrew סחר , and is interpreted *scindere, secare se in orbem, inde notio circinandi, mox gyrandi, et hinc à motu versatili, fascinavit, incantavit,* signifies in the Koran *the glimmering of twilight:* a sense deducible from the shapeless glimpses of objects when hurried round with the velocity here described, and very applicable to the sudden disappearance of Carathis, who, like the stone in a sling, by the progressive and rapid increase of the circular motion, soon ceased to be perceptible. Nothing can impress a greater awe upon the mind than does this passage in the original.

PAGE 193. . . . *they at once lost the most precious gift of Heaven—Hope*

It is a soothing reflection to the bulk of mankind that the commonness of any blessing is the true test of its value. Hence, Hope is justly styled "the most precious of the gifts of Heaven," because, as Thales long since observed—οἶς ἄλλο μηδὲν, αὐτὴ πάρεστιν—it abides with those who are destitute of every other. Dante's inscription over the gate of hell was written in the same sense, and perhaps in allusion to the saying of the Grecian sage.

Strongly impressed with this idea, and in order to complete his description of the infernal dungeon, Milton says:—

> where . . .
> . . . hope never comes,
> That comes to all.
> *Paradise Lost,* i. 66.

THE VAMPYRE

A Tale

Extract of a Letter to the Editor

from Geneva

"I breathe freely in the neighbourhood of this lake; the ground upon which I tread has been subdued from the earliest ages; the principal objects which immediately strike my eye, bring to my recollection scenes, in which man acted the hero and was the chief object of interest. Not to look back to earlier times of battles and sieges, here is the bust of Rousseau—here is a house with an inscription denoting that the Genevan philosopher first drew breath under its roof. A little out of the town is Ferney, the residence of Voltaire; where that wonderful, though certainly in many respects contemptible, character, received, like the hermits of old, the visits of pilgrims, not only from his own nation, but from the farthest boundaries of Europe. Here too is Bonnet's abode, and, a few steps beyond, the house of that astonishing woman Madame de Stael: perhaps the first of her sex, who has really proved its often claimed equality with the nobler man. We have before had women who have written interesting novels and poems, in which their tact at observing drawing-room characters has availed them; but never since the days of Heloise have those faculties which are peculiar to man, been developed as the possible inheritance of woman. Though even here, as in the case of Heloise, our sex have not been backward in alledging the existence of an Abeilard in the person of M. Schlegel as the inspirer of her works. But to proceed: upon the same side of the lake, Gibbon, Bonnivard, Bradshaw, and others mark, as it were, the stages for our progress; whilst upon the other side there is one house, built by Diodati, the friend of Milton, which has contained within its walls, for several months, that poet whom we have so often read together, and who—if human passions remain the same, and human feelings, like chords, on being swept by nature's impulses shall vibrate as before—will be placed by posterity in the first rank of our English Poets. You must have heard, or the Third Canto of *Childe Harold* will have informed you, that Lord Byron resided many months in this neighbourhood. I went with some friends a few days ago, after having seen Ferney, to view this mansion. I trod the floors with the same feelings of awe and respect as we did, together, those of Shakspeare's dwelling at Stratford. I sat down in a chair of the saloon, and satisfied myself that I was resting on what he had made his constant seat. I found a servant there who had lived with him; she, however, gave me but little information. She pointed out his bed-chamber upon the same level as the saloon and dining-room, and informed me that he retired to rest at three, got up at two, and employed himself a long time over his toilette; that he never went to sleep without a pair of pistols and a dagger by his side, and that he never eat animal food. He apparently spent some part of every day upon the lake in an English boat. There is a balcony from the saloon which looks upon the lake and the mountain Jura; and I imagine, that it must have been hence he contemplated the storm so magnificently described in the Third Canto; for you have from here a most extensive view of all the points he has therein depicted. I can fancy him like the scathed pine, whilst all around was sunk to repose, still waking to observe, what gave but a weak image of the storms which had desolated his own breast.

The sky is changed!—and such a change; Oh, night!
And storm and darkness, ye are wond'rous strong,
Yet lovely in your strength, as is the light
Of a dark eye in woman! Far along
From peak to peak, the rattling crags among,
Leaps the live thunder! Not from one lone cloud,
But every mountain now hath found a tongue,
And Jura answers thro' her misty shroud,
Back to the joyous Alps who call to her aloud!

And this is in the night:—Most glorious night!
Thou wer't not sent for slumber! let me be
A sharer in thy far and fierce delight,—
A portion of the tempest and of me!
How the lit lake shines a phosphoric sea,
And the big rain comes dancing to the earth!
And now again 'tis black,—and now the glee
Of the loud hills shakes with its mountain mirth,
As if they did rejoice o'er a young earthquake's birth,

> Now where the swift Rhine cleaves his way between
> Heights which appear, as lovers who have parted
> In haste, whose mining depths so intervene,
> That they can meet no more, tho' broken hearted;
> Tho' in their souls which thus each other thwarted,
> Love was the very root of the fond rage
> Which blighted their life's bloom, and then departed—
> Itself expired, but leaving them an age
> Of years all winter—war within themselves to wage.

I went down to the little port, if I may use the expression, wherein his vessel used to lay, and conversed with the cottager, who had the care of it. You may smile, but I have my pleasure in thus helping my personification of the individual I admire, by attaining to the knowledge of those circumstances which were daily around him. I have made numerous enquiries in the town concerning him, but can learn nothing. He only went into society there once, when M. Pictet took him to the house of a lady to spend the evening. They say he is a very singular man, and seem to think him very uncivil. Amongst other things they relate, that having invited M. Pictet and Bonstetten to dinner, he went on the lake to Chillon, leaving a gentleman who travelled with him to receive them and make his apologies. Another evening, being invited to the house of Lady D—— H——, he promised to attend, but upon approaching the windows of her ladyship's villa, and perceiving the room to be full of company, he set down his friend, desiring him to plead his excuse, and immediately returned home. This will serve as a contradiction to the report which you tell me is current in England, of his having been avoided by his countrymen on the continent. The case happens to be directly the reverse, as he has been generally sought by them, though on most occasions, apparently without success. It is said, indeed, that upon paying his first visit at Coppet, following the servant who had announced his name, he was surprised to meet a lady carried out fainting; but before he had been seated many minutes, the same lady, who had been so affected at the sound of his name, returned and conversed with him a considerable time—such is female curiosity and affectation! He visited Coppet frequently, and of course associated there with several of his countrymen, who evinced no reluctance to meet him whom his enemies alone would represent as an outcast.

Though I have been so unsuccessful in this town, I have been more fortunate in my enquiries elsewhere. There is a society three or four miles from Geneva, the centre of which is the Countess of Breuss, a Russian lady, well acquainted with the *agrémens de la Société,* and who has collected them round herself at her mansion. It was chiefly here, I find, that the gentleman who travelled with Lord Byron, as physician, sought for society. He used almost every day to cross the lake by himself, in one of their flat-bottomed boats, and return after passing the evening with his friends, about eleven or twelve at night, often whilst the storms were raging in the circling summits of the mountains around. As he became intimate, from long acquaintance, with several of the families in this neighbourhood, I have gathered from their accounts some excellent traits of his lordship's character, which I will relate to you at some future opportunity.

Among other particulars mentioned, was the outline of a ghost story by Lord Byron. It appears that one evening Lord B., Mr. P. B. Shelly [sic], two ladies and the gentleman before alluded to, after having perused a German work, entitled *Phantasmagoriana,* began relating ghost stories; when his lordship having recited the beginning of "Christabel," then unpublished, the whole took so strong a hold of Mr. Shelly's mind, that he suddenly started up and ran out of the room. The physician and Lord Byron followed, and discovered him leaning against a mantle-piece, with cold drops of perspiration trickling down his face. After having given him something to refresh him, upon enquiring into the cause of his alarm, they found that his wild imagination having pictured to him the bosom of one of the ladies with eyes (which was reported of a lady in the neighbourhood where he lived) he was obliged to leave the room in order to destroy the impression. It was afterwards proposed, in the course of conversation, that each of the company present should write a tale depending upon some supernatural agency, which was undertaken by Lord B., the physician, and one of the ladies before mentioned. I obtained the outline of each of these stories as a great favour, and herewith forward them to you, as I was assured you would feel as much curiosity as myself, to peruse the *ébauches* of so great a genius, and those immediately under his influence."

Introduction

The superstition upon which this tale is founded is very general in the East. Among the Arabians it appears to be common: it did not, however, extend itself to the Greeks until after the establishment of Christianity; and it has only assumed its present form since the division of the Latin and Greek churches; at which time, the idea becoming prevalent, that a Latin body could not corrupt if buried in their territory, it gradually increased, and formed the subject of many wonderful stories, still extant, of the dead rising from their graves, and feeding upon the blood of the young and beautiful. In the West it spread, with some slight variation, all over Hungary, Poland, Austria, and Lorraine, where the belief existed, that vampyres nightly imbibed a certain portion of the blood of their victims, who became emaciated, lost their strength, and speedily died of consumptions; whilst these human bloodsuckers fattened—and their veins became distended to such a state of repletion, as to cause the blood to flow from all the passages of their bodies, and even from the very pores of their skins.

In the *London Journal,* of March, 1732, is a curious, and, of course, *credible* account of a particular case of vampyrism, which is stated to have occurred at Madreyga, in Hungary. It appears, that upon an examination of the commander-in-chief and magistrates of the place, they positively and unanimously affirmed, that, about five years before, a certain Heyduke, named Arnold Paul, had been heard to say, that, at Cassovia, on the frontiers of the Turkish Servia, he had been tormented by a vampyre, but had found a way to rid himself of the evil, by eating some of the earth out of the vampyre's grave, and rubbing himself with his blood. This precaution, however, did not prevent him from becoming a vampyre* himself; for, about twenty or thirty days after his death and burial, many persons complained of having been tor-

* The universal belief is, that a person sucked by a vampyre becomes a vampyre himself, and sucks in his turn.

mented by him, and a deposition was made, that four persons had been deprived of life by his attacks. To prevent further mischief, the inhabitants having consulted their Hadagni,* took up the body, and found it (as is supposed to be usual in cases of vampyrism) fresh, and entirely free from corruption, and emitting at the mouth, nose, and ears, pure and florid blood. Proof having been thus obtained, they resorted to the accustomed remedy. A stake was driven entirely through the heart and body of Arnold Paul, at which he is reported to have cried out as dreadfully as if he had been alive. This done, they cut off his head, burned his body, and threw the ashes into his grave. The same measures were adopted with the corses of those persons who had previously died from vampyrism, lest they should, in their turn, become agents upon others who survived them.

This monstrous rodomontade is here related, because it seems better adapted to illustrate the subject of the present observations than any other instance which could be adduced. In many parts of Greece it is considered as a sort of punishment after death, for some heinous crime committed whilst in existence, that the deceased is not only doomed to vampyrise, but compelled to confine his infernal visitations solely to those beings he loved most while upon earth—those to whom he was bound by ties of kindred and affection.—A supposition alluded to in the "Giaour."

> But first on earth, as Vampyre sent,
> Thy corse shall from its tomb be rent;
> Then ghastly haunt the native place,
> And suck the blood of all thy race;
> There from thy *daughter, sister, wife,*
> At midnight drain the stream of life;
> *Yet loathe the banquet which perforce*
> Must feed thy livid living corse,
> Thy victims, ere they yet expire,
> Shall know the demon for their sire;
> As cursing thee, thou cursing them,
> Thy flowers are withered on the stem.
> But one that for *thy crime* must fall,
> The youngest, best beloved of all,
> Shall bless thee with a *father's* name—
> That word shall wrap thy heart in flame!
> Yet thou must end thy task and mark
> Her cheek's last tinge—her eye's last spark,

---

* Chief bailiff.

And the last glassy glance must view
Which freezes o'er its lifeless blue;
Then with unhallowed hand shall tear
The tresses of her yellow hair,
Of which, in life a lock when shorn
Affection's fondest pledge was worn—
But now is borne away by thee
Memorial of thine agony!
Yet with thine own best blood shall drip
Thy gnashing tooth, and haggard lip;
Then stalking to thy sullen grave,
Go—and with Gouls and Afrits rave,
Till these in horror shrink away
From spectre more accursed than they.

Mr. Southey has also introduced in his wild but beautiful poem of "Thalaba," the vampyre corse of the Arabian maid Oneiza, who is represented as having returned from the grave for the purpose of tormenting him she best loved whilst in existence. But this cannot be supposed to have resulted from the sinfulness of her life, she being pourtrayed throughout the whole of the tale as a complete type of purity and innocence. The veracious Tournefort gives a long account in his travels of several astonishing cases of vampyrism, to which he pretends to have been an eye-witness; and Calmet, in his great work upon this subject, besides a variety of anecdotes, and traditionary narratives illustrative of its effects, has put forth some learned dissertations, tending to prove it to be a classical, as well as barbarian error.

Many curious and interesting notices on this singularly horrible superstition might be added; though the present may suffice for the limits of a note, necessarily devoted to explanation, and which may now be concluded by merely remarking, that though the term Vampyre is the one in most general acceptation, there are several others synonymous with it, made use of in various parts of the world: as Vroucolocha, Vardoulacha, Goul, Broucoloka, &c.

THE VAMPYRE

A Tale

It happened that in the midst of the dissipations attendant upon
a London winter, there appeared at the various parties of the lead-
ers of the *ton* a nobleman, more remarkable for his singularities,
than his rank. He gazed upon the mirth around him, as if he
could not participate therein. Apparently, the light laughter of
the fair only attracted his attention, that he might by a look
quell it, and throw fear into those breasts where thoughtlessness
reigned. Those who felt this sensation of awe, could not explain
whence it arose: some attributed it to the dead grey eye, which,
fixing upon the object's face, did not seem to penetrate, and at
one glance to pierce through to the inward workings of the heart;
but fell upon the cheek with a leaden ray that weighed upon the
skin it could not pass. His peculiarities caused him to be invited
to every house; all wished to see him, and those who had been accustomed to violent excitement, and now felt the weight of *ennui*,
were pleased at having something in their presence capable of
engaging their attention. In spite of the deadly hue of his face,
which never gained a warmer tint, either from the blush of modesty, or from the strong emotion of passion, though its form and
outline were beautiful, many of the female hunters after notori-
ety attempted to win his attentions, and gain, at least, some marks
of what they might term affection: Lady Mercer, who had been
the mockery of every monster shewn in drawing-rooms since her
marriage, threw herself in his way, and did all but put on the
dress of a mountebank, to attract his notice—though in vain;—
when she stood before him, though his eyes were apparently fixed
upon hers, still it seemed as if they were unperceived;—even her
unappalled impudence was baffled, and she left the field. But

though the common adultress could not influence even the guidance of his eyes, it was not that the female sex was indifferent to
him: yet such was the apparent caution with which he spoke to
the virtuous wife and innocent daughter, that few knew he ever
addressed himself to females. He had, however, the reputation of
a winning tongue; and whether it was that it even overcame the
dread of his singular character, or that they were moved by his apparent hatred of vice, he was as often among those females who
form the boast of their sex from their domestic virtues, as among
those who sully it by their vices.

About the same time, there came to London a young gentleman
of the name of Aubrey: he was an orphan left with an only sister
in the possession of great wealth, by parents who died while he
was yet in childhood. Left also to himself by guardians, who
thought it their duty merely to take care of his fortune, while
they relinquished the more important charge of his mind to the
care of mercenary subalterns, he cultivated more his imagination
than his judgment. He had, hence, that high romantic feeling of
honour and candour, which daily ruins so many milliners' ap-
prentices. He believed all to sympathise with virtue, and thought
that vice was thrown in by Providence merely for the picturesque
effect of the scene, as we see in romances: he thought that the
misery of a cottage merely consisted in the vesting of clothes,
which were as warm, but which were better adapted to the painter's eye by their irregular folds and various coloured patches. He
thought, in fine, that the dreams of poets were the realities of life.
He was handsome, frank, and rich: for these reasons, upon his entering into the gay circles, many mothers surrounded him, striv-
ing which should describe with least truth their languishing or
romping favourites: the daughters at the same time, by their
brightening countenances when he approached, and by their
sparkling eyes, when he opened his lips, soon led him into false
notions of his talents and his merit. Attached as he was to the romance of his solitary hours, he was startled at finding, that, except in the tallow and wax candles that flickered, not from the
presence of a ghost, but from want of snuffing, there was no foundation in real life for any of that congeries of pleasing pictures
and descriptions contained in those volumes, from which he had
formed his study. Finding, however, some compensation in his
gratified vanity, he was about to relinquish his dreams, when the

extraordinary being we have above described, crossed him in his career.

He watched him; and the very impossibility of forming an idea of the character of a man entirely absorbed in himself, who gave few other signs of his observation of external objects, than the tacit assent to their existence, implied by the avoidance of their contact: allowing his imagination to picture every thing that flattered its propensity to extravagant ideas, he soon formed this object into the hero of a romance, and determined to observe the offspring of his fancy, rather than the person before him. He became acquainted with him, paid him attentions, and so far advanced upon his notice, that his presence was always recognised. He gradually learnt that Lord Ruthven's affairs were embarrassed, and soon found, from the notes of preparation in —— Street, that he was about to travel. Desirous of gaining some information respecting this singular character, who, till now, had only whetted his curiosity, he hinted to his guardians, that it was time for him to perform the tour, which for many generations has been thought necessary to enable the young to take some rapid steps in the career of vice towards putting themselves upon an equality with the aged, and not allowing them to appear as if fallen from the skies, whenever scandalous intrigues are mentioned as the subjects of pleasantry or of praise, according to the degree of skill shewn in carrying them on. They consented: and Aubrey immediately mentioning his intentions to Lord Ruthven, was surprised to receive from him a proposal to join him. Flattered by such a mark of esteem from him, who, apparently, had nothing in common with other men, he gladly accepted it, and in a few days they had passed the circling waters.

Hitherto, Aubrey had had no opportunity of studying Lord Ruthven's character, and now he found, that, though many more of his actions were exposed to his view, the results offered different conclusions from the apparent motives to his conduct. His companion was profuse in his liberality;—the idle, the vagabond, and the beggar, received from his hand more than enough to relieve their immediate wants. But Aubrey could not avoid remarking, that it was not upon the virtuous, reduced to indigence by the misfortunes attendant even upon virtue, that he bestowed his alms;—these were sent from the door with hardly suppressed sneers; but when the profligate came to ask something, not to re-

lieve his wants, but to allow him to wallow in his lust, or to sink
him still deeper in his iniquity, he was sent away with rich charity. This was, however, attributed by him to the greater importunity of the vicious, which generally prevails over the retiring
bashfulness of the virtuous indigent. There was one circumstance
about the charity of his Lordship, which was still more impressed
upon his mind: all those upon whom it was bestowed, inevitably
found that there was a curse upon it, for they were all either led
to the scaffold, or sunk to the lowest and the most abject misery.
At Brussels and other towns through which they passed, Aubrey
was surprized at the apparent eagerness with which his companion sought for the centres of all fashionable vice; there he entered
into all the spirit of the faro table: he betted, and always gam-
bled with success, except where the known sharper was his
antagonist, and then he lost even more than he gained; but it was
always with the same unchanging face, with which he generally
watched the society around: it was not, however, so when he encountered the rash youthful novice, or the luckless father of a
numerous family; then his very wish seemed fortune's law—this
apparent abstractedness of mind was laid aside, and his eyes sparkled with more fire than that of the cat whilst dallying with the
half-dead mouse. In every town, he left the formerly affluent
youth, torn from the circle he adorned, cursing, in the solitude of
a dungeon, the fate that had drawn him within the reach of this
fiend; whilst many a father sat frantic, amidst the speaking looks
of mute hungry children, without a single farthing of his late immense wealth, wherewith to buy even sufficient to satisfy their present craving. Yet he took no money from the gambling table; but
immediately lost, to the ruiner of many, the last gilder he had just
snatched from the convulsive grasp of the innocent: this might
but be the result of a certain degree of knowledge, which was not,
however, capable of combating the cunning of the more experienced. Aubrey often wished to represent this to his friend, and beg
him to resign that charity and pleasure which proved the ruin of
all, and did not tend to his own profit; but he delayed it—for
each day he hoped his friend would give him some opportunity of
speaking frankly and openly to him; however, this never occurred.
Lord Ruthven in his carriage, and amidst the various wild and
rich scenes of nature, was always the same: his eye spoke less than
his lip; and though Aubrey was near the object of his curiosity,

he obtained no greater gratification from it than the constant excitement of vainly wishing to break that mystery, which to his exalted imagination began to assume the appearance of something supernatural.

They soon arrived at Rome, and Aubrey for a time lost sight of his companion; he left him in daily attendance upon the morning circle of an Italian countess, whilst he went in search of the memorials of another almost deserted city. Whilst he was thus engaged, letters arrived from England, which he opened with eager impatience; the first was from his sister, breathing nothing but affection; the others were from his guardians, the latter astonished him; if it had before entered into his imagination that there was an evil power resident in his companion, these seemed to give him almost sufficient reason for the belief. His guardians insisted upon his immediately leaving his friend, and urged, that his character was dreadfully vicious, for that the possession of irresistible powers of seduction, rendered his licentious habits more dangerous to society. It had been discovered, that his contempt for the adultress had not originated in hatred of her character; but that he had required, to enhance his gratification, that his victim, the partner of his guilt, should be hurled from the pinnacle of unsullied virtue, down to the lowest abyss of infamy and degradation: in fine, that all those females whom he had sought, apparently on account of their virtue, had, since his departure, thrown even the mask aside, and had not scrupled to expose the whole deformity of their vices to the public gaze.

Aubrey determined upon leaving one, whose character had not yet shown a single bright point on which to rest the eye. He resolved to invent some plausible pretext for abandoning him altogether, purposing, in the mean while, to watch him more closely, and to let no slight circumstances pass by unnoticed. He entered into the same circle, and soon perceived, that his Lordship was endeavouring to work upon the inexperience of the daughter of the lady whose house he chiefly frequented. In Italy, it is seldom that an unmarried female is met with in society; he was therefore obliged to carry on his plans in secret; but Aubrey's eye followed him in all his windings, and soon discovered that an assignation had been appointed, which would most likely end in the ruin of an innocent, though thoughtless girl. Losing no time, he entered the apartment of Lord Ruthven, and abruptly asked him his in-

tentions with respect to the lady, informing him at the same time
that he was aware of his being about to meet her that very night.
Lord Ruthven answered, that his intentions were such as he supposed all would have upon such an occasion; and upon being
pressed whether he intended to marry her, merely laughed. Aubrey retired; and, immediately writing a note, to say, that from
that moment he must decline accompanying his Lordship in the
remainder of their proposed tour, he ordered his servant to seek
other apartments, and calling upon the mother of the lady, informed her of all he knew, not only with regard to her daughter,
but also concerning the character of his Lordship. The assignation was prevented. Lord Ruthven next day merely sent his servant to notify his complete assent to a separation; but did not hint
any suspicion of his plans having been foiled by Aubrey's interposition.

Having left Rome, Aubrey directed his steps towards Greece,
and crossing the Peninsula, soon found himself at Athens. He
then fixed his residence in the house of a Greek; and soon occupied himself in tracing the faded records of ancient glory upon
monuments that apparently, ashamed of chronicling the deeds
of freemen only before slaves, had hidden themselves beneath the
sheltering soil or many coloured lichen. Under the same roof as
himself, existed a being, so beautiful and delicate, that she might
have formed the model for a painter, wishing to pourtray on can-
vass the promised hope of the faithful in Mahomet's paradise,
save that her eyes spoke too much mind for any one to think she
could belong to those who had no souls. As she danced upon the
plain, or tripped along the mountain's side, one would have
thought the gazelle a poor type of her beauties; for who would
have exchanged her eye, apparently the eye of animated nature,
for that sleepy luxurious look of the animal suited but to the taste
of an epicure. The light step of Ianthe often accompanied Aubrey in his search after antiquities, and often would the unconscious girl, engaged in the pursuit of a Kashmere butterfly, show
the whole beauty of her form, floating as it were upon the wind,
to the eager gaze of him, who forgot the letters he had just de-
cyphered upon an almost effaced tablet, in the contemplation of
her sylph-like figure. Often would her tresses falling, as she flitted
around, exhibit in the sun's ray such delicately brilliant and
swiftly fading hues, as might well excuse the forgetfulness of the

antiquary, who let escape from his mind the very object he had before thought of vital importance to the proper interpretation of a passage in Pausanias. But why attempt to describe charms which all feel, but none can appreciate?—It was innocence, youth, and beauty, unaffected by crowded drawing-rooms and stifling balls. Whilst he drew those remains of which he wished to preserve a memorial for his future hours, she would stand by, and watch the magic effects of his pencil, in tracing the scenes of her native place; she would then describe to him the circling dance upon the open plain, would paint to him in all the glowing colours of youthful memory, the marriage pomp she remembered viewing in her infancy; and then, turning to subjects that had evidently made a greater impression upon her mind, would tell him all the supernatural tales of her nurse. Her earnestness and apparent belief of what she narrated, excited the interest even of Aubrey; and often as she told him the tale of the living vampyre, who had passed years amidst his friends, and dearest ties, forced every year, by feeding upon the life of a lovely female to prolong his existence for the ensuing months, his blood would run cold, whilst he attempted to laugh her out of such idle and horrible fantasies; but Ianthe cited to him the names of old men, who had at last detected one living among themselves, after several of their near relatives and children had been found marked with the stamp of the fiend's appetite; and when she found him so incredulous, she begged of him to believe her, for it had been remarked, that those who had dared to question their existence, always had some proof given, which obliged them, with grief and heartbreaking, to confess it was true. She detailed to him the traditional appearance of these monsters, and his horror was increased, by hearing a pretty accurate description of Lord Ruthven; he, however, still persisted in persuading her, that there could be no truth in her fears, though at the same time he wondered at the many coincidences which had all tended to excite a belief in the supernatural power of Lord Ruthven.

Aubrey began to attach himself more and more to Ianthe; her innocence, so contrasted with all the affected virtues of the women among whom he had sought for his vision of romance, won his heart; and while he ridiculed the idea of a young man of English habits, marrying an uneducated Greek girl, still he found himself more and more attached to the almost fairy form before him. He would tear himself at times from her, and, forming a plan for some antiquarian research, he would depart, determined not to return until his object was attained; but he always found it impossible to fix his attention upon the ruins around him, whilst in his mind he retained an image that seemed alone the rightful possessor of his thoughts. Ianthe was unconscious of his love, and was ever the same frank infantile being he had first known. She always seemed to part from him with reluctance; but it was because she had no longer any one with whom she could visit her favourite haunts, whilst her guardian was occupied in sketching or uncovering some fragment which had yet escaped the destructive hand of time. She had appealed to her parents on the subject of Vampyres, and they both, with several present, affirmed their existence, pale with horror at the very name. Soon after, Aubrey determined to proceed upon one of his excursions, which was to detain him for a few hours; when they heard the name of the place, they all at once begged of him not to return at night, as he must necessarily pass through a wood, where no Greek would ever remain, after the day had closed, upon any consideration. They described it as the resort of the vampyres in their nocturnal orgies, and denounced the most heavy evils as impending upon him who dared to cross their path. Aubrey made light of their representations, and tried to laugh them out of the idea; but when he saw them shudder at his daring thus to mock a superior, infernal power, the very name of which apparently made their blood freeze, he was silent.

Next morning Aubrey set off upon his excursion unattended; he was surprised to observe the melancholy face of his host, and was concerned to find that his words, mocking the belief of those horrible fiends, had inspired them with such terror. When he was about to depart, Ianthe came to the side of his horse, and earnestly begged of him to return, ere night allowed the power of these beings to be put in action;—he promised. He was, however, so occupied in his research, that he did not perceive that day-light would soon end, and that in the horizon there was one of those specks which, in the warmer climates, so rapidly gather into a tremendous mass, and pour all their rage upon the devoted country.—He at last, however, mounted his horse, determined to make up by speed for his delay: but it was too late. Twilight, in these southern climates, is almost unknown; immediately the sun sets,

night begins: and ere he had advanced far, the power of the storm
was above—its echoing thunders had scarcely an interval of rest;
—its thick heavy rain forced its way through the canopying foliage, whilst the blue forked lightning seemed to fall and radiate at
his very feet. Suddenly his horse took fright, and he was carried
with dreadful rapidity through the entangled forest. The animal
at last, through fatigue, stopped, and he found, by the glare of
lightning, that he was in the neighbourhood of a hovel that
hardly lifted itself up from the masses of dead leaves and brush-
wood which surrounded it. Dismounting, he approached, hoping
to find some one to guide him to the town, or at least trusting to
obtain shelter from the pelting of the storm. As he approached,
the thunders, for a moment silent, allowed him to hear the dreadful shrieks of a woman mingling with the stifled, exultant mockery of a laugh, continued in one almost unbroken sound;—he was
startled: but, roused by the thunder which again rolled over his
head, he, with a sudden effort, forced open the door of the hut.
He found himself in utter darkness: the sound, however, guided
him. He was apparently unperceived; for, though he called, still
the sounds continued, and no notice was taken of him. He found
himself in contact with some one, whom he immediately seized;
when a voice cried, "Again baffled!" to which a loud laugh succeeded; and he felt himself grappled by one whose strength
seemed superhuman: determined to sell his life as dearly as he
could, he struggled; but it was in vain: he was lifted from his feet
and hurled with enormous force against the ground:—his enemy
threw himself upon him, and kneeling upon his breast, had
placed his hands upon his throat—when the glare of many torches
penetrating through the hole that gave light in the day, disturbed
him;—he instantly rose, and, leaving his prey, rushed through
the door, and in a moment the crashing of the branches, as he
broke through the wood, was no longer heard. The storm was now
still; and Aubrey, incapable of moving, was soon heard by those
without. They entered; the light of their torches fell upon the
mud walls, and the thatch loaded on every individual straw with
heavy flakes of soot. At the desire of Aubrey they searched for her
who had attracted him by her cries; he was again left in darkness;
but what was his horror, when the light of the torches once more
burst upon him, to perceive the airy form of his fair conductress
brought in a lifeless corse. He shut his eyes, hoping that it was but

a vision arising from his disturbed imagination; but he again saw the same form, when he unclosed them, stretched by his side. There was no colour upon her cheek, not even upon her lip; yet there was a stillness about her face that seemed almost as attaching as the life that once dwelt there:—upon her neck and breast was blood, and upon her throat were the marks of teeth having opened the vein:—to this the men pointed, crying, simultaneously struck with horror, "A Vampyre! a Vampyre!" A litter was quickly formed, and Aubrey was laid by the side of her who had lately been to him the object of so many bright and fairy visions, now fallen with the flower of life that had died within her. He knew not what his thoughts were—his mind was benumbed and seemed to shun reflection, and take refuge in vacancy;—he held almost unconsciously in his hand a naked dagger of a particular construction, which had been found in the hut. They were soon met by different parties who had been engaged in the search of her whom a mother had missed. Their lamentable cries, as they approached the city, forewarned the parents of some dreadful catastrophe.—To describe their grief would be impossible; but when they ascertained the cause of their child's death, they looked at Aubrey, and pointed to the corse. They were inconsolable; both died broken-hearted.

Aubrey being put to bed was seized with a most violent fever, and was often delirious; in these intervals he would call upon Lord Ruthven and upon Ianthe—by some unaccountable combination he seemed to beg of his former companion to spare the being he loved. At other times he would imprecate maledictions upon his head, and curse him as her destroyer. Lord Ruthven chanced at this time to arrive at Athens, and, from whatever motive, upon hearing of the state of Aubrey, immediately placed himself in the same house, and became his constant attendant. When the latter recovered from his delirium, he was horrified and startled at the sight of him whose image he had now combined with that of a Vampyre; but Lord Ruthven, by his kind words, implying almost repentance for the fault that had caused their separation, and still more by the attention, anxiety, and care which he showed, soon reconciled him to his presence. His lordship seemed quite changed; he no longer appeared that apathetic being who had so astonished Aubrey; but as soon as his convalescence began to be rapid, he again gradually retired into the same state of mind, and Aubrey perceived no difference from the former man, except that at times he was surprised to meet his gaze fixed intently upon him, with a smile of malicious exultation playing upon his lips: he knew not why, but this smile haunted him. During the last stage of the invalid's recovery, Lord Ruthven was apparently engaged in watching the tideless waves raised by the cooling breeze, or in marking the progress of those orbs, circling, like our world, the moveless sun;—indeed, he appeared to wish to avoid the eyes of all.

Aubrey's mind, by this shock, was much weakened, and that elasticity of spirit which had once so distinguished him now seemed to have fled for ever. He was now as much a lover of solitude and silence as Lord Ruthven; but much as he wished for solitude, his mind could not find it in the neighbourhood of Athens; if he sought it amidst the ruins he had formerly frequented, Ianthe's form stood by his side;—if he sought it in the woods, her light step would appear wandering amidst the underwood, in quest of the modest violet; then suddenly turning round, would show, to his wild imagination, her pale face and wounded throat, with a meek smile upon her lips. He determined to fly scenes, every feature of which created such bitter associations in his mind. He proposed to Lord Ruthven, to whom he held himself bound by the tender care he had taken of him during his illness, that they should visit those parts of Greece neither had yet seen. They travelled in every direction, and sought every spot to which a recollection could be attached: but though they thus hastened from place to place, yet they seemed not to heed what they gazed upon. They heard much of robbers, but they gradually began to slight these reports, which they imagined were only the invention of individuals, whose interest it was to excite the generosity of those whom they defended from pretended dangers. In consequence of thus neglecting the advice of the inhabitants, on one occasion they travelled with only a few guards, more to serve as guides than as a defence. Upon entering, however, a narrow defile, at the bottom of which was the bed of a torrent, with large masses of rock brought down from the neighbouring precipices, they had reason to repent their negligence; for scarcely were the whole of the party engaged in the narrow pass, when they were startled by the whistling of bullets close to their heads, and by the echoed report of several guns. In an instant their guards had left them, and, placing themselves behind rocks, had begun to fire in the direction whence the report came. Lord Ruthven and Aubrey, imitating their example, retired for a moment behind the sheltering turn of the defile: but ashamed of being thus detained by a foe, who with insulting shouts bade them advance, and being exposed to unresisting slaughter, if any of the robbers should climb above and take them in the rear, they determined at once to rush forward in search of the enemy. Hardly had they lost the shelter of the rock, when Lord Ruthven received a shot in the shoulder, which brought him to the ground. Aubrey hastened to his assistance; and, no longer heeding the contest or his own peril, was soon surprised by seeing the robbers' faces around him—his guards having, upon Lord Ruthven's being wounded, immediately thrown up their arms and surrendered.

By promises of great reward, Aubrey soon induced them to convey his wounded friend to a neighbouring cabin; and having agreed upon a ransom, he was no more disturbed by their presence—they being content merely to guard the entrance till their comrade should return with the promised sum, for which he had an order. Lord Ruthven's strength rapidly decreased; in two days mortification ensued, and death seemed advancing with hasty steps. His conduct and appearance had not changed; he seemed as unconscious of pain as he had been of the objects about him: but towards the close of the last evening, his mind became apparently uneasy, and his eye often fixed upon Aubrey, who was induced to offer his assistance with more than usual earnestness—"Assist me! you may save me—you may do more than that—I mean not my life, I heed the death of my existence as little as that of the passing day; but you may save my honour, your friend's honour."—"How? tell me how? I would do any thing," replied Aubrey.—"I need but little—my life ebbs apace—I cannot explain the whole—but if you would conceal all you know of me, my honour were free from stain in the world's mouth—and if my death were unknown for some time in England—I—I—but life."—"It shall not be known."—"Swear!" cried the dying man, raising himself with exultant violence, "Swear by all your soul reveres, by all your nature fears, swear that for a year and a day you will not impart your knowledge of my crimes or death to any living being in any way, whatever may happen, or whatever you may see."—His eyes seemed bursting from their sockets: "I swear!" said Aubrey; he sunk laughing upon his pillow, and breathed no more.

Aubrey retired to rest, but did not sleep; the many circumstances attending his acquaintance with this man rose upon his mind, and he knew not why; when he remembered his oath a cold shivering came over him, as if from the presentiment of something horrible awaiting him. Rising early in the morning, he was about to enter the hovel in which he had left the corpse, when a robber met him, and informed him that it was no longer there, having been conveyed by himself and comrades, upon his retiring, to the pinnacle of a neighbouring mount, according to a promise they had given his lordship, that it should be exposed to the first cold ray of the moon that rose after his death. Aubrey astonished, and taking several of the men, determined to go and bury it upon the spot where it lay. But, when he had mounted to the summit he found no trace of either the corpse or the clothes, though the robbers swore they pointed out the identical rock on which they had laid the body. For a time his mind was bewildered in conjectures, but he at last returned, convinced that they had buried the corpse for the sake of the clothes.

Weary of a country in which he had met with such terrible misfortunes, and in which all apparently conspired to heighten that superstitious melancholy that had seized upon his mind, he resolved to leave it, and soon arrived at Smyrna. While waiting for a vessel to convey him to Otranto, or to Naples, he occupied himself in arranging those effects he had with him belonging to Lord Ruthven. Amongst other things there was a case containing several weapons of offence, more or less adapted to ensure the death of the victim. There were several daggers and ataghans. Whilst turning them over, and examining their curious forms, what was his surprise at finding a sheath apparently ornamented in the same style as the dagger discovered in the fatal hut;—he shuddered;—hastening to gain further proof, he found the weapon, and his horror may be imagined when he discovered that it fitted, though peculiarly shaped, the sheath he held in his hand. His eyes seemed to need no further certainty—they seemed gazing to be bound to the dagger; yet still he wished to disbelieve; but the particular form, the same varying tints upon the haft and sheath were alike in splendour on both, and left no room for doubt; there were also drops of blood on each.

He left Smyrna, and on his way home, at Rome, his first inquiries were concerning the lady he had attempted to snatch from
Lord Ruthven's seductive arts. Her parents were in distress,
their fortune ruined, and she had not been heard of since the departure of his lordship. Aubrey's mind became almost broken
under so many repeated horrors; he was afraid that this lady had
fallen a victim to the destroyer of Ianthe. He became morose and
silent; and his only occupation consisted in urging the speed of
the postilions, as if he were going to save the life of some one he
held dear. He arrived at Calais; a breeze, which seemed obedient
to his will, soon wafted him to the English shores; and he hastened to the mansion of his fathers, and there, for a moment,
appeared to lose, in the embraces and caresses of his sister, all
memory of the past. If she before, by her infantine caresses, had
gained his affection, now that the woman began to appear, she
was still more attaching as a companion.

Miss Aubrey had not that winning grace which gains the gaze
and applause of the drawing-room assemblies. There was none
of that light brilliancy which only exists in the heated atmosphere
of a crowded apartment. Her blue eye was never lit up by the
levity of the mind beneath. There was a melancholy charm
about it which did not seem to arise from misfortune, but from
some feeling within, that appeared to indicate a soul conscious
of a brighter realm. Her step was not that light footing, which
strays where'er a butterfly or a colour may attract—it was sedate
and pensive. When alone, her face was never brightened by the
smile of joy; but when her brother breathed to her his affection,
and would in her presence forget those griefs she knew destroyed
his rest, who would have exchanged her smile for that of the vo-
luptuary? It seemed as if those eyes, that face were then playing
in the light of their own native sphere. She was yet only eighteen,
and had not been presented to the world, it having been thought
by her guardians more fit that her presentation should be delayed
until her brother's return from the continent, when he might be
her protector. It was now, therefore, resolved that the next drawing-room, which was fast approaching, should be the epoch of her
entry into the "busy scene." Aubrey would rather have remained
in the mansion of his fathers, and fed upon the melancholy
which overpowered him. He could not feel interest about the
frivolities of fashionable strangers, when his mind had been so

torn by the events he had witnessed; but he determined to sacrifice his own comfort to the protection of his sister. They soon
arrived in town, and prepared for the next day, which had been
announced as a drawing-room.

The crowd was excessive—a drawing-room had not been held
for a long time, and all who were anxious to bask in the smile of
royalty, hastened thither. Aubrey was there with his sister. While
he was standing in a corner by himself, heedless of all around
him, engaged in the remembrance that the first time he had seen
Lord Ruthven was in that very place—he felt himself suddenly
seized by the arm, and a voice he recognized too well, sounded
in his ear—"Remember your oath." He had hardly courage to
turn, fearful of seeing a spectre that would blast him, when he
perceived, at a little distance, the same figure which had attracted
his notice on this spot upon his first entry into society. He
gazed till his limbs almost refusing to bear their weight, he was
obliged to take the arm of a friend, and forcing a passage through
the crowd, he threw himself into his carriage, and was driven
home. He paced the room with hurried steps, and fixed his hands
upon his head, as if he were afraid his thoughts were bursting
from his brain. Lord Ruthven again before him—circumstances
started up in dreadful array—the dagger—his oath.—He roused
himself, he could not believe it possible—the dead rise again!—
He thought his imagination had conjured up the image his mind
was resting upon. It was impossible that it could be real—he determined, therefore, to go again into society; for though he attempted to ask concerning Lord Ruthven, the name hung upon
his lips, and he could not succeed in gaining information. He
went a few nights after with his sister to the assembly of a near
relation. Leaving her under the protection of a matron, he retired into a recess, and there gave himself up to his own devouring thoughts. Perceiving, at last, that many were leaving, he
roused himself, and entering another room, found his sister surrounded by several, apparently in earnest conversation; he attempted to pass and get near her, when one, whom he requested
to move, turned round, and revealed to him those features he
most abhorred. He sprang forward, seized his sister's arm, and,
with hurried step, forced her towards the street: at the door he
found himself impeded by the crowd of servants who were waiting for their lords; and while he was engaged in passing them, he

again heard that voice whisper close to him—"Remember your oath!"—He did not dare to turn, but, hurrying his sister, soon reached home.

Aubrey became almost distracted. If before his mind had been absorbed by one subject, how much more completely was it engrossed, now that the certainty of the monster's living again pressed upon his thoughts. His sister's attentions were now unheeded, and it was in vain that she intreated him to explain to her what had caused his abrupt conduct. He only uttered a few words, and those terrified her. The more he thought, the more he was bewildered. His oath startled him;—was he then to allow this monster to roam, bearing ruin upon his breath, amidst all he held dear, and not avert its progress? His very sister might have been touched by him. But even if he were to break his oath, and disclose his suspicions, who would believe him? He thought of employing his own hand to free the world from such a wretch; but death, he remembered, had been already mocked. For days he remained in this state; shut up in his room, he saw no one, and eat only when his sister came, who, with eyes streaming with tears, besought him, for her sake, to support nature. At last, no longer capable of bearing stillness and solitude, he left his house, roamed from street to street, anxious to fly that image which haunted him. His dress became neglected, and he wandered, as often exposed to the noon-day sun as to the mid-night damps. He was no longer to be recognized; at first he returned with the evening to the house; but at last he laid him down to rest wherever fatigue overtook him. His sister, anxious for his safety, employed people to follow him; but they were soon distanced by him who fled from a pursuer swifter than any—from thought. His conduct, however, suddenly changed. Struck with the idea that he left by his absence the whole of his friends, with a fiend amongst them, of whose presence they were unconscious, he determined to enter again into society, and watch him closely, anxious to forewarn, in spite of his oath, all whom Lord Ruthven approached with intimacy. But when he entered into a room, his haggard and suspicious looks were so striking, his inward shudderings so visible, that his sister was at last obliged to beg of him to abstain from seeking, for her sake, a society which affected him so strongly. When, however, remonstrance proved unavailing, the guardians thought proper to interpose, and, fearing that his mind was becoming alienated, they thought it high time to resume again that trust which had been before imposed upon them by Aubrey's parents.

Desirous of saving him from the injuries and sufferings he had daily encountered in his wanderings, and of preventing him from exposing to the general eye those marks of what they considered folly, they engaged a physician to reside in the house, and take constant care of him. He hardly appeared to notice it, so completely was his mind absorbed by one terrible subject. His incoherence became at last so great, that he was confined to his chamber. There he would often lie for days, incapable of being roused. He had become emaciated, his eyes had attained a glassy lustre;—the only sign of affection and recollection remaining displayed itself upon the entry of his sister; then he would sometimes start, and, seizing her hands, with looks that severely afflicted her, he would desire her not to touch him. "Oh, do not touch him—if your love for me is aught, do not go near him!" When, however, she inquired to whom he referred, his only answer was, "True! true!" and again he sank into a state, whence not even she could rouse him. This lasted many months: gradually, however, as the year was passing, his incoherences became less frequent, and his mind threw off a portion of its gloom, whilst his guardians observed, that several times in the day he would count upon his fingers a definite number, and then smile.

The time had nearly elapsed, when, upon the last day of the year, one of his guardians entering his room, began to converse with his physician upon the melancholy circumstance of Aubrey's being in so awful a situation, when his sister was going next day to be married. Instantly Aubrey's attention was attracted; he asked anxiously to whom. Glad of this mark of returning intellect, of which they feared he had been deprived, they mentioned the name of the Earl of Marsden. Thinking this was a young Earl whom he had met with in society, Aubrey seemed pleased, and astonished them still more by his expressing his intention to be present at the nuptials, and desiring to see his sister. They answered not, but in a few minutes his sister was with him. He was apparently again capable of being affected by the influence of her lovely smile; for he pressed her to his breast, and kissed her cheek, wet with tears, flowing at the thought of her brother's being once more alive to the feelings of affection. He began to speak with all his wonted warmth, and to congratulate her upon her marriage with a person so distinguished for rank and every accomplishment; when he suddenly perceived a locket upon her breast; opening it, what was his surprise at beholding the features of the monster who had so long influenced his life. He seized the portrait in a paroxysm of rage, and trampled it under foot. Upon her asking him why he thus destroyed the resemblance of her future husband, he looked as if he did not understand her;—then seizing her hands, and gazing on her with a frantic expression of countenance, he bade her swear that she would never wed this monster, for he—But he could not advance —it seemed as if that voice again bade him remember his oath— he turned suddenly round, thinking Lord Ruthven was near him but saw no one. In the meantime the guardians and physician, who had heard the whole, and thought this was but a return of his disorder, entered, and forcing him from Miss Aubrey, desired her to leave him. He fell upon his knees to them, he implored, he begged of them to delay but for one day. They, attributing this to the insanity they imagined had taken possession of his mind, endeavoured to pacify him, and retired.

Lord Ruthven had called the morning after the drawing-room, and had been refused with every one else. When he heard of Aubrey's ill health, he readily understood himself to be the cause of it; but when he learned that he was deemed insane, his exultation and pleasure could hardly be concealed from those among whom he had gained this information. He hastened to the house of his former companion, and, by constant attendance, and the pretence of great affection for the brother and interest in his fate, he gradually won the ear of Miss Aubrey. Who could resist his power? His tongue had dangers and toils to recount—could speak of himself as of an individual having no sympathy with any being on the crowded earth, save with her to whom he addressed himself;—could tell how, since he knew her, his existence had begun to seem worthy of preservation, if it were merely that he might listen to her soothing accents;—in fine, he knew so well how to use the serpent's art, or such was the will of fate, that he gained her affections. The title of the elder branch falling at length to him, he obtained an important embassy, which served as an excuse for hastening the marriage (in spite of her brother's deranged state), which was to take place the very day before his departure for the continent.

Aubrey, when he was left by the physician and his guardians, attempted to bribe the servants, but in vain. He asked for pen and paper; it was given him; he wrote a letter to his sister, conjuring her, as she valued her own happiness, her own honour, and the honour of those now in the grave, who once held her in their arms as their hope and the hope of their house, to delay but for a few hours that marriage, on which he denounced the most heavy curses. The servants promised they would deliver it; but giving it to the physician, he thought it better not to harass any more the mind of Miss Aubrey by, what he considered, the ravings of a maniac. Night passed on without rest to the busy inmates of the house; and Aubrey heard, with a horror that may more easily be conceived than described, the notes of busy preparation. Morning came, and the sound of carriages broke upon his ear. Aubrey grew almost frantic. The curiosity of the servants at last overcame their vigilance, they gradually stole away, leaving him in the custody of an helpless old woman. He seized the opportunity, with one bound was out of the room, and in a moment found himself in the apartment where all were nearly assembled. Lord Ruthven was the first to perceive him: he immediately approached, and, taking his arm by force, hurried him from the room, speechless with rage. When on the staircase, Lord Ruthven whispered in his ear—"Remember your oath, and know, if not my bride to day, your sister is dishonoured. Women are frail!" So saying, he pushed him towards his attendants, who, roused by the old woman, had come in search of him. Aubrey could no longer support himself; his rage not finding vent, had broken a blood-vessel, and he was conveyed to bed. This was not mentioned to his sister, who was not present when he entered, as the physician was afraid of agitating her. The marriage was solemnized, and the bride and bridegroom left London.

Aubrey's weakness increased; the effusion of blood produced symptoms of the near approach of death. He desired his sister's guardians might be called, and when the midnight hour had struck, he related composedly what the reader has perused—he died immediately after.

The guardians hastened to protect Miss Aubrey; but when they arrived, it was too late. Lord Ruthven had disappeared, and Aubrey's sister had glutted the thirst of a VAMPYRE!

FRAGMENT OF A NOVEL

by Lord Byron

Fragment of a Novel

"June 17, 1816.

"In the year 17—, having for some time determined on a journey through countries not hitherto much frequented by travellers, I set out, accompanied by a friend, whom I shall designate by the name of Augustus Darvell. He was a few years my elder, and a man of considerable fortune and ancient family: advantages which an extensive capacity prevented him alike from undervaluing or over-rating. Some peculiar circumstances in his private history had rendered him to me an object of attention, of interest, and even of regard, which neither the reserve of his manners, nor occasional indications of an inquietude at times nearly approaching to aliena-tion of mind, could extinguish.

"I was yet young in life, which I had begun early; but my intimacy with him was of a recent date: we had been educated at the same schools and university; but his progress through these had preceded mine, and he had been deeply initiated into what is called the world, while I was yet in my novitiate. While thus engaged, I heard much both of his past and present life; and, although in these accounts there were many and irreconcilable contradictions, I could still gather from the whole that he was a being of no com-mon order, and one who, whatever pains he might take to avoid remark, would still be remarkable. I had cultivated his acquaint-ance subsequently, and endeavoured to obtain his friendship, but this last appeared to be unattainable; whatever affections he might have possessed seemed now, some to have been extinguished, and others to be concentred: that his feelings were acute, I had suffi-cient opportunities of observing; for, although he could control, he could not altogether disguise them: still he had a power of giving to one passion the appearance of another, in such a manner that it was difficult to define the nature of what was working within him; and the expressions of his features would vary so rapidly, though slightly, that it was useless to trace them to their sources.

It was evident that he was a prey to some cureless disquiet; but whether it arose from ambition, love, remorse, grief, from one or all of these, or merely from a morbid temperament akin to disease, I could not discover: there were circumstances alleged which might have justified the application to each of these causes; but, as I have before said, these were so contradictory and contradicted, that none could be fixed upon with accuracy. Where there is mystery, it is generally supposed that there must also be evil: I know not how this may be, but in him there certainly was the one, though I could not ascertain the extent of the other—and felt loth, as far as regarded himself, to believe in its existence. My advances were received with sufficient coldness: but I was young, and not easily discouraged, and at length succeeded in obtaining, to a certain degree, that common-place intercourse and moderate confidence of common and every-day concerns, created and cemented by similarity of pursuit and frequency of meeting, which is called intimacy, or friendship, according to the ideas of him who uses those words to express them.

"Darvell had already travelled extensively; and to him I had applied for information with regard to the conduct of my intended journey. It was my secret wish that he might be prevailed on to accompany me; it was also a probable hope, founded upon the shadowy restlessness which I observed in him, and to which the animation which he appeared to feel on such subjects, and his apparent indifference to all by which he was more immediately surrounded, gave fresh strength. This wish I first hinted, and then expressed: his answer, though I had partly expected it, gave me all the pleasure of surprise—he consented; and, after the requisite arrangement, we commenced our voyages. After journeying through various countries of the south of Europe, our attention was turned towards the East, according to our original destination; and it was in my progress through these regions that the incident occurred upon which will turn what I may have to relate.

"The constitution of Darvell, which must from his appearance have been in early life more than usually robust, had been for some time gradually giving away, without the intervention of any apparent disease: he had neither cough' nor hectic, yet he became daily more enfeebled; his habits were temperate, and he neither declined nor complained of fatigue; yet he was evidently wasting away: he became more and more silent and sleepless, and at length so seriously altered, that my alarm grew proportionate to what I conceived to be his danger.

"We had determined, on our arrival at Smyrna, on an excursion to the ruins of Ephesus and Sardis, from which I endeavoured to dissuade him in his present state of indisposition—but in vain: there appeared to be an oppression on his mind, and a solemnity in his manner, which ill corresponded with his eagerness to proceed on what I regarded as a mere party of pleasure little suited to a valetudinarian; but I opposed him no longer—and in a few days we set off together, accompanied only by a serrugee and a single janizary.

"We had passed halfway towards the remains of Ephesus, leaving behind us the more fertile environs of Smyrna, and were entering upon that wild and tenantless tract through the marshes and defiles which lead to the few huts yet lingering over the broken columns of Diana—the roofless walls of expelled Christianity, and the still more recent but complete desolation of abandoned mosques—when the sudden and rapid illness of my companion obliged us to halt at a Turkish cemetery, the turbaned tombstones of which were the sole indication that human life had ever been a sojourner in this wilderness. The only caravansera we had seen was left some hours behind us, not a vestige of a town or even cottage was within sight or hope, and this 'city of the dead' appeared to be the sole refuge of my unfortunate friend, who seemed on the verge of becoming the last of its inhabitants.

"In this situation, I looked round for a place where he might most conveniently repose:—contrary to the usual aspect of Mahometan burial-grounds, the cypresses were in this few in number, and these thinly scattered over its extent; the tombstones were mostly fallen, and worn with age:—upon one of the most considerable of these, and beneath one of the most spreading trees, Darvell supported himself, in a half-reclining posture, with great difficulty. He asked for water. I had some doubts of our being able to find any, and prepared to go in search of it with hesitating despondency: but he desired me to remain; and turning to Suleiman, our janizary, who stood by us smoking with great tranquillity, he said, 'Suleiman, verbana su,' (*i.e.* 'bring some water,') and went on describing the spot where it was to be found with great minuteness, at a small well for camels, a few hundred yards to the right: the janizary obeyed. I said to Darvell, 'How did you know this?'—He replied, 'From our situation; you must perceive that this place was once inhabited, and could not have been so without springs: I have also been here before.'

" 'You have been here before!—How came you never to mention this to me? and what could you be doing in a place where no one would remain a moment longer than they could help it?'

"To this question I received no answer. In the mean time Suleiman returned with the water, leaving the serrugee and the horses at the fountain. The quenching of his thirst had the appearance of reviving him for a moment; and I conceived hopes of his being able to proceed, or at least to return, and I urged the attempt. He was silent—and appeared to be collecting his spirits for an effort to speak. He began—

" 'This is the end of my journey, and of my life;—I came here to die; but I have a request to make, a command—for such my last words must be.—You will observe it?'

" 'Most certainly; but I have better hopes.'

" 'I have no hopes, nor wishes, but this—conceal my death from every human being.'

" 'I hope there will be no occasion; that you will recover, and——'

" 'Peace!—it must be so: promise this.'

" 'I do.'

" 'Swear it, by all that——' He here dictated an oath of great solemnity.

" 'There is no occasion for this. I will observe your request; and to doubt me is——'

" 'It cannot be helped,—you must swear.'

"I took the oath, it appeared to relieve him. He removed a seal ring from his finger, on which were some Arabic characters, and presented it to me. He proceeded—

" 'On the ninth day of the month, at noon precisely (what month you please, but this must be the day), you must fling this ring into the salt springs which run into the Bay of Eleusis; the day after, at the same hour, you must repair to the ruins of the temple of Ceres, and wait one hour.'

" 'Why?'

" 'You will see.'

" 'The ninth day of the month, you say?'

" 'The ninth.'

"As I observed that the present was the ninth day of the month, his countenance changed, and he paused. As he sat, evidently becoming more feeble, a stork, with a snake in her beak, perched upon a tombstone near us; and, without devouring her prey, appeared to be steadfastly regarding us. I know not what impelled me to drive it away, but the attempt was useless; she made a few circles in the air, and returned exactly to the same spot. Darvell pointed to it, and smiled—he spoke—I know not whether to himself or to me—but the words were only, ''Tis well!'

" 'What is well? What do you mean?'

" 'No matter; you must bury me here this evening, and exactly where that bird is now perched. You know the rest of my injunctions.'

"He then proceeded to give me several directions as to the manner in which his death might be best concealed. After these were finished, he exclaimed, 'You perceive that bird?'

" 'Certainly.'

" 'And the serpent writhing in her beak?'

" 'Doubtless: there is nothing uncommon in it; it is her natural prey. But it is odd that she does not devour it.'

"He smiled in a ghastly manner, and said faintly, 'It is not yet time!' As he spoke, the stork flew away. My eyes followed it for a moment—it could hardly be longer than ten might be counted. I felt Darvell's weight, as it were, increase upon my shoulder, and, turning to look upon his face, perceived that he was dead!

"I was shocked with the sudden certainty which could not be mistaken—his countenance in a few minutes became nearly black. I should have attributed so rapid a change to poison, had I not been aware that he had no opportunity of receiving it unperceived. The day was declining, the body was rapidly altering, and nothing remained but to fulfil his request. With the aid of Suleiman's ataghan and my own sabre, we scooped a shallow grave upon the spot which Darvell had indicated: the earth easily gave way, having already received some Mahometan tenant. We dug as deeply as the time permitted us, and throwing the dry earth upon all that remained of the singular being so lately departed, we cut a few sods of greener turf from the less withered soil around us, and laid them upon his sepulchre.

"Between astonishment and grief, I was tearless."

A CATALOGUE OF SELECTED DOVER BOOKS
IN ALL FIELDS OF INTEREST

A CATALOGUE OF SELECTED DOVER BOOKS
IN ALL FIELDS OF INTEREST

AMERICA'S OLD MASTERS, James T. Flexner. Four men emerged unexpectedly from provincial 18th century America to leadership in European art: Benjamin West, J. S. Copley, C. R. Peale, Gilbert Stuart. Brilliant coverage of lives and contributions. Revised, 1967 edition. 69 plates. 365pp. of text.
21806-6 Paperbound $3.00

FIRST FLOWERS OF OUR WILDERNESS: AMERICAN PAINTING, THE COLONIAL PERIOD, James T. Flexner. Painters, and regional painting traditions from earliest Colonial times up to the emergence of Copley, West and Peale Sr., Foster, Gustavus Hesselius, Feke, John Smibert and many anonymous painters in the primitive manner. Engaging presentation, with 162 illustrations. xxii + 368pp.
22180-6 Paperbound $3.50

THE LIGHT OF DISTANT SKIES: AMERICAN PAINTING, 1760-1835, James T. Flexner. The great generation of early American painters goes to Europe to learn and to teach: West, Copley, Gilbert Stuart and others. Allston, Trumbull, Morse; also contemporary American painters—primitives, derivatives, academics—who remained in America. 102 illustrations. xiii + 306pp.
22179-2 Paperbound $3.00

A HISTORY OF THE RISE AND PROGRESS OF THE ARTS OF DESIGN IN THE UNITED STATES, William Dunlap. Much the richest mine of information on early American painters, sculptors, architects, engravers, miniaturists, etc. The only source of information for scores of artists, the major primary source for many others. Unabridged reprint of rare original 1834 edition, with new introduction by James T. Flexner, and 394 new illustrations. Edited by Rita Weiss. 6⅝ x 9⅝.
21695-0, 21696-9, 21697-7 Three volumes, Paperbound $13.50

EPOCHS OF CHINESE AND JAPANESE ART, Ernest F. Fenollosa. From primitive Chinese art to the 20th century, thorough history, explanation of every important art period and form, including Japanese woodcuts; main stress on China and Japan, but Tibet, Korea also included. Still unexcelled for its detailed, rich coverage of cultural background, aesthetic elements, diffusion studies, particularly of the historical period. 2nd, 1913 edition. 242 illustrations. lii + 439pp. of text.
20364-6, 20365-4 Two volumes, Paperbound $6.00

THE GENTLE ART OF MAKING ENEMIES, James A. M. Whistler. Greatest wit of his day deflates Oscar Wilde, Ruskin, Swinburne; strikes back at inane critics, exhibitions, art journalism; aesthetics of impressionist revolution in most striking form. Highly readable classic by great painter. Reproduction of edition designed by Whistler. Introduction by Alfred Werner. xxxvi + 334pp.
21875-9 Paperbound $2.50

DESIGN BY ACCIDENT; A BOOK OF "ACCIDENTAL EFFECTS" FOR ARTISTS AND DESIGNERS, James F. O'Brien. Create your own unique, striking, imaginative effects by "controlled accident" interaction of materials: paints and lacquers, oil and water based paints, splatter, crackling materials, shatter, similar items. Everything you do will be different; first book on this limitless art, so useful to both fine artist and commercial artist. Full instructions. 192 plates showing "accidents," 8 in color. viii + 215pp. 8⅜ x 11¼.   21942-9 Paperbound $3.50

THE BOOK OF SIGNS, Rudolf Koch. Famed German type designer draws 493 beautiful symbols: religious, mystical, alchemical, imperial, property marks, runes, etc. Remarkable fusion of traditional and modern. Good for suggestions of timelessness, smartness, modernity. Text. vi + 104pp. 6⅛ x 9¼.
                                                          20162-7 Paperbound $1.25

HISTORY OF INDIAN AND INDONESIAN ART, Ananda K. Coomaraswamy. An unabridged republication of one of the finest books by a great scholar in Eastern art. Rich in descriptive material, history, social backgrounds; Sunga reliefs, Rajput paintings, Gupta temples, Burmese frescoes, textiles, jewelry, sculpture, etc. 400 photos. viii + 423pp. 6⅜ x 9¾.   21436-2 Paperbound $4.00

PRIMITIVE ART, Franz Boas. America's foremost anthropologist surveys textiles, ceramics, woodcarving, basketry, metalwork, etc.; patterns, technology, creation of symbols, style origins. All areas of world, but very full on Northwest Coast Indians. More than 350 illustrations of baskets, boxes, totem poles, weapons, etc. 378 pp.
                                                          20025-6 Paperbound $3.00

THE GENTLEMAN AND CABINET MAKER'S DIRECTOR, Thomas Chippendale. Full reprint (third edition, 1762) of most influential furniture book of all time, by master cabinetmaker. 200 plates, illustrating chairs, sofas, mirrors, tables, cabinets, plus 24 photographs of surviving pieces. Biographical introduction by N. Bienenstock. vi + 249pp. 9⅞ x 12¾.   21601-2 Paperbound $4.00

AMERICAN ANTIQUE FURNITURE, Edgar G. Miller, Jr. The basic coverage of all American furniture before 1840. Individual chapters cover type of furniture—clocks, tables, sideboards, etc.—chronologically, with inexhaustible wealth of data. More than 2100 photographs, all identified, commented on. Essential to all early American collectors. Introduction by H. E. Keyes. vi + 1106pp. 7⅞ x 10¾.
                              21599-7, 21600-4 Two volumes, Paperbound $11.00

PENNSYLVANIA DUTCH AMERICAN FOLK ART, Henry J. Kauffman. 279 photos, 28 drawings of tulipware, Fraktur script, painted tinware, toys, flowered furniture, quilts, samplers, hex signs, house interiors, etc. Full descriptive text. Excellent for tourist, rewarding for designer, collector. Map. 146pp. 7⅞ x 10¾.
                                                          21205-X Paperbound $2.50

EARLY NEW ENGLAND GRAVESTONE RUBBINGS, Edmund V. Gillon, Jr. 43 photographs, 226 carefully reproduced rubbings show heavily symbolic, sometimes macabre early gravestones, up to early 19th century. Remarkable early American primitive art, occasionally strikingly beautiful; always powerful. Text. xxvi + 207pp 8⅜ x 11¼.   21380-3 Paperbound $3.50

ALPHABETS AND ORNAMENTS, Ernst Lehner. Well-known pictorial source for decorative alphabets, script examples, cartouches, frames, decorative title pages, calligraphic initials, borders, similar material. 14th to 19th century, mostly European. Useful in almost any graphic arts designing, varied styles. 750 illustrations. 256pp. 7 x 10.   21905-4 Paperbound $4.00

PAINTING: A CREATIVE APPROACH, Norman Colquhoun. For the beginner simple guide provides an instructive approach to painting: major stumbling blocks for beginner; overcoming them, technical points; paints and pigments; oil painting; watercolor and other media and color. New section on "plastic" paints. Glossary. Formerly *Paint Your Own Pictures*. 221pp.   22000-1 Paperbound $1.75

THE ENJOYMENT AND USE OF COLOR, Walter Sargent. Explanation of the relations between colors themselves and between colors in nature and art, including hundreds of little-known facts about color values, intensities, effects of high and low illumination, complementary colors. Many practical hints for painters, references to great masters. 7 color plates, 29 illustrations. x + 274pp.
20944-X Paperbound $2.50

THE NOTEBOOKS OF LEONARDO DA VINCI, compiled and edited by Jean Paul Richter. 1566 extracts from original manuscripts reveal the full range of Leonardo's versatile genius: all his writings on painting, sculpture, architecture, anatomy, astronomy, geography, topography, physiology, mining, music, etc., in both Italian and English, with 186 plates of manuscript pages and more than 500 additional drawings. Includes studies for the Last Supper, the lost Sforza monument, and other works. Total of xlvii + 866pp. $7\frac{7}{8}$ x $10\frac{3}{4}$.
22572-0, 22573-9 Two volumes, Paperbound $10.00

MONTGOMERY WARD CATALOGUE OF 1895. Tea gowns, yards of flannel and pillow-case lace, stereoscopes, books of gospel hymns, the New Improved Singer Sewing Machine, side saddles, milk skimmers, straight-edged razors, high-button shoes, spittoons, and on and on . . . listing some 25,000 items, practically all illustrated. Essential to the shoppers of the 1890's, it is our truest record of the spirit of the period. Unaltered reprint of Issue No. 57, Spring and Summer 1895. Introduction by Boris Emmet. Innumerable illustrations. xiii + 624pp. $8\frac{1}{2}$ x $11\frac{5}{8}$.
22377-9 Paperbound $6.95

THE CRYSTAL PALACE EXHIBITION ILLUSTRATED CATALOGUE (LONDON, 1851). One of the wonders of the modern world—the Crystal Palace Exhibition in which all the nations of the civilized world exhibited their achievements in the arts and sciences—presented in an equally important illustrated catalogue. More than 1700 items pictured with accompanying text—ceramics, textiles, cast-iron work, carpets, pianos, sleds, razors, wall-papers, billiard tables, beehives, silverware and hundreds of other artifacts—represent the focal point of Victorian culture in the Western World. Probably the largest collection of Victorian decorative art ever assembled— indispensable for antiquarians and designers. Unabridged republication of the Art-Journal Catalogue of the Great Exhibition of 1851, with all terminal essays. New introduction by John Gloag, F.S.A. xxxiv + 426pp. 9 x 12.
22503-8 Paperbound $4.50

VISUAL ILLUSIONS: THEIR CAUSES, CHARACTERISTICS, AND APPLICATIONS, Matthew Luckiesh. Thorough description and discussion of optical illusion, geometric and perspective, particularly; size and shape distortions, illusions of color, of motion; natural illusions; use of illusion in art and magic, industry, etc. Most useful today with op art, also for classical art. Scores of effects illustrated. Introduction by William H. Ittleson. 100 illustrations. xxi + 252pp.
21530-X Paperbound $2.00

A HANDBOOK OF ANATOMY FOR ART STUDENTS, Arthur Thomson. Thorough, virtually exhaustive coverage of skeletal structure, musculature, etc. Full text, supplemented by anatomical diagrams and drawings and by photographs of undraped figures. Unique in its comparison of male and female forms, pointing out differences of contour, texture, form. 211 figures, 40 drawings, 86 photographs. xx + 459pp. 5⅜ x 8⅜.
21163-0 Paperbound $3.50

150 MASTERPIECES OF DRAWING, Selected by Anthony Toney. Full page reproductions of drawings from the early 16th to the end of the 18th century, all beautifully reproduced: Rembrandt, Michelangelo, Dürer, Fragonard, Urs, Graf, Wouwerman, many others. First-rate browsing book, model book for artists. xviii + 150pp. 8⅜ x 11¼.
21032-4 Paperbound $2.50

THE LATER WORK OF AUBREY BEARDSLEY, Aubrey Beardsley. Exotic, erotic, ironic masterpieces in full maturity: Comedy Ballet, Venus and Tannhauser, Pierrot, Lysistrata, Rape of the Lock, Savoy material, Ali Baba, Volpone, etc. This material revolutionized the art world, and is still powerful, fresh, brilliant. With *The Early Work,* all Beardsley's finest work. 174 plates, 2 in color. xiv + 176pp. 8⅛ x 11.
21817-1 Paperbound $3.00

DRAWINGS OF REMBRANDT, Rembrandt van Rijn. Complete reproduction of fabulously rare edition by Lippmann and Hofstede de Groot, completely reedited, updated, improved by Prof. Seymour Slive, Fogg Museum. Portraits, Biblical sketches, landscapes, Oriental types, nudes, episodes from classical mythology—All Rembrandt's fertile genius. Also selection of drawings by his pupils and followers. "Stunning volumes," *Saturday Review.* 550 illustrations. lxxviii + 552pp. 9⅛ x 12¼.
21485-0, 21486-9 Two volumes, Paperbound $7.00

THE DISASTERS OF WAR, Francisco Goya. One of the masterpieces of Western civilization—83 etchings that record Goya's shattering, bitter reaction to the Napoleonic war that swept through Spain after the insurrection of 1808 and to war in general. Reprint of the first edition, with three additional plates from Boston's Museum of Fine Arts. All plates facsimile size. Introduction by Philip Hofer, Fogg Museum. v + 97pp. 9⅜ x 8¼.
21872-4 Paperbound $2.00

GRAPHIC WORKS OF ODILON REDON. Largest collection of Redon's graphic works ever assembled: 172 lithographs, 28 etchings and engravings, 9 drawings. These include some of his most famous works. All the plates from *Odilon Redon: oeuvre graphique complet,* plus additional plates. New introduction and caption translations by Alfred Werner. 209 illustrations. xxvii + 209pp. 9⅛ x 12¼.
21966-8 Paperbound $4.00

A HISTORY OF COSTUME, Carl Köhler. Definitive history, based on surviving pieces of clothing primarily, and paintings, statues, etc. secondarily. Highly readable text, supplemented by 594 illustrations of costumes of the ancient Mediterranean peoples, Greece and Rome, the Teutonic prehistoric period; costumes of the Middle Ages, Renaissance, Baroque, 18th and 19th centuries. Clear, measured patterns are provided for many clothing articles. Approach is practical throughout. Enlarged by Emma von Sichart. 464pp.   21030-8 Paperbound $3.50

ORIENTAL RUGS, ANTIQUE AND MODERN, Walter A. Hawley. A complete and authoritative treatise on the Oriental rug—where they are made, by whom and how, designs and symbols, characteristics in detail of the six major groups, how to distinguish them and how to buy them. Detailed technical data is provided on periods, weaves, warps, wefts, textures, sides, ends and knots, although no technical background is required for an understanding. 11 color plates, 80 halftones, 4 maps. vi + 320pp. 6⅛ x 9⅛.   22366-3 Paperbound $5.00

TEN BOOKS ON ARCHITECTURE, Vitruvius. By any standards the most important book on architecture ever written. Early Roman discussion of aesthetics of building, construction methods, orders, sites, and every other aspect of architecture has inspired, instructed architecture for about 2,000 years. Stands behind Palladio, Michelangelo, Bramante, Wren, countless others. Definitive Morris H. Morgan translation. 68 illustrations. xii + 331pp.   20645-9 Paperbound $2.50

THE FOUR BOOKS OF ARCHITECTURE, Andrea Palladio. Translated into every major Western European language in the two centuries following its publication in 1570, this has been one of the most influential books in the history of architecture. Complete reprint of the 1738 Isaac Ware edition. New introduction by Adolf Placzek, Columbia Univ. 216 plates. xxii + 110pp. of text. 9½ x 12¾.
21308-0 Clothbound $10.00

STICKS AND STONES: A STUDY OF AMERICAN ARCHITECTURE AND CIVILIZATION, Lewis Mumford.One of the great classics of American cultural history. American architecture from the medieval-inspired earliest forms to the early 20th century; evolution of structure and style, and reciprocal influences on environment. 21 photographic illustrations. 238pp.   20202-X Paperbound $2.00

THE AMERICAN BUILDER'S COMPANION, Asher Benjamin. The most widely used early 19th century architectural style and source book, for colonial up into Greek Revival periods. Extensive development of geometry of carpentering, construction of sashes, frames, doors, stairs; plans and elevations of domestic and other buildings. Hundreds of thousands of houses were built according to this book, now invaluable to historians, architects, restorers, etc. 1827 edition. 59 plates. 114pp. 7⅞ x 10¾.
22236-5 Paperbound $3.00

DUTCH HOUSES IN THE HUDSON VALLEY BEFORE 1776, Helen Wilkinson Reynolds. The standard survey of the Dutch colonial house and outbuildings, with constructional features, decoration, and local history associated with individual homesteads. Introduction by Franklin D. Roosevelt. Map. 150 illustrations. 469pp. 6⅝ x 9¼.   21469-9 Paperbound $4.00

THE ARCHITECTURE OF COUNTRY HOUSES, Andrew J. Downing. Together with Vaux's *Villas and Cottages* this is the basic book for Hudson River Gothic architecture of the middle Victorian period. Full, sound discussions of general aspects of housing, architecture, style, decoration, furnishing, together with scores of detailed house plans, illustrations of specific buildings, accompanied by full text. Perhaps the most influential single American architectural book. 1850 edition. Introduction by J. Stewart Johnson. 321 figures, 34 architectural designs. xvi + 560pp.
22003-6 Paperbound $4.00

LOST EXAMPLES OF COLONIAL ARCHITECTURE, John Mead Howells. Full-page photographs of buildings that have disappeared or been so altered as to be denatured, including many designed by major early American architects. 245 plates. xvii + 248pp. 7⅞ x 10¾. 21143-6 Paperbound $3.00

DOMESTIC ARCHITECTURE OF THE AMERICAN COLONIES AND OF THE EARLY REPUBLIC, Fiske Kimball. Foremost architect and restorer of Williamsburg and Monticello covers nearly 200 homes between 1620-1825. Architectural details, construction, style features, special fixtures, floor plans, etc. Generally considered finest work in its area. 219 illustrations of houses, doorways, windows, capital mantels. xx + 314pp. 7⅞ x 10¾. 21743-4 Paperbound $3.50

EARLY AMERICAN ROOMS: 1650-1858, edited by Russell Hawes Kettell. Tour of 12 rooms, each representative of a different era in American history and each furnished, decorated, designed and occupied in the style of the era. 72 plans and elevations, 8-page color section, etc., show fabrics, wall papers, arrangements, etc. Full descriptive text. xvii + 200pp. of text. 8⅜ x 11¼.
21633-0 Paperbound $5.00

THE FITZWILLIAM VIRGINAL BOOK, edited by J. Fuller Maitland and W. B. Squire. Full modern printing of famous early 17th-century ms. volume of 300 works by Morley, Byrd, Bull, Gibbons, etc. For piano or other modern keyboard instrument; easy to read format. xxxvi + 938pp. 8⅜ x 11.
21068-5, 21069-3 Two volumes, Paperbound $8.00

HARPSICHORD MUSIC, Johann Sebastian Bach. Bach Gesellschaft edition. A rich selection of Bach's masterpieces for the harpsichord: the six English Suites, six French Suites, the six Partitas (Clavierübung part I), the Goldberg Variations (Clavierübung part IV), the fifteen Two-Part Inventions and the fifteen Three-Part Sinfonias. Clearly reproduced on large sheets with ample margins; eminently playable. vi + 312pp. 8⅛ x 11. 22360-4 Paperbound $5.00

THE MUSIC OF BACH: AN INTRODUCTION, Charles Sanford Terry. A fine, nontechnical introduction to Bach's music, both instrumental and vocal. Covers organ music, chamber music, passion music, other types. Analyzes themes, developments, innovations. x + 114pp. 21075-8 Paperbound $1.25

BEETHOVEN AND HIS NINE SYMPHONIES, Sir George Grove. Noted British musicologist provides best history, analysis, commentary on symphonies. Very thorough, rigorously accurate; necessary to both advanced student and amateur music lover. 436 musical passages. vii + 407 pp. 20334-4 Paperbound $2.25

JOHANN SEBASTIAN BACH, Philipp Spitta. One of the great classics of musicology, this definitive analysis of Bach's music (and life) has never been surpassed. Lucid, nontechnical analyses of hundreds of pieces (30 pages devoted to St. Matthew Passion, 26 to B Minor Mass). Also includes major analysis of 18th-century music. 450 musical examples. 40-page musical supplement. Total of xx + 1799pp.
(EUK) 22278-0, 22279-9 Two volumes, Clothbound $15.00

MOZART AND HIS PIANO CONCERTOS, Cuthbert Girdlestone. The only full-length study of an important area of Mozart's creativity. Provides detailed analyses of all 23 concertos, traces inspirational sources. 417 musical examples. Second edition. 509pp.
(USO) 21271-8 Paperbound $3.50

THE PERFECT WAGNERITE: A COMMENTARY ON THE NIBLUNG'S RING, George Bernard Shaw. Brilliant and still relevant criticism in remarkable essays on Wagner's Ring cycle, Shaw's ideas on political and social ideology behind the plots, role of Leitmotifs, vocal requisites, etc. Prefaces. xxi + 136pp.
21707-8 Paperbound $1.50

DON GIOVANNI, W. A. Mozart. Complete libretto, modern English translation; biographies of composer and librettist; accounts of early performances and critical reaction. Lavishly illustrated. All the material you need to understand and appreciate this great work. Dover Opera Guide and Libretto Series; translated and introduced by Ellen Bleiler. 92 illustrations. 209pp.
21134-7 Paperbound $1.50

HIGH FIDELITY SYSTEMS: A LAYMAN'S GUIDE, Roy F. Allison. All the basic information you need for setting up your own audio system: high fidelity and stereo record players, tape records, F.M. Connections, adjusting tone arm, cartridge, checking needle alignment, positioning speakers, phasing speakers, adjusting hums, trouble-shooting, maintenance, and similar topics. Enlarged 1965 edition. More than 50 charts, diagrams, photos. iv + 91pp.
21514-8 Paperbound $1.25

REPRODUCTION OF SOUND, Edgar Villchur. Thorough coverage for laymen of high fidelity systems, reproducing systems in general, needles, amplifiers, preamps, loudspeakers, feedback, explaining physical background. "A rare talent for making technicalities vividly comprehensible," R. Darrell, *High Fidelity.* 69 figures. iv + 92pp.
21515-6 Paperbound $1.00

HEAR ME TALKIN' TO YA: THE STORY OF JAZZ AS TOLD BY THE MEN WHO MADE IT, Nat Shapiro and Nat Hentoff. Louis Armstrong, Fats Waller, Jo Jones, Clarence Williams, Billy Holiday, Duke Ellington, Jelly Roll Morton and dozens of other jazz greats tell how it was in Chicago's South Side, New Orleans, depression Harlem and the modern West Coast as jazz was born and grew. xvi + 429pp.
21726-4 Paperbound $2.50

FABLES OF AESOP, translated by Sir Roger L'Estrange. A reproduction of the very rare 1931 Paris edition; a selection of the most interesting fables, together with 50 imaginative drawings by Alexander Calder. v + 128pp. 6½x9¼.
21780-9 Paperbound $1.25

POEMS OF ANNE BRADSTREET, edited with an introduction by Robert Hutchinson. A new selection of poems by America's first poet and perhaps the first significant woman poet in the English language. 48 poems display her development in works of considerable variety—love poems, domestic poems, religious meditations, formal elegies, "quaternions," etc. Notes, bibliography. viii + 222pp.

22160-1 Paperbound $2.00

THREE GOTHIC NOVELS: THE CASTLE OF OTRANTO BY HORACE WALPOLE; VATHEK BY WILLIAM BECKFORD; THE VAMPYRE BY JOHN POLIDORI, WITH FRAGMENT OF A NOVEL BY LORD BYRON, edited by E. F. Bleiler. The first Gothic novel, by Walpole; the finest Oriental tale in English, by Beckford; powerful Romantic supernatural story in versions by Polidori and Byron. All extremely important in history of literature; all still exciting, packed with supernatural thrills, ghosts, haunted castles, magic, etc. xl + 291pp.

21232-7 Paperbound $2.00

THE BEST TALES OF HOFFMANN, E. T. A. Hoffmann. 10 of Hoffmann's most important stories, in modern re-editings of standard translations: Nutcracker and the King of Mice, Signor Formica, Automata, The Sandman, Rath Krespel, The Golden Flowerpot, Master Martin the Cooper, The Mines of Falun, The King's Betrothed, A New Year's Eve Adventure. 7 illustrations by Hoffmann. Edited by E. F. Bleiler. xxxix + 419pp.

21793-0 Paperbound $2.50

GHOST AND HORROR STORIES OF AMBROSE BIERCE, Ambrose Bierce. 23 strikingly modern stories of the horrors latent in the human mind: The Eyes of the Panther, The Damned Thing, An Occurrence at Owl Creek Bridge, An Inhabitant of Carcosa, etc., plus the dream-essay, Visions of the Night. Edited by E. F. Bleiler. xxii + 199pp.

20767-6 Paperbound $1.50

BEST GHOST STORIES OF J. S. LEFANU, J. Sheridan LeFanu. Finest stories by Victorian master often considered greatest supernatural writer of all. Carmilla, Green Tea, The Haunted Baronet, The Familiar, and 12 others. Most never before available in the U. S. A. Edited by E. F. Bleiler. 8 illustrations from Victorian publications. xvii + 467pp.

20415-4 Paperbound $2.50

THE TIME STREAM, THE GREATEST ADVENTURE, AND THE PURPLE SAPPHIRE— THREE SCIENCE FICTION NOVELS, John Taine (Eric Temple Bell). Great American mathematician was also foremost science fiction novelist of the 1920's. *The Time Stream,* one of all-time classics, uses concepts of circular time; *The Greatest Adventure,* incredibly ancient biological experiments from Antarctica threaten to escape; The *Purple Sapphire,* superscience, lost races in Central Tibet, survivors of the Great Race. 4 illustrations by Frank R. Paul. v + 532pp.

21180-0 Paperbound $3.00

SEVEN SCIENCE FICTION NOVELS, H. G. Wells. The standard collection of the great novels. Complete, unabridged. *First Men in the Moon, Island of Dr. Moreau, War of the Worlds, Food of the Gods, Invisible Man, Time Machine, In the Days of the Comet.* Not only science fiction fans, but every educated person owes it to himself to read these novels. 1015pp.

20264-X Clothbound $5.00

THE RED FAIRY BOOK, Andrew Lang. Lang's color fairy books have long been children's favorites. This volume includes Rapunzel, Jack and the Bean-stalk and 35 other stories, familiar and unfamiliar. 4 plates, 93 illustrations x + 367pp.
21673-X Paperbound $2.50

THE BLUE FAIRY BOOK, Andrew Lang. Lang's tales come from all countries and all times. Here are 37 tales from Grimm, the Arabian Nights, Greek Mythology, and other fascinating sources. 8 plates, 130 illustrations. xi + 390pp.
21437-0 Paperbound $2.50

HOUSEHOLD STORIES BY THE BROTHERS GRIMM. Classic English-language edition of the well-known tales — Rumpelstiltskin, Snow White, Hansel and Gretel, The Twelve Brothers, Faithful John, Rapunzel, Tom Thumb (52 stories in all). Translated into simple, straightforward English by Lucy Crane. Ornamented with headpieces, vignettes, elaborate decorative initials and a dozen full-page illustrations by Walter Crane. x + 269pp.
21080-4 Paperbound $2.50

THE MERRY ADVENTURES OF ROBIN HOOD, Howard Pyle. The finest modern versions of the traditional ballads and tales about the great English outlaw. Howard Pyle's complete prose version, with every word, every illustration of the first edition. Do not confuse this facsimile of the original (1883) with modern editions that change text or illustrations. 23 plates plus many page decorations. xxii + 296pp.
22043-5 Paperbound $2.50

THE STORY OF KING ARTHUR AND HIS KNIGHTS, Howard Pyle. The finest children's version of the life of King Arthur; brilliantly retold by Pyle, with 48 of his most imaginative illustrations. xviii + 313pp. 6⅛ x 9¼.
21445-1 Paperbound $2.50

THE WONDERFUL WIZARD OF OZ, L. Frank Baum. America's finest children's book in facsimile of first edition with all Denslow illustrations in full color. The edition a child should have. Introduction by Martin Gardner. 23 color plates, scores of drawings. iv + 267pp.
20691-2 Paperbound $2.25

THE MARVELOUS LAND OF OZ, L. Frank Baum. The second Oz book, every bit as imaginative as the Wizard. The hero is a boy named Tip, but the Scarecrow and the Tin Woodman are back, as is the Oz magic. 16 color plates, 120 drawings by John R. Neill. 287pp.
20692-0 Paperbound $2.50

THE MAGICAL MONARCH OF MO, L. Frank Baum. Remarkable adventures in a land even stranger than Oz. The best of Baum's books not in the Oz series. 15 color plates and dozens of drawings by Frank Verbeck. xviii + 237pp.
21892-9 Paperbound $2.00

THE BAD CHILD'S BOOK OF BEASTS, MORE BEASTS FOR WORSE CHILDREN, A MORAL ALPHABET, Hilaire Belloc. Three complete humor classics in one volume. Be kind to the frog, and do not call him names . . . and 28 other whimsical animals. Familiar favorites and some not so well known. Illustrated by Basil Blackwell. 156pp.
(USO) 20749-8 Paperbound $1.25

EAST O' THE SUN AND WEST O' THE MOON, George W. Dasent. Considered the best of all translations of these Norwegian folk tales, this collection has been enjoyed by generations of children (and folklorists too). Includes True and Untrue, Why the Sea is Salt, East O' the Sun and West O' the Moon, Why the Bear is Stumpy-Tailed, Boots and the Troll, The Cock and the Hen, Rich Peter the Pedlar, and 52 more. The only edition with all 59 tales. 77 illustrations by Erik Werenskiold and Theodor Kittelsen. xv + 418pp. 22521-6 Paperbound $3.00

GOOPS AND HOW TO BE THEM, Gelett Burgess. Classic of tongue-in-cheek humor, masquerading as etiquette book. 87 verses, twice as many cartoons, show mischievous Goops as they demonstrate to children virtues of table manners, neatness, courtesy, etc. Favorite for generations. viii + 88pp. 6½ x 9¼.
22233-0 Paperbound $1.25

ALICE'S ADVENTURES UNDER GROUND, Lewis Carroll. The first version, quite different from the final Alice in Wonderland, printed out by Carroll himself with his own illustrations. Complete facsimile of the "million dollar" manuscript Carroll gave to Alice Liddell in 1864. Introduction by Martin Gardner. viii + 96pp. Title and dedication pages in color. 21482-6 Paperbound $1.25

THE BROWNIES, THEIR BOOK, Palmer Cox. Small as mice, cunning as foxes, exuberant and full of mischief, the Brownies go to the zoo, toy shop, seashore, circus, etc., in 24 verse adventures and 266 illustrations. Long a favorite, since their first appearance in St. Nicholas Magazine. xi + 144pp. 6⅝ x 9¼.
21265-3 Paperbound $1.75

SONGS OF CHILDHOOD, Walter De La Mare. Published (under the pseudonym Walter Ramal) when De La Mare was only 29, this charming collection has long been a favorite children's book. A facsimile of the first edition in paper, the 47 poems capture the simplicity of the nursery rhyme and the ballad, including such lyrics as I Met Eve, Tartary, The Silver Penny. vii + 106pp. 21972-0 Paperbound $1.25

THE COMPLETE NONSENSE OF EDWARD LEAR, Edward Lear. The finest 19th-century humorist-cartoonist in full: all nonsense limericks, zany alphabets, Owl and Pussycat, songs, nonsense botany, and more than 500 illustrations by Lear himself. Edited by Holbrook Jackson. xxix + 287pp. (USO) 20167-8 Paperbound $2.00

BILLY WHISKERS: THE AUTOBIOGRAPHY OF A GOAT, Frances Trego Montgomery. A favorite of children since the early 20th century, here are the escapades of that rambunctious, irresistible and mischievous goat—Billy Whiskers. Much in the spirit of Peck's Bad Boy, this is a book that children never tire of reading or hearing. All the original familiar illustrations by W. H. Fry are included: 6 color plates, 18 black and white drawings. 159pp. 22345-0 Paperbound $2.00

MOTHER GOOSE MELODIES. Faithful republication of the fabulously rare Munroe and Francis "copyright 1833" Boston edition—the most important Mother Goose collection, usually referred to as the "original." Familiar rhymes plus many rare ones, with wonderful old woodcut illustrations. Edited by E. F. Bleiler. 128pp. 4½ x 6⅜. 22577-1 Paperbound $1.25

Two Little Savages; Being the Adventures of Two Boys Who Lived as Indians and What They Learned, Ernest Thompson Seton. Great classic of nature and boyhood provides a vast range of woodlore in most palatable form, a genuinely entertaining story. Two farm boys build a teepee in woods and live in it for a month, working out Indian solutions to living problems, star lore, birds and animals, plants, etc. 293 illustrations. vii + 286pp.

20985-7 Paperbound $2.50

Peter Piper's Practical Principles of Plain & Perfect Pronunciation. Alliterative jingles and tongue-twisters of surprising charm, that made their first appearance in America about 1830. Republished in full with the spirited woodcut illustrations from this earliest American edition. 32pp. 4½ x 6⅜.

22560-7 Paperbound $1.00

Science Experiments and Amusements for Children, Charles Vivian. 73 easy experiments, requiring only materials found at home or easily available, such as candles, coins, steel wool, etc.; illustrate basic phenomena like vacuum, simple chemical reaction, etc. All safe. Modern, well-planned. Formerly *Science Games for Children*. 102 photos, numerous drawings. 96pp. 6⅛ x 9¼.

21856-2 Paperbound $1.25

An Introduction to Chess Moves and Tactics Simply Explained, Leonard Barden. Informal intermediate introduction, quite strong in explaining reasons for moves. Covers basic material, tactics, important openings, traps, positional play in middle game, end game. Attempts to isolate patterns and recurrent configurations. Formerly *Chess*. 58 figures. 102pp. (USO) 21210-6 Paperbound $1.25

Lasker's Manual of Chess, Dr. Emanuel Lasker. Lasker was not only one of the five great World Champions, he was also one of the ablest expositors, theorists, and analysts. In many ways, his Manual, permeated with his philosophy of battle, filled with keen insights, is one of the greatest works ever written on chess. Filled with analyzed games by the great players. A single-volume library that will profit almost any chess player, beginner or master. 308 diagrams. xli x 349pp.

20640-8 Paperbound $2.75

The Master Book of Mathematical Recreations, Fred Schuh. In opinion of many the finest work ever prepared on mathematical puzzles, stunts, recreations; exhaustively thorough explanations of mathematics involved, analysis of effects, citation of puzzles and games. Mathematics involved is elementary. Translated by F. Göbel. 194 figures. xxiv + 430pp. 22134-2 Paperbound $3.00

Mathematics, Magic and Mystery, Martin Gardner. Puzzle editor for Scientific American explains mathematics behind various mystifying tricks: card tricks, stage "mind reading," coin and match tricks, counting out games, geometric dissections, etc. Probability sets, theory of numbers clearly explained. Also provides more than 400 tricks, guaranteed to work, that you can do. 135 illustrations. xii + 176pp.

20338-2 Paperbound $1.50

"ESSENTIAL GRAMMAR" SERIES

All you really need to know about modern, colloquial grammar. Many educational shortcuts help you learn faster, understand better. Detailed cognate lists teach you to recognize similarities between English and foreign words and roots—make learning vocabulary easy and interesting. Excellent for independent study or as a supplement to record courses.

ESSENTIAL FRENCH GRAMMAR, Seymour Resnick. 2500-item cognate list. 159pp.
(EBE) 20419-7 Paperbound $1.25

ESSENTIAL GERMAN GRAMMAR, Guy Stern and Everett F. Bleiler. Unusual shortcuts on noun declension, word order, compound verbs. 124pp.
(EBE) 20422-7 Paperbound $1.25

ESSENTIAL ITALIAN GRAMMAR, Olga Ragusa. 111pp.
(EBE) 20779-X Paperbound $1.25

ESSENTIAL JAPANESE GRAMMAR, Everett F. Bleiler. In Romaji transcription; no characters needed. Japanese grammar is regular and simple. 156pp.
21027-8 Paperbound $1.25

ESSENTIAL PORTUGUESE GRAMMAR, Alexander da R. Prista. vi + 114pp.
21650-0 Paperbound $1.25

ESSENTIAL SPANISH GRAMMAR, Seymour Resnick. 2500 word cognate list. 115pp.
(EBE) 20780-3 Paperbound $1.25

ESSENTIAL ENGLISH GRAMMAR, Philip Gucker. Combines best features of modern, functional and traditional approaches. For refresher, class use, home study. x + 177pp.
21649-7 Paperbound $1.25

A PHRASE AND SENTENCE DICTIONARY OF SPOKEN SPANISH. Prepared for U. S. War Department by U. S. linguists. As above, unit is idiom, phrase or sentence rather than word. English-Spanish and Spanish-English sections contain modern equivalents of over 18,000 sentences. Introduction and appendix as above. iv + 513pp.
20495-2 Paperbound $2.00

A PHRASE AND SENTENCE DICTIONARY OF SPOKEN RUSSIAN. Dictionary prepared for U. S. War Department by U. S. linguists. Basic unit is not the word, but the idiom, phrase or sentence. English-Russian and Russian-English sections contain modern equivalents for over 30,000 phrases. Grammatical introduction covers phonetics, writing, syntax. Appendix of word lists for food, numbers, geographical names, etc. vi + 573 pp. 6⅛ x 9¼.
20496-0 Paperbound $3.00

CONVERSATIONAL CHINESE FOR BEGINNERS, Morris Swadesh. Phonetic system, beginner's course in Pai Hua Mandarin Chinese covering most important, most useful speech patterns. Emphasis on modern colloquial usage. Formerly *Chinese in Your Pocket*. xvi + 158pp.
21123-1 Paperbound $1.50

THE PHILOSOPHY OF THE UPANISHADS, Paul Deussen. Clear, detailed statement of upanishadic system of thought, generally considered among best available. History of these works, full exposition of system emergent from them, parallel concepts in the West. Translated by A. S. Geden. xiv + 429pp.
21616-0 Paperbound $3.00

LANGUAGE, TRUTH AND LOGIC, Alfred J. Ayer. Famous, remarkably clear introduction to the Vienna and Cambridge schools of Logical Positivism; function of philosophy, elimination of metaphysical thought, nature of analysis, similar topics. "Wish I had written it myself," Bertrand Russell. 2nd, 1946 edition. 160pp.
20010-8 Paperbound $1.35

THE GUIDE FOR THE PERPLEXED, Moses Maimonides. Great classic of medieval Judaism, major attempt to reconcile revealed religion (Pentateuch, commentaries) and Aristotelian philosophy. Enormously important in all Western thought. Unabridged Friedländer translation. 50-page introduction. lix + 414pp.
(USO) 20351-4 Paperbound $2.50

OCCULT AND SUPERNATURAL PHENOMENA, D. H. Rawcliffe. Full, serious study of the most persistent delusions of mankind: crystal gazing, mediumistic trance, stigmata, lycanthropy, fire walking, dowsing, telepathy, ghosts, ESP, etc., and their relation to common forms of abnormal psychology. Formerly *Illusions and Delusions of the Supernatural and the Occult.* iii + 551pp. 20503-7 Paperbound $3.50

THE EGYPTIAN BOOK OF THE DEAD: THE PAPYRUS OF ANI, E. A. Wallis Budge. Full hieroglyphic text, interlinear transliteration of sounds, word for word translation, then smooth, connected translation; Theban recension. Basic work in Ancient Egyptian civilization; now even more significant than ever for historical importance, dilation of consciousness, etc. clvi + 377pp. 6½ x 9¼.
21866-X Paperbound $3.95

PSYCHOLOGY OF MUSIC, Carl E. Seashore. Basic, thorough survey of everything known about psychology of music up to 1940's; essential reading for psychologists, musicologists. Physical acoustics; auditory apparatus; relationship of physical sound to perceived sound; role of the mind in sorting, altering, suppressing, creating sound sensations; musical learning, testing for ability, absolute pitch, other topics. Records of Caruso, Menuhin analyzed. 88 figures. xix + 408pp.
21851-1 Paperbound $2.75

THE I CHING (THE BOOK OF CHANGES), translated by James Legge. Complete translated text plus appendices by Confucius, of perhaps the most penetrating divination book ever compiled. Indispensable to all study of early Oriental civilizations. 3 plates. xxiii + 448pp. 21062-6 Paperbound $3.00

THE UPANISHADS, translated by Max Müller. Twelve classical upanishads: Chandogya, Kena, Aitareya, Kaushitaki, Isa, Katha, Mundaka, Taittiriyaka, Brhadaranyaka, Svetasvatara, Prasna, Maitriyana. 160-page introduction, analysis by Prof. Müller. Total of 826pp. 20398-0, 20399-9 Two volumes, Paperbound $5.00

JIM WHITEWOLF: THE LIFE OF A KIOWA APACHE INDIAN, Charles S. Brant, editor. Spans transition between native life and acculturation period, 1880 on. Kiowa culture, personal life pattern, religion and the supernatural, the Ghost Dance, breakdown in the White Man's world, similar material. 1 map. xii + 144pp.
22015-X Paperbound $1.75

THE NATIVE TRIBES OF CENTRAL AUSTRALIA, Baldwin Spencer and F. J. Gillen. Basic book in anthropology, devoted to full coverage of the Arunta and Warramunga tribes; the source for knowledge about kinship systems, material and social culture, religion, etc. Still unsurpassed. 121 photographs, 89 drawings. xviii + 669pp.
21775-2 Paperbound $5.00

MALAY MAGIC, Walter W. Skeat. Classic (1900) ; still the definitive work on the folklore and popular religion of the Malay peninsula. Describes marriage rites, birth spirits and ceremonies, medicine, dances, games, war and weapons, etc. Extensive quotes from original sources, many magic charms translated into English. 35 illustrations. Preface by Charles Otto Blagden. xxiv + 685pp.
21760-4 Paperbound $4.00

HEAVENS ON EARTH: UTOPIAN COMMUNITIES IN AMERICA, 1680-1880, Mark Holloway. The finest nontechnical account of American utopias, from the early Woman in the Wilderness, Ephrata, Rappites to the enormous mid 19th-century efflorescence; Shakers, New Harmony, Equity Stores, Fourier's Phalanxes, Oneida, Amana, Fruitlands, etc. "Entertaining and very instructive." *Times Literary Supplement.* 15 illustrations. 246pp.
21593-8 Paperbound $2.00

LONDON LABOUR AND THE LONDON POOR, Henry Mayhew. Earliest (c. 1850) sociological study in English, describing myriad subcultures of London poor. Particularly remarkable for the thousands of pages of direct testimony taken from the lips of London prostitutes, thieves, beggars, street sellers, chimney-sweepers, street-musicians, "mudlarks," "pure-finders," rag-gatherers, "running-patterers," dock laborers, cab-men, and hundreds of others, quoted directly in this massive work. An extraordinarily vital picture of London emerges. 110 illustrations. Total of lxxvi + 1951pp. 6⅝ x 10.
21934-8, 21935-6, 21936-4, 21937-2 Four volumes, Paperbound $14.00

HISTORY OF THE LATER ROMAN EMPIRE, J. B. Bury. Eloquent, detailed reconstruction of Western and Byzantine Roman Empire by a major historian, from the death of Theodosius I (395 A.D.) to the death of Justinian (565). Extensive quotations from contemporary sources; full coverage of important Roman and foreign figures of the time. xxxiv + 965pp. 21829-5 Record, book, album. Monaural. $3.50

AN INTELLECTUAL AND CULTURAL HISTORY OF THE WESTERN WORLD, Harry Elmer Barnes. Monumental study, tracing the development of the accomplishments that make up human culture. Every aspect of man's achievement surveyed from its origins in the Paleolithic to the present day (1964) ; social structures, ideas, economic systems, art, literature, technology, mathematics, the sciences, medicine, religion, jurisprudence, etc. Evaluations of the contributions of scores of great men. 1964 edition, revised and edited by scholars in the many fields represented. Total of xxix + 1381pp. 21275-0, 21276-9, 21277-7 Three volumes, Paperbound $7.75

ADVENTURES OF AN AFRICAN SLAVER, Theodore Canot. Edited by Brantz Mayer. A detailed portrayal of slavery and the slave trade, 1820-1840. Canot, an established trader along the African coast, describes the slave economy of the African kingdoms, the treatment of captured negroes, the extensive journeys in the interior to gather slaves, slave revolts and their suppression, harems, bribes, and much more. Full and unabridged republication of 1854 edition. Introduction by Malcom Cowley. 16 illustrations. xvii + 448pp. 22456-2 Paperbound $3.50

MY BONDAGE AND MY FREEDOM, Frederick Douglass. Born and brought up in slavery, Douglass witnessed its horrors and experienced its cruelties, but went on to become one of the most outspoken forces in the American anti-slavery movement. Considered the best of his autobiographies, this book graphically describes the inhuman treatment of slaves, its effects on slave owners and slave families, and how Douglass's determination led him to a new life. Unaltered reprint of 1st (1855) edition. xxxii + 464pp. 22457-0 Paperbound $2.50

THE INDIANS' BOOK, recorded and edited by Natalie Curtis. Lore, music, narratives, dozens of drawings by Indians themselves from an authoritative and important survey of native culture among Plains, Southwestern, Lake and Pueblo Indians. Standard work in popular ethnomusicology. 149 songs in full notation. 23 drawings, 23 photos. xxxi + 584pp. 6⅝ x 9⅜. 21939-9 Paperbound $4.00

DICTIONARY OF AMERICAN PORTRAITS, edited by Hayward and Blanche Cirker. 4024 portraits of 4000 most important Americans, colonial days to 1905 (with a few important categories, like Presidents, to present). Pioneers, explorers, colonial figures, U. S. officials, politicians, writers, military and naval men, scientists, inventors, manufacturers, jurists, actors, historians, educators, notorious figures, Indian chiefs, etc. All authentic contemporary likenesses. The only work of its kind in existence; supplements all biographical sources for libraries. Indispensable to anyone working with American history. 8,000-item classified index, finding lists, other aids. xiv + 756pp. 9¼ x 12¾. 21823-6 Clothbound $30.00

TRITTON'S GUIDE TO BETTER WINE AND BEER MAKING FOR BEGINNERS, S. M. Tritton. All you need to know to make family-sized quantities of over 100 types of grape, fruit, herb and vegetable wines; as well as beers, mead, cider, etc. Complete recipes, advice as to equipment, procedures such as fermenting, bottling, and storing wines. Recipes given in British, U. S., and metric measures. Accompanying booklet lists sources in U. S. A. where ingredients may be bought, and additional information. 11 illustrations. 157pp. 5⅝ x 8⅛. (USO) 22090-7 Clothbound $3.50

GARDENING WITH HERBS FOR FLAVOR AND FRAGRANCE, Helen M. Fox. How to grow herbs in your own garden, how to use them in your cooking (over 55 recipes included), legends and myths associated with each species, uses in medicine, perfumes, etc.—these are elements of one of the few books written especially for American herb fanciers. Guides you step-by-step from soil preparation to harvesting and storage for each type of herb. 12 drawings by Louise Mansfield. xiv + 334pp. 22540-2 Paperbound $2.50

Mathematical Puzzles for Beginners and Enthusiasts, Geoffrey Mott-Smith. 189 puzzles from easy to difficult—involving arithmetic, logic, algebra, properties of digits, probability, etc.—for enjoyment and mental stimulus. Explanation of mathematical principles behind the puzzles. 135 illustrations. viii + 248pp.
20198-8 Paperbound $1.25

Paper Folding for Beginners, William D. Murray and Francis J. Rigney. Easiest book on the market, clearest instructions on making interesting, beautiful origami. Sail boats, cups, roosters, frogs that move legs, bonbon boxes, standing birds, etc. 40 projects; more than 275 diagrams and photographs. 94pp.
20713-7 Paperbound $1.00

Tricks and Games on the Pool Table, Fred Herrmann. 79 tricks and games—some solitaires, some for two or more players, some competitive games—to entertain you between formal games. Mystifying shots and throws, unusual caroms, tricks involving such props as cork, coins, a hat, etc. Formerly *Fun on the Pool Table*. 77 figures. 95pp.
21814-7 Paperbound $1.00

Hand Shadows to be Thrown Upon the Wall: A Series of Novel and Amusing Figures Formed by the Hand, Henry Bursill. Delightful picturebook from great-grandfather's day shows how to make 18 different hand shadows: a bird that flies, duck that quacks, dog that wags his tail, camel, goose, deer, boy, turtle, etc. Only book of its sort. vi + 33pp. 6½ x 9¼.   21779-5 Paperbound $1.00

Whittling and Woodcarving, E. J. Tangerman. 18th printing of best book on market. "If you can cut a potato you can carve" toys and puzzles, chains, chessmen, caricatures, masks, frames, woodcut blocks, surface patterns, much more. Information on tools, woods, techniques. Also goes into serious wood sculpture from Middle Ages to present, East and West. 464 photos, figures. x + 293pp.
20965-2 Paperbound $2.00

History of Philosophy, Julián Marías. Possibly the clearest, most easily followed, best planned, most useful one-volume history of philosophy on the market; neither skimpy nor overfull. Full details on system of every major philosopher and dozens of less important thinkers from pre-Socratics up to Existentialism and later. Strong on many European figures usually omitted. Has gone through dozens of editions in Europe. 1966 edition, translated by Stanley Appelbaum and Clarence Strowbridge. xviii + 505pp.
21739-6 Paperbound $3.00

Yoga: A Scientific Evaluation, Kovoor T. Behanan. Scientific but non-technical study of physiological results of yoga exercises; done under auspices of Yale U. Relations to Indian thought, to psychoanalysis, etc. 16 photos. xxiii + 270pp.
20505-3 Paperbound $2.50

Prices subject to change without notice.
Available at your book dealer or write for free catalogue to Dept. GI, Dover Publications, Inc., 180 Varick St., N. Y., N. Y. 10014. Dover publishes more than 150 books each year on science, elementary and advanced mathematics, biology, music, art, literary history, social sciences and other areas.